Black Nazareth

Also by Rosemary Sturge

Death of a Daughter of Venice

A Storm in Summer

Black Nazareth

Rosemary Sturge

Copyright ©2017 Rosemary Sturge
Rosemary Sturge has asserted her right under the Copyright, Designs and Patents Act 1988 to be identified as the author of this work

This novel is a work of fiction. Names and characters are the product of the author's imagination and any resemblance to actual persons, living or dead, is entirely coincidental

This book is available and as an
e-book and in print from Amazon, and in print from
createspace.com

If you would like to contact the author please see her website
www.historical-novels.co.uk

Cover photograph
Korte Haven, Schiedam, in winter
By kind permission of Lida Bruinen, artist and photographer, whose generosity and help is greatly appreciated

This is dedicated to the inhabitants of the Dutch town of Schiedam who made myself and my husband welcome in their fascinating town in 2013

Principal Characters

Tomas	An eleven year old boy, 'van de Gracht', from a canal boat family
Henke van de Grote	Foreman of the Zakkendragers
Margriet	His wife, a madwoman
Pastor Jacob Winkelmann	A protestant pastor and poet (Dutch Reformed Church)
Ignaas van Damme	Tomas's stepfather
Cornelius de Haan	Chief of the Bridge Watchers
Clara	His wife
Anneke and Lotte	Their daughters
Mathilde (Mattie)	Their niece
Ambroos	A zakkendrager
Geert	A zakkendrager, Henke's deputy
Maurits	A baker
Augustijn	His assistant
Frans Rijnsburger	An apothecary
Hedy and Cees and their children	Boat people, known to Tomas
Maarten de Hoop and his wife, Margriet	Regents of the orphanage
Roel Mulder	Schoolmaster (or is he?)
Father Anthonis	Catholic Priest (the Haven Kerk)
Dries van Corte	Directeur of Sint Jacob's hospital and alms-house
Casper	Tomas's friend, an orphan, a hunch-back
Saskia	Tomas's friend, an asthmatic orphan girl with a withered leg.
Alexander Saunders (Xander)	A Scottish Doctor
Wim Rombouts	A lawyer
Anders Vos ('the Fox')	Detective from the Maréchaussée or Dutch National Police Force
Corporals Josef van Dyke and Joop Barends	His assistants
Aarte	A glass blower
Dieric	A cobbler
Piet	A "wharf rat"
Heer Wenders	Manager of the Walvisch Windmill
Dirk and Ruud	Ushers at the orphanage
Vrouw Dorte Schmit	Matron at the orphanage
Katjie	The cook
Roos	A maid
Vrouw Hauberk	A landlady

Other Characters: zakkendragers, barrel makers, shop keepers, orphans, orphanage staff, drunkards, binnenschippers (bargees), gin distillery workers, windmill operators, night watchmen, dogs

Glossary of Dutch words

Binnenschipper	Bargee, skipper of a sailing barge
Boot	Boat
Bootje	Rowing boat
Broodjes	Sandwiches
Brug	Bridge
Dwazen	Fools
Gemeentehuis	Town Hall, Council House
Gracht	Canal
Guildhuis	Headquarters of a guild or guilds
Heer	Mr
Hoogstraat	High Street
Kirstmis	Christmas
Koemarkt	Cattle market
Maréchaussée	Dutch National Police Force
Meester	Mister, or Master, roughly someone who is master of his trade
Ponds	old measurement for fruit and vegetables
Rakker	Slang name for a policeman, cf. 'rozzer' in English
Snert	Thick pea soup, 'winter soup'
Vrouw	Mrs
Waterpokken	Chickenpox
Weeshuis	Orphanage
Zakkendrager	Porter, sack carrier

Chapter 1

Tomas

The boy, Tomas, ran. The pain in his back and buttocks travelled with him, screaming at him to stop, begging him to consider a plunge into the waters of the gracht, the canal, but his bare feet carried him forward. Down the slope onto the Lange Haven, along the side of the brick-paved quay, to the slender wrought-iron bridge. He was sobbing aloud as he ran, he could hear himself, but his racing mind spoke firmly to his child's body in the voice of his dead mother. 'Be quiet! Don't snivel! Don't waste a breath! Keep *going*, the pain will stop.' He had no idea whether his step-father was behind him. He did not, dared not, look back. He must find somewhere to hide, to curl up like an animal hit by a cart – *like a beaten dog* – for he knew himself to be no more, no less. Until his wounds healed, then, wait, *just wait*, Ignaas!

It had happened before. Unless he got clear of him the man would try again. It would be worse. This last time the drunken bully had thrown aside the mooring pole with which he'd belaboured him, and scrabbled at his britches, ramming his body against Tomas's buttocks. Yelling with pain and fright – and shame, *oh, why should the shame be his?* Tomas had squirmed free, eyes bleared by tears of fury, and bolted across the boat's gang plank. Escaped. Now he must forsake water for land. Never go back.

He'd no strong notion of where to go, no plan, just the abused creature's desire to get away, but across the two bridges (thanks be to God they were closed, no boats lined up to pass through at this lantern-glow hour) he veered right beyond the lock towards the Palmboom, which was one of the tallest of the many windmills in Schiedam. In this town he knew folk steered their way about by these huge windmills which towered over buildings and people alike.

A yell behind him sent sharp shards of fear through his body. Ignaas must be following. Hide, hide! Seeing an open doorway ahead, and commanding his body and soul to God, for even if this dark, soot-stained entry was the gateway to Hell, nothing could be worse than what lay behind, he dived through it.

He was in a small passageway at the foot of a ladder-stair leading to the upper storey. The air was thick with maize dust, which flew into his open mouth so that he gasped for breath and stifled a sneeze. Beyond was another open door, a lighted room in which a group of men in blue smocks stood gazing at something out of his sight within the low-ceilinged chamber.

'Last drop! Last drop!' a man's voice boomed. 'Unloading the Goudbloem! Four hands needed. Them as wants a last chance of work tonight, pass yer ball!'

Several of the blue smocks stepped forward in the direction of the booming voice, offering up small brown wooden balls, each with a number painted on it. Tomas heard the clunk of these balls being dropped into a wooden container of some kind. Now he knew where he was. This was the Guild house of the zakkendragers!

He'd been in the town of Schiedam before, of course. Many times when Mama was alive and even before that with Papa, and even Grandpapa, whom he barely remembered. They were boat people, Tomas's family, canal folk, the van de Grachtes, as their name made clear. No town claimed them, they lived aboard the boat, sailed the rivers and the canals carrying whatever cargo people wanted transported. Often it had been maize or barley for the gin mills of Schiedam. When they got here, these sacks must be unloaded, taken on a wheeled handcart, or carried on the shoulders of these burly zakkendragers, to the corn exchange or the grain stores. The guild had strict rules, everyone knew that. No one else in the town was permitted to do this, and no sack dragger could take the work unless "his number came up."

This must be what was happening. He heard the thud of the wooden balls falling through the 'shoot,' and Booming Voice began calling the numbers, 'Five, twenty two, seventeen, nine! Ach, bad luck, Ambroos, fifteen left behind! Better luck next time!' Tomas ducked down onto a pile of sacking under the steep wooden stairway.

Good fortune for him, though. The zakkendragers were taking their last orders. Four numbers called; soon they would be on their way to unload the Goudbloem, which must be one of the boats tied up in the Schie basin outside. Then this particular team of men would be leaving the Guildhuis for the night, and with luck would

10

never notice him hidden in the hallway as they tramped out into the deepening twilight. And if Ignaas should spot them, stop them (which they wouldn't like, not with those heavy sacks bowing their shoulders) they would declare they hadn't seen him! It wouldn't be a bad place to sleep either, once his hurts eased.

Tomas positioned himself carefully, easing his painful buttocks. He wriggled onto his stomach on the pile of sacks, and peered out through the rungs of the ladder as the zakkendragers strode by. One, two, three, four, brisk and purposeful. The lucky ones! Then Ambroos the unfortunate, shoulders drooping, clumped out.

But where was Booming Voice? Come on, Booming Voice! Close the shutters! Snuff out the lanterns, take those keys from the pocket of your baggy britches and lock the door! Go home to your wife and children!

He'd reckoned wrongly however, about Booming Voice. After moving about in the room beyond Tomas's line of vision, tidying the place perhaps, straightening the benches, carefully latching the wooden shutters, he came striding through, a lantern held at waist height. Instead of continuing through the door though, he dropped a heavy wooden bar into place on the inside, and then turned back again, setting his foot on the first rung of the ladder. The man lived here! Tomas hadn't thought of that.

'Ach!' he said, seeing the boy lying almost beneath his feet, 'A visitor, eh? Who would you be?'

No use to play dumb. It might earn him another beating. 'Tomas,' he muttered, 'van de Gracht. From the Appelbloesem.'

'The Appelbloesem, eh?' Booming voice paused foot raised, searching in his mind for the boat Tomas named, and with a nod, finding it. Finding Ignaas at the helm. 'Not getting on with your step-dad?' He held up the lantern for a closer look at Tomas.

'He thrashed me.'

The man leaned forward, examining Tomas's face for lies or bruises. Tomas could have shown him the wheals on his back and the rope burns on his shoulders, but Mama had always said 'keep your body covered child, no matter who asks.'

'Thrashed you? For what reason?'

'I would not do what he wanted. He's stolen the Appelbloesem from me!'

'Ach! Surely not? Where was Anna, your mother?'

11

'Dead.' It was the first time Tomas had said it out loud. Mama. Dead. 'Sh-She got sick and Ignaas t-took her to the workhouse infirmary in D-Dordrecht! He said they'd make her better but they d-didn't!' He was weeping now although he had vowed he never would. He was eleven years old, and believed he had put away childish things.

The big man, one foot still on the bottom rung of the ladder, leaned over and offered his enormous hand to be shaken. 'Henke van de Grote,' he said. 'I'm sorry to hear that. Very sorry. She was a good woman, your mother.'

In the lantern light his pale eyes showed no sign of calculation. Tomas had learned to read men, and some women, by their eyes. And, in this particular town, by the smell of gin that hovered around them, or the lack of it.

It was worth the risk, he decided. 'Meester Henke, m-may... May I sleep here tonight?'

The big man pressed his lips together, and gazed upwards at the hatchway standing open above his head, considering this. Then he looked down at the pile of sacks on which Tomas lay.

'Here? Yes, *here*, you may,' he replied. 'I can't invite you upstairs. My wife... she... she gets upset. Doesn't take to strangers.' He hooked the lantern onto one of the rungs of the ladder in order to spread his huge hands, palms upward, in a gesture Tomas recognised. It meant, 'Well, that's the way it is, nothing to be done about it.' Then he said, 'No pissing on the floor though young fellow. There's a privy out back but you won't want to go there in the dark. I'll pass you down a bucket.' Saying no more, he unhooked the lantern and began to climb. His progress was slow, slower than Tomas would have expected from such a big, active man, the man whose voice had boomed so energetically amongst the zakkendragers. Tomas had the idea that Henke van de Grote did not particularly want to go up to his living quarters where the wife so easily upset awaited him.

Presently Tomas heard the man's boots tramping across the wooden boards above him, and then he was climbing another ladder, or stairway, and then another. This guild house must have several storeys. A key scraped in a lock, and suddenly there was a flurry of sound and movement above. Henke's voice, rumbled low, and a series of shrieks and squawks, reminded Tomas of Grandpa's grey and scarlet parrot, Prins. Ignaas had sold Prins in Utrecht although Mama had protested, softly, lest he raise his fist to her, that their parting with Prins would have broken the old man's heart. Despite the harshness of this distant voice however, Tomas knew it was no parrot, but a human being. And now a second set of feet came scrabbling down the ladders, and thudded softly on the boards above his head. Then there were scuffling sounds as though this person and Henke were wrestling.

'Sit, will you, woman! I'll find you something to eat, have no fear, I'll find you something! Yes, yes, you may have your gin now! Geert fetched a jug in at mid-day. Leave off pulling at me while I pour it!'

So. Henke had a drunken wife, a wife whose wits had been destroyed by gin. A wife he must keep locked in some upper room during the day lest she go reeling through the streets, falling into the canals. Even a boy of eleven knew what gin could do. It was common enough. Especially here in Schiedam, the town, so Tomas's mother had told him, they called Black Nazareth. He wondered what Henke was giving her to eat (If she would eat. Sometimes, he had already learned, drunkards will only drink). Would the thought come to the man that he, Tomas, might be hungry?

Seemingly it did not. Tomas lay for a long while, face down on the sacks. His back and buttocks still throbbed. His stomach growled in sympathy. He tried not to weep.

The woman upstairs must have slurped her gin. Now he could hear her making little mewling noises like a cat, and then he heard Henke walking slowly across the floor.

'Now sit by the stove and be quiet, Margriet,' he heard him say. 'I'm taking the scraps down for the ducks. Forgot to do it, earlier, it's been busy. The Goudbloem came in late off the Schie. By luck I still had some men... no, no! Sit quiet woman!'

There was a great scuffling above, and the woman cried out in her parrot's squawk once more. 'No, I've told you!' Meester Henke was grunting, breathing hard. 'If you will not sit quiet I must tie you to the chair! Last time I took you along you tried to run off. You fell and broke your wrist. 'Tis for your own good, Margriet!'

Henke now sounded quite breathless, and the woman continued to screech. He must be tying his wife up, and she was struggling against him. Tomas pulled one of the sacks over his head and stuck his fingers in his ears. Why was it, that grown men and women, who were meant to know how the world wagged, were so cruel to one another?

The noise of their struggle died away, the woman mewling softly, and after some minutes, Henke's boots appeared on the ladder above. He descended slowly, lantern in one hand, a bucket handle hooked over his arm, its base clanking against the steps.

'Here's the pail for you to piss in, youngster,' he said quietly, 'but first take out the scraps I've put in it, and this pot of watered jenever. You'll have an empty belly, no doubt?'

'Yes, sir, thank you sir,' whispered Tomas, 'but what about your ducks, sir?' By the light of the lantern he saw the man's eyebrows arch in alarm. Perhaps Henke hadn't realised that Tomas could hear every word that was spoken upstairs through the open hatchway. Now his large light eyes rolled up, worried about what he'd just said. 'Oh, never mind the ducks,' he dropped his voice to a murmur. 'I fed 'em earlier. I didn't want...' he jerked his thumb sharply upwards, '*her* to discover you were here. She's a sick woman, my wife, and takes strange fancies into her head. 'Tis best she doesn't know.'

'I'll be quiet as a mouse, no, a black beetle!' Tomas whispered back. 'Is... anybody else living upstairs?'

'Not at the present time. The zakkendragers all live out. Our four sons are gone, gone seafaring. 'Tis just as well.'

Henke might say this but Tomas could hear sadness in his voice. He understood, without needing to be told, that Henke didn't like being alone with his wife, her wits gone. Whether from gin or some other cause, Henke's wife was a mad woman.

'Can she not...' Tomas was unsure whether to say this. 'Can you not get a place for her in the asylum?' He knew that such places existed. Had, in some town, perhaps Rotterdam? – seen a half-naked man being hauled off, struggling against his captors, to a large and gloomy building. Tomas had asked his mother (thinking that the man had committed some crime) what the man had done to be thus treated. His mother had told him no, the man was a madman, and was being taken to the town asylum for his own safety. Thus Tomas knew how and where, though he little understood why, mad people were accommodated.

Henke merely looked at him for a while. 'You haven't been inside one of them places, have you, youngster? Margriet would be dead inside a week. Everyone tells me to do it, but I couldn't. She was a good woman when she had her wits.' He ducked his head, turned away, and began to climb the ladder without saying another word.

Chapter 2

Tomas

When Tomas woke, daylight was already poking its fingers round the heavy wooden shutters. It had been past one of the clock by the chimes of Grote Sint Jan before he slept, his body paining him, and his heart even more. He'd missed, too, the movement of the boat, gentle as its rocking would have been on the calm waters of the Lange Haven. Tomas had never before in his life slept on dry land. He sat up, carefully uncurling his body as he always did. He was well accustomed to a confined sleeping space, tucked away beneath the steps down into the hold of the Appelbloesem. What had woken him this morning was Henke's stockinged feet thudding quietly overhead. There was no sound from the mad wife, Margriet. Perhaps Henke had already imprisoned her in an upper room. Now the man was getting his breakfast. The smell of bacon frying drifted down through the trap door and curled up into Tomas's nostrils. He feared Henke must have forgotten his existence, but presently the big man's face appeared above the opening.

'Still here, young'un? I can spare you a slice off the pig's back, but I've no bread. Only stale stuff I'm keeping for the ducks.'

Tomas hauled his unhappy limbs to a kneeling position and peered upwards through the rungs of the ladder. 'Shall I run and get you a loaf, Meester?'

He had run errands almost from the time he had his first pair of britches, and knew that the willing running of them was the best way to curry favour with adults, and, at the same time stay clear of their fists. A slice of fresh bread to wrap around the promised bacon would be worth the painful effort. He knew also, although he didn't know this town very well away from the canals, that there was a bakery down by the Koemarkt. It might not be the nearest, there could well be one just over the lock in the Hoogstraat, but he decided not to ask. If he was careful around the narrow lanes that sloped down beyond the Cattle Market Bridge, he could check whether the Appelbloesem was still tied up just along from the Buitenhaven wharf. Surely Ignaas would not have sailed her in the dark? But you never knew what Ignaas would do when he was in drink.

Henke tossed him down a coin, which he missed, so that it rolled across the floor and lodged, end on, between two boards, but Tomas was sharp-eyed, and pounced on it in a moment, folding it into his palm. He didn't trust it to his pockets, which he knew from sad experience to consist of more holes than pocket. Mama would have sewn him new ones, but Mama…

'I'll be as quick as I can, Meester Henke!' he called up, keeping his voice low, in case the mad wife, Margriet, should after all be within hearing. Henke grunted assent.

After a struggle, he lifted the bar down from the outer door. Tomas supposed the zakkendragers would soon be here. Surely they should be here already? It must be late, to be so light on a November morning? But once he was outside, had rounded the curve of the basin and started up the slope of the lock towards the Lange Haven, there was still no one. So, perhaps it was the Sabbath? Tomas breathed in the cold damp air, and trotted, limbs stiff and protesting, up past the lock, and across the front of the Korenbeurs, the corn exchange, which stood silent, its doors barred – yes, now he was sure. If the doors of the Korenbeurs were closed it must indeed be the Sabbath.

At the huge new Haven Kerk, across the water, he deliberately did not look – although, last night, running in terror through the dark, he hadn't even thought about it. Today he averted his face, and ran a little faster, though the wounds to his back pulled and stung, where blood had glued them to his shirt. Of course he didn't believe what that boy had told him. This church had been built by the gin Meesters, 'about the time I was born,' Mama had said. 'Why? Because they had the money, and wanted to appear pious, and the old Catholic church that had stood there was gone. And, she'd added, because they and their wives lived in the fine-looking mansions that lined this part of the Lang Haven and up beyond it, on the Plantage, and didn't wish to go walking across the town through the poor, dirty, twisted streets, too narrow for any carriage, as the Protestants had to, to their old Kerk of Grote Sint Jan. 'Streets where you might, as like as not,' said Mama, 'at any moment get a bucket of slops thrown across your skirts by some slattern emerging from her filthy hovel.'

No, he didn't believe what that boy had told him about the

Haven Kerk, but he wasn't going to take a risk, not this morning. How Mama had laughed! Even Ignaas had laughed, when he told them what the boy – Piet, his name was – had said about it. *They'd* said it wasn't true. Very likely someone had told Piet that story, 'a boy like that, such a light fingered one *he* is.' Someone had said it to frighten Piet and his pals, the town's thieving little wharf rats, into good behaviour.

Boats were berthed bow to stern all along the canal banks today, ropes taut, chafing gently against the iron bollards, tarpaulins tied snug across their cargoes. One or two families had already thrown back their hatches, and the smell of pancakes and bacon bubbling in the frying pan was for once stronger than the reek of gin. A hundred chimneys, blackened with soot, stood cold and idle in Schiedam on the Lord's Day. The canvas sails of the enormous Walvisch windmill, the tallest one of them all, hung limp on their frames, its kruibok, the brake mechanism, held in Sabbath chains. Tomas felt the morning breeze blow soft but chill through his tattered shirt and patched britches. The occasional wintry leaf from the plane tree near the bridge flapped past like a tired bird and fell into the treacly waters with a gentle plop.

He scurried on, hopping clumsily over mooring ropes, his wounds protesting. He dodged amongst piles of empty barrels, and even the occasional tired sleeper, "sleeping off" last night's libations, never glancing across the water until he was level with the Zeeland and Gelderland grain stores, with their bell shaped gables, and their names painted white above the doors. Tomas had never been to school, but Mama had taught him his letters. He could spell *those* out he remembered with pride, when he was only six.

His family had seldom shipped cargoes from as far away as Zeeland to the south, or Gelderland to the east, but there was a lot of grain grown in those provinces, juniper too, on the inland heaths. He'd heard plenty of people say so. One day, he vowed, running up the nine-stepped stoop of Menheer Nolet's grand Italian mansion (it was too early for the gin Meester's servants to catch him doing it) and down the other side. One day he would sail the Appelbloesem to those far provinces. He would bring back a cargo worth – oh, a thousand guilders! – And tie up, proud as a king, in front of those very warehouses. But first he must somehow win back the Appelbloesem. The pain in his back and buttocks might have eased somewhat with sleep, but the pain in his chest, where Mama had told him his heart resided, twisted as sharp as a fish-gutting knife.

On silent soles he padded up the bank to the Koemarktbrug. It was closed, naturally, on the Sabbath. No Bridge Watcher, he was relieved to see. No boats moving on the Haven. No cattle being driven across into the market place or down to the slaughter houses by the sea harbour.

Yet here unexpectedly was an obstacle. A man lay sprawled in the middle of the bridge, arms and legs flung out north, south, east and west, smock torn to his waist, blood seeping from a gash down his belly. Tomas paused, hanging back by the bridge end, his heart beating fast. Dead? Perhaps. Drunk? Certainly, dead or alive he must have been drunk. A bottle had rolled away from the pocket in his britches, spilling a stream of gin which had soaked into the grimy planks. On bare, silent feet, Tomas crept closer, meaning to pass by. Henke's coin was warm in his fist, and he could see the sign board of the baker's shop on the other side.

Papa had always said, 'stay away from drunkards, give 'em a wide berth, son.' It was a long time now since Papa had died, knocked off the quay by a loose hawser in... Tomas wasn't sure now which town, but he still remembered the things Papa had said.

The problem here was, that although the Koemarktbrug was wide compared with other bridges in Schiedam, with fenced-in sides to allow for the push and jostle of a herd of cattle, the man, the drunkard, the maybe-dead'un, lay sprawled right in the middle of it. He was a big man too, tall and lanky, and it wouldn't be easy to pass without coming close to an out-flung arm or leg. The man's clogs had been kicked to his left side, and lay lodged, heel to toe across the space between his body and the side of the bridge. The rolling bottle was on his other side. Papa's words came into Tomas's head once more, 'Ach, clogs! Good wearing, good for the wet, but not for a fight! Too easily lost against boots, and hard to run away in!' This man must have been in a fight. And clogs had lost.

He crept forward, trying to pass between the man and the parapet. If he knocked against either clogs or bottle and set them clacking or clanking, the drunk – if he was a drunk, sleeping it off – might wake and make a grab for him. He rose onto the balls of his feet and inched forward; stepping lightly, but the planks of the bridge moved beneath him, and the man's eyes flew open, rolling up in his head. His mouth gaped, gin vapour assailed Tomas's nostrils, and a harsh sound emerged from the man's throat.

His mother, who had been a devout Christian as Papa said, "After her own fashion", had told him the story of the Good Samaritan, and urged her son to think that he, too, might help people in trouble. So, what would Mama do here? Tomas stared down at the fallen man. Now that he looked closer he realised he'd seen him before. He even knew his name. *Ambroos*. He was the zakkendrager whose numbered ball had fallen last through the shoot, and so was sent away from the Guildhuis yesterday evening without work.

'Get help, boy!' he croaked. Ambroos, of course, hadn't seen Tomas, hiding in the hallway.

'I'm going to the bakers,' Tomas whispered. 'They might be Catholics.' The man closed his eyes accepting this remark. The effort to ask for help seemed to have cost him all his strength. Tomas had no clear understanding of the differences between the Catholics and the Protestants, except that the Catholics kept the Sabbath less strictly. Always hungry, especially of late, he knew that after early attendance at their Mass, the Catholics would often open up their shops and take his cent in exchange for a slice of apple cake. And a loaf for Meester Henke. He hoped they might be willing to leave their work to help Ambroos.

'I'll ask them to send someone!' he promised, and ran lightly across the bridge, to where he could see a small clutch of women, pots and dishes in their hands, queuing to have the Maurits, the baker, cook their Sabbath meal in his ovens. Protestants these, he supposed. They didn't like to work on the Lord's Day, but it wasn't a day of fast, far from it.

Chapter 3

Henke van de Grote

Henke stood on the edge of the canal before the wide basin in front of the Guildhuis, hands in his britches' pockets, rocking back and forth from his toes to his heels, and watching his little flock of ducks as they swam around in circles, splashing and quacking.

'Enjoy it, my friends, enjoy it!' he murmured, chuckling. The feathered creatures paid no attention to him, bobbing and diving, snapping at one another's tail feathers, and attempting to take off in little flurries of flight. Which they could never achieve since their wings were clipped. Henke was fond of his ducks, but he did not intend to let them go free. On the Sabbath however, when there were no boats moving on the water, he always brought them from their pen in the yard, for a swim on the canal. Fourteen white ducks with orange beaks and yellow feet followed him in procession to the water's edge. Then, one after another, they flopped down into the water, quacking with joy, or so he imagined. An hour of freedom on the water each Sunday, in return for the bucket of grain and vegetable scraps he gave them daily, and for which they in their turn surrendered their eggs. Henke had collected four this morning. Not many, but enough. November wasn't a good time for laying. Presently, when the boy came back, he'd intended to fry them up with some more of the bacon, melt a little cheese on top, and place the whole on slices of rye bread. Margriet might like that too. She was still sleeping up aloft, stupefied with gin. It was the only way to ensure some rest for himself. Otherwise she would roam the Guildhuis all night like an angry ghost, hammering at the doors and rattling the shutters, trying to get out. Where did she think she could go, once outside? Would she walk the thirteen kilometres to Delft, where she'd lived as a girl?

He dismissed these unproductive thoughts, and considered Tomas instead. A good enough boy as far as he'd ever heard, and that Ignaas was a brute. Thrashing the lad, surely there was no need for that? Why Anna van de Gracht had agreed to marry the fellow, he couldn't think. Of course, when her man was killed she'd to marry *somebody*, or sell the boat. A woman and a young boy couldn't manage the Appelbloesem by themselves, but couldn't she have done better than this Ignaas van Damme? And now she was dead, poor lass, by Tomas's account, and her son cast upon his stepfather's mercy. With a grunt, Henke settled his seaman's cap down firmly over his large ears, and shifted the stem of his clay pipe from one side of his mouth to the other. Something, he decided, should be done about young Tomas. He'd heard things about Ignaas – things repeated in the tavern which he didn't care to think about. Maybe they were untrue, exaggerated by men gazing at the bottom of a glass or three, but still, if there's a nasty smell of smoke, it usually means someone's set a fire. What to do? He couldn't take the boy in, not with Margriet the way she was.

Some movement made him raise his eyes to the opposite bank. The canalised river flowed into a wide basin here, where the boats turned and unloaded in front of the Guildhuis, but not so wide that he couldn't recognise the man walking alone on the opposite side. Pastor Winkelmann. Henke thought of him as the Pastor, although he knew there must be several such in the town. To Henke this one was *the* Pastor because he lived close by, just across the lock, and was often to be seen in his loose black gown and white bands, wandering the banks of the gracht, head down, old fashioned shovel hat held in place with one hand against the wind, lips moving. Folk thought he was praying, but Henke had learned that this was not so. Pastor Jacob Winkelmann was a poet, and ambled about the town, reciting the verses he was composing, trying, he'd explained to Henke, 'to get the words to fit the metre' Henke wasn't devout, and was untroubled though intrigued by this strange behaviour.

'Hoy, Pastor! Heer Winkelmann!' he called across the water. 'I'm in need of your counsel! I can't leave the fowls. Can you come across?'

Jacob Winkelmann, who must be returning from an early service, raised a hand in acknowledgement. A pastor does not shout to his parishioners across a stretch of water, and certainly not on the Lord's Day. He might not be quite what the good burgers of Schiedam expected of their clergymen, but he knew how to behave. Presently he crossed over by the lock, and came round to join Henke on the deserted quay in front of the Guildhuis.

'Such fine birds! And how they enjoy their chance to swim!' he remarked, nodding towards the raft of ducks as they bobbed and squabbled on the water before him.

'I can only let 'em out on the Sabbath. I've tried at other times when things were quiet, but I lost too many,' Henke told him. 'Boats came in and didn't see 'em. I'd two crushed to their deaths against the embankment earlier in the year. They're good creatures. Good company, when I'm tied as I am.'

The Pastor, who knew about Margriet from their previous conversations, gave a little sigh of agreement and sympathy, and waited for Henke to say what he wanted today.

'It's about a boy,' Henke removed his pipe from his mouth, waving the stem before him. 'Tomas, his name is, Tomas van de Gracht. Off the boats. The Appelbloesem. Skinny little fellow, tow-headed, holes in his britches. I'd put his age at about ten, eleven? I don't suppose you'd know him. They come down the Maas mostly, five or six times a year, mebbe?'

'No, I don't think...'

'You might know of the mother, Anna. I believe she was a churchgoer. When they were here?'

Jacob Winkelmann pursed his mouth and scratched his ear, thinking through such of his congregation who might be off the boats. 'I don't think I do, but she may not come to Sint Jan's. Could she have been a Catholic? The Haven Kerk is handy for the boat people, depending where they're berthed. And much smarter than old St Jan's of course!'

'I doubt "smarter" would appeal to Anna. Anyway 'tis of no account, she's dead. According to young Tomas, she got sick and his step-father took her to the workhouse infirmary in Dordrecht, where she died.'

'And now? The boy lives on the boat with the step-father? Can they manage to sail her with just a man and a young boy?'

'Just about. The man'll manage the sails or pull the towing rope when the wind is down, and the boy can hold the tiller.'

'What is she? The Appelbloesem?'

'A tjalk? Friesian, I'd say, built just for the inland trade. Trim little boat, but it'd be hard for the boy to hold her steady. He's a wiry little fellow, but there's not much of him. And the man's brute.'

'Knocks the boy about?'

'Tomas ran off from him yester night after a thrashing. I let him bed down here, on the ground floor,' Henke pointed over his shoulder with his pipe stem towards the Guildhuis. 'Sent him off this morning to buy a loaf about an hour ago. He's not back yet. I'm just afraid the man, Ignaas van Damme, his name is, may've grabbed him back.'

'Perhaps he was in drink, and is now contrite?'

'I'm sure he was in drink. I'd doubt contrition. I've heard things about the man.'

Henke studied his boots, tapped the bowl of the pipe against the back of his hand, and took a deep breath. 'This is hearsay, Pastor. Tavern talk.'

'Amongst the zakkendragers?'

'Them and others. The zakkendragers see a lot. Hear even more. They're on and off the boats, in and out of the taverns and the grain stores all the time.'

'And you hear what they hear?'

'I do. I take much of it with a grain or two of salt, but I don't like what they say about Ignaas van Damme. They say he's a… Well, young lads should beware of him.'

'I see. And you fear he will… corrupt this boy, Tomas?'

'Not corrupt exactly, Pastor. That implies Tomas might be willing. Ignaas is big strong brute, and the boy would hardly be able to withstand him.'

Henke watched Pastor Winkelmann out of the corner of his eye. The man pulled his lips in, breathed in hard through his high bridged nose, and then let the breath out again by the same route. This would be the kind of human wickedness a pastor doesn't like to hear, but sometimes, nevertheless Henke reckoned, he needs to hear it. Are not pastors the guardians of public morals? Or, in his opinion, should be.

'How long did you say the boy's been gone?'

Henke pulled a watch on a chain out from under his smock. 'Three quarters, mebbe an hour?'

'You'd like me to look for him? Where would he go, to buy the loaf?' Henke was surprised by this offer. He hadn't thought of Pastor Winkelmann as a practical man, a man of action, not just a man of poetry – and sermons too, of course. He'd been thinking more of what the pastor might do for the boy in the days ahead.

'Ah, that I don't know; where he went – on the Sabbath? I didn't think to ask. He said he'd go, and off he scampered. Mebbe I'm worriting too much. Mebbe he couldn't find a bakery open.'

'The best would be Maurits', in the Koemarkt. Would he think of that? They should be open. They're papists. Shall I walk down and ask if they've seen him?'

'Are you able to do that, Pastor? It wouldn't interfere with your preaching?' Henke had a notion that Pastor Winkelmann might be the kind to forget a service he was supposed to conduct. 'I'd take it kindly. I'd go myself, but I need to bring the ducks in and my wife...'

'I can go,' said the clergyman. 'I've taken the early service and I don't have another until this evening. What will I say to the boy, if I find him?'

'That's the other thing I wanted to ask you about. I can't take him in, not for more than a night or two. Not with Margriet the way she is. I had to let him bed down on a pile of sacking in the hallway last night. Pastor, what *can* be done in such a case?'

Jacob Winkelmann shrugged. 'Difficult. I suppose there are no other relatives? I could recommend him for the town weeshuis ... well, the burgers may object. If the family aren't from Schiedam, they won't have paid any taxes here I'd imagine. There's the Catholic one, but you think the mother was Protestant? At eleven he's too young to be apprenticed. I'll think about it, as I walk.'

He turned and strolled away. Henke began to call to his ducks, drumming on a pail with a wooden spoon. The ducks were always loath to leave the water, but they loved their food. So first one and then another lumbered onto the little landing stage Henke had caused to be built for the bootjes, the row boats, (and for ducks, though he never mentioned that). They followed the man with the pail back to the yard and another week in captivity. Not so different, now he brought it to mind, to the little processions of orphaned children he often saw about the town, obediently following their ushers to church and back again.

Henke had lost his own parents when young. It had been lucky for him, he realised, that he'd had an aunt willing to take him in, although he hadn't always felt so at the time.

It had eased his conscience to speak of Tomas to the Pastor, but it hardly eased his mind. Whatever befell the boy, Henke couldn't imagine him happy. Confined to the orphanage or brutalised by Ignaas. Though surely the first must be better than the second?

Chapter 4

Tomas

As Tomas approached the bakery on the Cattle Market square, he recognised one of the boat women in the queue, Hedy, fat and full of smiles. Their families' boats plied similar waterways, they might meet often or not for months on end. His mother had liked her, and had always been glad to exchange news whenever they did meet up. He'd played with Hedy's children on quaysides in towns and villages up and down rivers and canals all over South Holland. Not so much of late, as she had four little girls, and now he was eleven, almost a man in his own eyes, Tomas thought it beneath his dignity to play with hoops and peg dolls. However, Hedy was "off the boats," one of "his people." He ran straight to her, and, although she was deep in conversation with two other women, tugged at her sleeve. Mama would have said, 'Wait, Tomas! Wait until the grownups have finished their talk,' but this was an emergency.

'Tante Hedy!' he whispered, urgently. His mother had taught him always to call her friends *tante*, or *oom*, as a mark of respect to older people, even though Hedy was not his aunt, nor was her man, Cees, his uncle. Her response astonished him.

'Tomas! Heaven help us! What are you doing here, child?'

'Oh, Tante Hedy, there's man. On the bridge. He's been cut! With a glass or a knife or something. All down his belly. He's bleeding, he might die! Please come!'

'But... you shouldn't be here, Tomas!' Tante Hedy wasn't listening. Her fat cheeks blanched, her chins wobbled, and her round blue eyes darted away towards the wharf, hidden behind the lanes that ran off the market place. Tomas saw her shock but failed to understand it to begin with, his mind full of Ambroos, dying on the bridge.

'Please! Tante Hedy!'

The two elderly women she'd been gossiping with now turned and regarded him with anxious, bulging eyes. They made noises in their throats like hens about to lay, 'Kr..ooo! Kr..ooo!'

'What man is this, little fellow?'

'A drunkard most likely dearie, pay no attention.'

'Someone's injured? Who, where?' Spare Maurits, in his ample white apron and baker's hat, had stepped out of the doorway, perhaps to tell his customers that the ovens were hot and ready. With him came the wonderful smell of warm bread. Tomas's stomach growled in longing.

'On the bridge, Meester! I-I think his n-name is Ambroos!' Confused by Hedy's reaction, which seemed to have nothing to do with his own concern, Tomas began to stammer. Then, belatedly, he realised what she'd said, and gaped at her, her meaning finally dawning.

'The Appelbloesem's... *gone?*'

'Unless I'm mistaken. She'll be through the locks with the wind behind her, and onto the Maas by now. Oh, perhaps I am mistaken, child! Perhaps it was some other... Here, I'll run and look!' She thrust her pie plate into Tomas's hands, and ran, her fat buttocks wobbling beneath her skirts, across the corner of the square, past the site for the new elementary school, disappearing into a narrow alley that led down to the water. Maurits had already trotted away too, down to the bridge to see what had happened to Ambroos, whom he evidently knew. The two women, clucking and crooning with concern, placed their pot roasts on the bakery's stoop and hurried after him, skirts and aprons flapping about their knees in the wind. Tomas remained, bewildered, grasping the edges of Hedy's pie plate, unable to decide who to follow.

Surely Hedy *was* mistaken? Even Ignaas, even Ignaas with his senses befuddled by strong drink, as they must have been, wouldn't set sail single-handed? Had they not struggled with the capricious wind these last few days, with Tomas pressing the whole weight of his body against the tiller to hold Appelbloesem steady, to steer a straight course, coming down from Rotterdam, whilst Ignaas cursed on the tow ropes? His heart was hammering behind his ribs. Tears were beginning to prick behind his eyelids, though he blinked them away. What should he do? His head felt heavy as though it was full of uncooked pies. The baker and the women were hastening to help Ambroos. Let them save his life if they could. Should he leave go of Hedy's pie and ...? Then he saw someone crossing the square purposefully coming directly towards him, as though he meant to speak to him. Holding his hat in place with one hand as clergymen often seemed to find necessary, Pastor Winkelmann was making his way across the open, breezy space under a cold sky. The haven was sheltered by tall houses and grain stores, but the wide space of the cattle market was this morning swept by a strong easterly wind beneath scudding broken clouds. The ends of the man's long white bands danced about his neck. Was this man coming to see him, or to see Maurits? Tomas didn't know him. Most of the ministers he had seen on Mama's excursions to church had dressed as this one did, but she'd sometimes pointed out the Catholic ones, who dressed in a different way. No white bands but a dangling cross, and a sash fixed high around the chest.

He remembered that Mama had told him, should he ever find himself in difficulties, 'Ask one of the ones with white neck bands. Although they are all good men… or supposed to be,' she'd added, rather doubtfully. Tomas wondered if this one, now approaching, was a good man, and if so, what he should ask of him.

'Tomas?' called the Pastor from some distance away. 'Are you Tomas van de Gracht?'

'Yes, Sir,' mumbled Tomas.

'Is there some problem?' The man came closer and peered down at Tomas over gold-rimmed nose pinchers 'I understand you came to buy a loaf for Henke at the Guildhuis.' He looked at the pie plate. 'Henke thought you would come back more quickly than this. You haven't lost the money he gave you have you, Tomas?'

'No, Sir! If you please, Sir, I'm still waiting. The baker, Meester Maurits… isn't here.'

'I see. Where is he, do you know?'

'Yes, Sir. He's gone to see to Ambroos, the man that's been hurt.'

'Hurt? Hurt where?'

'In his belly, Sir. He's been cut.'

'Yes, boy, but *where?*'

'On the bridge, Sir! The ladies went too. Hedy went to see about the Appelbloesem, and she gave me this pie to hold.'

Tomas and Pastor Jacob Winkelmann, (whose name Tomas did not yet know) stared at one another in bafflement, neither knowing what to do with the other.

Into their bewildered silence came Augustijn, Maurits' fat apprentice, who had all the while been working away in the back of the shop, pulling the loaves from the oven on his long wooden paddle, and piling them onto the counter. Puzzled by the emptiness of the shop, and the non-appearance of the pies and pot roasts he expected to place next into the hot ovens, he'd come to find out what was happening. On the doorstep he nearly trampled them, knocking against one of the pots with the toe of his clog. Augustijn said a bad word. Then he registered the presence of Tomas and the Pastor, crossed himself, and flushed scarlet.

'Wha's goin' on?' said Augustijn, who had a bad case of adenoids, 'where'd 'e go? Meest' Maurits?'

'I *believe*, I understand, he has gone to assist an unfortunate man who has been attacked...*cut*, I think you said?' Pastor Winkelmann addressed this last question to Tomas, who nodded, too awe-struck by the presence of the pastor, and the girth of fat Augustijn, to risk speech.

'An' the w'men went too?'

'So Tomas here says. I do pray they can help this unfortunate fellow, whoever he is...'

'Yer wan' tha' cooked?' Augustijn interrupted, looking at Tomas and ignoring Pastor Winkelmann.

'Yessir, that is... it's not mine. Hedy off the Wildegans, it's her pie. She went... to see about the Appelbloesem. *I* want to buy a loaf, Meester. Please? For Meester Henke van de Grote at the Guildhuis. He sent me.' He held out his coin as proof of the genuineness of his errand.

'A 'right,' said Augustijn. 'Come in, bu' don' kick them pots. Fool w'men musta left 'em!' He had evidently made up his mind to pretend not to see the Pastor standing there. Tomas was shocked by this rude, behaviour but the clergyman seemed to find it unremarkable.

'I'm Pastor Winkelmann,' he now told Tomas, clapping a hand briefly on the boy's shoulder. 'I came to look for you. Henke was worried about you. I'll walk back to the Guildhuis with you once you've bought the loaf. Tomas looked back at him doubtfully as he entered the shop. He had learned to be wary of unknown men, and he didn't understand why Augustijn had treated the Pastor as he had. This man was a clergyman. Mama would have said trust him, treat him with respect. But Augustijn hadn't, so should he? The pastor's vague and rather watery grey eyes behind his nose pinchers did not inspire confidence. Why had he come looking for him, and why did he want to walk back with him to the Guildhuis?

Chapter 5

Cornelius de Haan

When Tomas emerged from the shop, a warm loaf clasped in his arms, he saw that the pastor was still waiting there, but in the act of raising his hat to someone who was just emerging from the front door of a tall narrow house by the bridge. A man in a frock coat and top hat, with a gleaming silver chain stretched tight across his bulging stomach. Tomas wouldn't have recognised him, dressed as he was in his Sabbath Day finery, but when the Pastor called his name and strode forward to greet him, then he knew him. The Bridge Watcher! The man Ignaas had quarrelled with, only yesterday.

'Cornelius!' Pastor Winkelmann called. He signalled Tomas to follow him and strode across the roadway. Tomas, doubtful, but under the impression that they were about to walk back to the Guildhuis together, followed him.

'Cornelius the Rooster thinks he's cock of the dunghill!' Ignaas had spat, when Cornelius refused to open the bridge and let the Appelbloesem through. He'd said it was too late in the day. Told Ignaas he must lower the mast and scull under it if he was set on mooring inside the Haven tonight, and what a business *that* would have been, lowering the mast between just the two of them.

Cornelius de Haan, though his ancestors might have lived close to a chicken coop, and thus bestowed on him his name, was a man of importance, in his own eyes if not in anyone else's, Tomas understood *that* well enough. Cornelius was Schiedam's chief Bridge Watcher, and tyrant of the waterways. With him today was his little round dab of a wife in an ugly coat of emerald green, his two plump daughters in purple capes and muffs trimmed with rabbit fur, and a tall thin girl in a cloak of sober brown, her face completely hidden inside the brim of what even a boy like Tomas could recognise as an old-fashioned bonnet. If asked he would have guessed she must be their maid or a governess.

Someone must have told Cornelius about the man lying injured on the bridge, *his* bridge. Now, in his Sunday-best clothes, he was bustling forth to investigate this outrage.

The de Haan family had been about to leave for church when Sara, their housemaid, who'd been shaking out a counterpane from an upper window, came tumbling and scrambling downstairs, showing a great deal of her darned stockings in a most undignified fashion, to report what she had seen.

'If you please, Menheer, there's a dead'n on the bridge, Menheer!' His bridge! It was quite useless for his dumpy wife, Clara, heavily corseted inside her "emerald," and his two chubby daughters, Anneke and Lotte, in their "violet", to protest that they 'would be late for the service.' This must be looked into, and immediately! Cornelius was deaf to all arguments. Mathilde, his tall skinny niece, didn't offer any. Nor would he have welcomed them. She was, in his eyes, a poor relation.

Thus it was, followed by a gaggle of querulous womenfolk (and a silent Mattie) that Cornelius erupted onto the market place, hat in hand, his coxcomb of hair quivering with indignation, to discover who could have had the audacity to lie down and die on the Koemarkt Bridge.

It was something of a surprise to him to be hailed, almost immediately, by Pastor Winkelmann. This would have been embarrassing too, if the pastor had been aware the de Haans had intended on this particular Sabbath, to go to the later service at Grote St Jan's which would be taken by the kapalaan, the curate. Lately Clara and the girls had been agitating to try the young man, who gave a livelier sermon.

'*I* never know what Pastor Winkelmann is on about,' Clara had complained. 'They say he writes poetry, but his sermons are as dull as dyke water. The Reverend Aalbers has such a beautiful speaking voice, it quite stirs you up!'

'Such dowdies they are at the early service at Sint Jan's, too,' said Miss Anneke, 'Nothing but dreary bombazine, and hardly even any decent lace to be seen.'

Cornelius had resisted this pleading for weeks, but today he had succumbed to their entreaties. However, it seemed the St Jan's was not to enjoy their patronage at all today. Hearing Pastor Winkelmann calling out to him, he halted, and waited for him to cross the square and join him.

'Is this true what our maid Sara tells us? That there's a corpse on the bridge?' he demanded, seeing that the pastor had urgent news to impart.

'Oh, not a *corpse*, at least one hopes, one *prays*, not,' replied the clergyman, falling into step beside him. 'This lad came running,' he indicated Tomas, 'to tell the baker that there's a man lying injured there. Maurits and some of the women have gone to see what can be done. I fear, Cornelius,' he said, glanced around at Cornelius's womenfolk, 'that it may be quite a distressing sight. The boy says his stomach has been cut open. Perhaps the ladies would prefer to go on to the church...?' Cornelius's wife and daughters were now hurrying eagerly in their wake.

Cornelius waved a dismissive hand. He knew well enough that his wife and daughters might have aspirations to attend a more stylish service but he also knew that no sermon, however stirring, could compete with a man with his stomach cut open.

'We may be able to help!' beamed Clara, now pattering at the minister's elbow. 'We should all attempt to be good Samaritans should we not, Pastor? I know you have several times preached on that theme. Mathilde! Go back, child, and bring some of that sheeting you were cutting up for rags. And a bowl of water. Papa, give her the front door key so that she doesn't need Sara to leave off bed-making to let her in.'

Mattie, invisible inside her shabby poke bonnet, took the key, and turned on her heel. Pastor Winkelmann watched her go, but said nothing. Cornelius, who'd passed over the key without even glancing at her, was hurrying on.

'I'm in two minds, Pastor,' he muttered out of the corner of his mouth as though he did not want his wife and daughters to hear, although he had made no attempt to stop them following him. 'If this man is dead, or dies, then a crime has been committed, a very serious crime! Obviously I must inform the authorities. I am, as you know, a member of the Town Watch, by reason of my role as Chief Bridge Watcher. Should I send to Rotterdam for the Maréchaussée?' he pondered, naming the national law enforcers.

'The military police?' Pastor Winkelmann was startled. 'The responsibility for such action surely does not fall on you alone, Cornelius? I'd imagine you can safely leave that to the Committee. Why, I hardly think this can have been anything more than the result of a drunken altercation. Do you not?'

Cornelius made no reply to this, but puffed his way onto the bridge, where Maurits, the two housewives and a tall young man, who might have been considered handsome, but for a strawberry birthmark marring one cheek, were bending over Ambroos.

'What's happened here? Who is this fellow? Is he still breathing?' Cornelius, who never normally hurried in the execution of his duties, was by this time himself struggling to catch his breath.

The tall young man straightened up, challenging Cornelius's round amber eye with his own slanting blue ones. 'He's alive, and it's not, I think, too serious. A nasty jagged cut, done with a serrated knife or a broken bottle perhaps, but the bleeding has more or less stopped. Whoever did this missed the main artery, thanks be to God.' The young man's name was Frans Rijnsberger, and he too was dressed for church in a neat frock coat, a little on the short side for his gangly frame. He carried a worn but well brushed top hat, and the silver-top of his cane was only a trifle tarnished. Cornelius's daughters, who were inclined to admire him, though deploring the too-short coat, squeaked in pretended alarm, at the same time pushing themselves forward.

'That's your opinion as a medical man, Heer Rijnsburger?'

'As an apothecary, I'm not a doctor,' replied Frans Rijnsburger.

'I'm well aware of that!' snapped Cornelius. 'The question here, *the questions*, are who attacked the man, and what are we to do with him? He cannot remain here!'

'Obviously not,' said the apothecary shortly. 'What say you, Pastor Winkelmann, Sint Jacob's? I'd imagine he's a guild member? The zakkendragers? They'd pay for medicines and dressings? Does he have a wife, family?' He spoke directly to the pastor, making it obvious to a furious Cornelius that he was disinclined to parley further with him.

Cornelius wasn't going to be ignored by this upstart of a pill dispenser, and butted in. 'The zakkendragers, yes, yes! They'll have a cart or a barrow. Someone must fetch one of them at once.' He pointed his beak of a nose at Maurits. 'Isn't he one of yours?' he demanded, implying that Ambroos was a papist, and that as Maurits was also of that faith, it was up to him to do something. Maurits, however, knew his own worth (after all, was he not the best patronised baker in the town?) and refused to be intimidated.

'Your niece is here,' he remarked pacifically, nodding towards the approaching figure. 'Aarte, the glassblower has a handcart, and lives close. I'm sure he'd lend it, as it's an emergency.'

Mattie carried a chipped blue delft bowl of warm water. Since this had taken two hands, the bundle of torn sheeting she'd lodged beneath her arm. Rather than drop it onto the ground, she now pressed this into Tomas's arms on top of the loaf of bread, thus drawing attention to his presence. Tomas would have preferred to be almost anywhere but here, and had been trying to remain invisible in the shadow of Pastor Winkelmann's black coat. Now, alas, Cornelius noticed him properly for the first time.

The Bridge Watcher didn't know Tomas by name, but he certainly knew him by sight. Hadn't he seen this boy's cheeky grin only yesterday, aboard that boat he'd refused to open the bridge for? With that foul-mouthed binnenschipper they called Ignaas? Yes! And was it not all too likely that the drunken bargee had committed this criminal act? Slashed this unfortunate man's stomach during an inebriated quarrel? Cornelius had absolutely no evidence of this, but felt it behoved his status to produce the criminal, or a likely suspect at least. Who better than that man who'd ranted and raved on the deck of his boat and called him rude names? A man who was not even from this town? A dirty binnenschipper with a filthy tongue that was Ignaas van Damme.

'Here, you!' he darted forward and seized Tomas's shoulder. 'Where's your father?'

All eyes turned to Tomas, except those of Mattie, who silently handed the bowl of water to Frans Rijnsburger, and relieved Tomas of the rags.

'*Where* is your father?' Cornelius gave Tomas a shake.

'He's dead, Sir,' said Tomas, clinging onto the loaf and staring up at Cornelius fearfully.

'No boy! Don't lie!'

'It's true, Sir. He died... a long time ago.'

'Nonsense! I saw you with him yesterday.'

'No, Sir!' Tomas's lip trembled and tears started in his eyes.

'I believe the man you saw would be the stiefvader,' interrupted Pastor Winkelmann hastily. 'Do you know where your *step*-father is, Tomas?'

To Cornelius he added, 'You think that man, Ignaas van Damme, had something to do with *this*?'

'I'd certainly want to question him!' gobbled Cornelius. 'That is, the Watch Committee will want to question him! He's a notorious drunkard. An undesirable! A quarrelsome fellow! He was taken up here last spring for threatening someone with a knife! I would almost take my oath he'd something to do with this!'

Cornelius must have known very well that he'd no proof that Ignaas had done anything at all, but his sense of his own importance was great, and he liked to appear to know more than he did. He wanted to find someone to blame, and a suspect from outside the town was always the popular choice.

Support for this view came quickly. 'Tch! A terrible fellow, that one. My husband told me he pulled a knife in the Linderboom tavern,' offered one of the housewives, and her companion chimed in, 'Oh, yes, a terrible fellow!'

Pastor Winkelmann repeated his question to Tomas. 'Do you know where Ignaas is?'

'No, Sir. Hedy went to see.'

'Hedy?'

'She's... she's off the boats, sir, the Wildegans.' Tomas swallowed another sob. 'She thought... she thought the Appelbloesem was...gone.'

'Yes, that's what she said, that the boat was gone,' confirmed the first housewife, nodding her head like a mechanical toy, 'while we were queuing at the bakery. This woman, I wouldn't know her name, but the boy called her Hedy. She told him she *thought* the boat had sailed, but she went running off to look.'

'Went to warn the man more like, if he *wasn't* already gone,' said Cornelius nastily.

'But how could he sail? On the Sabbath? Surely all the locks are closed?' queried Clara de Haan. Cornelius glowered. He had often wished his wife would not question his word so often and so publicly, but this time at least he had an answer.

'Bribery! He'll have bribed the lock keeper to let him through so he could get onto the Maas. Isn't that right, boy?' he said, giving Tomas's boney shoulder another painful squeeze.

Tomas shook his head, sniffed, and shifted the loaf under his arm so that he could wipe his eyes and nose on one of his frayed cuffs.

'I doubt if Tomas knows any more than we do...' began the Pastor.

'The immediate need is to get this man medical help.' Frans Rijnsburger looked up and spoke with some force. He had all the while been crouched over Ambroos, taking cloths as they were passed to him by Mattie, dipping them in the bowl, and using them to wipe away blood from the man's stomach, exposing and cleaning the long jagged cut. 'If he dies we may never know who did this. If he lives... no doubt he'll tell us himself. Speculation seems to me to be pointless. We must get him over to Sint Jacob's without more delay.'

Cornelius frowned, perhaps feeling himself to have been wrong footed here. *He* should have thought of it – had he not been voted onto the board of governors of the infirmary? Did he not give generous donations to Sint Jacob's, the town's hospital and alms house? He felt a sense of ownership of that handsome building, and took pride in his association with it.

But before he could recover lost ground by pointing this out, Pastor Winkelmann interrupted. 'Wisely spoken, Heer Rijnsburger, I'll go straight away and find the glassblower, and borrow his handcart.' And with this he walked off.

Tomas stared miserably after him. Although he hadn't made up his mind whether to trust the clergyman, being left in the custody of the Bridge Watcher, whom he knew to be Ignaas's enemy and therefore his, filled him with dread. Cornelius seemed convinced that Ignaas had done this to Ambroos. Perhaps he had. Perhaps he hadn't. Tomas didn't know how Cornelius could know for sure, or why blame seemed to be falling on him. He tried, stealthily, to wriggle free from the Bridge Watcher's grip.

But Cornelius wasn't having it. 'You, you young scoundrel, are going nowhere! I shall keep you at my house until that villain turns up! He'll come back for you, and then, mark my words; I'll put him before the Watch Committee.'

Although Cornelius couldn't have known it, the idea that Ignaas might come back for him frightened Tomas more than the thought of imprisonment in Cornelius's house. Surely they would at least give him breakfast? He suspected Ignaas wouldn't have gone beyond the Eastern locks anyway. If Ignaas had money he drank it. There would be none left over for bribing Sabbath-day lock keepers. Maybe he hadn't sailed at all. Maybe Hedy had found him and was speaking to him even now. With a final desperate jerk he freed himself from Cornelius's grasp; and thrust the loaf at Mattie, whose hands were now empty of the rags. 'Please Miss, give this to the Pastor!' he whispered to her desperately, and set off running as hard as he could.

Chapter 6

Tomas, Casper and Saskia

Tomas's original notion was to stay close to the canal, and make his way back to the zakkendragers' Guildhuis, but having parted with the loaf he now realised he couldn't. He'd shoved it into the arms of the young woman in the brown bonnet afraid that if he took it Cornelius would accuse him of having stolen it, and send someone in pursuit. But how could he now face Henke without either loaf or money? Henke had been kind, and he just hoped Pastor Winkelmann would take it to him.

Instead of running down onto the canal bank therefore, he swerved across the corner of the cattle market into the mouth of the Hoogstraat. Mama – or perhaps it was Papa, had once told him that the High Street in Schiedam was indeed the highest part of the town, built on a ridge formed when an embankment was constructed long ago to prevent the Schie, then untamed, from flooding the town as it flowed out to the sea. The Hoogstraat of today was lined with shops, a barrel-maker's, a glass blower's and a number of small warehouses. Six days a week it was a busy thoroughfare, but on the Lord's Day it was deserted. For which Tomas was at first glad, lest Cornelius send hue and cry after him, but which he then realised made him all too visible to anyone watching from a window. Even on the Sabbath, perhaps particularly on the Sabbath, those who lived above these shops might be looking idly out at passers-by and asking themselves, 'Why is that boy running? What has he done?'

But where could he go? Where could he hide this time? Short passageways to his left led steeply down at intervals to the Lang Haven. Longer, winding ones snaked off to the right, twisting through grimy alleys lined with tumbledown houses and workshops. Here lived many of the poor of Schiedam, the walls of their hovels stained dark with smoke and grime from the gin distillery chimneys. Tomas turned sharply into one of these passageways and stumbled to a halt. The bank on which these sorry dwellings perched fell away steeply, and before him the ways divided, going right and left. If he took the right hand way he feared it might just take him back to the cattle market. If he took the left hand way, where would that lead him? He could easily become lost in a maze of unfriendly streets. Whilst he deliberated, and as if to confirm his fears, a large surly dog which had been sleeping in a doorway, rose to its feet and snarled at him, fangs bared. Turning right it would mean passing close to it. Tomas took the opposite way.

At the foot of the slope he veered to the left and slewed to a halt again, surprised. At the bottom of the incline, over the roofs of the tumbledown dwellings and ramshackle workshops towered the roof of a handsome red brick building. Drawing closer he saw a broad front entrance flanked by columns. On each side of its pediment and cupola, outlined against moving clouds in the washed-out November sky, were perched two painted wooden figures. Statues. Not the figures of saints or angels that Tomas had occasionally seen in churches or cemeteries. These were two children, a boy on the right, and a girl on the left. He was dressed in a brown coat and knee britches, a cap on his head. She wore a brown dress and a white bonnet and apron. This must be the town orphanage, the weeshuis. Any town of any size to call itself one had an orphanage. A place his mother had feared.

'I won't let them take you *to one of those*, Tomas,' she'd said, trying to comfort him when Ignaas had blacked both their eyes for returning late from picking blackberries. 'Anything is better than that dearest, anything!' Mama had spent a sad year in an orphanage in Utrecht until her father, having married again, came to reclaim her. When Tomas had asked what was so terrible about the weeshuis she hadn't wanted to talk about it, saying only that that the punishments were harsh, and that some of the ushers were always 'trying it', with the older girls.

'And we were shut up in that place like prisoners,' she'd added. 'We were made to sew and embroider until our eyes hurt with straining and our fingers bled. Sometimes we never left the building, except to go to church, for weeks on end. At least on the boat we're free. We can roam where we will in the fresh air and under the sky!' Except that Ignaas hadn't liked them doing that.

Lately, when Ignaas's drinking and the beatings and fumblings had become so much worse, Tomas had wondered if the weeshuis could really be so bad. This one was a very fine-looking building. He walked closer. The broad double doors were thrown open just now, and a well-polished checkerboard-tiled floor gleamed within. The sharp scent of lye soap wafted out into the morning air. As he stood watching, a tall man made taller by a stove-pipe hat strode out, followed by a crocodile of youngsters dressed, like the statues high above them, in brown. First boys, then girls, then a brace of ushers. Then tiny children surrounded by clucking nursemaids, who hurried them along, setting them back on their feet when they tumbled over. On their way to church no doubt, just as Mama had described. But Tomas couldn't help noticing that their clothes were in good repair, if showing occasional careful darns and patches, and their cheeks were plump and pink with health. He wondered what the orphanage fed them for breakfast. And if there might be any left?

He took a few hesitant steps towards the entrance, fully expecting a maid or a manservant to come and close the big doors once the crocodile had disappeared around the corner. No one came. The doors stood open, inviting. A sudden surge of hunger in his belly swamped Mama's voice in his head saying 'Tomas! You mustn't steal from those poor children!' Yet the thought of whatever scraps might be left from an orphan's breakfast, was making him dizzy with longing. He had parted with the loaf without realising how hungry he was. Dare he step inside to see what he could find? What was the worst that could happen? Someone would spy him and chase him out. And if they didn't, might there be some cranny – a cupboard, a storeroom? Within this great building there must surely be somewhere he could hide? Neither Ignaas nor Cornelius the cockerel would ever think to look for him in the orphanage!

He stepped over the threshold, and the sudden cold from the marble tiles made his bare toes curl. His heart pattered inside his chest. Beneath the clean scent of soap there was a musty smell – of cabbage, boiled milk and children's feet. Off this main entrance hall corridors stretched right and left. Boys and girls, thought Tomas, remembering what Mama had said. 'They keep the boys and girls apart, but it wasn't the boys we had to fear, it was the men, the ushers.' Tomas, from his own unhappy experience, wondered if the boys had feared the ushers too.

He peered hesitantly down each corridor, heart beating faster now. In the left hand one, at some distance, a woman stood with her back to him. She wore a white cloth wound around her head and carried a big stoneware jug under one arm. Perhaps she was on her way to shut the front doors, and had been distracted by the person to whom she was speaking through an open doorway. She didn't look round. Quickly, knees knocking, Tomas dodged down the opposite corridor, which was empty. Behind one door as he passed, he heard the sound of a baby wailing. Someone was making cooing sounds, though to no avail. Then, heart jumping on hearing, as he thought, a doorknob turn somewhere close at hand, he ducked into an empty room.

This proved not to be empty after all. It was small ante-room, hardly more than an alcove, off what he was later to discover was the main dining hall. This was a place where perhaps the grown-ups in charge sat to eat, a little apart but still able to see and hear how the orphans might be behaving themselves as they sat at long wooden tables in the main part of the room.

'And who might *you* be?' The voice was high and reedy. Tomas halted in mid-step and swivelled, ready to run for it. Then he realised that the speaker was not, as he'd thought from the rasping sound, some fearsome old man, but a boy, seated in a wooden chair which had wheels. He was small, wizened. His head with its large Punchinello nose was almost dwarfed by the hump of his crooked spine. He sat at a table, a plate of bread liberally spread with beef dripping before him. On the other side of the table, her head thrown back, eyes strangely half-open, half-closed, so that the whites flickered beneath her drooping eyelids, lolled a girl. She was breathing shallowly, her chest wheezing on every intake of breath.

'Don't mind Saskia,' said the hunch-back, 'it's her asthma. Always comes on when it's time for church. I'm Casper Meijer, cripple of this parish. Who are you?'

'Er...Tomas. Tomas van de Gracht.'

'Oh, off the boats. I see. Are you hungry?' he watched Tomas's face for a moment and then said, 'Help yourself. I've had what I want and Saskia here doesn't eat when her chest's playing up. This is our dear Regent's apology. To me. I'm forbidden the comfort of religion lest some young wife should be distressed by the sight of me in church, and her child be born a monster as a result. Stupid superstition. Two or three girls admitted here have given birth, much to the Regent's wife's displeasure, and not one of their brats had so much as a birth mark. Do have some bread and scrape. The dripping's fresh today, I recommend it.'

Thus encouraged, Tomas took a slice and crammed it into his mouth.

'Hey, that's rude!' The girl, Saskia, sat up suddenly, her breathing miraculously restored. 'You'd get in awful trouble if the maids or the ushers sees you stuffing food into your gob like that.'

'I would imagine Tomas would prefer that they didn't see him at all,' drawled Casper in his grating thread of a voice. Tomas was beginning to understand that Casper, despite his small twisted frame, hardly bigger than that of a child of eight, must be much older than he looked. 'Tomas is on the run. Am I right?'

His mouth full (Mama had always cautioned against speaking with a mouthful) Tomas nodded.

'You can't run away to the weeshuis!' interrupted Saskia, bolt upright now, and clearly shocked. 'Children run away *from* the weeshuis. At least they try to. They always get caught though.'

'So, Tomas must have some good reason for doing the opposite. What is it Tomas?'

'My step-dad,' Tomas mumbled, swallowing bread and dripping. 'He ... beat me, and now the Bridge Watcher thinks he's done a murder. He, I mean the Bridge Watcher, wants to hold me by him until Ignaas, that's my step-father, comes back. Then he can catch him and put him up before the Watch Committee.'

'The Bridge Watcher?' said Saskia. 'You mean that man with the key on a silver chain who comes to open the Appelmarktbrug? He's rotten to his apprentice, Wilhelm. Boxes his ears until they're sore! I seen 'im when I went with one of the kitchen maids to get flour from one of the windmills! Wilhelm used to be one of ours,' she added, by way of explanation.

'Saskia's an Orphan Watcher,' explained Casper, dryly. 'She can name all our ex-residents, from as far back as she's been here, and tell you where they're placed as apprentices around the town. But *did* this man, your steifvader, murder someone, Tomas? Do sit down and have another slice. Regent de Hoop likes to see me eating heartily. It makes him feel better. As you can perhaps understand, finding an apprentice "place" for *me* has proved impossible. Tell me about this murder. Does the man with the key on a silver chain imagine you were your father's accomplice?'

'Dunno,' mumbled Tomas through another mouthful of bread and dripping. He wasn't sure what an accomplice was. 'Dunno know if Ignaas had anything to do with it. Old de Haan doesn't know it either, he just hopes it was Ignaas, 'cos he hates him. Ignaas always bawls him out.'

'Have some milk to wash that down,' offered Casper, nodding towards a pottery jug. 'It's got a slug of gin in it. You look as though you need it.'

'Anyway, it's *not* a murder, 'cos the man, Ambroos, isn't dead.' Tomas continued, once he'd swallowed a draught. 'His belly's cut open, but the Apothecary fellow said he could get better if they took him to… some place. The Infirmary.'

'Sint Jacob's. Yes,' Casper pulled a face, 'where I shall no doubt end my days. Straight from childhood to old age with nothing in between. But never mind. Continue. The Watch Committee want to catch Ignaas and the Bridge Watcher wants to hold you until they do? He wants to use you as bait, I suppose, like a when they catch tigers in the jungle. I read that in a book the Regent lent me. They tie a goat to a tree and wait for the tiger to come for it. So… how shall we go about hiding you?'

'I thought maybe there'd be a cupboard here? Or a storeroom?'

'We could give you a uniform!' interrupted Saskia. 'Then if anyone spots you, say at the end of a corridor, they wouldn't know you ain't a new boy, not straight away they wouldn't. O' course, you'd need your hair cut. And you ought to get a bath. You stink a bit, you know?' She wrinkled her nose, 'Like you've been lying on something rotten. Come along with me, I know how to get into the clothes cupboards! She slid from her chair, all trace of painful breathing gone. However, Tomas now saw that she limped. There was an iron brace on one of her legs.

'Go with her,' said Casper, 'while nearly everyone's at Sint Jan's. A uniform is a good idea, but if they catch me in there the game would be up. Saskia can always shove you in a cupboard if she hears someone coming, and say she's there because she wet her drawers. She does sometimes when her asthma's really bad. At least she used to, when she was younger. There's hardly anyone around just now, they're all at church. But one of those idle kitchen maids will be along here in a while to collect the dishes, and we can't have her setting up a screech!'

'I don't want to get you two into trouble,' mumbled Tomas, doubtfully, 'if I could just hide in a cupboard somewhere? Just for a day or so, until – until all this goes away?'

'Don't worry about it!' Casper waved a dismissive hand. 'What could they do to us? The Regent won't cane a cripple like me, and he doesn't cane the girls. All they can do to Saskia is send her out as a maid to some family up on the Plantage, which they're going to do anyway, as soon as she's twelve, which isn't many months off.' He grinned his wide-mouthed Punchinello grin. 'I've lived here nearly fourteen years and I think this is one of the most interesting things that has happened in a long time. A stowaway on the good ship, Burgerweeshuis! Good to have you on board, Midshipman Tomas!'

Tomas had never placed his trust in other children before. He'd never had much to do with them. Sometimes he'd played for a while with a group of youngsters in one of the towns or villages where the Appelbloesem tied up. More often however, the children he met there had been name callers, stone throwers, best avoided. But he liked these two. He raised a hand to his brow in salute, as he had seen the seafarers do aboard the great ships in Rotterdam harbour. 'Aye, aye, Captain!' he said, grinning, and trotted after Saskia.

Chapter 7

Frans Rijnsburger

Frans Rijnsburger the Apothecary had lived in Schiedam for three years. Although an "off comer", a native of Rijnsburg, about twenty kilometres to the north, he'd been here long enough to have established a small business along the Nieuwe Haven (a hardly fashionable, but never-the-less respectable neighbourhood). And long enough to irritate a good many of the stolid burgers of Schiedam with his forthright opinions on medical matters. He was especially active around Sint Jacob's, the town's infirmary and alms house. Those same burgers having had the last guilder wrung out of their pockets for its construction, wished, he well knew, to hear no more of it. Frans however went on insisting that despite the classical beauty of its assembly hall, and the awe inspiring tones of its splendid organ, (both of which he believed benefitted its patrons a good deal more than the residents) the medical side was underfunded and ineffectively run.

Even more dangerously as he should have realised, in the eyes of the likes of Cornelius de Haan, he'd had time to establish himself as something of a favourite with the ladies. Although his ill-fitting coats and prominent birthmark might be regrettable, and his eccentric habit of propelling himself along the canal banks to visit his patients on a two-wheeled wooden contraption he called a *laufmachine* or velocipede, (surely those things would never catch on?) he was able to trade on a certain charm of manner. He was known to be particularly kind to small children and the elderly. The ladies of the town all swore by a special tonic he concocted himself from mysterious ingredients. This had proved highly efficacious for the whoops and croups of infancy and the painfully constricted chests of old age. Clara de Haan had dosed her aged mother with it for years. So successful was this remedy, that the old lady had passed away only last February, not far short of her eightieth birthday.

Since Cornelius had heartily disliked his mother-in-law, referring to her, out of his wife's hearing, as 'that cantankerous old moo-cow,' it will be understood that Frans was not popular with the

Chief Bridge Watcher. Now, insisting on the necessity of getting this wounded sack porter to hospital, and refusing to be side tracked by Cornelius's hunt for the attacker, he'd made himself doubly so.

And about to be trebly so although even Frans himself had not yet realised this. Right there on the cattle market bridge, Frans Rijnsburger had fallen in love. This had never happened before. Regarding himself as a scientist and, above all, a rational man, he would have dismissed out of hand "love at first sight," as affecting only those made up of an ill-disciplined bundle of emotions. But when Mathilde de Haan, clutching the loaf that Tomas had thrust into her arms, had gazed up at him from within the concealing brim of her bonnet, he had fallen head first with a mighty splash, into the deep dark pool of her eyes. Later, he might acknowledge to himself that Mattie was a plain girl in many respects. A little too tall, a little too thin, her chin was too pointed for beauty. Her nose... well, her nose was quite a surprise, but her eyes! Mattie had the most beautiful eyes he'd ever encountered.

A man who slips on vegetable peelings on his morning walk may at first deny this loss of dignity, even to himself. Then he looks around to see if anyone else has noticed, before attempting to carry on as though nothing has happened. In this manner, Frans Rijnsburger shrugged his shoulders within his too tight coat and looked about him. He must not be distracted! He had a patient bleeding to death here.

Happily, he now saw Pastor Winkelmann approaching across the marketplace, together with Aarte the glassblower, pushing a handcart. He was pleased to see it was a flat-bedded cart with low sides, intended for transporting jeroboams from workshop to distillery. Ideal. He shook off the toils of enchantment and hurried to organise lifting Ambroos carefully onto it.

Together with Maurits, Pastor Winkelmann, and the glassblower himself, this was achieved. Cornelius, who was sulking, didn't offer any assistance. The ladies, with the exception of Mattie, who watched silently and proffered more rags once Ambroos was settled, simply provided a chorus of 'oohs', 'ahs' and 'be carefuls!' to the proceedings.

'And now,' said Frans, 'what's the best route? The most level route? Avoiding steps and steep slopes? I've managed to slow the bleeding, but any unnecessary jolts and jars must be avoided.'

'Straight up the Hoogstraat, got to be,' said the glassblower, firmly. 'There's a bit of a dip at this end as you come off the bridge, and the paving's none too even just before you turn in at the gates of Sint Jacob's.' Since a glassblower knows more than most about transporting delicate articles, even Cornelius was disinclined to argue.

'I would like, if you're agreeable, Mevrouw',' said Frans, addressing Clara de Haan with elaborate courtesy, 'to borrow your niece for the length of the journey? I've explained to her the necessity of keeping the wound from bleeding too much, and she can place fresh pads if needed.' He could, of course, do this himself while Pastor Winkelmann pushed the cart, but some compulsion he hadn't yet examined made him want to keep Mattie beside him.

'But where's Tomas?' demanded the Pastor, suddenly peering about him in surprise as though he expected to find the youngster beneath his coat tails. 'Where is the boy?'

'Gone. Went running off, the young devil!' snarled Cornelius. 'I wanted to keep him by me until that steifvader of his turns up. *I* couldn't go running after him, not with my chest!' (He breathed heavily, to illustrate the parlous state of his chest) 'And no one else was willing to put themselves out!' (He turned his fierce cockerel eyes on Frans Rijnsburger and Maurits in turn) 'So off he went. But he won't go far. He'll be hiding out somewhere, sneaking in at someone's back door and pinching something to eat, as like as not. Those little devils off the boats are all the same. I'll soon get word of him!'

'But Cornelius, he was on a legitimate errand for Henke van de Grote at the Guildhuis,' said the Pastor, doubtfully. 'Henke had taken him in overnight, and sent him out for a breakfast loaf.' He could deduce, from what Henke had told him that Tomas had good reason not to want to stay with the Bridge Watcher until Ignaas turned up to claim him. However, he hesitated to start explaining this to Cornelius. There were ladies present, who must surely find such information distressing. One had to think of their sensitivities. 'I suspect he's frightened of his step-father,' he ventured, 'some ill-treatment there, I understand.'

He became aware that someone was tugging at his sleeve, and turned to find Mattie thrusting a loaf at him.

'This is for Meester Henke,' she murmured. 'The boy gave it to me, for you to give to him.'

Pastor Winkelmann had never heard Mattie speak before, and broke into a delighted smile on discovering that this niece of the de Haans was not, as he'd presumed, deaf and dumb. Frans Rijnsburger, who was waiting with impatience to start conveying his patient to Sint Jacob's, was surprised to find himself consumed by a pang of jealousy because she had spoken to Winkelmann and not to him.

'Come on! This man needs to be in the hospital! Who cares where the boy has got to! Let us get going, for Heaven's sake.'

Interest in Ambroos' fate waned at this point. Maurits set off back to his neglected bake house. The two housewives, recalling their pot roasts, went with him. Clara de Haan and her daughters decided they might as well abandon the idea of going to church, and stroll instead by the Lang Haven – where they might be in time to scrutinise the fashionably attired Catholic fraternity as the congregation from the Haven Kerk dispersed. The glassblower, who was an atheist, reminded Frans that he wanted his property back when he'd finished with it, and trudged off home. Cornelius de Haan remained on the bridge, gazing fiercely seawards, as though he expected Ignaas to sail into view at any moment, armed to the teeth like a pirate chieftain.

'I'm grateful to you, Juffvrouw Mathilde,' said Frans, formally, as they steered the trolley slowly along the Hoogstraat. 'And to you, Pastor,' he added hastily, acknowledging that Jacob Winkelmann had stayed to help. 'I didn't want to attempt this on my own.'

He'd hoped to coax a reply from the girl, but none came. She walked alongside the improvised conveyance, ducking her head to peer down at Ambroos' wound, a pad of clean rags at the ready in her hand. Frans wondered if she was short-sighted. Those eyes! It would be a shame to hide them behind spectacles and perhaps, he thought, Miss Mattie knew this. Ambroos remained unconscious, although now and then his eyelids fluttered.

The morning had moved on, and already the scent of roasting Sunday dinners floated out onto the street. Not everyone paid Maurits to cook for them. Passing one of several small dwellings that lined either side of the Hoogstraat, they heard raised voices, followed by a yell of pain and angry shouting, thumps and slaps.

Pastor Winkelmann flinched.

'There's so much drinking, leading to violent behaviour amongst the poorer classes in this town,' he said with a sigh. 'I fear for so many of our people, especially the women and the children. No wonder they call our town Black Nazareth, for it is surely the very opposite of the holy place where our Lord grew up!'

As if to illustrate this text, a door was flung open, and a heavy cooking pot sailed in an arc above their heads. It bounced off the further wall and clattered to the ground, narrowly missing the trolley and its burden.

'Take this young boy, Tomas,' Jacob Winkelmann continued, inhaling to calm himself and glancing around nervously, lest other heavy objects follow. 'I'm sure Bridge Watcher de Haan, without intending to, frightened him just now. Tomas ran off from his step-father yesterday because of his brutality. I have all this from Henke van de Grote of the zakkendragers. I'm sure the last thing the boy wants is to be re-united with that man.'

'There was blood on his shirt, Sir,' announced Mattie, nodding as she turned her head to address this to the pastor, 'Stripes of blood, as though he'd been beaten with a stick, poor boy.'

Frans felt another sharp stab of jealousy. Why does she speak to *him* and not to me? He knew he was being ridiculous. It was natural enough, was it not, for a young unmarried woman to feel more comfortable speaking to an older clergyman than to a young man she didn't know?

But she's going to know me, he vowed. The de Haans shall not prevent it. Although I'm sure they'll try, for she's very useful to them. A needy relative. I don't suppose they ill-treat her, but they don't appreciate her. Look how they sent her back alone to fetch rags and water! Not one of them offered to help. They're using her as a maidservant to whom they need not pay wages. Someone to carry their parcels when the women go shopping! Then he gave his wits a shake. This was foolishness. He should be looking for an heiress – or at the very least a girl with good family connections, someone who could help him make a success of his business. This was what he'd always intended. The last thing he needed was a penniless bride.

'Here we are. We must take this turn gently,' he warned, as they approached the tall wrought-iron gates at the front of Sint Jacob's

Infirmary.

They paused, considering how to manage this. The glassblower's cart had but two wheels, it was designed to move in straight lines. Before they could position it satisfactorily however, a bent, elderly man in a uniform cap, and a greatcoat that was too large for him, suddenly hobbled forward to block the entrance.

'Can't come in with that!' he stated in a high, cracked voice.

'Nonsense, Klaas! You know me, Frans Rijnsburger the apothecary. Did I not prescribe drops for your eyes only last week? *This* man has been badly injured, and I need to get him to Heer Doctor Saunders as quickly as possible. He's already lain in the open half the night.'

The old man thrust his chin forward like a lizard darting at a fly, and peered into Frans' face. 'Could be,' he acknowledged. 'Could 'ave been you got them drops for me, and they did ease my eyes a little, but I've my instructions, see? Them as is needing urgent medical attention should use the lower side gate. Directeur van Corte isn't wishful to have folks bleeding and dying in the main court. It upsets folk.'

Despite the chilly breeze of the November morning, a number of people were promenading in the courtyard in front of the enormous stone columns that guarded the main entrance. Some even sat huddled on the shallow steps before the entrance doors, wrapped in blankets. Frans had often wondered if Bouwmeester Giudici (that fashionable Italian architect of fifty years ago), had supposed himself to be another Bernini, designing a frontage for Saint Peter's in Rome, when he came up with this stately facade for what was, after all, just a small town hospice for the sick and aged.

'Preposterous!' he snapped at old Klaas, waving a hand to indicate that he had seen the loiterers. 'Most of these people here are too blind to see in front of their noses, and those that aren't are in their second childhoods! What do they care whether a sick man is carried past them? To take this man by another entrance would mean wheeling him either up steps or down a steep slope. He needs to lie flat.'

'Ah, 'tis all very well for you to say that, Meester Apothecary,' said Klaas. 'But I should lose my place if I let you by. Heer Directeur has given strict instructions. "It's offensive to the ladies," says he, "to have the sick and dying thrust into their society without warning.'"

'The *ladies* he has in mind aren't here!' protested Frans, whose temper was about to boil over. 'He's thinking of the burgers' wives you old fool! Not these poor old grannies shuffling about in their nightgowns!'

'If you and I, Heer Rijnsburger,' interrupted the soft voice of Mathilde de Haan, 'were to walk in front and to the side of the trolley, we could enter by that small door in the right wing without anyone coming close enough to see who or what is being wheeled in.'

'Why yes!' confirmed Pastor Winkelmann. 'Miss de Haan makes an excellent suggestion. Come now, Klaas, old fellow, you know *me*, Pastor Jacob Winkelmann from Sint Jan's? I come here twice a week to take services in the chapel. You must recognise my voice?' He took the old fellow gently by the elbow. 'I can vouch for Heer Rijnsburger, and Miss de Haan is a most estimable young lady. If Directeur van Corte should make the slightest difficulty, be assured we would speak up for you. All three of us.' So saying he delved in the pocket of his coat and produced a small coin which he pressed into old Klaas's hand, at the same time moving him gradually aside so that they could pass.

Frans Rijnsburger found that he was absolutely furious. Whilst waiting for the little Scottish doctor to be called away from his post-Church whisky-and-soda, he had plenty of time to examine his own state of mind. He was furious with the ancient gatekeeper for being an exasperating old nuisance. He was furious with Mattie for making a sensible suggestion, and in doing so showing him up as a fool for making a fuss. He was furious with Pastor Winkelmann too... for something or other. Probably for being a good Christian and handling the old man with love and tact. But most of all he was furious with himself for displaying his own bad humour. He had demeaned himself, and in front of a girl he was determined should think well of him.

Ambroos was still alive, perhaps even breathing a little easier. Miss Mathilde would now be walking home, escorted, at least as far as the Appelmarkt Bridge, by Jacob Winkelmann. Pastor Winkelmann must be approaching forty, and had never shown, in the three years Frans had known him, the slightest inclination to neglect either his calling or his poetic muse for courtship. But Frans couldn't help seeing him in the role of a rival.

Xander Saunders, the stout little Scottish doctor, with his thinning ginger hair and his pot belly, found him seated on a window ledge in the operating room, chewing the head of his cane and brooding.

'Now, young Frans,' said he, in his bad Dutch, 'why so filled with gloom? He lives, this patient of yours! I stitch him up, and the good God being willing, he survives another forty years more.'

Chapter 8

Tomas and Saskia

Tomas was taking a bath. This was not something he cared for at all, but Saskia, finding a tub in the laundry which still had two or three inches of water in it, had been insistent. "Cos you niff,' she remarked brutally, 'you niff like you're mouldy, and they'll find you out by the smell, like they did when Atie let that stray dog in and it was sick in the kitchen store cupboard. It's a lucky chance for you,' she pointed out. 'The kitchen porter's supposed to empty that tub right out, and upend it so it all goes down the drain, 'cos it's too heavy for the maids. Should've done it, Friday, but he's a lazy devil and didn't finish the job. So you take a good wash all over, while I find you some clothes from next door.'

Tomas resented this bossy little girl, but something told him Mama would have said the same. Mama was keen on washing too. When he was a tiny boy she had dumped him regularly in her own, smaller, wash tub once she'd finished the week's clothes' wash. Latterly she'd been too sick to insist, and it hadn't mattered while the warm days lasted. He'd swum naked and slick as a fish, in the river or the canal wherever the boat tied up.

He was relieved that Saskia didn't stay to watch, but took herself off, her gait uneven on her withered leg, into the storeroom next door to find a suit of clothes she thought might fit him. Lately he liked to be private. Not just because of Ignaas. Didn't like it when Hedy's eldest, Eva, stood and stared with her thumb in her mouth, one time when he had stripped off on a sunny September day and jumped into the canal beyond Leerdam.

He crouched in the cold suds and scrubbed at himself with the piece of rag Saskia had found for him. Cupped his hands and poured water over his head, and then examined the water for lice to drown. Didn't find any. 'They like strong blood,' someone had told him. Perhaps his blood wasn't as strong as it used to be. They said that could happen if you didn't get regular meals.

There was a towel drying on a rack overhead. He had to jump to catch a corner of it and drag it down to dry himself.

'Someone'll puzzle where *that's* gone,' said Saskia, stumping in with her arms full of garments. 'Just toss it in the tub. Let them think it fell in off the rack. Here, try this lot. I'll look the other way while you pull on your underdrawers.'

Orphans, Tomas discovered, wore an awful lot of clothes. Woollen vest and long underdrawers, spencer, wool stockings, garters, wool shirt, serge knee britches, waistcoat, neck cloth, jacket and cap. Stout *boots*. Tomas had never worn anything on his feet. Cap to be kept in pocket while indoors? Dressed in all of this Tomas felt bundled up like a bale of wheat straw, and wondered if he would be able to run if he had to. He protested that the jacket was too big and Saskia went and found another, which had two buttons missing, but they agreed that didn't matter. She also produced, from the pocket of her apron, a comb and a pair of scissors.

'You got crawlers?' she demanded, advancing with these.

'No! I used to, but my blood's got thin, I think.'

'I'll just cut the front since I've only got scissors,' she said. 'Stand still.'

'Do you have to?'

'Yes. Or you won't look right. All the boys has their hair shaved close in case of crawlers. It's a rule.'

'Why not girls then?' he asked, grumpily, as she sheared hanks off his fringe. Saskia wore her blond hair in two pigtails, doubled up, but peeping from under a close fitting white linen cap. 'We do when we're babs. Then we're let to grow it. Lotta combing each other out and we has to wear caps all the time,' she replied, taking another couple of slashes at his hair. 'There! Just let me getta broom and pan, and sweep up, and we'll go and find Casper. He'll know where it's best for you to hide out.'

'Is Casper the oldest boy here?'

'Yes. He's thirteen, going on fourteen. Bin here since he was just a bab. A lot here don't like him 'cos they reckon he's got a curse laid on him, being a hunchback. Also he's clever. He can read any books they give him. And his tongue! Sharp as a knife! The bullies are afraid to cross 'im. Regent de Hoop says he's gotta good brain. He could have been a lawyer or a doctor of medicine mebbe, if he hadn't been born a cripple. I reckon the Regent's right, too. Casper's my friend,' she added, proudly, 'An' I'm his. I push him about. Wherever he wants to go, s'long as it's not upstairs. Only reason I'm hanging on here. They've got a place for me on the Plantage. You know it? A big park, they tell me. Where the smart folks live, over the other side of the Nieuwe Haven? Fambily with a girl my age that's had some illness that's made her too weak to walk. Liesbeth, her name is. Miss Liesbeth van Doran. I'm to be her maid and *com-pan-ion,*' she boasted. 'I'll live in. It's good place for me, but I don't want to leave Casper, and I don't have to until I'm twelve.'

They left the laundry room and went stepping quietly through empty corridors. Tomas felt awkward and clumsy in his too large boots. They found Casper where they'd left him. To Tomas's disappointment someone had been and removed the plate of bread and dripping. After so much washing, and the effort of donning all these clothes, he could have used more sustenance. Casper was reading a linen bound book, a pair of ill-fitting spectacles perched on his oversized nose. Seeing them in the doorway, he removed these, folded them, and stuck them in an inner pocket of his jacket.

'That's better, Tomas. You'd pass at a distance, in a poor light,' he said, looking Tomas over critically. He sniffed the air. 'You smell a lot better too.'

'He's had a bath,' said Saskia, proudly. 'We found a tub with some water left in it, in the laundry. So he's as clean as we can get him, for the moment. What d'you think of his rig out?'

'Good. Convincing. But the cap Tomas? *Not* in your pocket. It bulges. Fold it as flat as you can, and button it inside your coat. That's better. That's what I do. We're supposed to hang them on pegs in the lobby near the Regent's office, but I can't reach, and you might need to leave us in a hurry.'

'So, where's he to hide out? Have you thought?' Saskia demanded. 'They'll be back from church soon.'

'I've given it my best attention,' Casper replied, solemnly, 'and I think he'd be safest in that walk-in storeroom next to Matron Schmit's office. Just across from me,' he added. 'I used to sleep in the dormitory with the other boys, but they complained. I cough a lot, clearing my chest, and sometimes I choke, and can't get my breath. So they decided to make a small cubicle for me downstairs, near to Matron, so she doesn't have to be fetched if I'm taken sick. The Regent's given me a bell to ring. And the ushers don't have to carry me up and down stairs anymore. Across from me there's a storeroom nobody uses much. It's full of old matrasses and bedframes and such. I haven't been inside, only looked in from the doorway, but I'm sure *you* could wriggle in amongst them. Would you mind that?'

'Course not,' said Tomas. 'I can sleep anywhere.' But even as he said it, he wondered how long he would have to remain hidden inside in this storeroom. It would be a bit like being trapped on the boat below deck in a jammed lock in driving rain. He'd never liked that shut in feeling. Something of these thoughts must have passed as shadows across his face, because Casper asked, 'Can you read?'

'Some,' he said, doubtfully.

'I'll lend you a book. It's a book of children's rhymes. Not too difficult.' He produced a tiny leather bound book from somewhere under his jacket tails. 'I liberated this from the schoolroom cupboard a couple of months ago!' he grinned. 'I caught one of the little 'uns chewing on it!'

'Oh, I always liked that one!' said Saskia. 'It's ever so old, too. You can see by the pictures. Nobody wears clothes like that nowadays, and even the printing of the words is old fashioned. I couldn't figure some of the words out.'

'Well, Tomas can try. And you can have one of my spinners too, Tomas. It'll help to pass the time.' From a pocket he produced a piece of stiff paper, a circle, but with its edges cut to form an octagon, each 'edge' having a number from one to eight written on it. To this, he added a thin spindle of wood which he poked through a central hole. He placed the point of the spindle on the scarred table beside him, and twisted the stick with a flick of his fingers. The little homemade top spun in place for several moments before it developed a wobble. He grinned at Tomas, 'One of the older boys brings me the spindles,' he said. 'He's apprenticed to a carpenter. He thinks he's keeping me from putting a curse on him!'

'Eight! I guess it'll fall on eight!' squeaked Saskia, who must have seen this many times before. It fell with number '7' at the bottom, touching the table.

Casper chuckled. 'Wrong again, Saskia! You always guess wrong. Yours to keep you amused,' he added, handing it to Tomas. 'Come on, Sas, we need to take him to his new home. Time's getting on.'

Saskia seized the back of the wheeled chair, hauled it round with some difficulty, and began to push him out into the corridor.

'But… won't I need a candle or something?' Tomas asked,

hurrying after them, still feeling exceedingly clumsy as he clattered along in those second-hand boots. He was so used to the darkness below the Appelbloesem's deck, he was sure he'd need a light if he was to read.

However, the storeroom had a window. If he balanced on the toe-caps of the boots he could even see out. There wasn't a lot to see, but it helped to pass the time. A stretch of grass, a few scrubby alder trees, almost bare of their leaves now. There might have been flowers, daisies, clover he thought, but that season was past. A fence around the orphanage's ground, houses beyond. Poor looking houses, and what might be a gin mill or a warehouse. Just a small one, if it was a distillery. He'd heard someone telling his stepfather that there had been nearly two hundred in the town at one time, although nobody seemed very sure how many there were nowadays. Two hundred distilleries, that was a lot of gin! Even Ignaas couldn't drink that much. Between the thin branches of the trees he could see, in the distance above the house tops, part of a grey stone building with high arched windows. He thought it might be Grote Sint Jan's, which must be somewhere close by. The children had returned very soon after Casper and Saskia left him. They'd hidden him in here not a moment too soon.

As the orphans clattered noisily past, (boys he was sure, wearing heavy boots like the ones Saskia had given him) men's voices, the ushers, calling on them to be quiet, be quick, wash their hands before the midday meal, he'd held his breath.

He wasn't locked in. Casper had said the door was never locked, that was how he knew what was in here. In one way that felt good. Tomas wouldn't have liked the sensation of being sealed in, trapped. In another, he feared the suddenness with which someone could thrust the door open and catch him unawares.

'On my better days I can move my chair using my hands to turn the wheels,' Casper had explained before he left him, 'just enough to get me along this corridor without having to ask one of the ushers, or wait for Saskia. Naturally, with a large snout like mine, I've felt the need to poke it in anywhere I can get to! I know what's in all these rooms,' he chuckled. 'Saskia likes to know too! Girls aren't supposed to come into the boys' wing, but they let Saskia, because they know she's bringing or fetching me.'

'I'll bring him again after lunch,' Saskia had promised, jiggling about on her good foot anxiously. Time had been passing. 'He's supposed to rest in the afternoon, but he often doesn't. You'll have to say you're tired today, Casper, so we can fetch Tomas something to eat.'

How were they going to do that? Tomas didn't know, but he found he trusted these new friends. Casper seemed to have all the answers. Casper would think of something. This room he was in had a stuffy odour. It reminded him of their living quarters below deck on the Appelbloesem when there was a bad spell of winter weather, and Mama hadn't been able to wash and air their clothes and bedding. Familiar, and somehow comforting. He subsided onto an old torn and stained mattress, and laid the book and the spinning top neatly on the floor in front of him. He wasn't used to sitting still, having nothing to do. No tasks around the boat. No errands to run. Idly, he spun Casper's homemade top on the bare floor, and guessed three. Once, that would have been for his family, Tomas, Mama and Papa. And it fell on three. Me, Casper and Saskia, he decided. This must be a good omen?

Chapter 9

Jacob Winkelmann, Mathilde de Haan, and Henke van de Grote

'I pray that this poor man, Ambroos, will survive,' said Pastor Winkelmann, as he and Mattie walked together down the street called Appelmarkt (although all kinds of fruit were sold there in their season) and down the slope to the Lang Haven. 'It was very fortunate, was it not, that Frans Rijnsburger came along when he did, and was able to take charge of the situation? A most capable young fellow!' He had been searching for the last few minutes for something to say to her, and hoped she would respond. She didn't. Whatever opinions Mathilde de Haan had, it seemed she habitually kept them to herself. One could not even begin to guess, he thought, what she might be thinking, her face completely hidden deep inside her bonnet's brim. He tried to remember exactly when it had been that he first saw her about the town, trailing silently in the wake of Cornelius and his family. Three years? Five? To begin with he hadn't noticed her at all, supposing, he now thought rather ashamedly, that she must be either their maidservant or a deaf and dumb relative.

Reaching the bridge, he spoke again. 'Will you be alright, walking back alone? You see I feel I ought to take this loaf to the Guildhuis straight away. Henke must be wondering what has happened to his breakfast! I hope I may find young Tomas there too.'

'Perfectly alright, Sir,' she replied, gravely. 'I trust you'll find that poor boy safe. My aunt and my cousins were going down to the Haven to take a walk, having missed the service at St Jan's. I expect I'll meet up with them.' She turned her head to scan the quayside. 'There's rather a crowd, the congregation's just leaving the Nieuwe Kerk, but I expect I'll find them. Good day to you, Menheer!'

With this she began to walk, giving no sign that she intended to hurry. He had the impression that despite her words, it would not trouble her if her relatives had already returned home. Perhaps, he thought, she values time to herself. She must seldom have that luxury. Jacob Winkelmann understood this, none better. Although he carried out his duties as pastor as diligently as he was able, he knew himself to be a failure. The lives and loves and sorrows of his congregation simply did not command his interest, only his compassion. He longed, so often, to be free of their importuning. Of their neediness. Of their squabbles. Of their unchristian behaviour to one another. Husbands who drank and beat their wives. Wives who drank, or scolded. Men *and* women who were interested only in appearances, in wealth, in holding positions of importance in the town. People who lived in comfort, yet blamed the poor for their poverty. Who, whilst thinking themselves pious, gave grudgingly, if at all, to schemes for their relief. How he longed to be free of them all. Free to worship God and write his poetry!

As he crossed over the graceful wrought-iron Appelmarkt bridge and then its twin sister, the Korenbeurs bridge, where the Lange and Korte Havens came together before the corn exchange and the lock, he found himself wondering, as he had occasionally in the past, if a wife might be a help and a consolation? Having a dedicated housekeeper, a devout and conscientious elderly woman, he'd never felt the need of one. By no means a man of earthly passions, he found everything about human love difficult. Celibacy, he was more at home with. As a minister in the Dutch Reformed church, a wife and family were, of course, permitted, even encouraged. But for forty years God and poetry had been sufficient for Jacob Winkelmann. However, as he walked down the slope and around the edge of the Schie basin to the Guildhuis, he found himself wondering if Mathilde de Haan might not make an excellent wife. Calm. Practical. Discrete. The very opposite of those flipperty-gibbets her cousins, who had nothing in their heads but thoughts of clothes and young men. Presumably she had very little money of her own. Otherwise the de Haans might not have felt obliged to take her in. That was no obstacle. His father had owned two ocean-going vessels, and made his fortune shipping barrels of gin across the North Sea to the Port of London. Jacob Winkelmann did not resent the fact that his elder brother had scooped the bulk of that considerable inheritance. He'd been left in comfortable circumstances. Sufficient to buy Mattie a new bonnet with a narrower, more fashionable brim, for the wedding, he thought, smiling to himself. Then it dawned on him that he had never yet, in those three, (or was it five?) years in which he'd been aware of her, seen the girl's face full-on, only a glimpse of the tip of her nose and a rather sharply pointed chin. Might she be, in fact, extremely ugly? Hadn't he heard a whisper that she was disfigured in some way? He was shocked at his own reaction to these thoughts. Had not Christ healed the leper, and shown His love and pity for the cripple? Could Jacob Winkelmann, His faithful servant, do less? But as a poet, and a man, he was forced to acknowledge that ugliness was an anathema. Beauty was important to him. This was a depressing discovery. As he trudged to the Guildhuis door and raised his hand to knock, it seemed Mattie's chance of an advantageous marriage (for the townsfolk would certainly have seen it that way) had melted clean away.

There was no immediate answer to his knock. He waited patiently, realising that Henke might be on the upper floor, attending to his sick wife. He didn't like to think that he might be tying her up, although Henke had confessed that he sometimes did this, 'to keep her safe.' Jacob Winkelmann found this understandable and perhaps even wise, but none the less disturbing. He knocked again, and after another long pause, yet again. Still no reply. This was vaguely troubling. On a working day, when the zakkendragers were frequently sitting or standing about indoors waiting to be called to work the boats, Henke must, and did, go out and about. He'd seen him on the quays, supervising teams loading and unloading. He must also meet with distillers' representatives, collect payments, settle disputes, and visit the widows of former workers. Henke, he supposed, had plenty of friends and old comrades amongst the zakkendragers whom he could trust to sit with Margriet if she was calm enough to be left. To take her food and drink. To ensure that she didn't fall into the fire, or try to run off. But this was Sunday, and Henke was not a regular church goer. Where would he go on a Sunday?

All Jacob Winkelmann could think was that *someone*, (news flew around this town by apparently supernatural means) must have come to tell Henke about Ambroos, and he'd locked Margriet in, and walked across the dam to the infirmary. He'd quite convinced himself that this must be the case, when he happened to push gently against the door, and it swung open. This wasn't a good sign. If Henke had gone out, leaving Margriet alone in the building he would surely have locked the door? He might, of course, have locked her in an upper room. Jacob Winkelmann knew he did this, but Henke had also told him that it was never for more than a few minutes if no one else was around. He'd confessed to the pastor that he always feared she would harm herself in some way, if only by hurling herself against the door. Once, in a frantic state, she had broken an upper window and cut her wrists quite badly. Henke had said he'd never been sure whether this had been the accidental result of demented rage, or if she had actually been trying to kill herself.

He stepped nervously inside the Guildhuis's hallway and called out. If he should encounter Margriet, a furious whirling dervish of a woman as he recalled, from the rare occasions she had been visible, what would he do? The Bible told how the Lord Jesus had calmed the man possessed by unclean spirits who shouted in the synagogue, by force of His Holy personality alone. Jacob Winkelmann knew he didn't have his Master's divine command. Much as he would have liked to heal the sick, whether of body or mind, he had never discovered any gift for it.

'Meester Henke? Henke? Mevrouw Margriet?' he called out nervously, but no one answered. His voice echoed in the tall building seemingly empty of life. He glanced into the downstairs room where the numbered balls in their box and the 'shoot' contraption stood idle. The zakkendragers' lanterns were lined up on one of the trestle tables, their wicks trimmed and ready for an early start on Monday. Ladders used for unloading the bigger boats hung against the wall. He put Tomas's loaf down on one of the tables, and went and stood beneath the hatch-way to the upper floor. He called again, louder. There was no reply.

Was he was being foolish? He ordered himself to review what he knew of Henke. The ducks! Might he be attending to his ducks in the yard at the rear of the building, and have taken Margriet with him? Henke had mentioned in the past that he tried to take her out into the fresh air for short walks on days when she was sufficiently quiet and amenable. This surely must be one of those days.

The ducks were in the walled courtyard behind the big square building, in a special pen that Henke had built for them, separated off from the barrels, ladders, ropes and grappling hooks which were kept there. There was also a small rowing boat for retrieving items that fell into the basin. The pen was thickly lined with straw, and there were shallow enamelled dishes containing maize and water at one end. The ducks were mostly asleep, huddled together for warmth. Some of them opened round yellow eyes and looked at him, ruffled their feathers, and then settled down to sleep again. There was no sign that Henke and his wife had been here this last hour.

Baffled and uneasy, the pastor walked back around the building. The Guildhuis stood empty, its door unbarred. As he wavered, wondering what to do, he saw several people walking by on the towpath on the other side of the canal basin. They seemed familiar, if only by sight. Catholics, he decided, who had been to Mass at the Haven Kerk, and were now returning to their homes somewhere further along the Schie. The fact that they were Catholic and that shouting across the water was considered rude, especially for one of his cloth, made him shrink from calling out to ask if they had seen Henke. Everyone in Schiedam must know Henke van de Grote by sight, even those who'd never had cause to speak to him.

Instead, he walked round to the lock and stationed himself below the Corn Exchange Bridge. There, he felt confident he would see anyone who approached from either direction and on either side of the canal. The water was quite high. There must have been a lot of rain further inland during the previous week. The Schie was pushing hard against the lock gates. He supposed that someone would come down later today and ease the flow. Although in theory the lock keepers took the Sabbath as a day of rest, when God sends high water it waits for no man. Once the light began to fade they could, and frequently did, declare the Sabbath over, and reopen their locks.

Jacob Winkelmann now stared down into the water, which was creating eddies and tiny whirlpools against the gates, thrusting up swirls of foam and little floating islands of autumn leaves. He fell to wondering whether Tomas's step-father, the much reviled Ignaas, really had bribed one of these industrious men to open the eastern locks which would let him up on to the Maas.

Unlike Cornelius he doubted whether the binnenschipper would return to claim Tomas. Certainly he couldn't sail the boat far without help, but on the other hand he must fear that Tomas, having run, would tell people why. As Mathilde de Haan (here she was, creeping into his thoughts again!) had pointed out, the evidence of a cruel beating was there for anyone who had eyes to see. Of course, people would say parents have a right to chastise their children, but not to the extent of covering a young boy's back with bloody wheals.

What little he'd seen of Tomas had given him a better opinion of the boat child's character than Cornelius would be willing to acknowledge. The boy had carried out Henke's errand honestly. He'd been the one to fetch help for Ambroos. When threatened with incarceration and being handed over to Ignaas, he'd fled, understandably, but not before doing his best to make sure that Henke's loaf was delivered.

No, decided the worthy Pastor, staring into the black waters of the canal, the boy was a good boy, deserving, and he must try to discover some way to help him. He searched his mind for charitably-inclined parishioners who might be persuaded to sponsor him. Find him a place in the weeshuis, give him an education. And, in time, contrive a suitable apprenticeship. It was unfortunate that Tomas's family were outsiders who lived an itinerant life, answering to no one and paying, he imagined, no taxes. He could well envision the response of many here in wealthy Schiedam. 'He wasn't born here; he's not one of us! Why should we pay for some water gypsy's brat?'

Deep in thought, his eyes followed the swirling currents of the pent up river. A larger than usual vortex was being created against the wooden supports of the lock gate. Something was being pushed up from the depths towards the surface. Jacob Winkelmann was visited by a sudden horrid presentiment.

Then, from the far bank, a voice hailed him.

'Pastor! Have you seen her?' Henke was running, stumbling onto the bridge from the lower end of the Hoogstraat. Other men ran after him, their heads moving from side to side as they gazed around, troubled, searching.

'Have you…seen…Margriet?' Henke was breathless, his face contorted with anxiety. 'She's missing. I've…we've been looking everywhere.'

'I'm…afraid so,' said Jacob Winkelmann, his voice sinking to a shocked whisper. He pointed down into the water. 'I fear this is she, poor woman. God save her soul!'

Margriet's cap had been lost. Her hair had come unbound and floated away from her body on the surface of the water, two thin plaited ropes of grey. If she'd been wearing shoes they were gone. There were holes in the heels of her stockings. Air, trapped between her stained linen apron and her dark woollen gown was escaping and rising up in tiny columns of bubbles.

Henke stood for a moment, then gave a single howl of anguish and began to heave dry sobs. 'Dead! Drowned! I was only gone a quarter hour. Hardly more! I went to see about Ambroos... one of the lads came... said he heard it in the bakery... She was asleep! I locked the door...from the outside.' His voice trailed away to a hoarse whisper. 'I could swear I locked the door!'

Chapter 10

Mathilde de Haan

After leaving Pastor Winkelmann behind at the bridge, Mattie walked sedately for just a few paces, and then paused. As the pastor had guessed, she had no desire to catch up with her aunt and cousins. These times when she was free to walk about the town on her own, wrapped up in her own thoughts, were very precious to her. She suspected – no, she *knew*, that some of the townspeople pitied her, watching her forever being dispatched on errands for Aunt Clara and her cousins. She did find their demands tedious, but to be away from them – returning ribbons Anneke and Lotte had decided did not match closely enough. Purchasing items Aunt Clara had forgotten to ask the grocer to deliver, taking her uncle's letters to the post office, his notes about town business to the offices of the Watch Committee. All these provided opportunities to be alone, away from the endless *chatter, natter and mindless blether* (Oh, unkind Mathilde!) she had to endure every day in the de Haan household.

Was she thankful to Uncle Cornelius and Aunt Clara for taking her in when her parents were killed? No, wicked girl, she knew very well she was not! How shocked kindly Pastor Winkelmann would be if he could see into her ungrateful heart. How astonished that conceited Frans Rijnsburger would be too, if he knew how she coveted his occupation! '*I* could do that,' she thought. 'I could do what he does, just as well as he. Better. I could have been an apothecary, even a doctor like Papa. Papa often said so, had I not been born female!'

If Mama and Papa had not been killed on her seventeenth birthday, she believed she might have achieved something, a significant life of her own. If the medical profession was closed to her, she might still have been a librarian, a teacher! Here we are she frequently thought, more than half way through the nineteenth century. Surely it should be possible for a young woman with a mind and a will to have a career? True, *Mama* hadn't been able to contemplate anything other for her only daughter than marriage to a suitable man.

'Mattie dear, married life can be very rewarding!' she'd coaxed, when Mathilde voiced these opinions. 'To bring your own child into the world! To have the satisfaction of being a support to your husband!'

But Mattie, although she loved her father dearly, couldn't see "satisfaction" in being a support to a man. Even dearest Papa could be extremely trying, careless as he was of his clothes, of mealtimes, of appointments. Always needing Mama to be sewing on buttons, calling him from his laboratory and reminding him to eat his soup before it went cold. Despatching him through Amsterdam in a cab at the last minute to visit patients he'd entirely forgotten about.

The strings of her bonnet had grown worn and thin. She could feel them chafing beneath her chin as she walked back up through the Appelmarkt in the pale winter light. The wind tugged at them. They would pull into knots if she wasn't careful. Soon she must ask Aunt Clara for money to buy new ones. Then Aunt Clara, who was kind-hearted as well as foolish, would start the old argument again.

'Mattie, my love, that bonnet! So old fashioned. It's positively shabby! You *must* have a new one; I'm quite mortified to be seen out with you, wearing it. I'm sure people must think we're too mean to buy you another.' What other people might think was Aunt Clara's constant anxiety.

'It was Mama's,' she would reply, listlessly, 'it's all I have to remember her by. There's plenty of good wear in it yet.' Neither of them mentioned nowadays, although both of them knew it, that she wore it to hide the scar that crept from her cheek up the side of her nose. In those first terrible months after the accident she'd worn a veil as well. The scar, red and angry, had marred her face, so that people had backed away from her, their eyes registering pity and distaste – no matter how hard they tried to disguise it. Only this morning, when she had been forced to speak directly to Frans Rijnsburger, she'd seen what she'd supposed was shock in his eyes. So she hid herself inside the deep brim of Mama's best bonnet. Over time it had become a safe place, not only to hide her disfigurement, but also her thoughts and feelings. She could be private, free even, surrounded by those she regarded as chattering idiots.

Looking ahead now, she saw Aunt Clara and her cousins in the distance. They'd been strolling amongst the wealthier, though not necessarily Catholic, citizens who congregated close to the Haven

Kerk. This part of the Lange Haven, in the vicinity of the new church and some of the more elegant houses, was the place for those with social ambitions to see and been seen on a Sabbath day morning. Clara was exchanging gossip with two of her especial cronies. Her daughters, Anneke and Lotte, stood beside her, prayer books clutched in their plump mittened fingers, apparently waiting obediently for Mama, but actually glancing slyly around them, noticing who was there and what they were wearing. They were hoping to catch the eye of any of the young men who were accompanying their parents. Mattie was pleased to note that they didn't seem to have noticed her.

She turned quietly on her heel, and slipped back up the slope onto the Hoogstraat. As the High Street exactly followed the gentle curve of the canal, she would be able to walk home in parallel with Aunt Clara and her daughters. She might even, if her aunt stopped along the way as she frequently did to greet friends, arrive first.

Home! Her Aunt and Uncle's house wasn't her home and never could be, but it was all she had. Melancholy, depressed spirits, always hovering close, descended on her once more. *Why* had she survived the accident when her parents had not? If Papa had lived he would have been sad and sorry to lose his wife and daughter, but at least he would still have had a reason to continue living. He would have had his work, healing the sick. He would have had his research, discoveries which might have helped so many desperately ill people in the future. Discoveries she had been helping him, in her small way, to make. If *she* had died, then Mama and Papa would have been a comfort to one another. As it was, she had been thrust cruelly back into a life, a world, that had no need of her, where she could see no future for herself. Witness that young man's response to her, this morning, she thought. Her disfigurement had shocked him – and he a medical man! Four years ago she had known that she was not a beauty, but Mama had encouraged her to believe that she had pretty eyes and a pleasant smile. Certainly no one she met *then* had backed away from her, as they had tended to do since "the accident." (Mattie, alas, always believed the worst, refusing to countenance the idea that Frans Rijnsberger's reaction might not have been horror and dismay at all).

Then she was reflecting, she had been Papa's helpmeet, working alongside him in his laboratory. They'd been on the brink of thrilling discoveries. *Now* all she was able to do was to attempt invisibility as a helpmeet to her Aunt Clara and her silly, *silly* cousins! Oh, that she had died with Mama and Papa!

The man sprang out of nowhere. One moment she was walking along the deserted Sunday morning High Street, wrapped up in her sorrows. The next he'd seized hold of her and was holding a knife at her throat: A knife with a sharp point and a curved and jagged blade.

'Where is 'e?' the ruffian demanded, 'Where's Tomas?'

Mattie gulped in terror, trying to wriggle from his grasp. Suddenly she didn't want to die after all.

'I seen yer wiv him! I seen yer talking to him, on the bridge!' He grasped her shoulders harder, and she could feel the prick of the tip of the blade against the skin of her throat. Gin fumes gusted hot and damp in her face.

'I don't know!'

'Yer do! I seen yer wiv him! 'E wus talking to yer! 'E handed something over to yer to hold, and then 'e ran off. I wus watching, standing by where they're building that new school. Yer sent him on some errand. Yer *know* where the boy's gone!'

'I don't!' she gasped, terrified now. 'He...ran away. My uncle is the Bridge Watcher, and he wanted to keep him with us because... he thought you would come back. You're his steifvader, and you treat him cruelly! That's why he ran off. He was frightened because if you came back you would beat him!' The street was deserted, the nearby shops blind behind their Sabbath day shutters. No one to hear her cries for help.

'Very likely I would,' agreed the man, shaking Mattie until she felt her brain within her skull might work loose. 'Deserves it for running off, 'e does. How am I supposed to manage the boat wiv out 'im? 'Tis no business of yours *what* I does. 'E's my son. I took 'im and his mother on, and what thanks do I get? She takes sick and dies on me, and 'e runs off.' He gave Mattie another violent shake. 'So where is 'e? Where d'yer tell 'im to go?'

'I didn't! He...gave me the loaf he'd bought for someone...at the zakkendragers' Guildhuis, then he ran away! My uncle...'

'Cornelius the cockerel!' Ignaas van Damme's face darkened from dull red to almost black. Veins stood out across his brow. 'He'd better not hide that boy from me, or I'll...'

Mattie never heard what Ignaas van Damme would do to Cornelius, for he loosened his grip on her shoulders, gave a quick jab of the knife to her ribs, and let go of her. She fell to the ground, all consciousness slipping away.

It was Dries van Corte, Director of Sint Jacob's Infirmary who found her as he cut across the Hoogstraat from a private Sunday morning excursion. Finding the young woman, whom he recognised but couldn't have named for the life of him, unconscious on the brick paving, he assumed she'd fainted. It wasn't until he had hammered on the door of the nearest house and persuaded one of the barrel-makers' wives to let him carry her in and lay her on her sofa, that he noticed the darker stain of blood spreading through the brown cloth of her outmoded cloak, and onto the hem of his immaculate silver-grey frock coat.

Chapter 11

Tomas and Schoolmaster Mulder

Tomas had made a comfortable nest for himself amongst the torn mattresses and old bed frames in the weeshuis storeroom. He'd never intended to stay here for more than a night or two. However, his new friends Casper and Saskia seemed so pleased to have him, so eager to find ingenious ways to smuggle food out of the dining hall for him that three days later he was still there. True, it was often tedious, waiting alone in that stuffy room. Casper had made him another spinning top with higher numbers printed around it, and urged him to entertain himself with addition, subtraction and multiplication. (He found Tomas knew nothing of division, Mama's instruction never having reached so far). True, he'd lent him several books, some with lithographs, purloined from the schoolroom stock. True, the food they brought, though sparse – a hunk of bread, sometimes spread with dripping, an apple or two, a sliver of cheese – was sustaining life. But the mornings were long and dull. His back was fast healing and he longed to be outside running about, active, as he always had been. Casper had informed him that all the children above the age of seven years and below the age of twelve were in the orphanage school until noon. Most of the boys over twelve, with the exception of Casper, went each day to their apprentice places straight after breakfast, and returned each evening to sleep. The older girls, as Saskia had already explained, were sent mainly to positions as live-in servants and didn't return at all except on their days off, and then only if they had nowhere else to go. Thus, said Casper, the orphanage kept an eye on their youngsters as they made the transition from childhood to their adult lives.

'I'll give it to old de Hoop,' he said, 'he does try to see that no one is mistreated, or not too much, and that they're reasonably happy in their work.'

Tomas was surprised. This was rather better than Mama had led him to believe. He supposed this must be a particularly good weeshuis. Maarten de Hoop must be a good Regent.

'But he can't find anything for you?'

'No. He thought I might try tailoring.'

Saskia went into peals of laughter at this. 'Tomas, you should have seen it! They put him in with us girls in the afternoons to learn to sew! It was so funny. He was hopeless! I always had to thread his needles.'

'It appears I'm long sighted, and I didn't have my spectacles then, Sas! Anyway, I could have sat in the tailor's backroom and sewed, not that I showed much aptitude for it, I admit, but I suppose I'd have improved with practice. The customers need never have set eyes on me, but the tailor said he hadn't the time to be a nursemaid. Not on top of his own work. So the plan had to be abandoned. Really, the only way I could go out to work would be if someone came with me to push the chair and take me to the privy whenever I needed it. The weeshuis can't spare anyone on a regular basis, and no employer wants to pay a second person just to take care of me. Also, I nearly died of congestion of the lungs back in January and they don't rate my chances of surviving another winter.'

He seemed remarkably cheerful about this, although it saddened Tomas to think he might lose his new friend. Winter, he knew, was already on its way.

Afternoons were better. Once the orphans had eaten in the dining room, they were allowed an hour of freedom outside, the boys kicking a bunch of rags about in lieu of a football, the girls turning a length of washing line, and singing loud skipping chants to drown out the boys' excited yells. Tomas dared to raise his eyes above the windowsill from time to time to watch. Casper of course could take no part in the football, and during this recreation period he would get Saskia to bring him to his room, "to rest." There Tomas would join him, crouching down in a corner or even rolling under the bed if Matron's voice was heard in the corridor outside. Sometimes Saskia stayed while Tomas ate whatever she'd purloined, but now and then, once she had delivered the food safely, she went to join the other girls out of doors.

While Tomas ate, Casper explained things. Tomas soon knew who everyone was within the orphanage, even those he hadn't yet seen. Sometimes Casper read aloud from a book he was studying. Sometimes he expounded on things that had been taught during the morning's lessons. Casper's role, Tomas gathered, was not to learn, since he already knew everything the school could teach, but to help the other children as an assistant to the Master. This he enjoyed, although, he acknowledged, ruefully, some of the little ones were frightened to come close to him so that he could show them how to write, or how to form their figures.

'You're a much more satisfactory pupil,' he assured Tomas, handing him a slate and a piece of chalk which he had brought along by dint of stuffing it up the back of his jacket. 'I feel I can get somewhere with you! I wish you could come along to the schoolroom with the rest of us. I'd like your opinion on this new Master we've got. De Hoop's been teaching us himself since our old Master retired, but now his wife's got sick or something and gone away – at least that's what we've been *told* – he's too busy, and we've got this new fellow, Heer Mulder. He's good, in a way, although he keeps striding about with the cane in his hand as though he's going to beat the living daylights out of anyone who gives a wrong answer. Everyone's scared to say a word! I don't quite know what to make of him.'

Tomas fervently hoped never to meet such a one, but the very next morning, returning from the privy where he'd gone to get a drink from the stand pipe (Casper and Saskia hadn't found a way to smuggle liquids to him) Heer Mulder, arriving rather late to take the class, caught sight of him in the corridor.

'Hoy, you, boy!'

Terrified, Tomas froze on the spot.

'Why aren't you in the schoolroom?'

'I went...to the privy, Sir,' Tomas whispered, wishing the tiles that lined the corridor could slide apart and swallow him. He didn't know who this man was, but seeing the cane in his hand, guessed this must be the new Master. Heer Mulder had never seen Tomas. He was wearing orphanage uniform. The new Master assumed he was a genuine inmate.

'Come along then!' he growled. 'You're late. I'm late myself, Regent de Hoop having stopped to speak to me as I came in. He's leaving almost immediately for Amsterdam. So on this occasion boy, *and this occasion only*, I excuse you!'

He placed his hand on Tomas's jacket collar and piloted him before him into the big schoolroom. The pupils, who'd been chatting amongst themselves, the boys dipping small balls of paper into the ink wells and flicking them at their friends, the girls fiddling with one another's caps and hair, fell silent and rose to their feet.

'Goed Morgan, Heer Mulder, Goed Morgan, iedereen!'

'Goed Morgan, iedereen,' replied Heer Mulder gravely. 'Class, you may sit. Now young man, where's your place?' There was no obvious empty seat that Tomas could see. The children sat on long benches with sloping desk tops before them. Girls next to the windows, boys by the door. Only Casper sat alone at a small table at right angles to the teacher's own desk, fashioned at the right height for his wheeled-chair to fit under it.

Heer Mulder repeated the question and added another. 'Where's your place, boy? What's your name?' Tomas tried to open his mouth, but no sound emerged.

'Sir, he's called Tomas, Sir,' piped up Saskia.

'He's new, Sir,' drawled Casper. To Tomas's astonishment, many of the orphans now nodded their heads vigorously. 'He's new,' they agreed. They were used to newcomers being suddenly thrust into their midst.

'He ain't in our dormitory, though,' supplied one of the boys, puzzled. He looked to be about Tomas's age.

'That's 'cos he's *in-fect-ious*, Felix!' said Saskia, leaning bossily across the dividing aisle. 'He's gotta sleep downstairs 'cos he's got crawlers, Sir! Under his *skin*! The worst kind!' she added with malicious glee.

Heer Mulder, who had been standing with his hand resting on the back of Tomas's neck, hastily removed it.

'He can fetch a stool and sit by me, Sir,' Casper offered. 'I don't mind if he scratches himself. You only catch 'em off the bed clothes, you know, Saskia?' Heer Mulder, whose expression suggested he knew nothing, and wished to know nothing, about the orphans' sleeping arrangements, signalled agreement. Tomas collected a stool from under the window and joined his friend.

'Right!' commanded the teacher, taking his cane in both hands and bending it back and forth to demonstrate how flexible it was, meanwhile walking up and down the room between the rows of desks. 'Mental arithmetic! Felix, seven times eight?' Felix stuttered out the wrong answer. So did Klaas, so did Eduard, so did Adrien. Saskia got it right. 'Casper, twelve times twenty seven?' Tomas's mouth fell open in horror at the magnitude of this sum, but Casper came straight out with the answer. Casper knew all the answers.

'Tomas, five times five?'

'T-twenty f-five, S-sir,' Tomas stammered.

'Correct! Mieke, twice twelve?' The girl next to Saskia got that one right, and slouched on the bench with a relieved smile on her face. All the time, Heer Mulder strode back and forth with his cane in his hands, but even when children answered wrongly, as many did, and Tomas expected the cane to be applied, it never was.

'All show?' Casper wrote on Tomas's slate, when the lesson changed to spelling, and Heer Mulder was writing the words he wanted them to memorise on the blackboard. Then he whispered behind his hand. 'He's pretending he's going to use that cane, but he won't. It's like he's pretending to be strict. It's almost like he's *pretending* to be a teacher!'

Since Tomas had never been to school before he felt unable to express an opinion on Heer Mulder.

At twelve, the class was dismissed and the orphans trooped off to the dining hall. Tomas sidled back to his storeroom and waited anxiously for Casper and Saskia to arrive.

'Did any of the children say anything? Did they tell on me?' he demanded anxiously, when they appeared.

''Course not,' said Saskia, handing him a rather squashed lump of cheese she'd concealed in her fist. 'I told them, you're *in-fect-ious*! And you *did* keep wriggling and scratching yourself, so they believe it's true!' She giggled.

'Well, this vest thing itches. I'm not used to wearing so many clothes.'

'Your story was quite inspired, Sas,' said Casper, solemnly. 'Orphans do sometimes get admitted and there's a scare on that they've got something catching,' he explained for Tomas's benefit. 'I reckon you're safe for the rest of the week. Of course you'll have to come to school, you realise that? Otherwise this Heer Mulder will ask where you are.'

'That's alright. I liked it,' mumbled Tomas through a mouthful of bread and cheese. 'I liked that *geography*. When he got that big map thing out and hung it over the blackboard? I liked seeing all the rivers drawn out like that. It was …interesting.' He smiled at the thought. All the rivers, *his* rivers, the Maas, the Rijn, the Waal, the Schie, laid out like that, as though he was looking down on them, as though he was a bird, flying high overhead.

'Yes, you clever clogs! Knowing big words like 'con-flu-ence'!' grumbled Saskia 'When we did geography with the Regent we only did "principal towns and cities".'

'Rivers and canals are Tomas's field of expertise,' said Casper seriously. Saskia and Tomas looked at him. Neither knew what a field of expertise was, but Casper didn't explain. Tomas had learned that this was often Casper's way. He expected you to pick up an understanding of what he meant from the other things he talked about.

'There's lot of news by the way,' the crippled boy went on. 'Although I don't know what it all means. While I was stuck in the hallway in my chair just now, waiting for Saskia to come out of the dining hall...we're dismissed one table at a time,' he added for Tomas's benefit, 'two of the ushers were talking. They never notice I'm there, listening. They think because I'm crippled I must be deaf and dumb! Anyway, there's big news from the town. Which is, Tomas, that as well as your steifvader being suspected of trying to murder that zakkendrager, the Chief zakkendrager's wife's throat is cut, *and* someone stabbed the Bridge Watcher's niece on her way home from the hospital, and her life is despaired of!'

'They can't think Ignaas did all that!' cried Tomas, alarmed. 'I thought he was gone, anyway, onto the Maas.'

'I'm sure he didn't do *all* those things,' soothed Casper, seeing Tomas's agitation, 'although grownups always like to have someone to blame. But maybe he *isn't* gone. They've found the boat.'

'The Appelbloesem! Is she alright?'

'They didn't say. Just that she'd been found, up near some lock.'

'Well, *I* think there's something unusual going on here in the orphanage as well,' said Saskia, who wasn't so interested in what happened beyond her own familiar walls. 'I keep my ears open too, you know, particularly when I'm going back down the corridor from bringing Casper here. I walk very slowly past *Matron's* room.' She grinned, pleased with her own cunning. 'The door's often open a bit, and she's in there, talking to one of the maids, Roos, who's her particular crony. I don't know what it's about, but *something's* going on, something to do with the Regent...' she paused for effect, '*and Vrouw de Hoop!* Something about the Regentess going away to Amsterdam, and the Regent's going after her! I couldn't hear anymore,' she added. 'It was disappointing.'

Casper nodded, looking wise. 'That'll be why things are slipping a bit. The dining hall was rowdy today but the Regent never came in, although I'm sure he'd normally hear from his office. Maybe he's gone already. No one takes much notice of the ushers,' he told Tomas, 'they swish those canes, but the Regent only allows one swipe on the back of the legs. *This* is why nobody's found out about *you*, why we can smuggle you into school. Heer Mulder doesn't know you shouldn't be there, and the Regent's been too distracted to check up. Mevrouw de Hoop must be really ill – or something. Heer Mulder's got us all well in hand, so the Regent's letting him get on with it.'

'I'm sad about Margriet,' said Tomas. He wasn't much concerned about Heer Mulder and the Regent, '*and* about Heer de Haan's niece. I don't know her name, but she seemed nice. I liked her. And I wish I could see the Appelbloesem, to see if she's all right.'

'Who's Margriet?' demanded Saskia.

Tomas told them again about Henke and his mad wife, and about finding Ambroos on the bridge. Although he'd already told about it, and how Cornelius de Haan had tried to arrest him, this was the first time he'd given a thought to Mattie, standing there with the loaf in her hands, watching him go.

'This is exciting!' said Saskia, happily, 'Murders happening in our town!'

'I expect Henke's wife just fell in the canal and drowned,' Tomas sighed. 'She was a mad lady. He'll be sad about it, though. I just hope Ignaas *isn't* here. If he's gone for good then Cornelius the cockerel won't want to catch *me* anymore.'

Chapter 12

Anders Vos

'Sergeant Vos!'

Anders Vos, who had been gazing out of the window at the mist of early rain glazing the cobbled streets of Rotterdam spun round and snapped to attention.

'Yessir!'

His commanding officer, the Big Cheese, angled himself into a chair at his plain, standard army-issue desk. He didn't offer Vos a seat. Vos stood to attention and waited for the axe to fall. He had no idea why he'd been summonsed, but an early morning summons was, in his experience, never good news. He thought there was bound to be an axe in it somewhere.

'How well do you know Schiedam, Sergeant?'

'Not at all, Sir, I'm afraid, never been there.' Windmills, he thought trying hastily to summon up *anything*, that he might know about the town. They had, he believed, a lot of windmills. They made gin there. He couldn't imagine where this could be going.

'Hmm, perhaps just as well,' said his superior, exploring his chin with thumb and forefinger for patches of stubble he'd missed when shaving. 'It may be best to send someone who doesn't know the place. Who can look at things with a fresh eye. *Where* are you from again?'

'Groningen, Sir.'

'Up there, eh? Well, they won't be able to say, "What do you expect from those dwazen in Rotterdam?"'

'There's some rivalry, Sir? Between the two towns?'

'You could say that. We build ships. They build ships too, but not so many as formerly, and none big enough for anything but coastal waters these days. They *used* to fish for herrings and charge a great deal too much for 'em. Perhaps they still do. Then about a hundred years ago they started building gin distilleries. And windmills! Great brick monsters that tower above the town. Walk through Schiedam on a sunny day when the sails are turning, and you feel seasick on dry land! And that's before you start drinking the local product!'

80

'You want me to go there, Sir?'

'I think you're the man for the job. The town Watch Committee has asked us to send someone – must really have the wind up. They've never asked for the Maréchaussée before in my time. Never had anything they couldn't handle themselves, or so they claim.'

'They don't like the police?' Vos knew many people didn't. The Dutch national police force had grown out of the military. Most people still saw them as a branch of the army, oppressors, men with guns who didn't understand local sensibilities. Small Dutch towns liked to manage their own affairs. They had Watch Committees made up of the great and the supposedly good, who had their own powers of arrest and punishment for offenders. For most small places that was enough to keep the peace. In Vos's experience they only ever called in the Maréchaussée for bloody insurrection.

'You must realise how they are in these tin-pot places, Vos,' said his superior, echoing this thought. 'You know, "*He* got drunk and peed on Vrouw Von Assen's washing? Two weeks in the Steen on bread and water! *She's* a bawdy who fornicated with Hanjie the cobbler behind the town hall? Send her to the women's house of correction, one month. Case dismissed." That's how they work.'

'Yes Sir.' Vos stopped himself from pointing out that he knew all this, even though he came from Groningen. 'So what do they want? That is, what do they think *the police* can do that they can't?'

'About that I'm not entirely clear,' confessed the Big Cheese, picking up a sheet of paper from his desk and peering at it long-sightedly. 'They sent an excitable fellow from the Watch Committee – he's their Chief Bridge Watcher it appears – and from what I can make out, they've had a spate of attacks on townspeople. One woman dead, her throat cut – that one was someone's drunken wife who sounds as though she was no great loss. One sack porter with his stomach cut open. Probably came up against some other toper in a brawl. He's thought to be recovering. *And*, and this sounds to be the only real mystery, a young woman stabbed on her way home from an errand of mercy, or so Heer Bridge Watcher claims. She's his niece, so he would say that. Probably some jealous lover boy he knows nothing about. She was still alive yesterday, although they're not optimistic.'

'They believe one person carried out all three attacks, Sir?'

'Heer Bridge Watcher does. He has it in for a binnenschipper called...' he consulted his papers, 'Ignaas Van Damme. So far they haven't caught him, although they've managed to impound his boat.'

'Not a local man?'

'No. Typical ruffian, "off the boats" as they say. Transports cargo back and forth inland, mainly between Schiedam, Rotterdam and Dordrecht, but will go anywhere he's paid to go.'

'Known trouble maker?'

'Sure to be.' The Big Cheese extended his arm and peered some more at his sheet of paper. 'That fool Barends took these notes. I can't read his scrawl.'

'Do they have any evidence that this van Damme is involved, Sir? Apart, that is, from local prejudice?'

'No. Several nasty rumours, but that's all. Something here about a...stepson. The man has a stepson who's disappeared. It's thought this Ignaas van Damme is looking for him. He's said to ill-treat the lad, but can't sail the boat without his help.'

'Probably hopped onto someone else's boat then, Sir,' growled Vos, 'if he's got any sense, and got out of town. How am I expected to find this villain when they can't?'

The Commander looked pained. 'You came with a good reputation, Vos. Anders the Fox they called you. You sniffed out that fellow that murdered his mother-in-law in Altmeer.'

Yes, Sir.' Vos decided not to remind him that it hadn't gone down well. He was the Burgemeester. They'd just elected him, and when he was arrested they'd had to go through the whole process again.

'Well, go to Schiedam and discover some crime this Chief Bridge Watcher fellow has committed. Then I won't have him ranting and raving in my office again. Oh, and take van Dyke and Barends with you. Show of force and all that.'

'Yessir,' said Vos, his heart sinking.

'Take the train. Report to the Gemeentehuis. The Burgemeester and the Watch Committee are expecting you.'

'Yessir. Are we to return to barracks tonight?'

'Not unless you solve the crime and arrest the criminal. They'll fix you up with somewhere to stay.' The axe had fallen.

'Yessir,' Vos sighed, unable to conceal his misgivings.

Josef van Dyke was a dour elderly man, a former soldier serving out his time in the police. Unlike the artist of the previous century Vos noted he did not have a beard, but had instead a long and drooping moustache which gave him a mournful expression. He boarded the train as though he had been ordered up to the front to face enemy cannons. Joop Barends was a young fellow, a newish recruit, keener than French mustard but in Vos's opinion, quite useless. He was delighted to be travelling by train.

'My first time! Never been on one before,' he burbled. 'Have you, Sir?'

'Yes, Corporal,' said Vos, shortly. How did they think he got around the country? By stage coach? The first steam-hauled train had arrived in the Netherlands nearly twenty years previously, but he supposed there were still many people who had never travelled on one. Now he thought about it, he recalled that there had been a nasty smash four or five years ago which had made many people nervous. Three people killed. At Schiedam, as it happened. No doubt this was why van Dyke was acting as though he was up before the firing squad.

'Only a short trip, we'll be there less than half an hour…' he began to say, rallying his troops. His voice was drowned by the whistle of the locomotive and the great whoosh of steam from the engine as the train pulled out of the station.

Vos had intended to give his men a briefing during the journey, explain to them why they were ordered to Schiedam, and what he was expecting they would achieve there. All that was required of *these two* was to provide back up, and help with the apprehension of this man, Ignaas van Damme, should he prove recalcitrant. The noise of the train in motion, plus the clouds of dirty smoke and cinders which flew in at the open window of their carriage made this impossible. By the time Barends had wrestled the window shut, and the noise had abated to a less ear-shattering level, they were in Schiedam.

His first impression was that it was a dirty little town. They passed tall chimneys belching steam, and small houses lining narrow streets, their facades stained and blackened. Poor looking people were going about their business as though their feet hurt. There was even a drunk, so early in the day, lying sprawled in a gutter. There must be money, surely, though, in the midst of so much industry? Two more prosperous fellows, finely dressed with comfortable paunches, turned their heads and crossed the street to avoid the sight of the drunkard. Once they reached the centre Vos began to notice larger houses, several storeys high with tall windows and elegant gables. Yes, there was money here, without a doubt.

Vos and his two colleagues marched into town, three abreast, uniform buttons and epaulettes gleaming in the sporadic November sunlight. Pistols visible at their hips. The arrival of the invaders, Anders Vos thought wryly, as several startled citizens turned to observe these outsiders and scuttled quickly away. Now all Schiedam knows the police have been sent for, he thought, and our villain – if he is a villain – will know it too. Vos was by no means convinced that all the three crimes he'd been told of, or indeed any of them, had necessarily been committed by this Ignaas van Damme. It was all too easy, in his experience, for a community to adopt a scapegoat, and have no interest in finding the real culprit. He assumed that he and his colleagues had been summonsed just for show. The burgers of Schiedam, he told himself, were about to learn that Anders den Vos didn't do things "just for show."

Reaching the Gemeentehuis, a neat little seventeenth century building in the middle of a cobbled square, they were denied admittance. A civil wedding ceremony was in progress in the upper rooms, and a master from the local weeshuis had brought a group of orphaned children to learn about "civic government" in the offices below.

When Vos protested that the Burgemeester and members of the Watch were expecting to meet with him here, the porter said 'Oh, *that* meeting. The Burgemeester, he's taken to his bed with the gout, and only two of the Watch are coming. They sent word they'll be here shortly. I'll send this schoolmaster fellow on his way, and then you can wait downstairs.'

Thus it was, had he only known it, that Vos could have solved the mystery of the missing boy, stepson of the main suspect, there and then. At the porter's urging, Roel Mulder, jovial schoolmaster, and his class of seven to twelve year old orphans marched out of the town hall and went on their way. At the back of the group, pushing a horribly deformed child in a wheeled chair was a wiry, tow-headed boy. He alone amongst the children did not turn to stare curiously at the policemen, seeming fully intent on his task of pushing the chair as smoothly as possible over the cobblestones.

'Ach!' whispered Saskia, who had hobbled back in the line to supervise, although she was meant to be walking with the other girls, 'That was close! I'll wager them policemen have come to catch your steifvader, Tomas! You want to keep your head down!'

'I am!' Tomas hissed in reply.

Fortunately for these youthful conspirators, Vos was busy claiming possession of the downstairs room, and gave them no thought at all.

In the event two members of the Watch committee, Cornelius de Haan, and a man named Matthias, who owned and ran a small distillery, and in addition, representing The Church, the Reverend Jacob Winkelmann, came to meet with Anders Vos.

Cornelius immediately started repeating, volubly, everything which he'd already (Vos assumed from the notes he'd been given) told his superior officer. Out of the corner of his eye he could see Barends picking his finger nails, and van Dyke's shoulders sagging along with his moustache. He held up a hand to stem the flow.

'I have notes here. It will save my time and yours if I summarise.' Matthias the distiller grunted assent.

'Firstly,' commenced Vos, 'a woman named Margriet van de Grote was found floating up against the Schie lock, close to her home, with her throat cut. She is dead, obviously. The weapon hasn't been located. The exact time of the attack is unknown, but her husband insists he left her alone for less than half an hour. Secondly, a man named Ambroos, family name unspecified, a sack porter by trade, was found with a severe gash to his stomach on the Cattle Market Bridge. He was removed, unconscious, to the town infirmary, where he remains. This must have occurred *before* the fatal attack on Vrouw van de Grote, because it was in order to visit this injured man that her husband left her alone at home. Or so he says. *Thirdly*, a young woman, Mathilde de Haan, who'd assisted the apothecary – and I believe *you*, Pastor? – to convey this same Ambroos to the hospital, was later found in the street, having been stabbed in the...er, ribcage. She's still alive, Heer de Haan?'

'Yes,' sighed the Bridge Watcher, filling his chest with air and letting it go in a dramatic rush, 'but we don't hold out much hope, poor girl.'

'And don't forget the boy,' interjected the Pastor. 'A boy has disappeared, Tomas, the step-son of this Ignaas van Damme, whom I gather is the main suspect. No one knows what has become of him.'

'He might be dead too,' offered the gin distiller, who seemed cheered by the idea.

'No great loss if he is,' growled Cornelius, 'he can't be anything but vicious with Ignaas van Damme as his father.'

'I feel that's rather ...unchristian, Cornelius!' chided the Pastor. 'Tomas is only the stepchild of this Ignaas. I've met the boy and he didn't seem at all vicious. I only wish we knew what has become of him.'

'*So*, we have one murder, two serious attacks and a missing person,' summarised Anders Vos, holding up his hand once more to stem the flow. 'You're all united in naming a suspect, a bargee named Ignaas van Damme. Detaining and questioning him must be our priority. I shall now tell you how I intend to handle things. Firstly, my two assistants will go out and about in the town, asking people if they've seen this man. Their presence will, I hope, reassure people who may fear further attacks. If they encounter van Damme he will be detained, brought back here, and put under interrogation. I myself will go immediately to Sint Jacob's Infirmary to interview the man Ambroos. I understand he's now conscious and recovering?'

'I met Father Anthonis from the Haven Kerk in the street this morning,' confessed Pastor Winkelmann, who seemed embarrassed to have hobnobbed with a rival priest. 'He'd been to visit the man, who's one of his flock. He told me Ambroos is recovering, but seemed quite confused about the whole affair. Although he named this Ignaas, Father Anthonis wasn't sure whether he knew this of his own knowledge – or whether the idea has been put into his head by others – those who have been caring for him, or have visited him.'

Vos couldn't restrain a grunt of exasperation at this. The whole town had made up their minds that the guilty party was Ignaas van Damme, and whilst they might be right, he, Vos, had not only to apprehend the man, but also provide proof. And both could be extremely difficult.

Chapter 13

Tomas and Casper

Tomas was, to his surprise, nearly a week after seeking sanctuary in the orphanage, now an established inmate. Somehow, he'd no clear idea why, the place had accepted and absorbed him. He asked Casper to explain.

'The children see you every morning in the schoolroom,' he said, 'so they've got used to you, and Heer Mulder has never said anything, so of course they think it's all right. He's new too, so he doesn't know you aren't supposed to be there. Children do arrive unexpectedly from time to time; he'll have been warned of that. Usually they've been living with foster parents, out on farms on the polders, but they're sent back as they grow older. It's a bit unusual for a farm family to keep a boy until he's as old as you are, Tomas – old enough to be useful about the place – and then send him back, but it can happen. Then they all know that Saskia's one of the biggest earwiggers that ever breathed, so they believe her that you've got some kind of skin disease, and you're banned from the dormitories and the dining hall.' He burst out laughing. 'Rumour varies as to whether what you have is scabies, eczema, impetigo, or even, *leprosy*!'

Some of the ushers were certainly aware of Tomas's existence, but with the Regent gone away, and no return date settled, Casper thought they must believe his admission had been their employer's last act before leaving. Certainly nobody had so far asked Tomas where he'd come from, who had sponsored his place here, or where he was, in fact, sleeping. It seemed no longer necessary for him to hide in the storeroom, so one evening after dark; he dragged one of the pallets through to Casper's room and stored it, during the daytime, beneath his friend's bed.

'It's nice to have a roommate,' said Casper, 'I hope my coughing and wheezing doesn't disturb your sleep?'

'Not at all!' said Tomas, beaming, because his friend had said it was nice to have him there. He'd never had a real bed of his own, only at best, a straw-stuffed sack in a corner below the Appelbloesem's deck. The worn mattress he'd liberated from the orphanage store seemed to him quite luxurious. Casper's rasping breaths he found almost comforting. Hearing them when he woke during the night reminded him where he was, safe from Ignaas's drunken assaults.

'This place is falling apart, you know?' Casper went on, sounding troubled. Tomas had taken on the responsibility of helping him out of his day clothes, into his nightshirt, and into bed. After the first shock of seeing how bent and twisted his friend's body was, it ceased to trouble him. Casper was Casper, his friend.

'One of the ushers is supposed to come and help me,' Casper said, apologetically, 'but they'll try any excuse to get out of it. They hate seeing my deformity. I think they believe it might be catching. Matron's supposed to check me too, night and morning, so they hope *she's* helping me, but how often has she been to see me this week?'

'Err, twice?' said Tomas, who'd had to roll under the bed and hide on each occasion. 'I thought she smelt awfully of gin,' he added.

'That's what I thought too,' said Casper. 'It's getting worse. Your foot was sticking out from under the bed this morning, but she never noticed. She doesn't even know you're here, and if she finds out now she won't say a thing. She'll think she's *supposed* to know, but she was too drunk to remember the day you were admitted.'

'She's a drunkard?'

'Sozzled, most days, but she used to be very good at hiding it. I think Regent de Hoop must have warned her plenty of times, but she's got worse. Much worse. You know how easy it is for people to get drink here in Schiedam, don't you?'

'I suppose. It's what they make here, isn't it? Anyone can buy it, really cheaply?' Tomas thought about Henke, allowing mad Margriet a ration of gin so that she would sleep. And Ignaas, whom drink made so ugly, and who was always so much worse in Schiedam than any of the other towns they visited.

'They don't even have to buy it,' said Casper. 'Do you know how they make it?'

Tomas considered. 'Not really,' he admitted. 'I know we bring grain in on the boat, and sacks of juniper berries. And I've seen boats and carts on the quays off-loading other stuff. Stuff that's come into the harbour on the ocean-going ships, like...sugar?'

'I don't really know either,' confessed Casper grinning his Punchinello grin. 'Perhaps we should petition Heer Mulder to take us to visit a distillery? Local commerce, now we've done local government! Anyway, they must use a lot of hot water, because they say all the women in the town – housewives, maidservants, whoever, – are free to go into any of the distilleries with a jug and get hot water any time they want to – and somehow, I don't know quite *how*, they manage to turn on a different tap and take jugs full of gin instead. That maid, Roos, she's called, she gets it for Matron Schmidt. You must have seen her going by the schoolroom windows with a big copper jug? She's like me, deformed. One shoulder higher than the other, and a squint, but alas, she doesn't share my charming personality! She *says* she's going for hot water, but I'm sure she isn't. If she was, why are we washing ourselves under the cold stand pipe? If the Regent was here, he'd be onto it. Those two would be pitched out the door! Maarten De Hoop wouldn't stand for it.'

Tomas kept hearing mention of the missing Regent and his wife. He asked Casper where they'd gone and why. Casper shook his head. He didn't know. 'It's pretty worrying,' was all he could say. 'Maybe Saskia will find out. She's busy listening at all the doors!'

But even Saskia, who still took charge of pushing Casper in his chair to the dining hall and back each meal time, and then stayed for a chinwag with them, didn't know. Saskia, as always, had plenty of other things she wanted to talk about.

'That was scary, yesterday, when Heer Mulder took us to the Gemeentehuis and the police were there!' she said, handing over Tomas's lunch time ration of bread, cheese and broth, (On a tray this time). Saskia had persuaded the kitchen maids to "send" lunch to that "poor boy with the skin disease." 'I thought they'd arrest you there and then, Tomas!' she prattled on. 'Anyway, I said to Heer Mulder, when we were walking back afterwards, that I thought it was really interesting, going out like that, and *he* said if we behaved ourselves and learned our lessons properly, he might take us out to visit one of the windmills. Maybe right to the top! So we could see the whole town laid out below us, like the maps he showed us. He said he's never been up one, and he didn't suppose we had. We never used to go out like this when old Heer

Vanderleur was teaching us, *or* the Regent. I think it's much more interesting than ordinary lessons.'

'You would, because you're such a scatterbrain, Saskia!' snorted Casper. 'I'm not sure the Regent would allow this "going out" if he was here. He certainly wouldn't take me. Look how he won't let me go to church in case it upsets people? I tell you, I'm suspicious of this Heer Mulder. I'm not even sure he's a proper teacher; he's enjoying himself too much. That's not natural. Anyway, a windmill is no good for me. Or you, I'd have thought. They must have stairs, but they'd never carry me up so high! Have you ever been in one here in Schiedam, Tomas?'

'I've been inside one. Well, sort of,' said Tomas. 'The Palmboom I think it was. It was a long time ago, before my Papa died. We called to see a friend of his.'

He thought about it, recollecting what little he remembered. 'I only saw inside the door on the ground floor. They were unloading sacks of grain and pulling them up to the next floor with ropes and … do you two know what a block and tackle is? A hoist?' There were, he was beginning to realise, some things a boat child knew that the weeshuis children had no notion of.

'So we could fasten your chair with ropes, Casper, and pull you up!' said Saskia, when Tomas tried to explain how the hoist worked. Picturing it, she dissolved into a fit of mirth.

'No thanks! I know they don't expect me to last much longer, but I don't want to die by falling from a great height!' he replied, which sobered Saskia instantly.

'Oh, Casper, don't! Don't talk about dying!' she wailed. 'Just don't!'

When Saturday came around lessons in the morning were followed by "the weekly bath" Great wooden tubs were filled with water that was, at least, warm, and first the girls and then the boys filed through, with the maids soaping the girls and washing their hair, and then handing over to the ushers, who repeated the process for the boys. Casper, it appeared, was always left to the last. It was obvious to Tomas that he dreaded it.

'Shall I come with you? I could help with your clothes and then I could go in the bath after you? Because of my skin disease?' he suggested, giggling. He was almost beginning to believe he really *did* have scabies, 'crawlers under the skin,' as Saskia had told everyone. Tomas personally thought taking a bath once a week was quite unnecessary, if it was what the orphans did, and to support Casper, he was willing to face the ordeal.

'I'd be glad if you'd come,' Casper agreed. 'It's one of the ushers, Dirk. He's big and strong and he can lift me in and out of the tub single-handed, so the others just leave him to do it, but he always says something, or pulls stupid faces, mocking me because I'm a cripple. He thinks it's funny to pretend he's going to drop me. If you're there he might behave in case you tell someone.'

'I would too!' said Tomas stoutly, valiant for his friend, although if the Matron was a drunkard and the Regent and his wife were gone, there didn't seem to be anyone to tell. He wondered, from his own unfortunate experiences with Ignaas, what else this Dirk might be inclined to do.

Dirk was a big, ugly lad whose tongue seemed too large for his mouth, so that Tomas found his speech hard to follow. What he did was haul off Casper's clothes, drag him roughly from his chair and dump him unceremoniously in the bath tub. Casper wasn't particularly hurt by this harsh treatment, but Tomas burned with anger to see his friend treated in this demeaning fashion.

'Hey! You mind what you do!' he snarled at the usher. 'If you hurt my friend I'll tell on you, you big bully!'

'Wha's s'pposed to be mather wi' *you*, anyway, y'young runth?' Dirk demanded of him, once Casper was safely back in his chair. 'How come ye're such big mates with thith cripple? *An'* how come you haf t'go lasth?'

'None of your business. I've got a skin complaint,' said Tomas.'

Dirk might be big and strong in body, but Tomas had decided he was somewhat slow in the wits department. Dirk aimed a backhanded swipe at him, but he didn't have with him the cane that the ushers used, and Tomas dodged him easily, sticking out his tongue, although as he did so he realised he was probably making an enemy. When the Regent returned Dirk would be the first to demand to have Tomas's hide tanned for cheek, whereupon his stay in the weeshuis would come to an abrupt end. But, he consoled himself, since that would be bound to happen sooner or later, did it matter?

'*You* can apply the lotion, if you like' he told Dirk, grandly,

91

stepping out of the tub and handing him a bottle and clean rag. 'See, on all these red splotches?'

'What *was* that lotion, and where did you get it?' Casper chuckled, wrinkling his nose as Tomas trundled him back to his room. 'I recognise the smell, but I'm sure it's not for scabies, if that's what you're supposed to have.'

Back in Casper's room, Tomas carefully checked the stopper, and stood the bottle back on the ledge where he'd found it. 'It's some medicine of *yours*. I thought I ought to have been given *something* to dab on my skin. Mama did that when I had waterpokken one time. Since Saskia's told everyone that I've got a skin disease, I needed something. I had to scratch myself in as many places as I could while I was in the water, just so I'd have some red patches to show that Dirk,' he grumbled.

He wasn't really cross with Saskia. He couldn't, he realised, be cross with her for very long. She was so full of good humour and mischief… and kindness towards Casper, whom so many of the children shunned.

Casper now burst out laughing so hard that he then fell into a painful fit of coughing. 'I *knew* I recognised the smell!' he gasped. 'It's some brew Heer Rijnsburger the apothecary made up to loosen the mucus on my chest! Matron used to make me take spoonfuls of it, but it didn't do a great deal of good. When you're as twisted out of shape as I am, *nothing* does much good.'

'Why *did* your back grow all twisted?' Tomas suddenly found himself asking once they lay in bed that night. 'Didn't you get enough nourishment when you were a baby?' He remembered his mother saying that about a child from one of the boat families who was always ailing, and eventually died.

Casper said nothing for a moment. Tomas was afraid he'd hurt his friend's feelings, but then he sighed deeply and said, 'No idea. The Regent had plenty of doctors to me. One of them, some expert, was supposed to come all the way from Amsterdam, but the train crashed and he was killed, so he never got here. One said it's an inherited weakness. He said I was of "poor stock" and my parents shouldn't have been allowed to breed – not that anyone knows who my parents *were*. The apothecary though, suggested I might have had consumption as a baby, but it burned itself out.

That seemed the most sensible suggestion to me.'

'Casper, I shouldn't have asked, I'm sorry,' said Tomas in the dark.

'Don't be. I'd rather you asked than you thought I was some sort of evil goblin. Or a devil's familiar. A lot of them do think that, you know? Dirk does, I'm sure. Some of the adults are worse than the children.'

'I shouldn't have cheeked Dirk, should I?'

'Why? What can he do about it?'

'Tell the Regent about me when he comes back.'

'Tomas, *everyone's* going to tell the Regent about you when he comes back! I wonder what he'll say?'

Chapter 14

Vos, Barends and van Dyke

Vos strode into the very small room in the town hall that had been, grudgingly, assigned to him as an office for the duration of his investigation. There, to his astonishment, he found Corporals Van Dyke and Barends standing guard over a family of six. This consisted of a very fat woman, a very thin man, and four almost identical little girls, each one twelve months shorter than the last, and who would probably all be as plump as their mother one day. All six of them were huddled side by side on a bench.

'Witnesses, Sir!' growled sour van Dyke.

'We thought we'd better bring them in, Sir,' corroborated an eager Barends, heels clicking together, chest puffed out with pride. 'They admit they *know* the suspect. Everyone else denies knowing anything about him!' he consulted his notebook. 'They're Hedy and Cees van de Meer, Sir.'

Vos bit back his growl of frustration. He'd been to interview Ambroos, and had used on him his most persuasive techniques, but the wretch had clammed up. Effectively, he had denied knowing whether it was Ignaas or someone else who had slashed his stomach open. As Pastor Winkelmann had implied, and Vos was now forced to accept, Ambroos must have been too far gone in drink to have any clear memory of what had happened. A largely wasted trip and now his two irksome underlings seemed to have had all the luck.

'We haven't seen Ignaas since Sunday!' wailed the woman, Hedy, squeezing two large tears out over the pouches of fat below her eyes. 'I thought he was gone, truly I did! I told young Tomas he was gone. My husband here said he'd only go as far as the lock, it being the Sabbath, so he went to find him. I was so worried about Ignaas leaving Tomas behind. He found the boat, but Ignaas wasn't there! We haven't seen hide nor hair of him since. Truly, Sir, we haven't!'

'S'fact,' confirmed her skinny spouse, Cees. 'M'wife was worried about the boy, so I walked up to the lock. The Appelbloesem was there alright, just as I said she would be, but no sign of him. I went below too, and looked around. What a mess! Dirty old drunkard!

'T'would break Anna's heart to see the state it's in, if she was still alive.'

'I believe the boat's been impounded by the town authorities?'

'S'right,' replied the laconic Cees. 'Tied up on Westvest is what they say.'

'With someone guarding it, day and night, Sir!' breathed Barends excitedly, 'Orders of the Watch. He wouldn't even let *us* on board, Sir.'

Thank the Lord for that, thought Vos. If these two fools had gone rampaging all over the Appelbloesem without specific instructions there would have been no clues left to find, supposing there were any in the first place.

'So, this is Saturday, and you haven't seen Ignaas since last Sunday?' he said to the van de Meers.

'Can't say we *saw* him then,' replied Cees. 'Saw the boat go by as we ate our Sabbath breakfasts. Since then, we've been up to Rotterdam with a dozen barrels for one of the smaller companies here, Matthias and sons. Brought back a load of timber for van Zwolle the cooper. As m'wife says, we didn't see hide nor hair of Ignaas.'

'But you'd recognise him if you saw him in the street?'

'Sure to, but we ain't. Mebbe, seeing he's in trouble with you fellows, he's taken a sea passage? Signed on for South Amerikay or the Antilles?' suggested Cees.

'Perhaps. But the Watch Committee has reported one woman dead, and two serious attacks against townsfolk. They seem very certain this Ignaas van Damme is the culprit, so you can see we have to keep on making enquiries.' As he said this, sounding like a stuffed shirt even to his own ears, Vos was wondering if Cees was right. All three attacks had taken place on the previous Sunday, none had been reported since. Was it not perfectly possible that Ignaas, sobering up and realising he'd be wanted, had signed on a fast clipper bound for Curacaos on Monday? He could easily have got a lift on a boat or a cart to the main harbour. In which case he was wasting his time looking for him.

'And what about poor little Tomas? What's happened to that boy?' demanded Hedy. 'My heart bleeds for him, losing his mother and being left with that brute! For he *is* a brute, and you know it!' She gave her husband a sharp kick on the shins as she said this last.

'Woman, we can't take the lad! I've told you a dozen times! We can hardly move below deck as it is!' said Cees, trying to shuffle along the bench, out of reach of her clog.

'How old is this boy?' Vos had somehow been picturing a youth in his teens, but now realised he'd never been given an exact age for the missing Tomas.

Hedy and Cees didn't seem too sure. Hedy worked her way back through where she had been when she had her eldest, and how long before that she might have first have seen Anna van de Gracht with her baby. 'Ten? Twelve?'

'Eleven,' announced the eldest daughter, Eva. 'He says.'

'As young as that?' Vos had been wondering if Ignaas had found his missing stepson, and that both were now "bound for the Rio Grande" or somewhere equally beyond the long arm of the Netherlandish law. 'If Ignaas *has* shipped out, he'd hardly take along a boy as young as that. Would he? Could he?'

Cees shook his head. 'Doubt it. A bit too young even for cabin boy. Supposing they didn't already have one.'

Hedy began to cry. 'Oh, that poor little soul! I do declare that dreadful man has killed the poor mite and hidden his body!'

At this the four little girls began to cry too. The tiny room became full of the reverberations of their wailing and sobbing. Vos threw up his hands and chased the whole family out.

'Didn't we do right to apprehend them, Sir?' asked Barends, rather hurt by this speedy dismissal. 'They're only ones who claimed even to know what this Ignaas looks like. And now they'll probably sail off somewhere on their boat, and we won't be able to pull them in again if we need them.'

'And they did have *one* piece of evidence you might want to hear, Sir,' droned van Dyke, apparently equally disappointed in his superior. When Vos permitted himself to raise and enquiring eyebrow he went on, 'A motive, Sir, of sorts, for the dead woman, Margriet van de Grote. That Cees fellow says Ignaas was once sweet on her. In his younger days. Hers too, of course. In Delft. She lived in Delft. A tavern keeper's daughter she was. And this Ignaas wanted to marry her, but her father thought he was a wastrel, so she married van de Grote instead.'

'And after twenty odd years he seeks her out and cuts her throat?'

'It might have been an act of mercy, Sir,' volunteered the ineffable Joop Barends. 'Everyone says this Margriet was stark raving mad, Sir! What with gin, and her brain rotting away. He might have wanted to put her out of her misery.'

'I would have thought it more likely that the husband would do that,' said Vos, who did indeed wonder if blaming the death of Margriet on Ignaas was merely opportunistic. He made a note on his cuff to interrogate Henke as soon as possible. 'Were any other connections with the victims mentioned?' The two men shook their heads.

'Of course the young woman, Matilde de Haan, could simply have rejected his advances or even someone else's advances and got stabbed for her pains. I've seen the zakkendrager, Ambroos, at the infirmary, and I believe that affair was just a gin-fuelled brawl that got out of hand. It *could* have been this Ignaas or someone else entirely. He was too stupid-drunk to know who attacked him. A hopeless witness and we'd never prove anything anyway.'

'So, what do we do now, Sir?' the zealous Barends demanded.

Vos winced. He was finding it hard to think of anything these two idiots might do that wouldn't make matters worse.

'I'd like you, van Dyke, to make enquiries – tactfully – amongst neighbours of the de Haan family, about the niece, Mathilde. Her uncle declares her to be a good quiet girl of a retiring disposition, who seldom strayed far from home, and had no particular bosom friends.' He scowled darkly. 'Personally, when someone tells me something like that about a young woman who has been subject to what may still prove to be a fatal attack, I am sceptical, *very* sceptical. Who were her friends? Did she have a lover? Find out.'

'Yessir,' said van Dyke. Neither his spirits nor his moustache appeared in anyway uplifted by this commission.

'And *you*, Barends. I want you to seek out some of the local scamps and ragamuffins. Question any youngsters you find hanging about on the quaysides, especially those youngsters from "off the boats". Do they know this boy, Tomas? Have they seen him, when and where?'

'Yessir! I'll soon nose him out!' promised Barends. 'Shall I... er, offer any reward for information received? A cent for gingerbread, for instance?'

'Only out of your own pocket,' Vos replied. 'Offer it to one, and you'd soon have twenty following at your heels, all eager to tell you they've seen Tomas and all of it tarradiddles. I myself,' he went on, 'am going to visit this Henke van de Grote. I need to know more about the circumstances of his wife, Margriet's, death. I'm by no means sure we've been told the whole story there.'

'I'm not sure about this Margriet that's dead,' said Barends, his foolish face puckered in concentration. 'Which one is she? Are we *sure* it's the drunken one? They were talking about a woman called Margriet this morning in the coffee house, weren't they van Dyke? *This* one the people here believe has run off with a lover.'

They'd spent part of the morning *in a coffee house*? Vos shook his head in despair.

'Not talking about *that* Margriet, they weren't! You weren't listening properly, lad,' grouched van Dyke. 'Too busy stuffing your face with spice cake. They were certain enough about the one *you* mean, Sir. Drinks and her wits are gone. She's definitely dead.'

'But they were talking about *someone*, and I'm sure her name was Margriet,' persisted Barends.

'The woman at the orphanage,' said van Dyke, 'the Regent's wife. *Her* name is Margriet too. They were saying that she's disappeared. But most of them think she's run off with a lover to Amsterdam,' he told Vos, 'that can't have anything to do with our case, can it?'

'Nothing at all I hope, so long as she *has* run off,' said Vos. 'We're not here to investigate runaway wives. If *she* turns up dead, that would be another matter.'

Chapter 15

Anders Vos and Henke van de Grote

Vos found Henke at the Guildhuis, though not immediately. It was another busy working day for the zakkendragers, most of the binnenschippers wishing to unload, load, and leave again as quickly as possible. A number of the porters were lounging idly before the Guildhuis, or seated within on benches, clay pipes in their mouths and tots of gin on the tables before them. They were waiting to have their numbers called.

Not having met the Chief of the zakkendragers, Vos naturally assumed the man calling out numbers as the wooden balls rattled through the shoot, must be Henke himself. He stood in the doorway for a moment, letting the man see him there, and watching for those signs of uneasiness which might indicate guilt. He was much inclined to think that mad Margriet's death was altogether too convenient.

'Six needed to unload the Eagle in front of the Korenbeurs!' the fellow was calling out in a shrill voice. The balls rumbled down through the hopper, one by one. 'Twelve, twenty-seven, nineteen, fourteen, seven, and twenty nine!'

Six men rose, pushed their beakers aside, and strode out, pleased and purposeful. Others grunted with dissatisfaction and pulled on their clay pipes. The balls were collected from the hopper and redistributed. Several men who'd been waiting outside now came in and sat down.

Vos pushed his way to the front and introduced himself.

'Henke van de Grote? Police. I need to have a word with you.'

The man looked alarmed, but this it turned out was not a sign of a guilty conscience. Several hefty zakkendragers stepped in to put Vos right. *This*, they told him, patting the man on the back with horny hands, was not Henke at all, but Geert, his second in command. It was explained, by way of several large calloused fingers jabbing upwards, that Henke was not at work today. In mourning for his wife he was, they laboured to inform him, and upstairs in consultation with the Pastor, no doubt arranging the poor woman's funeral.

And here, after climbing the ladder-stair to the upper room Henke used as kitchen and parlour, Vos finally found him. Also, as predicted, he found Pastor Winkelmann, which annoyed him although he tried not to show it. He would have preferred to have Henke alone for the purposes of interrogation. Obviously, a pastor could and indeed should, visit a bereaved member of his flock, but Vos didn't care for the clergy, and felt he had already seen this particular pastor, or at any rate been told about him, once too often. Wherever and whenever things happened in this town, it would seem this same cleric was a witness to them. And here he was again! Sitting at his ease, and smoking a splendid pipe of cherry-wood. As indeed was Henke. Between them on the bare scrubbed table-top was a child's clog containing tobacco. Rather a good blend, Vos deduced from the aroma. Although Henke grunted what might be taken for a welcome to the detective, and pulled out a chair for him, he didn't offer him a smoke.

'I'm sorry to trouble you at this sad time,' said Vos, once he'd introduced himself and laid his kepi on another chair, 'but we've been called in by the Watch Committee to investigate, amongst other things, the death of your wife. I've been given an account of her death by others. Various accusations have been made as to the likely culprit, but we don't want to make a mistake, do we? I'd like to hear the facts from you if I may? I realise that this must be painful for you, but I hope you'll help me understand clearly what happened?' He produced a note book, smoothed it open at a clean page, and held his pencil at the ready. This simple procedure often frightened wrongdoers into giving away more than they intended, but Vos saw no visible effect here.

Henke said nothing for several long minutes. He continued to draw on his pipe, his broad forehead creased, as though he was thinking the matter over and deciding what to say. Pastor Winkelmann opened his mouth once or twice apparently considering whether to speak, but when Vos frowned at him, closed it again. Vos didn't want this witness prompted.

'I don't know how it happened,' Henke finally said, laying down his pipe and spreading his large hands palm upwards on the table top in a gesture of defeat. 'I've tried and tried to make sense of it, but I can't.' His voice sounded hoarse, as though he had been using it too much, or perhaps not at all, over the last few days. 'You'll understand how my wife was? Folk'll have told you about her?'

'I understand,' said Vos, treading carefully, 'that she was not entirely... in her right mind?'

'That is so. She was fifty years old, the same as me. When she was about forty-three, her mind began to fail. She didn't remember things anymore. She used to cook and sew, none better, but gradually she forgot everything. Even our sons' names! Can you credit that?'

Vos shook his head, rather disturbed. He was forty-three himself – had just had a birthday. Now every time he forgot something he would worry that *his* mind was failing. 'I thought such things didn't come on until old age?'

'So did I' agreed Henke, 'I took her to some clever doctor in Rotterdam, hoping he could cure her, but no. He said sometimes it affects people in their thirties and forties, and Margriet was one of those unlucky ones. There was nothing to be done. I did my best...' he looked at Pastor Winkelmann for support.

'You did, man, you did,' agreed the clergyman, between puffs on his pipe.

'I tried to keep her safe. That was all I could do. I couldn't make her happy. She was lost in some terrible...' he glanced at the pastor and away again, quickly, 'She was lost in some terrible...*hell*. I'm not saying that to blaspheme. That's how it appeared to me. The only relief she seemed to get was from drinking. Sometimes, when she'd had her fill of strong gin she'd laugh. And laugh and laugh. Then she'd fall into a stupor and sleep for hours. That was a blessing to me, strange as you may think it. It was the only way I could get any sleep myself. Otherwise she'd roam the house all night, screaming and crying like a banshee, and trying to get out.'

Vos thought that if Henke *had* killed Margriet, he could understand it. As the tiresome Barends had suggested, it would have been a merciful release for the poor woman. And for her husband.

'Has she always liked her drink?' he asked, craftily. He wanted to find out if Henke knew that Ignaas had once courted her when she was living with her father the tavern keeper in Delft.

Henke said yes, Margriet had always liked a glass, but had never, previous to her illness, drunk to excess. He went on to explain about the tavern in Delft. Margriet had grown up there, and worked alongside her father as a serving wench.

'I understand she knew this Ignaas van Damme from there? The man people here in Schiedam seem to think may be the murderer? Did he ever come to see her?'

Henke seemed startled by the introduction of Ignaas's name. 'Never! She knew him. *Had* known him, but I don't suppose they'd laid eyes on one another for twenty years or more. He'd wanted to marry her, did they tell you that?'

'It was mentioned.'

Henke slapped his thigh and gave a short bark of laughter. 'He used to hang around the tavern. Spent all his money there! He asked her father... what a joke! Margriet wouldn't have looked at a ne'er-do-well like him, even if her father would have allowed it! No, he was sent off with a flea in his ear. He certainly never showed his face here!'

'Would she have known him now... recognised him? I mean, because of her illness? I'm just wondering...' Vos wasn't sure what he was wondering. 'Could Margriet have spotted the man from a window and... But if the door was locked...?'

The room grew still. Henke's broad, and Vos had to admit, honest face was creased in puzzlement.

'I don't know,' he said. 'I just don't know. I could have sworn I locked the front door. I don't lock it when I'm here, at home, just drop a heavy wooden bar and slide it into place. Margriet's never fathomed that. When I go out I can't do that, so I always lock it from without with a key. Perhaps this time I didn't. It wasn't locked when I got back. These things you do without thinking, don't you? Habitually? That's the word. Then you can't remember actually doing it. Margriet was asleep when I left. Snoring. I didn't lock the bedroom door. I'd no reason to think she'd wake within the half hour I thought it would take – *as it did take* – to go and see what was happening with Ambroos. An unlucky soul, Ambroos, always has been. He's a guild member. I needed to let them know that at Sint Jacob's. So they'd know his bills would be met, and that we'd bury him if he didn't survive. I'd only had half the tale from one of the other men, who'd heard it from Maurits at the Koemarkt bakery. I didn't know how bad things might be with him.'

'If perchance you did forget to lock up...? And if your wife did wake?' asked Vos, 'do you think she'd have known Ignaas, if he came here?'

Henke sat in silent thought, gently rubbing the bridge of his nose with a thick forefinger, before he replied. 'I honestly don't know, Sir. Sometimes, especially during the first few years of her illness, I'd say she was more at home in the past than the present. She did speak then of the people she'd known as a girl. She used to ask when she could go and visit her father, although he died the first year we were married. The two of us – *but that was years ago when the children were small* – used to laugh about Ignaas. She used to say she'd always had more sense than to look twice at a man like that. Why, she said he even used to knock his old mother about if she wouldn't give him money for his drink and his gambling at cards. She's never mentioned him in recent years though. She was a pretty girl, my Margriet; she'd plenty of admirers in the old days...' Henke's voice trailed away.

'But she might have recognised him,' said Pastor Winkelmann, breaking his silence. 'I'm thinking about young Tomas, the boy who's gone missing,' he said, turning to Vos. 'If we suppose she woke, and was looking out of the window, and saw this Ignaas van Damme with Tomas – perhaps beating the child? Perhaps even in the act of...killing him? We don't know what's happened to him. No one seems to have seen him since he ran away from Cornelius de Haan last Sunday. *Might* she have rushed down to intervene?'

The three of them contemplated this for a while without speaking. The clock on the wall chimed the hour. Below them they could hear Geert calling another set of numbers, and then the thump of boots and clogs as another team went forth to unload another boat.

'I couldn't say,' said Henke, at last. 'Once upon a time I'd have said, yes, Margriet hated any wrongdoing. She'd a fiery temper, my wife, when she was roused. When our boys were small, if she'd thought someone was ill-treating one of them, she'd have tackled him. Indeed she would! We paid for the boys to go to school – this was before the government started opening these new elementary schools that you don't have to pay for – and one of the masters caned our Wilhelm on his legs for talking in class. Wilhelm swore it wasn't him, and Margriet went down to the school and raised... but that was twenty years ago. I don't know if she even noticed what other people were doing anymore.'

Vos had given Jacob Winkelmann a look that combined aversion with admiration. He disliked interfering clergymen as a matter of principle, but the man was clearly no fool, and he had to acknowledge that this was an explanation he'd never thought of. He'd been inclined to believe that Tomas had merely run off, and would soon be found, or his whereabouts reported. If he hadn't taken refuge with Hedy and Cees, then with another family of boat people. The lad could be with them, up in Rotterdam or half way to Utrecht by now. Vos was still expecting Barends to return with news of this kind later today. The last thing he wanted was to entertain the possibility that Tomas was dead. But he had to face the fact that the pastor's theory was plausible. Ignaas catches up with Tomas and begins belabouring him – or killing him? – Mad Margriet either recognises Ignaas, or simply resents what the man is doing to the boy, and rushes out. Ignaas cuts her throat to prevent her reporting what she's seen. Not realising that Margriet, in her demented state, wouldn't have been sufficiently coherent to report it.

Anders Vos allowed himself a gusty sigh. 'I've a man out now, seeking information on this boy, Tomas,' he admitted. 'I've been expecting he'll come back and tell me someone knows where he is. I've been thinking it possible he would have gone to one of the boat families for help.'

'Perhaps he did,' said Jacob Winkelmann, humbly accepting this alternative explanation. 'Indeed I pray that may be so. The other was just an idea of mine. I hope I'm wrong.'

'So do I, but you could be right,' admitted Vos, depressed. He was thinking that he might have to ask permission to drag the Schie basin. Just because Margriet's body had floated to the surface almost straight away, didn't mean that Tomas's wasn't still lying on the bottom.

'I don't like to think of that happening to the poor boy,' said Henke after they had sat in silence for another space. 'Indeed I don't. He's a nice little fellow. But what you say does make it easier for me, in a way, to understand what happened to Margriet. Something like that *might* have penetrated her poor sick mind, and sent her running to try and stop it. When she was well, when she was *herself*, she would have, of that I'm certain. The shock of seeing that boy ill-treated. It might have jolted her poor brain into working again! She could even… have recalled where I keep a spare door key, d'you think? Behind the clock,' He nodded towards the grandmother clock ticking softly on the wall. 'I thought to look this morning and it isn't there.' He turned to Pastor Winkelmann. 'If she died trying to save the child, that was a good deed, wasn't it? Would that earn her a place in Heaven, d'you suppose?'

By way of reply the pastor leaned forward and placed his hand over one of Henke's enormous paws. 'Surely our Lord must see it that way,' he murmured, 'and whether it happened like that or not, I'm certain Heaven attaches no blame to Margriet for what she could not help, the loss of her reason.'

To Vos's embarrassment, Henke's large pale eyes now filled with tears. Jumping up and seizing his kepi, he bade the two men a hasty farewell. The whole interview had left him discomfited. This case was not going as he'd hoped or expected. It now appeared a lot less likely that Henke had killed his wife, and there seemed a real possibility that the missing boy was dead too. He might be forced to recommend that the canal to be dragged and his superiors in the Maréchaussée wouldn't like the expense of *that*.

Chapter 16

Mathilde de Haan, Clara de Haan, and Frans Rijnsburger

The room was dim and silent, the shutters closed. No domestic sounds were allowed to permeate this part of the upper floor. Dried lavender in a china bowl had been conscientiously stirred to mask the natural odours of the sick room. The girl in the bed lay on her back, her torso raised up on a pile of pillows, her dark chestnut hair spread out around her. Her bonnet hung from its strings on the bedpost. Clara de Haan had her finger to her lips as she led the visitor into her niece's chamber.

'You see how she is!' she whispered. 'Heer Doctor Saunders says the knife must have punctured her lung. He can only recommend complete rest and quiet, and that we all pray that it will heal. He wanted to move her to Sint Jacob's – into a private room of course – but we couldn't countenance the risk to her if she was moved. Poor child! She's been so unfortunate! Her father was my husband's elder brother. *They* were killed, you know, he and his wife? In that rail disaster just outside the station here, in '56. Mattie was thrown clear, and that's how she got the scar on her face. From the window-glass exploding, they said. Poor dear, she's so self-conscious about it, yet it's nothing to what it was.'

Frans Rijnsburger (for the visitor was he) made no immediate comment, but went and stood at the head of the bed, and looked down on the girl. She lay disconcertingly still on her lace-trimmed pillows. Her skin was almost as white as the starched linen. Her glorious eyes were closed. Long dark lashes, darker than her hair, formed feathery crescents on her blanched cheeks. The scarring, observed Frans the medical man had been caused by two deep cuts, which had healed to form two arcs joined at the centre. Over time their colour had faded to a pale coffee shade, and now the scar tissue resembled a mayfly which might have alighted on her face. The tip of one wing seemed to hover on her cheek, the other on her nose. He thought of the tattoos which sailors and their lassies sometimes caused, quite deliberately, to have pricked out on their skin. Frans the medical man thought whoever had sewn the cuts had done a neat job. Frans the would-be lover considered the result delightful.

'I hoped I could offer something to ease her suffering,' he murmured, 'but she seems peaceful enough just now. She doesn't ever show signs of being in pain?' He knew perfectly well that this was the case, having pestered Xander Saunders every day about her condition. Naturally, in scheming to gain admission to the sickroom, he hadn't mentioned this to Clara.

'Well... sometimes she's restless, as though she might be uncomfortable,' she said, doubtfully. 'Dr Saunders has prescribed laudanum to promote sleep and healing, but I suppose you know that?'

Frans did indeed know that, since he was supplying the drug. 'Laudanum in itself can sometimes make the patient restless,' he said. 'It affects different people in different ways. The dreams can be disturbing, frightening even. You're managing to give her liquids?' They were speaking in low voices. The girl's eyelids flickered. Frans wondered if she could hear what they were saying. If she knew he was there?

'Oh yes, we try to give her drinks of boiled water or a little gruel every two hours,' said Clara, 'and generally, if we stroke her throat she's able to swallow it. It seems so little, but Dr Saunders assures me that life can be sustained for months on such meagre fare.' Plump Clara de Haan sounded doubtful about this. Frans thought, meanly, that it would do the whole de Haan family good to subsist on gruel and water for a month.

'It's such a mystery, how it happened,' went on Clara.

'I can't help feeling responsible,' Frans confessed. 'As you know, Mevrouw, she came with me at my request to help convey the injured sack porter to Sint Jacob's. If I'd had the least suspicion that she might meet with danger, walking back through the town...'

'On the Sabbath too! It was so strange. Apparently she walked with Pastor Winkelmann as far as the Appelmarktbrug. He says he saw her begin to walk along the Lang Haven, having told him she'd catch up with me and my daughters near the Haven Kerk. In fact my daughter Lotte thought she caught a glimpse of her in the distance, coming towards us. Then more people must have spilled out of the church and formed a crowd on the quayside, milling about, discussing the service and exchanging news, and she disappeared from view.' Clara put out a hand and smoothed Mattie's brow. 'Poor child! She's never been one for crowds or a lot of company. I suppose she went back up to the Hoogstraat, thinking it would be quieter. I was surprised she wasn't home when we got here, especially when Lotte was so certain she'd seen her.'

'Then they came to tell you she'd been attacked?' Frans knew all this already, but he wanted to prolong his time at Mattie's bedside. He would dearly have liked to push Clara's hand away and stroke her brow himself.

'Directeur van Corte came himself! What a shock for the poor man, hurrying back from his devotions to his responsibilities at the hospital. To find our girl collapsed in the street! Of course, even then, we'd no idea how badly injured she was.'

'Hmm. It is indeed a mystery.'

Frans, knowing exactly whereabouts on the Hoogstraat that Mattie had been found, wondered why Directeur van Corte should have been carrying out those "devotions" in totally the opposite direction to Sint Jacob's, which naturally enough, had a chapel of its own. He decided not to point this out to Clara. There had been rumours about a certain attractive widow who lived over towards the Plantage... Frans was very conscious of his need as a young man, not from this town, to establish a satisfactory living. Knowledge like this could be useful if he needed to apply a little pressure in his dealings with the director of the hospital. The occasional hint to the man that he knew something to his discredit...? Discretion, however, was vital. Commonplace gossip and tittle-tattle must never pass his lips. He remembered, bleakly, the tittle-tattle that had caused his own family's downfall, and its lingering aftermath, which had obliged Frans himself to leave Rijnsburg.

'Well, if there's nothing I can do... nothing I can offer,' he said, realising that he had prolonged the visit as long as was reasonable, 'I must get back to my work. Do send for me at once if there is anything I can supply?'

He and Clara drifted from the room together, and Clara quietly closed the door. Neither of them saw Mattie's eyelids flutter open, or her lips form the words 'that fool,' before she floated down into laudanum induced slumber once again.

'My husband,' said Clara, as they carefully descended the steep, twisting staircase, 'is certain this terrible bargee, Ignaas somebody-or-other, must be the guilty party. Certainly the man has a bad reputation – for drunkenness and brawling to be sure – but why would he stab our poor niece? What had she ever done that he should take against her?'

Frans did not attempt to reply immediately. He was negotiating a dark bend on the stairs. He could imagine several reasons why someone might take against Cornelius, although not his niece. He'd often experienced a temptation to push that prosy old fool into the canal himself.

'These detectives from Rotterdam wonder if she knew something – or this Ignaas *thought* she knew something, about his step-son, Tomas?' he suggested, once they reached a better lighted portion of the staircase. 'You recall him? The boy who was on the bridge with us, when we were attempting to aid the wounded zakkendrager...?'

Frans had already been cornered in his shop and questioned by van Dyke. The policeman had made it clear he believed Mattie must have been meeting a lover, and thought Frans might know who he was. He, of course, had hotly denied that any such a person existed. Which hadn't seemed to convince the man. On reflection, Frans realised he'd been too vehement. Instead of persuading the lugubrious up-holder of the law that Mattie couldn't possibly have a jealous lover, he must have given the impression that *he* himself might well be the man, and therefore the prime suspect. Ridiculous! The whole thing was inexplicable. He hardly knew the girl. Although he would never admit it, this visit to the de Haan household (whilst Cornelius himself was out, at a Watch Committee meeting) was an attempt to learn more about the young woman who'd made such an impression on him. And he *had* learned something. He'd learned that her parents were dead, killed in the first ever rail crash in the Netherlands, four years ago. He'd learned that her father had been a doctor, a professional man, a fact which he could not help but find satisfactory. He'd learned that Mattie was self-conscious about the scar on her face. Also, he had to concede, he'd gained a more favourable impression of her aunt, who appeared genuinely concerned for her niece's recovery.

'Yes, I remember the boy,' admitted Clara, doubtfully, once they reached the front hallway, 'he ran away. Cornelius was frightfully cross about that. Why should Mattie know anything about him?'

'I doubt if she did... does. But Ignaas van Damme might think she did.'

'I don't believe she even spoke to him!'

'She didn't, but *he* spoke to her. Remember, Mevrouw? He said something to her as he handed her the loaf he'd bought from the bakery.'

'Why, yes! I was standing next to her. All he said was would she give it to Pastor Winkelmann to give to that man at the Guildhuis. The one whose crazy wife has been found with her throat cut!' she shuddered. 'It's *absurd* to think he was giving Mattie some... some kind of secret message! He was just a tiresome scamp of a boy! It's absolutely absurd!' Clara de Haan's several chins wobbled in outrage at the very notion.

'I'm sure you're right,' answered Frans, diplomatically as he took up his hat and cane from the hall table, signalling his intention to depart. 'Mevrouw, I thank you, and do call on me if I can help Miss Mathilde *in any way*, won't you? I hope we'll soon see her fully on the road to recovery.'

He would perhaps have said more, but just then he heard the aggrieved tones of Cornelius, coming in through the house from the back door. From what he could overhear, he gathered that Corporal Detective van Dyke had got around to questioning Mattie's uncle. Frans Rijnsburger prepared to make a hasty departure.

'I've never been so insulted!' he heard the Chief Bridge Watcher exclaim, as Clara's hand was arrested on the inner door knob. 'Suggesting that my poor niece was meeting some rogue – some *paramour* – behind our backs! Mattie of all people! Why, if we were Romans I'd say the poor child was ripe for a nunnery!'

Chapter 17

Corporal Barends and the Wharf Rat

Corporal Joop Barends was by no means a clever fellow. He knew his superior officers dismissed him as a nonentity, and a very junior nonentity at that. He was well aware of their disdain. More specifically, Andres Vos and Josef van Dyke had made no secret of the fact that they regarded him as a liability on the present case. But despite their discouragement he still revelled in the good fortune (actually a particularly large favour owed to his father) that had secured him his place in the Maréchaussée. He was young and he was optimistic. One day, he was certain, he would solve some baffling crime that had Anders Vos stumped, and *then* they would all discover his worth! *Then* they would pat him on the back, buy him a drink and, *glory of glories* promote him to sergeant! Ever hopeful, he said to himself as he strolled along Westvest, 'This might be the day!'

Today, Vos had given him his very own assignment; to find the binnenschippers' children and their pals, and question them about this lad, Tomas. No van Dyke breathing down his neck, no Vos pouring cold water on all his suggestions. With note book and pencil in his tunic pocket and his head high, he marched along the Korte Haven and turned onto the Westvest district which ran along the eastern bank of the Nieuwe Haven. He wouldn't be at all surprised if he found the boy first off. These bargees were reputed to be a clannish lot, little better than water-borne gypsies; most of them, but one of their little ragamuffins could surely be persuaded to let something out? Vos might be right to warn against using pennies-for-gingerbread as bribes, but Barends considered it would be worth quite a few if he could march back to Vos at the end of the afternoon, leading young Tomas by the ear!

To match his mood of confidence (or so he thought) the sun came out. The sails of the huge Walvisch windmill on Westvest, towering twenty six and a half meters above him, were already turning, their canvases slapping gently against the wooden frames. But the sudden burst of sunlight caused dark shadows to fall rhythmically across his path, a disconcerting sensation. He began to feel slightly seasick, and to experience that uncomfortable sensation where one is no longer able to walk in a straight line. Everyone in Schiedam is familiar with this effect, and adapts for it, but Joop Barends had never been there before. He found it alarming at first, but after a moment or two, highly amusing. This must be how happy drunkards felt, just after they'd imbibed one beaker too many! He himself was a very clean living young man.

'Oops!' he staggered a little in the direction of the canal, and put out a hand to steady himself against the high prow of a barge. He'd chosen to walk along Westvest because he knew the Appelbloesem was tied up here, and wanted another look at her. This was not she. This one was called... De Paardenbloem. Hmm, he wouldn't claim to be at all knowledgeable about botany, but he thought he might remember this one from childhood — yellow flower like a mop head. His nurse had told him he wasn't to pick them because they made you wet the bed.

Had the owner chosen the name because he had children who...?

'You! Geroff!' A voice roared from below the Paardenbloem's deck. The boat had, naturally, moved a little in the water under Barends' weight. A sturdy, not very clean figure emerged. 'Wha' yer want?' He was an elderly chap. Dirty blue smock, clogs. Grizzled beard. A Grandfather at least, he thought.

'Sorree! Not used to the... err... effect of the shadows from the windmill's sails flickering. Made me quite dizzy for a moment. I'm looking for a boy... Official business, Police, you know?' Barends realised he wasn't explaining himself well. He was flustered. 'I'm searching for a missing boy. His name is Tomas. Would you know him?'

'Nah,' said the skipper of the Paardenbloem, 'Never 'eard of 'im,' and then, as an afterthought, 'Police, eh? What's 'e done?'

'Oh, nothing. But *missing* d'you see? He's only a youngster. Eleven years old, I'm reliably informed. Nobody seems to have seen him since last Sunday. You haven't seen an eleven year old boy wandering about?'

'Nah. Not as I knows. Only bin 'ere since Thursday. Boys all over the place 'ere. Dunno one from another. Good thing 'twill be, to my mind when the government makes 'em all go to school!'

Barends, being a bachelor, had no opinion about this. He had

112

been carefully educated at home, where his tutors, so far as he recalled, had held him in much the same estimation as did van Dyke and Vos.

'O' course,' continued the old – *person*, well, you couldn't call him 'an old salt', since Barends supposed he was strictly an inland sailor – 'O' course, *I* grew up in an orphanage. We had to go to school there! Kept us busy every minute of the day, they did! No wandering off and getting into mischief! That's what this lad needs!'

'Couldn't agree more!' said Barends cheerfully, and moved on. The sun had retreated behind the clouds again, and though the Walvisch's sails spun quite rapidly in the stiffening breeze, there were no more shadows making him dizzy.

He walked further along the quayside. Ah! Here was the Appelbloesem, tied fore and aft, her gangplank pulled clear and upended on the deck. The guard he and van Dyke had encountered earlier wasn't there. Barends assumed he had gone home to lunch, taking his dog with him. He stopped and considered whether he could jump across from the quay onto the deck, a gap of about a metre.

'Yer'll fall in, Meester,' said a gruff but childish voice. 'Then you won't 'alf look silly!' Here, extremely ragged, filthy, wearing broken down boots without laces, but bright of eye, was a boy Barends judged to be roughly the right age.

'Ha! Could you be Tomas, by any chance?'

'Tomas? Nah. I'm Piet,' said the urchin. ''Oo'se Tomas?'

'A boy who lives, or used to live on this boat. About your age… perhaps a year or two younger.' Barends consulted his note book. 'Fairish hair. Slim build. Poorly dressed, bare-footed when last seen,' he recited. 'He lives, or used to live, with his steifvader, one Ignaas van Damme, on this boat. Do you know him?'

'Mebbe,' replied the ragamuffin. 'Wot's it worth?'

Barends gulped, shocked by the mercenary character of modern youth, although Vos had warned him how it would be.

'That depends,' he temporised. 'Do you know where he is?'

The boy Piet screwed up his lips, and considered. 'Nah, I ain't seen 'im,' he said. ''Oo wants 'im? If it's that Ignaas, ferget it. 'E's a right devil. I've 'eard 'e's bin amurderin' folk!'

'We, the police, are looking for *him* too, of course,' said Barends.

'Police!' Piet was horrified. 'Youse police?' He looked Barends up and down in alarm. 'Yer're kiddin', right? Thought you wus a soldier in that rig out. You're aimin' on *arrestin'* someone?'

'Ignaas van Damme, if I can,' said Barends, affecting modesty. 'But finding this boy, Tomas, is my immediate task. We want to interview him. He may have information that could lead us to his step-father.'

Piet gave this further thought. 'Nah, Tomas won't know nothin',' he decided. 'Waste of time askin' 'im. Wet behind the ears 'e is. Prob'ly believes in Sinter Klaas! 'E believed me when I said about the Eye. 'E's just a little kid.'

Barends was baffled. 'Eye, what eye? What are you talking about?'

'That Church. Yer must know it! Not the old one. The one on the Lang 'Aven.' Piet waved an arm towards the Lang Haven. 'We sez it to all the little 'uns. They got a big eye carved on the front. Yer seen it? High up, under the roof, right? We scares 'em all! Tells 'em that there eye is awatchin' 'em! And that eye belongs t'God! God'll send you to hell if 'e sees yer do anythin' bad!' Piet doubled up laughing at the thought of the terror he and his pals created. 'O' course it's all a lot o' nonsense,' he gasped, and then stood up, sobering himself. 'I'd bet Tomas believed me. 'E's wet behind the ears, *'e is*,' he repeated.

Barends could make little of this. He tried asking Piet where he lived, but received a so ambiguous a gesture of the arm as to make him wonder if the boy had a home at all. Piet agreed readily enough that he didn't live on one of the boats, although he knew many of the families who did. But as to where Tomas might have gone (or his step-father) he had no suggestions.

'Pity, it would have been worth a cent to me!' said Barends.

Piet favoured him with an evil look, pulled his disgusting cap down over his grimy forehead and slouched off. Two boats' length further along the quay he stopped, turned, and came back until he was close enough to be heard, but not close enough for Barends to nab a hold of him.

'That Ignaas might be kippin' in the barrel-maker's yard,' he hissed. 'I 'eard that. Don't know as 'e's there no more, though. Likely 'e's movin' around, since ye fellows is after 'im.'

Barends fished in his trouser pocket for a cent and tossed it to him. It was expertly caught. Only after Piet disappeared down the alley next to the windmill did it occur to him that there must be more than one barrel-maker in Schiedam.

Still, it was information! Valuable information and he'd like to see Anders Vos deny it! He licked his pencil. He turned to a clean page in his note book. He wrote "interrogate barrel-makers, possible sighting of JVD? Witness reliable? Doubtful, but investigate." Satisfied, and generally rather pleased with himself, he closed the note book, pocketed it, and took a step back – and fell into the canal with a mighty splash.

Chapter 18

Andres Vos, Josef van Dyke and Joop Barends

The Burgemeester had fixed for the detectives to stay in a lodging house run by his mother-in-law. It was a tall dismal building on a corner of the Korte Haven, which couldn't be said to have many amenities. However, they had the whole of the top floor to themselves, and this included as well as sleeping quarters, a room containing a table and three chairs (one with a wobbly leg, on which Barends was currently perched, naked, and wrapped in a blanket). The landlady had sent up a hot if uninspiring meal of stamppot, and the policemen, having eaten it, were smoking cheroots (Vos and van Dyke) and sharing their reports. Barends' clothes were being dried; it was hoped, downstairs over the kitchen range. He was drinking hot gin and lemon and was sure he was getting a cold.

Vos, being the superior officer, gave the report of his activities first.

'Henke van de Grote,' said he, 'husband of Margriet van de Grote, deceased. I interviewed this person of interest at his home, which is the Guildhuis of the Zakkendragers next to the Schie basin. The Reverend Jacob Winkelmann was also present throughout the interview. Van de Grote seems genuinely distraught at the loss of his wife. This despite the fact that he states that she has been astray in her wits for seven years or more, and that a doctor in Rotterdam had pronounced her incurable. He admits she had known Ignaas van Damme when she was a young woman living in Delft, and that the man had once wished to marry her, but he believes she had not seen him or heard from him in twenty years. Pastor Winkelmann put forward the theory that this Margriet might have seen van Damme mistreating or even murdering his step-son Tomas, and rushed from the house to intervene.'

'I've known murderers act distraught,' interposed van Dyke, morosely, 'especially when it's in the family. Frustration overcomes them, they kill their relative, and then they genuinely *are* sorry. Even convince themselves they didn't do it.'

'It's possible,' admitted Vos, 'though I'm inclined to think unlikely in this case. However frustrated he was with her craziness, why would he take her outside to cut her throat, where anyone passing might have seen him do it?'

'Blu...stains? Di'nt want 'em in th'house?' muttered Barends his nose buried in a vast handkerchief. Vos ignored him.

'I'm less convinced than I was that van de Grote did away with Margriet,' he hurried on to say, 'although not dismissing it entirely. The clergyman's notion has some merit, perhaps. They do say lunatics can sometimes be shocked out of their lunacy. Henke says his wife, before she lost her wits, *was* the kind of woman to intervene if she saw a child being mistreated. However, there's no evidence so far that any of this happened. Let's hear from you, Corporal van Dyke. Is Mathilde de Haan still living, for a start?'

'They say so. I didn't get to see her,' gloomed van Dyke between drags on his cheroot. 'The Aunt wouldn't let me into the sickroom.'

'Who did you see?'

'Her Aunt. Her Uncle. Her cousins. Heer Frans Rijnsburger, the apothecary. Maurits the baker, Aarte, the glass-blower, and two elderly ladies who attend the same church as the de Haans. I haven't caught up with the Pastor yet. I presume he's the same fellow you saw, Sir?'

'Yee-s,' agreed Vos, '*he* turns up everywhere. But then he's a pastor, people expect it. What do these other people have to say about Miss Mattie?'

Van Dyke consulted his note book. Barends sighed, glumly aware that his own was now a sodden mush.

'*One*: Clara de Haan,' van Dyke recited in a staccato fashion, 'States she's fond of the girl. Very quiet – Miss de Haan that is. Lost her parents in the rail crash here a few years back. Turned in on herself, the aunt says. Very self-conscious about a scar on her face. They've tried to "bring her out," but without success. So says Aunt Clara. No admirers that she is aware of.'

Two: the Misses Anneke and Lotte de Haan. I saw them together. Pair o' silly wenches, those two are. Not much concerned about their cousin's fate, or if they are they're hiding it well. Did she have an admirer? They nearly choked themselves sniggering over that. Not that they know of. "Mattie isn't interested in men," pipes up Miss Anneke, "Papa says if we were papists she could go to Ghent and join the Beguines."'

'*Three, four and five*: The baker, the glass-blower, and the two old biddies. They, the old women and the baker, know nothing about Miss Mattie except that she is Cornelius de Haan's niece, his brother's child. There has been some tragedy in her life, she seldom speaks. Her face is always hidden inside an old fashioned bonnet... That's all they could tell me.'

'It doesn't sound as though she would be likely to have... a follower?' queried Vos.

'No, Sir, but I reckon she does, all the same' said van Dyke, pleased. He paused, stubbing out his cheroot, perhaps to add an element of suspense to his meagre findings. Josef van Dyke was, in his own gloomy fashion, just as eager as Barends to put one over Anders Vos. 'That apothecary fellow, Frans Rijnsburger, he's sweet on her alright! Nearly went for me when I suggested she might be seeing some fellow her family didn't know about!'

'Might she have turned him down, if she's the next best thing to a nun?'

Van Dyke thought about this, whilst tapping his pencil on his teeth. Barends wriggled and caused his chair to rock unsteadily. Vos supposed that he was irritated, perhaps because his own pencil was at the bottom of the gracht.

'But would he stab her?' van Dyke went on, 'With a serrated knife? He's got sharp knives a plenty in his shop, I saw them. Uses them to chop the ingredients for his medicinal remedies, but none of those I saw had serrated edges. Anyway, he claims he stayed at the hospital with the injured zakkendrager. He was in consultation with the doctor, or so he maintains, at the time the girl was attacked. He must know we can check if that's true. Also, I'd say this Frans Rijnsberger is a young fellow with a fairly high opinion of himself. The ladies all like him, I hear. The girl would've had to have turned him down a tidy number of times before he'd believe she wouldn't have him – I'd say he's the kind, even if she'd given him no encouragement that would go to her uncle and make an offer for her. Evidently he hasn't, or it would surely have been mentioned.'

Barends began some comment about the apothecary's passion being perhaps of recent origin, but he was overcome with a fit of sneezing. Vos grimaced. The lad was nothing but a nuisance. He wondered what excuse he could manufacture to have him sent back to barracks.

Barends became aware that Vos and van Dyke were regarding him with exasperation, and tried to stifle the latest explosion. 'I hope you're not going to cough and sneeze all night,' grumbled Van Dyke, 'since you're bunking next to me.'

'What about the uncle? Cornelius de Haan?' asked Vos. 'What did *he* have to say?'

Josef van Dyke blew out his moustaches with a sigh. 'I could have filled a whole notebook with the things that man said,' he replied, 'but I didn't think you'd find most of it relevant. First off, he was insulted that I was questioning him about Miss Mathilde. According to him his niece is a paragon of virtue, who would never dream of meeting a member of the opposite sex in a clandestine manner. I would have liked to ask if he could say the same of those two daughters of his, but I managed to hold my tongue. There is no possible doubt in his mind that the girl was attacked by this Ignaas van Damme. *Why*, he has nothing better than a guess. According to him this van Damme is a monster of depravity who might do anything. He seems to believe the man may have tried to murder the girl just because she's his niece. To spite *him*, as it were. He has, of course, not a shred of evidence to support this.'

'And I suppose he may be right,' conceded Vos. 'Although on balance I'd still go for the thwarted lover.'

'Wh' did the glass-bl'er' say?' spluttered Barends.

Van Dyke glared at him. 'What makes you think the glass-blower knows anything to the point, young'un?' he growled. 'He's a grouch. He's seen the girl but never spoken to her. He said she could have a hundred lovers for all he knew, but he's never seen her out and about except on her own, or with members of the family. He only saw her last Sunday because he lent his cart to Heer Rijnsberger. At least I saw and questioned all *my* possible suspects. Unlike *you*, I refrained from diving into the canal and ruining a perfectly good uniform coat and trousers!'

Barends huddled down into his blanket, mortified by this attack. 'I only asked because...I wanted to know,' he said, hurt. 'I think this case of ours is proving tremendously interesting!'

'What *did* you achieve, if anything?' Vos asked.

'M-managed to question a youth called Piet...' Barends began, choking back another fit of coughing, "bout Tomas.'

'But you didn't find him!' Vos sighed and shook his head.

'No... bu' the youth,' atishoo! The youth said he'd heard...' atishoo!' 'That va' Damme...was hiding,' atishoo! In a barrel-maker's yard.'

'*Which* barrel-makers' yard?' demanded Vos and van Dyke in chorus.

'D-don't know,' sniffled Joop Barends, sadly. 'I forgot to ask him that.'

Chapter 19

Roel Mulder and Maarten de Hoop

Whenever Roel Mulder, a footloose fellow of thirty-seven, found himself in a new town (as happened quite frequently) and someone asked him how he earned his crust, he answered at random. Often he claimed the livelihood of the character he had most recently played upon the stage. Although he knew many people would regard this as reprehensible, Mulder loved to perform and was very conscientious in his roles, even when those roles were not for the stage but assumed for the purposes of mild deception. Indeed, whenever he was lucky enough to snare a genuine acting part, he researched it meticulously. He observed, if he could, the character's daily toil. He attempted to master – if the part required it – some of his skills, and was able to demonstrate them nightly. He had, until an unfortunate occurrence some five weeks previously, been performing at a theatre in Amsterdam. A fine part! That of a cruel schoolmaster who ill-treats his pupils. The play was based on an episode 'lifted' by the dramatist from the novel, "Nicholas Nickleby" by the well-known English writer, Charles Dickens. The inhabitants of the Netherlands had certainly heard of Heer Dickens. His novels had been translated into Dutch some twenty years before, but the dramatist (of whom they were most unlikely to have heard) hoped that few of them would have actually read them. And that they would not, therefore, realise the extent of his appropriation. Roel Mulder had shared those hopes, and indeed the play had been going rather well, until a drunken night-watchman had burned the theatre down.

The manner of Roel Mulder's arrival in Schiedam was thus. He'd heard vague rumours of a theatre company in Rotterdam who might be casting. He owed his landlady in the Jordaan district of Amsterdam a sizable amount in back rent. It therefore seemed a good time to pay a visit to a relative who lived "in the Rotterdam area."

On closer inspection of her address he was dismayed to discover that his distant cousin actually lived in Schiedam (which is not Rotterdam at all, and in his opinion never would be) However, he was not in a position to turn down free board and lodgings, and so he entrained for Schiedam.

On arrival, he was further dismayed to discover that his relative, a highly respectable matron, mother-in-law to the Burgemeester, was in fact a lodging-house keeper. She was happy enough to accommodate her cousin Roel, but neither his board nor his lodgings would be free. This was a bad blow. The train fare from Amsterdam had wiped out most of what little money he had. Even a trip on the horse-drawn tram into Rotterdam to find the theatre would tax his means. Moreover, a missive from the fellow thespian who had given him the tip followed him within days, and served to dash his hopes further. The theatre in Rotterdam would not in fact be auditioning for another six weeks. Six weeks! And he with barely a feather to fly with. There was nothing for it but to find some alternative employment (preferably, of course, with good remuneration) to while away the time. Enquiries amongst his widowed cousin's lodgers were not, initially, encouraging. There were vacancies for distillery hands, windmill operatives, and sail makers. Roel Mulder had never been cast in any of those roles, and couldn't pretend to be familiar with these trades. It was beginning to look as though he might have to skedaddle from the lodging house at the dead of night, and seek less costly accommodation. The only option seemed to be a hostel for foreign sailors washed up by the tides, or local men too permanently sozzled to be hired for anything at all. Once he might have settled for that, but as youth receded a comfortable bed to sleep in became more important than it had once been. This was an unattractive prospect.

Roel Mulder, however, was not a man to fall easily into despondency. Strolling idly along the Hoogstraat one morning in the direction of the town hall square, he happened to overhear a conversation between two well-dressed men in silk hats who were walking ahead of him.

'I don't know what to do,' said the first. 'I must believe my wife has taken leave of her senses! The man is a rogue. I don't know what he can have promised her that persuaded her to run off with him!'

'Has he managed to filch some of his employer's stock of diamonds?' asked the other. 'Is that the attraction?' Roel Mulder thought this second man placed emphasis on the word *diamonds* with a trace of bitterness, as though they were on his mind. A mistress, he imagined, had perhaps been pressing him for some.

'Certainly not!' said the first fellow jabbing angrily at the brick sets with the tip of his cane. 'He's nothing but the jeweller's sales clerk! And young enough to be Margriet's son! If only I could see her, talk to her! Make her see how foolish this is. I'm sure I could persuade her to return.'

'Why not?' drawled his companion, 'if you really want her back. Why don't you go to Amsterdam? Be firm, man! Drag her back where she belongs.'

'Ah, if only I could. But I don't have a schoolmaster for the orphanage since old Vanderleur retired; I've been doing his work myself. Who would teach the orphans whilst I'm gone? Even if I caught up with Margriet straight away – Amsterdam's such a big place – it could be two or three days before I return.'

At this point the two men turned into a coffee house in the square and took seats. Roel Mulder walked on a few paces, hesitated, turned as though making a sudden decision, and followed them in. Without glancing at them, he advanced into the shop and took a place at a table a little to the rear. Both men were absorbed in their conversation, and the interior of the little café was dimly lit. Its walls were lined with dark brown wood, and the window drapes were of thick lace which cut out the morning sunlight. He was confident that they hadn't taken particular notice of him, and was thus able to listen freely to what they said. A stout waitress with a mole on her cheek came and took his murmured order for a cup of 'Java'. Java was cheaper than Mocha. Roel Mulder, whose budget was constrained even when in work, had made a study of such matters. Presently the woman brought it, and he was able to eavesdrop, once more, on the talk at the near-by table. As is often the case in real life conversations, as opposed to those manufactured by playwrights, the participants were going over the same ground as before.

'If only I could *see* Margriet, talk to her…'

'Surely you can leave the orphanage for a day or two…?'

'If it were not for the children's schooling…'

'Is there no one who could take the lessons, if you left instructions?'

'No. I couldn't trust the ushers. Most of them are poorly

educated fellows. You must know how it is, from your experience at the hospital? Good men are difficult to find in this town. They can all get better money working in the distilleries. The children run rings around them as it is. Their idea of discipline is to lash out indiscriminately with the cane. I have to watch them constantly.'

Roel Mulder listened to this with interest whilst pretending to study the pages of the local Dagblad. Meanwhile he was manufacturing a plausible history for himself. Presently, when the man he'd deduced held some important post in the hospital showed signs of paying for his coffee and leaving, he arose.

'Excuse me, Sir,' he said, addressing himself to he-whose-wife-had-run-off, 'My name is Roel Mulder. Am I right in thinking you are the Regent of the orphanage?'

Maarten de Hoop, startled, confirmed this. Standing before him, Roel Mulder felt confident he would see a man in his late thirties, a man with a pleasant if unmemorable face, quietly if not smartly dressed. A man who might well be a clerk or a civil servant in the lower ranks – or a schoolmaster.

'I could not help overhearing a little – just a little – of what you said, Sir. Do I understand that you're looking for a master for the orphanage?'

'Why…yes. That is so. Are you a master?'

'I am, Sir, and currently unemployed. I had my own little school you see, just outside Amsterdam, but the owner of the premises I was renting decided to sell up, and what with the new government elementary schools opening up in every parish…' Roel Mulder sighed one of his most affecting sighs. (He had played Melancholy Jacques in a rather poorly translated version of As You Like It) 'If I could be of assistance to you…?'

'There you are, Maarten,' said the director of the hospital, waving a careless glove as he hurried out of the door, 'the answer to your problems. Sign this fellow on for a trial period!'

Maarten de Hoop was a cautious man. He invited Roel Mulder to be seated. He asked him how long he had been teaching. Roel plumped for five fictional years. The Regent mentioned that the governors of the weeshuis would require written recommendations. He explained, diffidently, that it would take a little time to secure these. He reiterated his willingness to start immediately if the Regent wished. At the end of half an hour, Roel Mulder was engaged as master to the children of the orphanage.

Sometimes, he thought, as he made his way back to the lodging house, he scored his greatest triumphs when he wasn't treading the boards at all. What a shame that there had been no audience today to admire his skill, his finesse. Why the great Johannes Jelgerhuis himself could hardly have played that scene better!

All he had to do now, he reflected, was convince his elderly cousin that now he'd secured employment her money would be forthcoming – eventually – and to visit one of the general emporiums in the town to purchase a suitable cane. An actor cannot play his part without the right props. A nice flexible whangee, yes that was the ticket! Such a pity the one he'd been using twice nightly in Amsterdam had gone up in flames with the building. Of course, he mused, the cane would be a *prop*, a threat to ensure good behaviour. Not, if he could avoid it, to be actually applied to those infant posteriors. As a small boy he had suffered many beatings. He'd become a fluent liar to avoid more. Those canings must, when he thought about it, have set him on the road to chicanery, a talent he now practiced both on the stage and off.

He tossed his Malacca in the air and caught it. A fine cane for walking, (he had twirled it, together with a sinister moustache, as the villain in more than one melodrama) but a shorter, more flexible version was what he needed for his latest role. Now, what should he teach these young imps? He laughed out loud at the thought. Roel Mulder, schoolmaster, a most excellent jest! If only his own schoolmasters could see him now!

Chapter 20

Roel Mulder and his pupils

'No, I cannot begin to guess when the Regent will return, Felix,' said Heer Mulder, for the fourth or fifth time that morning. His youthful pupils seemed to him unduly anxious to know the answer to this conundrum. Personally, the longer the Regent stayed away searching for his missing wife, the better it suited this temporary pedagogue. If he were to return, Roel Mulder would have to either manufacture letters of recommendation from the parents of those imaginary pupils in that moneyed suburb of Amsterdam, or make a hurried departure. This last, he was unwilling to do. Greatly to his surprise (and it would have surprised a good many people who knew him) he was enjoying himself hugely teaching the orphanage children. Every lesson was a little performance, and he prided himself that these performances were getting better day by day. Already he had been teaching for almost week – a fine run and there seemed no immediate reason why the show should close. True, he had not yet received any payment, but his cousin seemed to have accepted his assurances that she would be recompensed eventually, and as the weeshuis provided a hot mid-day meal he had no immediate need of ready guilders.

'But Sir,' said Felix, who was a persistent child, 'everything's going wrong without him!'

'Going wrong?' Roel Mulder contorted his face into a mixture of alarm and indignation. 'Going wrong!' he spluttered, eyes popping. 'What do you mean, Boy? Eh? Eh? Are my lessons unsatisfactory? Have you failed to learn anything since I arrived?'

Here, he was recreating the facial expressions he had used in a tragi-comedy where the villain had accused the innocent hero of stealing his watch (hoping to have him incarcerated, in order to ravish the hero's beautiful beloved).

'N-no, Sir,' stammered Felix, duly terrified. 'I d-don't mean, *you*, Sir! I m-mean in the weeshuis. We...' His voice trailed away, unable to explain what he meant.

'Felix means we haven't had any clean clothes issued to us this week, and we've had soused herring three times,' drawled Casper.

'We're not blaming you, Sir. It's just that the ushers and the cooks get in a muddle when Heer and Vrouw de Hoop aren't around to supervise. We thought you might be able to tell them what to do. Or speak to the governors, maybe?'

The orphans were used to a regimented existence, and found the sudden breakdown of this, arising within days of the Regent's departure, unsettling. Tomas, who wasn't used to such a well-ordered life, and thus took each day as it came, couldn't understand what all the fuss was about. So what if no one issued clean clothing at the appointed time? Who cared if soused herring arrived on his plate three days in a row? In what he was beginning to think of as his "old life" aboard the Appelbloesem he'd often (particularly of late) worn the same clothes for weeks if not months. He was happy just to sit down to a meal three times a day and rise from his seat again with a full belly. However, if Casper and Saskia were worried, he was prepared to worry along with them. He'd now graduated not only to the schoolroom but the dining hall. Maids and ushers were ceasing to ask his name. When at first they did, Saskia regaled them with her splendid fabrication about how he had been quarantined with a skin disease but was now cured by some wondrous lotion provided by Heer Rijnsberger. In Casper's room after lunch the three children had laughed a good deal over the supposed efficacy of Casper's chest medicine, applied to the skin.

The orphanage building was, it was undeniable, beginning to look neglected. The maids skimped their work. Dust balls and muddy smears from outdoor boots marred the tiles in the hallways. The ushers spent a lot of their time smoking home-rolled cheroots outside the laundry door. Nobody had seen Matron for days. She had apparently barricaded herself in her room, to be visited only by the maid, Roos. This was particularly worrying for Casper.

'If I get sick,' he said, 'who's going to send for the doctor?'

'I'll go,' said Tomas, loyally, 'if you can tell me his name and where to find him. I'll run straight there and get him.'

'His name is Doctor Saunders, but I don't know where he lives,' said Casper, sounding, for once, despondent. Tomas didn't know the town very well, but he'd come to realise that the weeshuis children were even less familiar with it than he was. Weekly trips to church and back were all most of them knew with any certainty. This, he now understood, was why the outing to the town hall with their new teacher had caused such excitement.

'They'll know at the Infirmary,' offered Saskia, trying to cheer Casper up. 'I can tell Tomas how to get there – *I think*. We passed by when we walked to the gemeentehuis.

You remember, Tomas? Well, Heer Mulder *said* it was. It's got those big iron gates. Oh, and the apothecary might know where the doctor lives. He calls here sometimes to see if the babies are croupy, even if nobody sends for him.'

'I know *him*,' said Tomas. 'Heer Rijnsburger. I know what he looks like. I told you. He was there that day when old de Haan was after me! I don't know where he lives, not exactly, but it must be over towards the Nieuwe Haven. If I ask, people will tell me where to find his shop. Just say the word, Casper, and I'll run and get him!'

With these assurances Casper, who understood better than any of them how dangerous the situation might become if the orphanage remained leaderless, had to be content.

However, he took the opportunity when it arose, to encourage Heer Mulder to intervene. 'The ushers *respect* you, Sir, because you're a teacher, you've had an *education*,' he told him as the other children filed out at the end of the morning, and he waited for Saskia or Tomas to push his chair. 'I'm sure if you spoke to them they'd mind you, the maids too. Just sort of make it known that you'll tell the Regent when he returns if they skimp their work.'

Roel Mulder was at first alarmed by this touching faith in his abilities. When he had inveigled his way into this job he'd certainly not foreseen that he might be required to *run* the orphanage. However, when soused herring appeared once again at lunch time, he saw that this strange, clever, crippled boy was right. *Someone* needed to take charge, and that someone had better be himself. Normally, lessons over, he ate lunch and then took himself off to spend the afternoon as he pleased, but today he decided to speak to the kitchen staff.

How should he present himself? What role had he played that might lend itself to tackling these domestics? He decided on the "family lawyer", stern but fair. He had once performed in a play where the leading character, having gone bankrupt, shot himself. Gloomy Scandinavian stuff, if he remembered rightly. He'd played the part of the notary who has the job of breaking this news to the man's retainers, making it clear that they were to be "let go" and the salaries owed to them were unlikely to be paid. That would strike the right note, he thought. He breezed into the kitchen, interrupting the post luncheon clatter of plates and pots being scraped and scrubbed.

'Ladies... and err, you, boy!' he declaimed. Instant attention! They stopped what they were doing and all eyes turned his way. Amazing! He certainly hadn't encountered this response too often during his stage appearances. Once, in Haarlem he recalled, a small audience had munched apples noisily throughout, almost drowning his impassioned speech as the cruel father turning his erring daughter out into the snowy night.

'Now as you are all aware,' he began, 'Regent de Hoop was called away at short notice to err... deal with family matters. He didn't expect to be gone for more than a few days, and he didn't, therefore, give me any precise instructions (he felt it best to be cautious on this point. Maarten de Hoop had given him no instructions other than for the conduct of the schoolroom).

'Clearly his errand has taken him longer than he intended, and I am aware that this may have created some difficulties for you?' *Dramatic pause, wait to see what they say.*

'Oh yes, Sir!' said the head cook, Katjie, a snaggle-toothed woman, her head swathed in a grubby cloth. 'I don't know what to do. I should be ordering. We're running out of everything except a couple more barrels of herring. But Vrouw de Hoop always looked over the orders with me, and the Regent paid the tradesmen. He didn't leave me any money, Sir.'

'Ah.' He saw that he had been right to cast himself as that family lawyer, the one smiling a sympathetic smile as he informed those faithful retainers that their salaries could not be forthcoming. 'I see your problem, Mevrouw. Unfortunately Regent de Hoop, didn't, as I say, anticipate being absent so long, and he didn't entrust to me a key to the cash box.'

He wasn't even sure there was a cash box. However, there must be money somewhere on the premises. He wasn't in any hurry to make contact with the governors (who must know) since the last thing he wanted was to draw their attention to his own irregular status. However, while his busy brain worked on the problem, Katjie came up with a suggestion.

'I could make out an *order*, Sir,' she proposed, doubtfully, 'and perhaps *you* could look it over, Sir, and see if I spelled everythin' right? And speak to the trades people? Explain the *situ*-ation.'

'Yes indeed, Mevrouw,' he said, exhaling in considerable relief, 'let's do that.' If there was one thing Roel Mulder knew he could do, and do well, it was persuade a tradesman to accept that he wasn't going to be paid on the nail.

There, that first confrontation had been easier than he thought. There'd been no need even to hint to the kitchen workers that he might "tell tales" when the Regent returned. Obviously they'd worked that out for themselves. The ushers were a surlier bunch, and the maids followed their lead, but by adopting the persona of that stern father tossing his erring daughter out into the snowstorm, he managed to gain their agreement to improve things. Floors were mopped. Clothing was collected, washed and redistributed, furniture was moved, firewood chopped, water boiled. Those of the older lads, the apprentices, who had gained the idea that the absence of the Regent and his wife meant permission to make a row in the dormitories, were shown the error of that assumption. Things did not run quite so smoothly as before (occasional appearances of Matron, pale and trembling, didn't inspire confidence) but he was satisfied that he, Roel Mulder, had prevented them from sliding into complete anarchy. Maarten de Hoop might not have asked him to do anything other than teach, but surely he'd done as the man would have wished? He wondered, not too hopefully, whether the Regent might show his appreciation, if and when he returned, by increasing the remuneration owed to him. He decided not to be too optimistic on that score.

On Sunday, by popular demand (at any rate by *demand*) it was Heer Mulder who led the cavalcade to Sint Jan's. "Cos yer can make 'em be'ave, Sir,' explained that great oaf of an usher, Dirk. Roel Mulder was not a church goer by choice, although he regarded the Sabbath as a welcome day of rest. During the sermon he began to feel that it would be a sin if the governors didn't offer him some additional payment.

When it was explained to him that Casper was not permitted to attend, he'd been inclined to insist that this was nonsense, but Casper himself said he preferred to stay behind, and nominated Tomas to stay with him.

'Because,' Casper told Tomas, as soon as the church party was off the premises, 'if Pastor Winkelmann is preaching up there in the pulpit looking around at everyone, as Saskia says he does, and he recognises you, he's bound to say something, and then what?'

Then what, indeed?

'I suppose sooner or later they'll find out and chuck me out,' Tomas replied gloomily. 'Then I don't know what I'll do. Even if I could get the Appelbloesem back, I can't sail her without a grown-up to help me. I just wish I could *see* her. See that she's all right. They've never caught Ignaas – at least we haven't heard that they have, so I suppose she's still tied up on Westvest. I do so wish I could see her!'

'Tomorrow perhaps you will!' said his friend. 'Heer Mulder's going to take us to the windmill if stays fine. The Walvisch. He's fixed it with the miller. He told me, I think to make me feel better about not going to church. As if I cared about that! If we're over at the Walvisch it can't be far from your boat, can it?'

'No, she might be close by. I'll show her to you! And if she isn't, I'll run up the ladders to the very top of the mill, and look out to spy where she is!' Tomas laughed out loud, so excited was he at this prospect. Then he noticed Casper's face. Casper had never run up a ladder. His friend was nearly fourteen years old, and had never been able to walk more than a couple of steps on his own two feet.

'I…I'd love to show you, Casper,' he said, his face falling in dismay. 'She's beautiful boat, our Appelbloesem. She belonged to my family, to my grandfather. I'll get her back one day, and then…'

'I hope you will, Tomas. It's something for you to aim for,' said Casper, his voice sounding strange and hollow. He turned his head away, and Tomas realised he was trying not to cry.

Chapter 21

Anders Vos confronts Frans Rijnsburger

'So, we think this Frans Rijnsburger might be the jealous lover? Miss Mattie, not fancying the cut of his jib, having turned him down?' demanded Vos over supper (stamppot again, and a rather mean serving of sausage). The three detectives had been in Schiedam for several days now and their investigation wasn't progressing. It wasn't progressing at all.

'We've asked around,' confirmed van Dyke, masticating brown bread and butter, his moustache rising and falling as he chewed, 'there doesn't seem to be anyone else with the slightest interest in the girl. She's still living, by the way. The de Haans are convinced she's at death's door, but we spoke to this Doctor Saunders – he's foreigner, his Dutch is atrocious – and he thinks she may pull through. At least that's what I understood him to say.'

'When she recovers, we can ask her if it was Ignaas!' said Barends, brightly.

'Ambroos recovered. At least he's recovering, but we're no wiser,' van Dyke retorted.

'Ambroos was off his head on gin when he was attacked. I hardly think Miss Mattie was,' said Vos, 'and as you say, Barends, *if* she regains consciousness, we may get confirmation. Or not. Rijnsburger does have an alibi, but it's not watertight. This Dries van Corte fellow is remarkably vague about the exact time he found her. Says he didn't have his pocket watch. No reports of sightings of Ignaas?'

'We've trailed around all the barrel-makers' yards,' said van Dyke, '*and* we've been to church and sat through a very tedious sermon by that pastor fellow, so we could mingle afterwards, but everyone denies having seen him. I reckon that lad, Piet, was making it up. Wanted to put one across young Barends!' he grinned, unpleasantly, at Joop Barends. 'Took you for a sucker, mate!' he jeered.

Joop Barends had long come to this conclusion himself. It had been a mistake to offer that cent bribe. Piet had made the story up, just to earn it. Or had he? He wasn't sure. He squirmed, an unwise proceeding as he was again seated on the chair with the wobbly leg. He heaved himself to one side, struggling to regain his balance. Also his uniform trousers had shrunk. Their turn-ups no longer met the top of his boots. His tunic too, felt tight across his chest and back. Life was uncomfortable and his ankles were cold.

'Is Rijnsburg in North or South Holland?' he asked suddenly.

'South, why?' demanded Vos.

'Oh, just I thought he might be a foreigner like that doctor.'

'Both North and South Holland are provinces of the United Netherlands,' said Vos, restraining with difficulty the urge to grind his teeth. 'Even it was in the Northern province he wouldn't be a foreigner, Barends!'

'Oh. It's just that people talk about him as though he was a foreigner. "The apothecary," they say, "the one from Rijnsburg."' Barends hastily caught van Dyke's eye. He didn't want to reveal to Vos that they had once again been gathering most of their information in the cosy warmth of a coffee house.

'Does he actually come from Rijnsburg?' asked van Dyke. 'Barends is right. They *do* talk about him as though he was foreign – or something. And it does seem a bit of a strange thing to do, to come and set himself up here. Why here? Rijnsburg's a tiddling little place, but why not Valkenburg, why not Haarlem? Why not try Amsterdam or Rotterdam, if he really wants to make something of himself?'

'He may not come from Rijnsburg. It could have been his grandfather who lived there fifty years back. Napoleon, you know. We can ask him,' said Vos.

The other two men nodded their understanding. Napoleon had been the one to insist that everyone must have a last name, a family name; stupid bureaucratic Frenchman. The inhabitants of the Low Countries had never bothered much with such things before the French invasion, half a century ago. Family names were for those whose families were important – Kings and dukes and the like. Most ordinary folks had simply identified themselves by the name of the town they came from, or the most memorable natural feature of the countryside outside their cottage door. Dyke, meer, veldt, bosch, or their profession, Boer, Muller. Or Slager, Bakker, Kandelaar maker, if it kept those tiresome Frenchmen happy.

'I'll ask young Meester Frans where he hails from,' Vos

repeated. 'I want to see him anyway. I'll go tomorrow morning. You two go down to the Guildhuis and get talking to the zakkendragers. Don't approach them if they're actually working, but they all seem to spend a lot of time sitting around waiting for their numbers to be put through the shoot before they're called. See what you can pick up. I'm fairly certain in my own mind that Henke van de Grote didn't murder his wife, but there may be things they could tell us... Henke himself told me they know most of what goes on in the town. They're up and down the quays, on and off the boats, in and out of the grain stores and the distilleries. It stands to reason that they hear a lot of gossip. They'll know all the boat people too, of course. See what you can get from them.'

Van Dyke and Barends exchanged dismayed glances. There were no coffee houses down by the basin, and over the last couple of days a biting wind had risen, blowing in off the North Sea. Hanging around to try to get into conversation with those tough burly zakkendragers, who almost certainly didn't much care for the police, held no appeal.

'We should have been issued with greatcoats,' grumbled van Dyke, smearing the last slice of bread around his plate to mop up the gravy, 'if we're going to be out in all weathers.'

Vos ignored him. 'I don't suppose, amongst the gossip you two picked up in the churchyard (Vos was not a church goer, but this did not prevent him from ordering his subordinates to attend) there was any mention of sightings of the missing boy? No? I suppose that's too much to hope for. I'm beginning to think he's either with his stepfather somewhere, whether willingly or not – or he's dead.'

'I'd say that binnenschipper was right, that fellow Cees with the fat wife and all the daughters. They've jumped a clipper, and are half way to the Indies. We'll never catch them,' said van Dyke ever the pessimist.

Next morning, after making enquiries of the landlady, Vos set out along Westvest, looking for the Apothecary's shop.

'He's strange one,' Vrouw Hauberk, proprietor of the lodging house told him, 'makes up his own cures and potions and what-have-you, but people do say they work. Some folks swear by him, but I don't know. Nice looking fellow apart from the birth mark on his face, but somehow he seems a bit... I can't describe it. Always very pleasantly spoken, but keeps himself to himself.'

'Does he actually hale from Rijnsburg?' he asked her. But the burgomaster's mother-in-law didn't know.

Out in the open, striding along the canal bank, Vos began to understand van Dyke's yearning for his greatcoat. An Artic wind, sweeping in from the Channel soon had him ramming his cap down over his ears and hunching into his tunic collar. Winter was coming. In a few weeks they'd be skating on these canals. If, he thought, Ignaas was sleeping rough, whether curled inside a barrel laid on its side, or in some workman's shed or loft, he wouldn't be doing it in comfort.

Ahead of him the sails of the Walvisch were spinning rapidly. However, today the sun was concealed by a layer of cloud, so the bellying canvases cast no distracting shadows. He passed a number of moored boats, some being unloaded by gangs of sack porters, but saw no familiar faces.

Just before the windmill, he spotted the Appelbloesem bobbing gently on the wind-ribbed water. Van Dyke and Barends had eventually been allowed to examine the hold and the living quarters, but had found nothing useful. They confirmed Cee's opinion that Ignaas and his step-son had been anything but careful housekeepers. They'd spoken too, to the fellow the Watch Committee were paying to keep guard.

'He saw someone, it *could've* been Ignaas,' Corporal van Dyke reported, 'some man came and stood looking at the boat, but the dog barked and he scarpered. No useful description. It *might* have been Ignaas, but it was dark… and he was drunk. The watchman, that is. He admitted it. Said he'd have gone ashore and tackled him if he'd been sober.'

'And he said a woman stopped earlier, and had a good look, a woman in a dark cloak. He didn't know who she was,' said Barends, 'but she *laughed*. A bit weird he thought.'

'Nothing to do with the case!' snapped Vos. 'We're looking for Ignaas, not some nosy woman.'

They'd also reported that this watchman kept a vicious dog, which if loose, would certainly discourage anyone from trying to board her. Barends had a rent in the knee of his uniform trousers to prove it. Drawing close now, Vos could hear it barking frantically.

Viewing her in the bright morning light, Vos agreed with Henke's assessment that the Appelbloesem was a trim vessel, if on the small side. It would be difficult, he judged, to make any great amount of money from the quantity of cargo she could carry. A hard way to make a living, but he was well aware that many of the bargees worked small boats. That family of six that his men had hauled in for questioning very likely lived on one no larger than this. It was a traditional way of life, one the binnenschippers were proud of, even if they barely scraped enough to keep body and soul together. Water gypsies, that's what they were, although they wouldn't care for that description. The watchman's dog was beginning to sound as though it would strangle itself in its attempts to break free and kill Vos so he walked on past the mill.

Looking back over his shoulder at the sound of childish voices, he saw the tail end of a crocodile of youngsters in traditional orphanage uniform being escorted in through the main door on the landward side of the great windmill. That schoolmaster again, thought Vos, rather he should have that job than me! Vos was not fond of children.

Soon, to his surprise, he came across a young man conforming to the description he'd been given of Frans Rijnsberger, clad in a dirty smock and standing on top of a step ladder painting the name board above the shop.

'Heer Rijnsberger?' he called up to him, a note of doubt entering his voice. Vos, being a detective, was busy deducing that the business mustn't be too profitable. Evidently if this was Rijnsberger, the fellow couldn't afford to employ someone to paint his signboard. Frans, loaded brush in hand, balanced the bucket of paint on the top step and looked down.

'I am he,' he replied. 'What do you want? Pills and medicines I don't dispense before noon on Mondays except in situations of emergency.' Then he must have noticed Vos's uniform. 'You're another policeman. What do you want this time?'

'I want you to come down off that ladder, stop waving that brush about, and answer some questions,' snapped Vos. The last thing he needed was Frans splattering paint all over him. Barends had already ruined one Maréchaussée uniform. The top brass in Rotterdam would be livid.

Frans laid the paintbrush across rim of the pail and began to descend.

'Will it take long?' he demanded, 'I want to finish this before the rain comes on. If it's about what happened to poor Miss de Haan, I can't tell you any more than I told your colleague. I was at the hospital with a patient when she was attacked, as I've already explained – *several times*.' He was a very tall young man and he looked down his rather fine nose at Anders Vos.

'Ah, but were you?' said Vos, nettled by his haughty manner. 'Heer van Corte, the *gentleman* (Vos laid some stress on the word gentleman, hinting that he didn't consider Frans to qualify for that description) who discovered the young lady lying in the street, says he didn't have his timepiece on him, so we don't have any precise idea when the attack took place. Had you quarrelled with Miss de Haan for some reason? After you left the hospital you could have caught up with her...'

"I hadn't. I didn't,' Frans interrupted, his colour rising, his birth mark standing out dark and livid across his cheek bone. 'Miss de Hann is a most estimable young lady, and I would never... I'd no reason... I hardly knew her.'

'Yet the Reverend Winkelmann says you specifically asked her to accompany you to the Infirmary. If you hardly knew her, why was that?' Vos had not, in fact, interviewed the Pastor. He felt he'd seen quite enough of that amiable Man of God. The information had come to him second hand (or possibly third or fourth) from the coffee house gleanings of Barends and van Dyke.

Frans heaved an ostentatious sigh. 'As I told your colleague, Miss de Haan struck me as an eminently practical young lady. Not one to succumb to the vapours at the sight of blood. I needed her to keep applying the pad to the man's wound. Heer Winkelmann and I had enough to do manoeuvring the cart through the streets. Of the people present on the bridge she struck me as the best choice. I'd never spoken to her previously. In an emergency with a man losing blood from a serious wound one must select the most competent seeming persons to assist.'

'Not because you were in love with Miss de Haan and she'd repelled your advances?'

Frans Rijnsberger said nothing for a moment. 'Miss de Haan is a charming young lady,' he said, carefully. Too carefully? 'But we hardly know one another. Last Sunday was the first time I'd even spoken to her.'

Vos judged that he'd get no more from pressing him on this

point for the present. After all, what could he prove? If he could come up with someone who had seen Frans talking with Miss Mattie on some other occasion, and expose him as a liar… Instead he changed the subject. 'That day on the bridge,' he began, 'there was a young boy present, Tomas, his name is, step-son of a binnenschipper called Ignaas van Damme. I understand the boy ran away, apparently not wishing to be detained by Heer de Haan. Since then, no one seems to have seen the lad. Have you any idea what became of him?'

'No. I've no idea where he went, or where he is,' said Frans Rijnsberger, 'and if I had, I wouldn't tell you! That boy had been ill-treated! It's no wonder he didn't care to be detained by de Haan.'

'You seem…antagonistic to me, Heer Rijnsberger,' mused Vos with eyes half closed. 'Have you had reason to form a dislike of the police?'

'No, I'm a busy man. I told you, I want to finish this painting before the rain comes.'

Vos looked up at the slow moving clouds overhead, at the trees by the canal, their nearly bare branches swaying back and forth; the shed leaves at their roots stirring in the sharp breeze. Certainly it would rain, once the wind died down, but not yet, possibly not even today.

'I won't keep you then,' he said, and turned away. Then, employing a technique he had often found useful in the past when questioning suspects, he turned back, as though a thought had just that moment come to him. 'By the way… do you actually come from Rijnsberg?'

'Of course,' said Frans. 'Why do you want to know?'

'No reason, just idle curiosity.'

'Got you there, young fellow!' Vos said to himself. The bright colour had faded from Frans' cheeks as though he had suffered a shock, and a look of anxious enquiry replaced his air of self-importance. Vos walked away. His superiors in the Maréchaussée didn't lightly sanction the expense of sending of telegrams, but he thought one to his chief seemed fully justified. Someone ought to go to Rijnsberg, or at least speak to the authorities there, and find out what Meester Frans had been up to. Perhaps he could send van Dyke or Barends?

Chapter 22

An Account of Our Visit to a Windmill

Roel Mulder found that although he was enjoying being a schoolmaster, like performing in a long running play (not that this had happened to him very often) he soon began to tire of saying and doing the same things time after time, day after day. Reading, writing, arithmetic, spelling tests, little excursions into geography and history – they were all very well, and he prided himself that some of the children had actually learned something under his tutelage. But he longed to get out of the stuffy confines of the classroom. To be shut in one room with twenty youngsters, especially since the orphanage routines for bathing and washing clothes seemed to have faltered, made going out into the fresh air all the more desirable.

'Right, kinder,' said he, lining them up. 'Button your coats; pull on your hats and mittens, there's cold wind.'

'Are we going to church, Sir?' quavered Felix, who seemed never quite to know where he was or what was happening.

'No, Felix, we are going to visit a windmill. Schiedam has many windmills, many exceedingly large windmills. Even you, Felix, must have noticed this? The windmills grind the corn which is then conveyed to the distilleries on which the economy and prosperity of this town depends. But do you know how a windmill works? Have you ever visited one?' He addressed the entire crocodile with these last two queries. 'No, and you should, and today I have arranged with the miller for us to see around his mill. You will take note of what you see and hear, and on our return you will all be set to write an account of our visit.' A few sighs and groans greeted this news, but Heer Mulder ignored them.

'Sir is it all right for me to come?' queried Casper, who suspected that had the Regent been there, permission for this would have been denied.

'Certainly,' Roel Mulder replied. 'Tomas will push your chair, and Adrien and Felix can assist if they are needed. Dirk here will walk at the rear of the line and can keep an eye on all of you.' Dirk, the big lout of an usher, looked morose. Everyone knew he would have preferred to remain behind in the orphanage, smoking and making coarse banter with the maids.

'*I* can help Tomas,' said Saskia, a slight note of jealousy evident in her voice. The teacher allowed his eyes to rest on her leg iron, but made no comment.

The morning was indeed cold, the sky pale and studded with tiny clouds. Roel Mulder marched his flock up over the spine of the Hoogstraat, down to and across the Appelmarktbrug and along the Lang Haven at a brisk pace. The little town was busy, the chimneys of its many distilleries cast a pall of smoke above the rooftops, and the creak of wooden cranes and the rumble of barrels being rolled along gangplanks and stowed on barges filled the air. The smell of gin hung heavy over everything; catching at the back of the children's' throats and making them cough. Tomas, once again at the back of the line, was concerned for Casper's weak chest. However Casper, enveloped almost up to eyebrows in a rug that Saskia had filched from his bed at the last minute, croaked from within its folds that he supposed he must be prepared to suffer for this chance to see more of the world. 'Before I leave it,' he added. Although Saskia, and nowadays Tomas too, begged him not to talk of dying, Casper continued to speak of it in matter-of-fact terms.

Although diligent in trying to push his friend's chair as smoothly as possible, Tomas frequently glanced about him at the boats tied up on the Lang Haven, and the people on the bustling quayside, in case he should see Ignaas, though he feared this less and less, since a whole week had now elapsed. Surely Ignaas must have taken himself off out of Schiedam now that he was suspected of murder and the boat had been confiscated? Tomas had no idea where his step-father would go, but if asked to guess, would have said Dordrecht, if only because they'd frequently gone there to seek work. If Ignaas could stay sober one of the larger boats would take him on as crew. Much as he hated and feared his stepfather, Tomas knew he was skilful around a boat.

Once the file of orphans had negotiated the narrow Walvisstrat passageway through to Westvest, he tried to look around for the Appelbloesem, but Heer Mulder wouldn't permit stragglers and Dirk swished his cane at them, hurrying them towards the curved brick belly of the Walvisch and in through the wide doors. Just as they were approaching the mill Tomas thought he saw a man in uniform ahead of them on the towpath. That policeman they had last seen at the Gemeentehuis! Ignaas might be gone (he hoped) but this man was still here. Looking for Ignaas, or looking for him? The man gazed back over his shoulder for a moment. Tomas ducked his head and trusted that the man had no idea what he looked like.

Inside the growling stomach of the great windmill the air was thick with dust and chaff, and filled with the sound of the creaking sails and the rumble of the grinding wheels. Casper, ever sensitive to what might irritate his chest, dived down beneath the folds of his rug until only his eyes beneath the peak of his orphanage cap were visible.

'I can't stay in here,' he croaked to Tomas and Saskia who had gravitated to his side now that the crocodile had become a shuffling crowd around Heer Mulder and the millwright.

Meester Wenders, the miller, was a stout fellow with a red face and good loud voice. Although not usually called upon to speak to children he was well used to haranguing his work force. He showed no hesitation when the schoolmaster urged him to address the orphans, but mounted onto a wooden hand cart, and with great rapidity began to spout facts and figures about the workings of the machinery, the size and weight of the grinding wheels, the dimensions of the sails, and the number of bags of grain delivered, ground, and dispatched to the distilleries each week. Even Heer Mulder looked daunted by these outpourings, and Felix, when the miller at last paused for breath, wailed 'Oh Sir, I *can't* remember all that!'

'I shall make some notes for you,' said the teacher, hastily producing a note book and a pencil from an inner pocket. 'Then all of you may copy them from the blackboard when we return. Err…perhaps Heer Wenders; we should climb up to view these grindstones at closer quarters? I don't want to hold up your work people here for too long…' The faces of the mill hands, who were enjoying an unusual moment of idleness, fell.

The miller, evidently feeling that he'd hardly broached his subject, seemed about to wave this suggestion away. Just then however, the great doors were thrown open once more and a chain of zakkendragers trudged in, the heavy sacks across their shoulders bowing them nearly double. These they proceeded to toss into untidy piles on the floor, raising thick clouds of dust into the air.

Heer Mulder, aided by the lugubrious Dirk, began to hurry his pupils up a series of steep wooden ladders leading first to the floor above, and then on up towards the top of the mill.

'*I'm* not going up *there*,' declared Saskia, plumping herself down on a sack of grain, and thrusting out her iron-bound leg. 'My leg iron's rubbed a hole in my stocking from walking here so quickly, and I can feel my chest getting tight. You go if you like, Tomas. I'll stay with Casper.'

Tomas was torn. Part of him wanted to climb nimbly up to see what could be seen, including, he hoped, the Appelbloesem moored below. Part of him felt he ought to stay with Casper whose breathing was growing increasingly harsh in the confines of the dusty room. The porters meanwhile were bringing in more and more sacks and throwing them down, grunting with effort and calling out to everyone to stand clear. Great spirals of chaff and dust rose into the air, fell to the floor, and were stirred again by the feet of departing men, only for other men to take their places.

'You two go outside,' said Tomas. 'You can't breathe properly in here.'

'We'll get into trouble,' said Saskia.

'Not if we don't go far,' Casper wheezed. 'Heer Mulder won't want me expiring right here. Let's go and look for Tomas's boat.'

Negotiating their way out past the incoming sack porters wasn't easy. The men were usually so bent over under the weight of the sacks across their shoulders that they could only see the floor in front of them, and so anxious to drop these loads that they barged forward regardless, swearing when Casper's wheeled chair got in the way. Tomas, more fluent in their deplorable language than his companions, barged and swore in return until they were safely outside.

'I'll tell you all about it when I've been up there!' he promised them, before turning and running back inside. Despite those clumsy orphanage boots, agile as a monkey, he began to climb the nearest ladder. Heights and steep ladders had no terrors for him. Tomas had first shinned up the mast of the Appelbloesem, barefoot, when he was six years old.

The first floor contained the miller's living space, barely curtained off from the access ladders. Like Henke at the zakkendragers' Guildhuis, Heer Wenders lived above his workplace.

Vrouw Wenders, who was trying to sooth a fractious baby at her breast, was less than pleased to see Tomas running by. She'd already had her privacy invaded as Roel Mulder and his class trooped by, and now here was yet another boy dashing past. Tomas ignored her squawks of protest and hurried up the next steep stairway. He passed the Wenders' sleeping quarters, and ran on up to the grain store where he found the orphans gathered around the miller. He was expounding how the milled grain arrived from above by the great 'spout' and was, even as they watched, being bagged by a team of perspiring mill workers.

'On the floor above us, the steenzolder,' Heer Wenders was declaiming above the noise of men and machinery, 'where we will be going shortly, it is ground in two circular stone troughs. You will see how the sails drive the poles and the cogs which turn the grindstones, which in turn grind the ears of barley to a coarse powder. For use in gin making it doesn't need to be ground so finely as if we were making bread flour. Then it descends through this shoot or spout you see before you, and the men catch it, bag it, and thrust it to one side until we have sufficient to send to one of the distilleries. *Then* we lower the sacks through the opening in the floor on your right, ready for distribution. The opening on the left, on the other hand, is where the corn still to be ground is hoisted up and stored until it is sent to the floor above us…'

Certain screeching and grating sounds from this left hand opening now added to the cacophony, as the mill hands on the lower floor began to hook the newly arrived sacks onto the pulleys. They rose on up through the various floors of the mill to the place where they would, sooner or later, be emptied into the steenkoppels, the stone grinding troughs. Tomas couldn't help grinning, seeing the faces of the children, and Heer Mulder's too, as they stood with their mouths open whilst this torrent of words (and grain dust) poured over them. The noise of the grinding wheels, the shouts and grunts of the workers both above and below made it impossible for anyone to stem the flow of the miller's peroration. But this suited Tomas exactly. *His* aim was to creep past them all unnoticed, up one floor and out onto the balkon that ran around the upper third of the mill, just below the tips of the great sails. He knew, without needing Heer Wenders to tell him, that this was where the kruibok, the brake, was situated. It was here that the miller or his assistants came when they needed to stop the sails to adjust or repair the canvases on their frames, or check the huge wooden spars that reinforced the sails and the sail cap. A broad fenced balcony ran right around the mill at this point, and from this he was sure he'd be able to look down and see the Appelbloesem on the canal below.

The first thing he spotted on the bank just beyond the mill, was Saskia, waving frantically and Casper, struggling to remove a hand from his enveloping blanket, to point at a boat. They'd already found the Appelbloesem! He waved back.

'I'm coming!' he called, jumping up and down in excitement, and then spinning on his heel to run back inside.

A hand fell on his shoulder, a rough calloused hand that grabbed hold of him and would not let him go. A hand that was all too familiar.

'So there you are you little devil! What 'yer doing here, dressed up like a workhouse brat?' Ignaas van Damme growled, transferring his grip to the scruff of Tomas's neck and pulling the collar of his coat so tightly that it cut into his throat. Tomas cried out and squirmed. 'Lemme go!' he tried to shout although Ignaas was choking him, hoping Heer Mulder or one of the mill workers might come to his rescue, but the squealing of the hoists and the rumbling of the grindstones doing their work drowned his stifled cries.

Explaining it to Casper later, they pondered on what had given him away.

'I don't think he knew it was me to begin with, when I first went out there. It must have been hearing me call down to you. He wouldn't have expected to see me in this uniform, and with my hair cut short – and I think I'm a bit fatter than I was before I came to live at the weeshuis.'

'You're right, he must have recognised your voice,' said Casper.

Ignaas! So Ignaas had been hiding out in the windmill all along. Thomas supposed he must have sneaked inside while the workers were preoccupied, and made a hiding place for himself amongst the sacks of meal which were waiting to be ground. From the balkon he too had been keeping an eye on the Appelbloesem, scheming, there was no doubt in Tomas's mind, how he might steal her back.

Twelve metres beneath them on the canal bank Saskia and Casper could see what was happening, but were powerless. 'Leave him, leave him you horrible man!' screamed Saskia, but no one inside the mill could possibly have heard her. Ignaas was squeezing his neck so tightly now that Tomas struggled to breathe. His head pounded painfully. He was afraid he was about to die.

    Whether Ignaas did intend to strangle him, he never learned. Just then, below in the grain store, one of the workmen with a particularly powerful set of lungs yelled something loud and urgent – perhaps a warning to those below as a sack dropped from the hoist – and Ignaas, visibly alarmed and fearing he was about to be discovered, thrust Tomas away from him so violently that the boy was hurled against the guard rail, and being small and light in weight, catapulted over it, out into the sharp morning air.

Chapter 23

Tomas in Flight and What Came After

It all happened in the wink of an eye. At one moment Tomas was struggling to breathe, unable to free himself from Ignaas's cruel grip, at the next he was falling through the empty air. Despite the speed at which he was tumbling there was time for him to notice that the clouds had parted a little and there were patches of milky blue overhead, and that a sharp breeze was turning the white canvas sails above him, casting faint shadows on the ground. There was time for a swift stab of fear. Would he land on the brick towpath and break all his bones, or in the canal where he might break only a few? Then, just as suddenly, his flight was halted by an abrupt and painful landing amongst the branches of a tree. The lesser twigs slowed his fall as he tumbled through them, but still the eventual collision between his head and stomach and a sturdy branch knocked all the breath out of his body. For a moment he must have lost consciousness. Slowly he came to, and finding where he was, clung on for dear life. Under the tree, Casper and Saskia were gazing up at him through the ruined veil of its yellow and bronze foliage.

'Are you alright?' enquired Saskia, conversationally. 'Shall I go and fetch someone?'

'I'm...alright,' Tomas gasped. 'I think. I'm just...getting my breath, from crashing into this tree...'

'Curl up, and keep still!' hissed Casper urgently, in his rusty scrape of a voice, 'because that policeman is coming back. There are still enough leaves on this tree, just about. He won't see you if you keep quite still.'

Voss, strolling back along the canal, thinking about the telegram he intended to dispatch with regard to the mysterious Frans Rijnsberger, was naturally puzzled to see in the distance two children, one in a wheeled chair, gazing up into the branches of a tree. By the time he drew level with them, Saskia had spun Casper's chair around and pushed it forward onto the towpath.

'And what might you two be doing here?' he demanded. He was a policeman, first last and always.

'Oh, Sir, please Sir, we're taking a walk,' said Saskia and Tomas, trying to remain still and invisible in the fork of the tree, could imagine how wide she was stretching her round blue eyes. 'Our teacher said we could, (Saskia, the world's *best* liar!) because he's taken the other children to visit the mill, but you see we two are cripples, so we can't climb up the ladders like the others.' With this Tomas sensed that she'd hitched up her skirts and the hem of her drawers to display her leg iron. 'We saw a little cat in that tree, so we've been calling to it,' she added, 'but it's jumped down now, and run away.'

Vos the policeman knew a fibber when he met one, no matter how round, blue and guileless her eyes, but he couldn't for the life of him imagine what she was fibbing about.

'Hmmp!' said he, 'Well, don't stray too far. I'm sure your schoolmaster wouldn't want you to go beyond calling distance.'

'Oh, *no*, Sir,' replied Saskia, innocence poured like syrup over her every syllable, 'I'm just taking poor Casper here to look at the pretty boats.'

She was lying. Vos knew it, but since he couldn't imagine that this little girl had anything to do with him or his current enquiries, decided it was better to ignore it. What, after all, could a couple of crippled kinder be up to that was any concern of his? And the child in the wheelchair, the really deformed boy, was beginning to shake alarmingly beneath his blanket. Going to go into convulsions? Vos definitely didn't want to be there if that happened. He considered himself to be a fairly brave man. He had tackled a gang of fleeing robbers in Rotterdam, disarmed a madman with a knife in Deventer, rescued a woman and a drowning donkey in Waalwijk, but he was uneasy around the crippled and deformed. Seeing this hunch-backed boy made him feel quite ill.

'Very well,' he grunted. 'Be sure to stay away from the water's edge. Don't let that chair run away with you, will you, young lady? One of my men wasn't looking where he was going the other day and fell in. Quite ruined his clothes, and now he's taken a nasty cold in the head.'

'Oh, no, Sir!' said Saskia, who couldn't hold back a little chirrup of laughter at the thought of a policeman falling into the canal. 'I'll be *ever* so careful!'

She and Casper watched as he strode away along the tow path

and on in the direction of the Korte Haven.

'Sas!' growled Casper, emerging from the folds of his rug once Vos was a tiny figure in the distance, 'You are *the* most appalling storyteller! "I'm just taking poor Casper to see the pretty boats," *you wretch!* My chest really hurts now from trying so hard not to laugh! That policeman must have thought I was having a conniption fit.'

'Well, I had to say *something*. We couldn't let him find Tomas,' said Saskia, 'he might have arrested him.'

'Perhaps I should have let him,' said Tomas, swinging down from a branch in a shower of gilded leaves, and dropping onto the grass beside them. 'Then I could have told him to arrest Ignaas – *if* he's still up there.'

'That was *him*, your steifvader, attacking you? Is that why you jumped off the balkon?' asked Casper.

'I didn't *jump*. He pushed me, Ignaas! He's hiding up amongst the sacks of grain in the maalzolder. Or he was. He... caught me, and he nearly killed me. Strangled me. But someone in the mill shouted out, really loudly, and he must have thought they were coming. He gave me such a shove that I couldn't save myself. Before I knew what was happening I was falling over the rail. It was lucky for me that this tree was here.' He rubbed his stomach. It hurt, but that was nothing. He could still feel his stepfather's fingers gripping his throat.

'Should you run after the policeman? Tell him Ignaas is in the mill?'

'I'm not sure I've enough puff to run fast enough catch him, and if I did, it's probably too late.' Tomas was clutching at his sore stomach and gulping for air to refill his lungs. Everything hurt. He felt discouraged.

He'd found it always took such a long time to explain things to grown-ups. Even Mama had often proved difficult to convince that something was so urgent that she must drop what she was doing and come *now*. Like that time, he recalled, when Prins, Grandpa's clever parrot, managed to get his cage open and flutter up through the hatch onto the yardarm.

'By the time I'd explained about Ignaas to that policeman, *and* got him to believe me, and come back, Ignaas would probably be gone,' he said, sighing despondently, and then regretting it because his chest was so bruised and sore. 'I expect he's run down the ladders already and away. The mill people wouldn't be expecting it, so he could probably run past them and they'd be too surprised to stop him, if they even noticed him with all the noise going on in there.' He was discovering that his legs and arms were shaking. Almost all parts of him must be covered in bruises.

'Seeing you in those clothes, Ignaas now knows you're living at the weeshuis,' Casper pointed out.

'I suppose...or maybe not. He said I was dressed like a workhouse brat. So maybe he doesn't know there's a difference. Anyway, he couldn't just walk into the weeshuis and kill me, could he?'

'Normally I'd say no. But with Heer de Hoop away...'

'Heer Mulder would *probably* save you,' offered Saskia, thoughtfully. 'I think he'd try, especially if Ignaas came in lesson time. He doesn't like lessons interrupted. He was really angry with Ruud the other day when he came barging in wanting money to pay that farmer who brings our milk. Anyway, surely Ignaas must think you're dead already if he pushed you over the balkon? You *would* have been killed if the tree hadn't been there to catch you. I shouldn't think he stayed around to find out,' she added, a little uneasily, gazing around to reassure herself that Ignaas wasn't hiding in the bushes close by, waiting to spring out at them.

'I *think*,' Tomas said slowly, 'he might have done it because he was so surprised to see me there, and afraid I'd start shouting and give him away. Which I *would* have of course, if I could have made anyone hear me! Perhaps he didn't really mean to kill me,' he added, trying to convince himself as much as the other two. 'Ignaas needs help to sail the boat, although if he caught me he'd certainly beat me as hard as he could.' He shuddered. He didn't want to think about, let alone explain to his friends, that there were other reasons Ignaas might want to keep him alive and in his power.

'Yes, your boat,' said Casper. 'This is it over here, isn't it? The Appelbloesem?'

'Yes!' cried Tomas, rousing himself, despite his injuries and his strong desire to lie down beneath the friendly tree. 'Let me show her to you!'

The three children approached the boat. Fierce barking broke out as they drew close, although they couldn't see the dog which was below deck.

'A guard dog,' said Casper. 'Someone has set him to stop Ignaas or anyone else taking the boat.'

'That was a good plan,' said Tomas, who was examining the mooring ropes and the furled sails with a critical eye. 'Listen to that! It must be a biter! Ignaas would cut through these ropes with one of his knives in less than a minute, but he hates dogs. He's scared of them. Biters. He got bitten really badly once when we were up in Sloop. He's got a big scar on his leg, even now.'

The dog, a mastiff with a brindled coat, which had somehow managed to chew through the stout rope by which it was tied, suddenly bounded up through the hatch and hurled itself to the side of the boat, snarling and barking.

'Hey! Stop that!'

The hound, astonished perhaps by Casper's peculiar croaky voice emerging from the bundle of blankets, ceased its onslaught of noise, and stood panting and bewildered on the deck, its tongue hanging out.

Tomas and Saskia burst out laughing. 'I didn't know you were a dog tamer, Casper,' said Saskia.

Casper grinned, his wide Punchinello mouth stretching from ear to ear. 'Well, now,' he said, 'I knew there must be something I was good at! Not that I've ever tried it before.'

The dog whined. Casper's rusty voice seemed to worry it. Was this a human being in the wheeled chair? Or was it some strange animal the dog had never encountered before?

'Here boy! Friends?' said Saskia, rooting beneath her skirts and producing one of the hard spice biscuits the orphans were given from time to time as a treat. The dog, who had been kept on short rations to encourage him to make a meal of any intruders, took it from her and swallowed it in a couple of slobbery bites.

'You would be amazed, Tomas,' commented Casper, 'if you knew what Saskia probably has hidden in the leg of her drawers. If we should ever find ourselves cast away on one of those desert islands I've read about, we needn't fear starvation. Have you got anything else that the dog would like, Sas? If so, provided Tomas can scramble across and reach the gangplank we could go on board.'

Tomas saw that his friend's eyes were glistening with excitement. 'I've never been on a boat,' he explained, 'just fancy!

I've lived all my life in a country of canals and waterways, and never left dry land. This might be my only chance…ever.'

It was not to be.

Other sounds rose above the creak and swish of the Walvisch's sails.

'You three!' bellowed Heer Mulder in the voice he was want to use to reach the back row of the upper gallery, 'what are you doing down there?'

The three of them looked round and up. The dog turned tail and disappeared back below deck. Roel Mulder and the class of orphan children were all out on the windmill's balcony, gazing down at them. Felix, over excited by the morning's activities, had climbed onto the rail and looked to be in danger of following Tomas's trajectory into the tree.

Saskia, ever resourceful, cupped her hands around her mouth and called up to the schoolmaster.

'We're waiting!' she shouted, 'for you, Sir!'

'Damnation, damnation, damnation!' hissed Casper. Tomas had never heard him use a bad word before. 'I really wanted to see your boat, Tomas.'

Chapter 24

Anders Vos in Pursuance of his Enquiries

When he returned to the lodging house, Vos was only mildly surprised, though not at all pleased, to find his two assistants back already and huddled around the pot-bellied stove in their quarters. Joop Barends' cold seemed to have ripened into a fever, and van Dyke too was coughing into a large checked handkerchief.

'You two are back early,' he commented disapprovingly. 'Did you learn anything from those zakkendragers?'

'Not what you'd call … a great deal…' van Dyke began to say, but was overcome by a fit of coughing.

Oh, thought Vos, this is wonderful. These two are hardly useful at the best of times, but now what must they do but go sick on me!

'We spoke to…*cough! cough*! We spoke to the man, Geert. He seems to be the second in…*cough, cough*…command down there. Van de Grote was away at his wife's funeral. He said…*cough, cough*…that the mad woman, Margriet, was more inclined to escape from the Guildhuis than Henke realised. Sly and crafty she was, the way some mad people can be. It was his opinion that she had a key hidden about her person, and she would get out sometimes if Henke left her alone in the building. Once or twice this Geert found her wandering along the edge of the canal bank, and took her back.'

'And never told her husband?'

'So he… (*cough! cough*!) says. Seems she'd get all agitated, and cling to him, and sort of beg him not to. Like she knew she shouldn't be out, and she was afraid Henke would find out. Geert said she sometimes seemed frightened of Henke, although he couldn't think why she should be. But then sometimes he believes she thought Henke was her father, called him Pappje. She was all muddled up, he said, like mad people are. She was in her second girlhood mebbe, and was back in the days when she lived in Delft and would creep out of her father's house to meet some young man Pappje didn't approve of.' Van Dyke fell into another bout of coughing.

'Such as Ignaas van Damme!' said Vos, raising his voice above this fusillade. 'Typical female! "No, no, I never gave him the time of day" she says to her father and her husband, but all the time she may have been meeting him – or hoping to meet him – on the sly.' Vos was, always had been, and intended to remain, a bachelor.

'Geert told us she was a good woman, so far as he knew, before her illness. He'd never heard otherwise, and he never saw Henke raise a hand to her, nor shout at her. He'd the patience of a saint, according to Geert.'

'Strange,' croaked Barends whose cold seemed to have taken away his voice, 'that she could find the key and turn it in the lock, yet Henke told you she never worked out how to take down the wooden bar.'

'Folks in their second childhood are ... like that,' said van Dyke, spluttering into his nosewipe, 'they recall something they used to do, thirty years ago... but can't fathom some simple mechanism that was installed in recent times. And if he went out, the bar wouldn't be in place. He'd lock the door from outside. As he said he did. Isn't that what he told you, Sergeant?'

Vos took a chair (the one with the wobbly leg, so he hastily moved to perch on the edge of the table) while he thought about this. Little as he might want to believe it, it now looked as though Pastor Winkelmann's theory had more than a small amount of merit. Margriet *had* known how to let herself out of the Guildhuis in Henke's absence. If she *had* seen Ignaas from her window she might have gone out, either to meet him (imagining she was a girl again, going to meet the young man her father had forbidden her to see) or because she saw him ...attacking?...murdering, Tomas?... or? Or?

He gnawed on his bottom lip as he thought about this. It might have been anything at all. Something had attracted her attention when she woke and looked down from her window – or perhaps not even that. Henke had hurried out to discover what had happened to Ambroos. He thought he'd left Margriet sleeping soundly, but there must have been some fuss and bother, some noisy activity, doors opening and closing, when someone (who? did it matter who?) came rushing to fetch Henke. Mad Margriet could well have been disturbed from her slumbers. Later, she came downstairs and let herself out, maybe looking for Henke, maybe for no reason what so ever. It was all very unsatisfactory, and unless there were witnesses, how could he ever find out? Witnesses. He scowled at Barends and van Dyke. They ought all of them to be out scouring the neighbourhood for those witnesses. It had been the Sabbath and growing close to the time of the midday meal. The area would have been largely deserted. Surely though there must have been *someone*, someone who lived nearby, who'd seen something? Neighbours who knew Mad Margriet by sight might be able to say they'd seen her, and with whom she'd met.

He considered sending Barends and van Dyke out anyway, but dismissed the notion. He could see for himself that these two were only capable of huddling over the stove, shivering. If he sent them out again now they would skimp the task, anxious only to return to their beds with, if Vrouw Hauberk could be persuaded to provide them, a hot stone and a hot gin toddy apiece.

'Meanwhile,' he informed them, '*I* have been and interviewed the apothecary, Frans Rijnsberger,' and my impression is that there is definitely something odd about that young fellow. I *may* need to send one of you to Rijnsberg to check up on his family, but that can wait. I'll dispatch a telegram to headquarters. They may be able to do it over the wire if he is already known to the authorities there. He was nervous when I questioned him, and got quite aggressive when the subject of his home town came up. It may be nothing at all to do with our inquiry. As I've said before, we all know how some witnesses can be. There is something he doesn't want us to know, although it may have nothing to do with our current investigation. You both know the kind of thing – he got some girl in the family way. Or he stole a sum of money from his previous employer, something like that. However, he's not, I believe, our *immediate* concern. We …*I* must follow up this new lead on Mad Margriet as soon as possible.'

He looked out of the window. Rain clouds filled the sky, just as Frans Rijnsberger had predicted. A disheartening drizzle was beginning to fall, making the roof tiles glisten on the opposite side of the canal. Although it was still early, a lamp glowed in the front window of one of the tall spout-gabled houses that lined the Lang Haven, visible at an angle from this window on the other side of the water. The bare branches of a tree were beginning to jostle each other in the rising wind.

'I suppose I can't prevail on either of you to wrap up warm and come with me?'

By way of reply van Dyke fell into another fit or coughing, and Joop Barends, who had fallen asleep, canted dangerously from his chair against the side of the hot stove.

'No, I suppose not. *Barends! Wake up!* You'd better go to your bed man, before you burn yourself!'

Donning his kepi and overcoat once more, and as an afterthought winding a woollen scarf around his neck, Vos tramped out into the gloomy afternoon. He wished he had an umbrella. He had a growing suspicion that there must be a hole in one of his boots. Before he had walked twenty yards his left foot was much colder than the right. The drizzle was turning to serious rainfall, large drops began to pock mark the surface of canal. Pools of water were gathering in the hollows where the brick paving of the quay had sunk. Dead leaves, black and sodden with water, made the going slippery. Would anyone even be willing to come to their door to answer questions when he knocked? By the time he had walked fifty yards he changed his priorities. Before he did anything else he must visit a cobbler. He stopped a youth pushing a handcart over the bridge and asked where he might find one.

'Below the Hoogstraat Meester, jus' above the weeshuis,' grunted the fellow, and trundled on. Vos crossed the canal, walked up to the Hoogstraat and sought further directions from a woman taking in chrysanthemums from in front of her shop lest the rain spoil them.

'Dieric, down there aways,' she grumbled, waving an unhelpful arm.

Presently, after taking two wrong turns, Vos found Dieric hammering nails into a lady's shoe heel in his cramped, one-room booth at the bottom of the slope. The cobbler was a tiny man with sleek fair hair and rosy cheeks. With his baggy britches, his striped waistcoat and his peaked seafarer's cap Vos thought he looked the image of a traditional "Dutch boy." Only his reddened nose, crisscrossed with veins, and the wrinkles around his eyes showed that he was a boy no longer.

'An' wha' can I do f'you, Sir?' he muttered through a mouthful of nails.

Clinging to the doorpost, Vos stood on one leg whilst he removed his boot. 'Sprung a leak,' he said, proffering it.

'Ha! And you want me to put my finger in the dyke?' chuckled the little man, removing the nails and dropping them into a glass jar. Vos was baffled by this remark, since the story of the (supposed) little boy who saved his town from drowning, a children's tale that had achieved recent popularity in North and South Holland, had not yet reached Groningen (and if it had, would have been received with great scepticism, for they are not at all romantic in Groningen).

'Patch it if you can or give me a new sole, whatever will stop the water getting in, I'd be most grateful,' he replied, choosing to ignore the cobbler's whimsicality.

'You don't have children?' enquired the cobbler, his head on one side, eyes quizzical. 'No, I'm guessing not. You haven't heard about this tale an American lady has written about a clever little Dutch boy who saves all his neighbours by plugging a hole in a dyke with his finger? No?'

'No,' said Vos, repressively.

'Ach well, 'tis a charming tale if not very believable. Do take a seat, Sir, while I see what I can do.'

From beneath his work bench Dieric produced a wooden box that had once held gin bottles, on which Vos, rather unwillingly, settled his posterior. The hut, for it was hardly more than that, was so small that being seated would bring Vos's nose uncomfortably close to the cobbler's elbow as he worked his hammer. The alternative was to stand outside in the rain with one boot missing, so he made the best of it.

'You have children, I take it?' he asked, realising that he had been rather sharp with the little cobbler. After all, Vos had always believed in "drawing local people out." One had to listen to a lot of nonsense of course, but sometimes useful nuggets emerged from what at first seemed like idle gossip. If this man had children, knew their friends amongst the other local children, perhaps he knew Tomas too? He really would like to be able to say what had happened to that boy before the time came to write his final report on the investigation.

But Dieric didn't have children. 'No, I never married,' the little man said, wistfully, cutting out a new leather sole with a few swipes of a sharp knife. Vos strained back on his stool, keeping his nose out of the way while this process took place. 'I live with my mother, down by the Schie dam. I'd like to have found a nice girl and had kinder, but I couldn't leave Mama, you see? Her health is so very poor.'

Vos, who was a bachelor and didn't care for children, grunted. However, something Dieric had said had caught his attention.

'You live down by the Schie dam, you say? Would you know Henke van de Grote and his wife?'

Dieric slapped glue onto the new sole and manoeuvred it into place before he replied.

'You're one of those detectives from Rotterdam, aren't you? Looking to find out who killed poor Margriet van de Grote?' He tapped in a few nails to hold the new sole in place. 'I was speaking to a couple of your lads this morning. I myself can't tell you anything. I come over here to the shop, even on a Sunday, just to do a little tidying up, but I told them Mother might have seen her. Mother used to know the van de Grotes quite well. 'Tis sad thing, what's happened to Mevrouw Margriet. She was a nice woman. She'd a sharp tongue mind you, but a nice woman all the same. I suggested to your fellows that they might go and ask Mother – she gets lonesome on her own all day whilst I'm here at my work – but they said they were both coming down with colds and didn't want to pass them on. Mother sits in the window most days watching the world go by,' he added, 'being such an invalid she can't get out, but I'd say she doesn't miss much.'

Vos noted with mild exasperation that van Dyke and Barends had completely failed to mention that they'd turned up a possible witness.

'I'll write you a little note if you like, to say I sent you? Once this glue dries and I tap in a few extra nails, you could pop round and ask her yourself,' said Dieric, eyeing Vos with his head on one side, like a robin on the lookout for bacon rinds.

'Thank you, I'd be grateful if you would,' admitted Vos, who knew from experience that old ladies can be difficult about strangers at the door.

'Best wait a while, whilst your new sole dries and the rain slackens off,' said Dieric comfortably, 'can I offer you a tot? No? Ach, I suppose you police fellows have to keep your heads clear.' So saying, the cobbler took down a flask he evidently kept on the shelf above his head amongst the glue pots and boxes of nails, and took a swallow of the contents.

This whole town is afloat on a tide of gin, thought Vos, they're all pickled in the stuff, (He did not admit to himself that on a cold wet afternoon like this one it might be an enviable state) and they're poisoning half of Europe!

Since he could go nowhere until his boot was ready he continued to perch on the wooden box, and Dieric went back to repairing the heel of the lady's shoe on which he had been working when Vos arrived.

'Although *this* won't be wanted in a hurry,' he remarked, holding it up for inspection before the pair of candles that stood guttering on a shelf. 'This lady, the owner of this shoe – is another Margriet. This one is the Regentess of the orphanage just along there.' He nodded towards the building further along the street. 'Mevrouw Margriet de Hoop *she* is – and she seems to have disappeared, gone to Amsterdam on some mysterious business!' Dieric chuckled. 'At least that's what her husband, the Regent; Menheer Maarten de Hoop is giving out. Seems this is not the first time she's taken off. He used to put it about that she'd gone to nurse her sick aunt, but that won't wash this time because the old lady died back in the spring... but you won't be interested in our little local peccadilloes.'

'Not unless it has any bearing on these mysterious attacks on townspeople,' said Vos. 'That's what we're here to look into.'

'Ah! Poor Miss Mathilde de Haan,' Dieric patted a pair of slender but shabby brown button boots lined up at the rear of the bench. 'Have you heard how she is? These are hers of course. And *these*, with the high heels, very unsuitable for a lady of her age I'd say, belong to her aunt, Mevrouw Clara de Haan. And these...' he reached behind Vos to seize hold of a pair of gentleman's patent leather boots, smart and well cared for, but obviously much worn, 'belong to Heer Rijnsberger, the apothecary. Quite a favourite with the ladies, he is. The young Miss de Haans, Miss Anneke and Miss Lotte, were in here the other day, bringing their Mama's shoes to be heeled, and you should have heard the squeals and giggles when they spotted Meester Frans' boots. The ladies seem to have a soft spot for that fellow, young and old alike!'

'I've met him,' said Vos, 'he didn't strike me at all favourably.'

'And the gentlemen don't care for him at all,' agreed the cobbler. 'Strange, isn't it?'

'I wondered,' said Vos, although he'd intended to leave this line of enquiry alone for the time being, 'if there was something going on between him and Miss Mattie?'

The cobbler thought about this. 'I never heard so,' he replied at length, 'Miss Mattie's never been one for the young fellows. A very serious young lady, not at all like those cousins of hers.'

'A very religious girl, is she?'

'No... No, I don't think so, not particularly. But serious minded you know? She called in here once on her way from the circulating library, and you should have seen the tomes she had in her basket! By some English lady author they were, translated into Dutch. In three volumes! Three volumes! I told her she'd ruin her eyes, reading so much, but she only cracked a *tiny* smile. I do hope she recovers, and then she can tell you who the villain was.'

'It would certainly be a help,' said Vos, pulling on his mended boot, 'because I'm not getting very far with it on my own.'

Feeling thoroughly sorry for himself he tramped out into the gloom laden afternoon, the sky brightening a little now in the west, to interview Dieric's mother.

Chapter 25

Three Orphans Talk Their Way Out of Trouble

Roel Mulder was giving his 'enraged father/cruel schoolmaster', a combination of parts he had played (or perhaps overplayed) upon the boards. The three miscreants, Tomas, Saskia and Casper, lined up before him in the empty weeshuis schoolroom, felt themselves to be in danger of being blown out of the door by the blast. Tomas trembled. Saskia, for once unsure she could fib her way out of this, blinked back real tears. Casper, huddled in his wheeled chair was struggling for breath, although his expression remained calm.

'Why? Tell me why boy!' Roel Mulder thundered. Tomas flinched. The temporary schoolmaster had been considerably alarmed to discover that the three children had strayed during the visit to the mill, but certainly had no intention of admitting it.

'*Why* didn't you tell me where the other two had gone?' he paused (dramatically) for effect, and also because he couldn't immediately think what his next line ought to be. Off the stage, as he was now realising, there was no prompter to suggest one.

'Sir, I...' Tomas gulped, his eyes sliding towards the cane which lay on the teacher's desk, easily within Heer Mulder's reach. 'I would have, but it was ... so noisy in there...' Tomas was not a good liar, he stumbled over his words. A free roaming tyke of the canals and riverbanks, it had never occurred to him that he ought to tell the teacher where he was going, or where the other two were.

'If you please Sir,' wheezed Casper, attempting to come to the rescue, 'you see Saskia and I couldn't manage the stairs in the mill, and I couldn't stay in the lower room because the dust affects my chest. Saskia too, she gets asthma. So she took me out into the fresh air, and Tomas followed you up. But then he came down to tell us what he'd seen, so we'd know what we were missing.'

'So that we didn't miss out too much,' added Saskia, with a quiver in her voice, which she hoped would melt the schoolmaster's heart. It had usually worked with the Regent, although she'd found it less successful with the female members of the orphanage staff.

Without any discussion between the children (since there had been no opportunity for any during the march back to the weeshuis and their arraignment before their irate teacher) an unspoken agreement had never the less sprung up. Neither Ignaas nor Tomas's descent via the tree would be mentioned.

Roel Mulder scowled ferociously at them. He was finding himself quite unable to come up with any suitable "line" to cover the situation; no part he'd ever played seemed to have provided him with one. The children of course were unaware of this.

'You see, Sir, Tomas hasn't been to school before,' Casper continued. 'He doesn't quite understand the rules yet – and I'm afraid I was at fault in not asking him to tell you where Saskia and I had gone.'

'You've never been to school, Tomas? How did that come about?' Roel Mulder, having run out of manufactured fury, was glad enough to change the subject. It was slowly dawning on him that he had not given sufficient thought, when deciding to take his pupils on a visit to the windmill, to the difficulties involved for the halt and the lame.

'No, Sir, I never did,' said Tomas lowering his head in shame. 'I…my parents lived on a boat. We never stayed in one place long enough for me to go to school…but I can read, Sir! Mama taught me, and I can do sums, 'cept long division, and Casper's showing me how to do those!'

'Good, I'm pleased to hear it.' Roel Mulder couldn't hide his relief at having moved onto other matters. 'Well, perhaps I should have realised that the visit to the mill was something of a waste of time for you, Casper, and you too, Saskia. However, the other children, including Tomas, shall tell you all about it once they have written their accounts. I had it in mind that next week we might visit the railway station to learn about the importance of up-to-date forms of transportation, but obviously I need to discover in advance whether it's accessible for you, Casper.'

'I'd like that,' said Casper solemnly, 'but as a matter of fact the Regent doesn't usually allow me to go out because the people here are superstitious and don't like to see deformed children. They complain, so if he's back I may not be allowed to go anyway. You haven't heard from him yet, Sir?'

'No. I'm beginning,' said Roel Mulder, frowning, 'to be slightly worried. I hope he hasn't met with an accident. He didn't give me the impression, when he left, that he'd be gone for more than a couple of days. Has he ever been away like this before?'

Casper and Saskia shook their heads.

'I'm the oldest inmate,' offered Casper, with a wry grin, 'and I never remember him going away for more than one night or perhaps two, not in all the time I've lived here.'

'He has relatives in other towns? Would you know? Roel Mulder felt rather uncomfortable asking for this information from a child, but he had formed the opinion during the short time he'd been involved with the weeshuis, that Casper was not only the oldest of his pupils, but easily the most intelligent. More intelligent, he'd have been prepared to wager, than many of the adults employed about the place.

'Not that I know of, Sir, I… err…' Casper jerked his head oddly, and twitched the corner of his mouth in a way that indicated to the teacher that he *could* say more, but believed it was unsuited to the ears of the younger children.

'Very well! Don't stray again when we go out, any of you!' Heer Mulder had decided to end the business. 'Tomas and Saskia wash your hands and go to the dining hall. Casper will remain here. I need to speak to him on his own. I'll send for someone to collect him shortly. Ask them to put food aside for both of us.'

Tomas and Saskia, relieved beyond measure to be "let off" scooted out of the door.

'He isn't going to *cane* Casper, is he?' Tomas asked anxiously, as they made their way to the dining room. Neither of them even considered wasting time on a diversion to wash their hands.

'Course not!' Saskia replied. 'He wants Casper to tell him about Vrouw de Hoop's lovers! He thinks because Casper is older than the rest of us it's all right to ask him. Although *I* know as much about it as he does and probably more!' she boasted.

Tomas thought about this. Life on the canals had been informative in many ways. He'd often overheard his parents and their friends talking casually about wives who had swapped one binnenschipper for another – about husbands who had other lady friends in towns along the waterways from Dortmund to Dordrecht. This information had never struck him as either interesting or important. It was just one of those things grown-ups liked to talk about.

'Does she have a lot of lovers?' he asked.

'Not a *lot*,' said Saskia, fairly, 'usually one at a time. Everyone knows she inherited some money from her grandmother, and she gets tired of being the Regent's wife and looking after us orphans, so she finds a gentleman friend and goes off with him to Rotterdam or Den Hague to have a good time.'

Saskia made this state of affairs sound perfectly reasonable, but Tomas had a feeling that his Mama would not have approved.

'So why doesn't she take the Regent, and they could have a good time together?' he asked, as they reached the door to the dining hall.

'Oh, the Regent doesn't like to go,' she replied, lowering her voice, although there was no need as the dining hall was in uproar. Without the Maarten de Hoop present to enforce discipline, the maids and ushers had given up all hope of getting the orphans to eat in silence – or even quietly. 'Heer de Hoop is *de-voted* to us. We are his Life's Work.'

'Why?' asked Tomas

Saskia shrugged, 'that's what he told Pastor Winkelmann. I heard him say it.'

'You wanted to tell me something, Casper?' Heer Mulder said, once the classroom door banged shut behind Tomas and Saskia. Roel Mulder had a wider experience of the world than many. He had on occasion shared lodgings with circus troops, with dwarves and hunchbacks amongst them, and though he'd never considered making one of these "freaks" his particular friend, he knew that whatever their physical abnormalities might be, they had as much in their noddles as most folks do, and was perfectly willing to listen to what Casper might say.

Casper was more circumspect than Saskia. He had, over his long years in the weeshuis, acquired a strong sense of what, as a child of the orphanage, he could and couldn't say to an adult, a teacher. He didn't allude to lovers. He explained carefully that Vrouw de Hoop *was* apt to go away, and sometimes, he believed, it was quite difficult to persuade her to return.

'She goes on visits, Sir, and sometimes the Regent goes to escort her back – but he's never been away for such a long time before. So I'm afraid some misfortune must have occurred, perhaps to both of them.'

'It's odd that he's sent no message.'

'Yes, Sir, that's why I think there must have been an accident.'

'Do you know how he intended to travel? By mail-coach or by train?'

Casper couldn't say. 'It's generally known though, Sir, amongst the ushers at any rate, that Vrouw de Hoop has gone to Amsterdam this time, so I suppose he went there to find her.'

'The train would be quickest, and there's been no word of any accidents on the railway. I'm sure we'd have heard if there had been. You've lived here for a long time Casper, and you're a sensible young fellow, so let me ask you something? You know how everything is supposed to work here. I'm just here to give you your lessons. I've never run an orphanage. Whom should I consult? Do you know the names of any of the Governors?'

Roel Mulder was very loath to approach any of the Governing body given his own irregular status, but already three people, Ruud, Katjie the cook, and the man who stoked the boilers had approached him asking for money to pay bills or placate tradesmen. Although personally never one to pay bills before he had to, if at all, in this situation he could see that things would soon be getting difficult, and he'd no answers to give.

Casper moved his large head slowly from side to side. He knew very little about the Governors, since the Regent usually kept him out of sight when these worthies came to "inspect" the weeshuis. He was fairly sure that Maarten de Hoop must mention him from time to time, particularly when soliciting funds, "some of our children are quite helpless cripples, you know." However, he'd long ago guessed that the Regent thought it best that the governors saw only the able-bodied, the rosy cheeked and the bright of eye on their visits, youngsters who would soon be going to their apprenticeships and therefore no longer a burden on the town.

'I *think* the Reverend Winkelmann is a Governor,' he told the teacher doubtfully. 'I know him because he comes to give us religious instruction – though he sometimes forgets, or comes on the wrong day. Heer Rijnsberger, the apothecary *isn't* a Governor, but he takes an interest in us. And the doctor, but he isn't a Governor either. Sir, I'm sure things would work better if you came and lived here until Heer de Hoop gets back The ushers and the maids *do* pay attention to you.'

The temporary schoolmaster regarded this proposal from his

young pupil with mixed feelings. It had its attractions. If he came to live in at the weeshuis he wouldn't have to pay for meals and board at his relative's lodging house. This would be a bonus, but on the other hand, the responsibilities would be considerable. Roel Mulder wasn't a man who cared for responsibility, had indeed made it his life's work to avoid it.

Chapter 26

Anders Vos Goes in Search of Further Clues and Suspects

'You did offer to help?' wheedled Clara de Haan. 'Mathilde seems restless, poor child. I think she's more aware of the pain than she was. Although I'm given to understand this may be a good sign?'

'*Anything* I can do, dear lady.' Frans Rijnsberger had finished his painting in good time, and was now seated behind the counter of his little shop, goose quill poised, going through his account books. He hadn't been expecting customers, the weather having turned as wet and surly as he'd predicted. His account books weren't telling him anything encouraging, so he was pleased to see an enormous umbrella bobbing along the quayside through the rain in the direction of his little shop – and even more pleased when this proved to be providing a shield from the elements to the aunt of his beloved.

Clara de Haan smiled and wriggled girlishly within her voluminous cloak, flattered to be called a "dear lady" by this personable young man.

'Doctor Saunders, as you probably know, tells us that little can be done other than keep her still and calm while her internal injuries have a chance to heal. He councils against giving her a higher dose of the laudanum, since he now feels she has a reasonable chance of survival – although I don't quite understand why the laudanum should matter...' she heaved a sigh that caused the artificial anemones on her bonnet to tremble.

'He's a good man. I'm sure he's right,' said Frans, sagely. He knew well enough that it behoves the proprietor of a pharmacy to be strong in support of a more highly qualified medical colleague, since he will, he hopes, be paid to provide the medicines the doctor recommends.

'Laudanum is an excellent nostrum in its way, but it can be addictive if taken over a prolonged period. The higher the dose, the more likelihood there is of this being a problem when the patient recovers. We wouldn't want Miss Mathilde to become addicted, would we?'

'Oh, *no!*' breathed Clara, horrified and thrilled in equal measure. She understood, vaguely, that laudanum was derived from opium, and that in wicked cities like London and Paris, such people as *opium addicts* existed. The idea that a member of her family might fall victim seemed to her too improbable to be seriously contemplated. 'Perhaps you have some other less... powerful but calming draught?'

'I'm sure I have something,' said Frans, his mind scurrying amongst the shelves carrying his stock without much enthusiasm. Boldly, on his visit to the sick room, he had promised Clara she had only to ask and he'd ride forth on his white charger to the aid of Miss Mathilde. Now, he had to prove as good as his word.

'Perhaps one of my special distillations...' he mused aloud, tapping his chin with the feathered end of his quill as an aid to thought. The tincture he had in mind was composed merely of the bark of the white willow soaked in gin (with, naturally, a certain amount of boiled water added) but Mevrouw Clara's mother and her arthritis had thrived on it for years. If he decanted some into a bottle and labelled it up in manner guaranteed to invoke confidence – with some of those smart new labels the printer at the far end of the Lang Haven had recently run off for him, it could hardly do harm.

He laid down his quill, slid from his high stool, and made for the shelving at the back of the shop. There he began hauling down the blue glass demi-johns and peering at their labels as though considering the perfect concoction. Clara de Haan laid her reticule upon the counter, and watched in open-mouthed admiration.

He really was a fine looking fellow if one discounted the birthmark, such delightfully broad shoulders! And the way his hair grew into an entrancing curlicue at the nape of his neck! It didn't surprise her that her daughters were inclined to sigh over this young man. If only she were twenty years younger – and not, alas, tied to Cornelius! (Mama and Papa had thought it such an advantageous match, and indeed she couldn't complain of Cornelius as a *provider* but Oh, so dull!) Entranced by the set of Frans' shoulders, she failed to notice that her damp reticule was leaking rainwater onto one his ledgers. She also failed to hear the shop door creak open. Anders Vos entered. He coughed, making both Clara and the apothecary jump.

'Beg your pardon, Mevrouw,' said Vos. 'Sorry to startle you.' He laid his military kepi carelessly upon the counter, where it proceeded to drip water from its peak onto the opposite page of Frans' ledger. 'Go ahead, Mevrouw, don't mind me,' he told Clara. 'I need a word with Heer Rijnsberger, but I'm happy to wait while you collect your remedy. Nothing serious, I hope? There are some nasty colds about, *very* nasty.'

He wondered if he might procure something to ease the colds of van Dyke and Barends, and get them back to work – provided it didn't cost too much. Otherwise he might as well be dealing with this crime wave on his own, and they could return to Rotterdam to spread their coughs and sneezes around the barracks.

Frans was not at all pleased to see Vos, and knowing that Vos (how *had* he divined it?) somehow knew how he felt about Mathilde de Haan, made him anxious in the extreme. He decided that he would say nothing, pretend even, that Vos wasn't here in the shop at all whilst he carefully dispensed the willow bark tincture into a small brown glass medicine bottle and corked it up. What could the wretched man want now? It annoyed him that his hand shook slightly as he poured.

'So kind, Heer Rijnsberger! I'm sure this will relieve my poor niece's suffering,' warbled Clara. She was nervous too. She hadn't met Vos before, but she'd immediately guessed who he was.

Vos hadn't previously encountered Clara de Haan, having assigned that duty to van Dyke, but at the mention of a sickly niece, he made a safe deduction. He bowed politely, and introduced himself.

'Vrouw de Haan? I believe you've met my junior officer, Josef van Dyke? In relation to the unfortunate attack upon your niece, Miss Mathilde de Haan? My name is Anders Vos, and I'm in overall charge of the investigation. I hope your niece continues to improve?'

'Oh, indeed, that is, a little,' gabbled Clara, thoroughly flustered. 'Doctor Saunders maintains that the fact that she's become more restless is a *good* sign, although… she seems to feel the pain more than she did. Heer Rijnsberger is very kindly making up one of his remedies. I'm sure it must ease her…'

'Try to get her to swallow a spoonful from time to time,

Ma'am,' said Frans, studiously ignoring Vos as he wielded his glue brush and fixed the label onto the bottle. 'I hope this will lessen the pain of her wound. Does she suffer with her head at all?'

'Oh, I think she *must*. She tosses about on the pillows so! But whether 'tis her head or her…chest that pains her, I cannot say. She must have hit her head when she fell to the ground after that dreadful man stabbed her…' Clara, discomfited by the presence of Vos, and the necessity to mention Mattie's chest, was becoming incoherent.

'I'd proscribe lavender water blended with Roman camomile for that,' said Frans, mendaciously, 'but I haven't sufficient lavender water made up just now. I'll crush some lavender seeds *when this man has gone*,' he added, 'and bring the mixture round to your house later this evening. How would that be, Mevrouw? I'd be happy to show you or one of your daughters how to make a soothing poultice for her brow with a soft piece of cloth.'

I'll wager you would, thought Vos to himself, but he stood politely by while Clara completed her purchase, retrieved her reticule and hurried out of the shop.

Both the men stood in silence for a space, listening to Vrouw de Haan's wet-weather clogs clip clopping along the canal bank through the drizzle.

'Bless me, she's left her umbrella,' said Vos, leaning across the counter in what Frans thought an overfamiliar manner. 'You'll be able to return it to her when you take the "whatever-it-is" you've promised her. I *hope*,' he said, laying stress on that word, 'you're paying due care and attention when you make up these potions of yours? I wouldn't like to hear that the young lady has suffered a setback. Not when things are looking more promising for her recovery.' He managed to instil these words with a hefty dollop of menace.

Behind his counter, his hands hidden, Frans gripped the sides of the stool in the hope that Vos wouldn't see him flinch. 'You've been talking to someone about me!' he accused.

'Yes. A Vrouw Rikila van Roosendaal. Unpleasant old party. Her name suits her. Rikila means "a stern ruler," I believe. She rules that son of hers with a rod of iron, poor fellow!'

'I've never heard of her.' said Frans shrugging, and hoping against hope to stop the detective in his tracks although he knew in his heart this was hopeless.

'No. She tells me she doesn't dose! *Never.* Doesn't trust Doctors, let alone apothecaries like yourself! Strange, that, when her son tells me she suffers such poor health that he can't leave her to set up his own establishment. Dieric, the cobbler? You know him alright. I saw your boots in his shop not two hours ago.'

'Certainly I know him, but I've never met his mother. I didn't even know he had one. He mends my shoes. We discuss the weather and economic conditions in the town. How can his *mother*, upon whom I've never set eyes, know something – or imagine she knows something – discreditable about me?'

'Because she has a sister living in Rijnsberg,' said Vos. He couldn't resist a little chuckle of triumph. Frans swallowed, but said nothing. 'Don't you want to defend yourself?' The silence continued. 'I'd have found out anyway,' said Vos. 'I was going to send someone to Rijnsberg to check up on you and your family.'

'How did you know there was anything to find out?'

'Oh, just… something about you, you know? Guilty conscience? You always seemed so uneasy when we questioned you. Even van Dyke spotted it.'

'I don't have a guilty conscience!' said Frans through stiff lips. 'My uncle made an accidental error. His eyesight was failing, but he wouldn't admit it. Everyone knew it was him. Nobody seriously blamed me for what happened, not even the victim's family, but it made it impossible for our dispensary to continue. I had to start again somewhere else. And since the apothecary's trade is the only one I know, I came and set myself up here.'

'Hmm, accidental error, that's not how Vrouw van Roosendaal described it. "Poisoning" was the term she used. Either you or your uncle – accidently maybe, or maybe through carelessness, poisoned the wife of one of the Clergymen in the town.'

'It wasn't poison!' Frans tried to keep his voice low and measured, despite rising panic. Oh, that this should come back to haunt him now, just when he'd got himself established at last in Schiedam!

'What happened was that this lady had a weak heart. Her medical man proscribed digitalis, a stimulant. In a low dose digitalis, which is derived from the leaf of the foxglove plant, is extremely beneficial for this purpose, and perfectly safe. Unfortunately, and I don't entirely blame my uncle because the dispensary was busy – and as I said his eyesight was failing – somehow too high a concentration was made up and sent to her. The heart was over stimulated, and unfortunately she died.'

'I doubt it's quite true that *nobody* blamed you. According to Vrouw van Roosendaal's sister, your uncle blamed you.'

'That was his habit,' said Frans sadly, his shoulders slumped in defeat. 'Anything that went wrong in the shop, misplaced ingredients, miscounted pills, missing orders, he could never admit his mistakes. Even when we proved to him – not just me, but his wife, his other assistant, the errand boy even – that the writing on the label his. He would never believe it, at least to begin with. He bawled us all out, made wild accusations in front of customers, and then the truth would slowly sink in.'

'And between you, you convinced the old fellow on this occasion too,' said Vos, leaning on the counter, happily allowing his cynicism to colour his response.

Frans subsided onto his stool, pressed the palms of his hands into his eyes despairingly, and leaned forward on his elbows. 'You think I'm lying, don't you? And now you're going to spread this around – that I was once accused of being a poisoner, and not to be trusted. I might as well pack my bags and leave on the evening train. You'll have it all over Schiedam by morning.'

'Why would I do that? No, your dark secret is safe with me,' said Vos with a grin more wolf than fox. 'At least for the moment,' he added lest Frans should think he was a soft touch. 'Unless, of course, I find that you've given up poison and are killing your patients with sharp knives instead.'

'I showed all my knives to your assistant, none are bloodstained or missing. I can show you too if you like.'

'Might as well,' said Vos. He was inclined to believe Frans' account of the accidental poisoning of the minister's wife in Rijnsberg. At least he was inclined to believe the poisoning *was* accidental, although blaming the old uncle's eyesight seemed rather too convenient. Vrouw Roosendaal was the kind he thought, (and probably her sister too) who believed the worst of everyone outside her immediate family circle. If *she* were to be poisoned he wouldn't hesitate to arrest the cobbler son. Or, on second thoughts, perhaps he'd leave him be. Apart from her insinuations about Frans, Vrouw

Von Roosendaal hadn't had much to contribute. No sighting of mad Margriet on the fateful morning. The only person she'd seen that she didn't recognise was a woman hurrying by, wrapped in a dark cloak whom the old lady had dismissed as 'probably a Catholic,' and therefore unworthy of notice.

'Might as well have a look,' he repeated. 'Exonerate you, eh? Besides,' he glanced out at the wet evening, 'it's coming down in torrents now. Unless I borrow Mama de Haan's umbrella, I'm going to get wet.'

Chapter 27

Roel Mulder Seeks Advice

'Of course, my dear fellow, any advice I can give, I'd be glad to…' Jacob Winkelmann, exhibited some surprise looking round the bare, rather dirty hallway of the weeshuis for somewhere to lodge his umbrella. On thinking it over, Roel Mulder had decided the Pastor was his best option. Unworldly, pastors were meant to be. Not too noticing he hoped, or only noticing those things, he, Roel Mulder, brought to his attention. Unlikely to question him too closely about his translation from out of work actor to schoolmaster. Plus, it had been unnecessary to ask any of the adults in the orphanage about him, to inquire where he lived for example, and thus reveal his almost total ignorance about the town and its inhabitants. Since Casper had told him that Jacob Winkelmann acted as the orphanage's chaplain, he thought it would appear natural that he should seek the man's guidance. It had been enough to say to the oaf, Dirk, 'Take this message to Pastor Winkelmann. Tell him I'd like to see him at his earliest convenience.'

'Come this way, Pastor,' he greeted his guest, taking his umbrella from him and propping it in a corner. 'The children are eating their supper.' Although the doors to the dining hall were fast shut on his orders, the hum of young voices was audible. 'It's been a trying day, so wet as you know throughout the afternoon, and although we were able to take an educational walk this morning there's been no opportunity since then for them to expend their energy. I'd hoped to conduct them in a little physical drill but the rain put paid to that.'

Roel Mulder was still deciding how to play this latest role. Humble, he thought, a humble clerkly, character? Ingratiating, anxious to please? But he mustn't overplay it. He must at the same time appear both efficient and authoritative. 'I think the Regent wouldn't take it amiss if we sat in his office while we talk?'

'I'm sure not,' replied the Reverend Winkelmann. 'You really have heard nothing from him…after how many days? I'm afraid, Sir, that I haven't quite grasped your name by the way. Dirk told it to me of course, but as I'm sure you are aware his speech is very thick – too large a tongue for his mouth, poor fellow. Regent de Hoop always says that's why he kept him on here as an usher. Not really employable in any situation where he has to communicate with strangers. Maarten is very protective of his geese with broken wings. Too protective in some ways.'

Roel Mulder, settling the man in the most comfortable chair in the Regent's office, considered that he'd be lucky to extract any useful advice from these ramblings. The pastor was now gazing around him as though he had never been in this room before although Governors' meetings must regularly be held here. It was a handsome chamber. He'd only been in it once himself – no, twice, once when he arrived to take up his new post, and once since in a fruitless search for guilden, stuiven, anything with which to pacify the dairyman who was menacing the cook for payment at the kitchen door.

He was about to make some comment about the striking group portrait on the wall of the seventeenth century town worthies who must have founded the weeshuis, when Jacob Winkelmann, nodding towards a statue above the ornate fireplace suddenly said, 'I do ask myself what the children make of *that*, when the Regent calls them in here to be reprimanded. I understand of course that she represents Charity, but why was it was felt necessary to show her as a figure with a naked bosom, I wonder? One suspects that some of the older boys may deliberately misbehave… Have you been bringing any, err… *miscreants* in here, Heer Err…?'

'Roel Mulder, Pastor. No, I haven't had any serious problems with the *children's* behaviour, and of course it was to teach the younger children that I was engaged.'

He'd decided it was best to hold to the fabrication he'd first told to Maarten de Hoop. Now, dragging the Reverend Winkelmann's attention away from the lady with the white marble bosom above the mantelpiece, he told it again. His little school for tradesmen's sons on the outskirts of Amsterdam (not, alas the most fashionable neighbourhood), the small profits he'd made in this enterprise despite all his hard work, the sudden wreck of his hopes when the owner decided to sell the building. To his ears it still sounded convincing. He was almost beginning to believe it himself.

'And so,' he said, adopting a brave if mournful expression which he had last made use of in a comedy in which (for once) he had played the wronged husband. (*"Dutch audiences do not easily respond to these 'farces' of which the French are so fond,"* the Amsterdam Courante had reported, the day before the show closed.) 'Regretfully, I'd decided to abandon Education and seek a position, perhaps as a clerk in the offices of one of the distilleries here. I am, needless to say, competent at ledger work and I write a good clear hand.' He'd thought of no such thing, but even as the words left his mouth he found himself wondering if he *should* have? After all, presumably the distillery clerks were regularly paid. 'However, when fate brought me into the orbit of Heer de Hoop…'

'Providential,' murmured Jacob Winkelmann, 'the ways of Providence are indeed wondrous. Our good Regent must have been overjoyed to secure your services at such short notice, Heer Mulder. How are you finding your pupils? A little slow perhaps, not so quick or so eager to learn as your Amsterdam tradesmen's sons?'

So the man was listening. Jacob Winkelmann wasn't quite so vague and unworldly as at first appeared. Time to tread carefully, Roel Mulder!

'Oh, as to ability, they are mixed. Some slow, some really quite able. But so it was in Amsterdam too, I assure you. Some of those tradesmen's sons are clever fellows; some would make you shake your head in despair. No, I'm perfectly satisfied with my *pupils*. My concern is with the continuing absence of Regent de Hoop. I accepted the position on the understanding that my sole responsibility would be to teach. Now that the Regent has been away for over a week, I find that I'm being asked – in effect – to run the orphanage.'

'Dear me, I'd heard of course that Maarten had gone away, but I imagined he must have returned by now. What instructions, precisely, did he give you?'

'Alas, hardly any, Pastor. I presumed, as everyone else seems to have done, that he only intended to be gone for a day or two. All he told me was to ensure that the children paid attention to their lessons, and that they were not to cheek the ushers. Nor was I to allow the ushers to strike the boys more than once upon the legs with their canes if they misbehaved. He gave me no instructions what-so-ever regarding the maids, the cook or the man who tends the stoves. He didn't leave me any money, or instruct me what to do if tradespeople came asking to be paid. Which, I may say, they are beginning to do.'

'The maids?' said Jacob Winkelmann, raising his eyebrows in surprise, 'surely the cook and Matrone Schmit can deal with the maids?'

'Ah, Matrone Schmit. I had been assuming that Mevrouw de Hoop attended to the children's health herself, and only discovered a few days ago that Vrouw Schmit, the matron, exists. I've been told, by Katjie the cook, that she is *ill*, and confined to her room. One of the maids, a girl called Roos, seems to make it her business to attend her.'

Pastor Winkelmann, who had been fishing about in the pocket of his coat for his pipe and tobacco, paused, an expression of alarm flitting across his amiable face, to be replaced by one of anxious displeasure. 'Oh, dear!' he said, shaking his head, 'If that's so I'm afraid...'

What he feared was interrupted by knocking at the door.

'Enter!' called Roel Mulder, after waiting a beat to see if the pastor would do so. The heavy door was pushed slowly open by a child in a state of agitation, her white apron stained with a large amount of some kind of sauce and her face blotched with tears. The child was Saskia.

'Heer Mulder!' she gasped, panting. 'Come to the dining room, quickly. We think Matron's gone mad! She's throwing the plates and smashing them, and... and she's hurt Casper!' As an afterthought she added, 'Please!'

The two men rose.

'I cannot imagine...' Roel Mulder began.

'I can, alas,' said the Pastor. 'They call this town Black Nazareth, because it is all too easy...' he glanced at Saskia, as if wondering whether to spare the child what he was about to say, but she was already limping out of the door and beckoning them to follow. He lowered his voice to a sepulchral whisper, 'Where it's all too easy to become *a drunkard.*'

They found the dining hall strangely hushed. The children still sat at their benches, their food bowls before them on the long tables, spoons suspended in mid-air. The maids and ushers huddled together in the doorway to the servery, mouths agape. When the two men entered, all eyes left the gaunt bedraggled figure of Vrouw Schmit who wavered dangerously on unsteady feet – she was surrounded by broken crockery, her long nightgown stained with gravy – and swivelled in their direction.

'Sir! Oh, Sir, make her stop!' wailed Felix, who'd taken himself and his food bowl under the table for safety.

Roel Mulder was not a man given to criticising the behaviour of others. Live and let live had always been his motto. He himself enjoyed a drink. A life upon the stage, he would have freely admitted, would be unsupportable without it. A drink before "going on" to quell stage fright – and fortify against the all too probable possibility that the play would be ill-received. A drink, or two or three, to enable him to relax afterwards – whether or not items of greengrocery had been hurled. But he counted himself fortunate that he had a hard head, and a strong sense of self preservation. He rarely drank to excess. He had known, however, plenty of thespians who did, often with disastrous consequences. Although ordinary folk might consider "the stage" the most easy-going of milieus, he'd found theatre managers ruthless towards those whom drink made unreliable. He had on several occasions been called upon to assist in the removal of an actor who'd over-indulged. Once, he recalled, he'd helped to drag Hamlet's Father's ghost off stage and dump him in a rainy back alley to cool off.

How should he play *this* scene? He glanced at Pastor Winkelmann, who seemed to have congealed on the spot. No help to be found there. Who should he be? A fierce paterfamilias? No, the children (and the ushers) had already seen that one. Enraged tyrant? He doubted he had the stature. A General leading his men in a charge on the battlefield? It would have to be that one. Mentally he donned the uniform. A high shako. Lots of gold braid, medals clanking on his chest, as he took a deep breath.

'Men!' he roared. 'Dirk! Ruud! Remove this woman! Take her to her room! And where's that girl? Roos? You, *miserable creature*! Go with her, lock the door, and stay with her until I give you leave!'

'Neee!' wailed the buck-toothed maid.

'Yaaah!' roared orphans, maids and menservants in unison. The ill-favoured girl slunk from the room, and the children began to bang their spoons on the tables.

'Enough!' bellowed Roel Mulder (the tyrant after all) and he raised his palms for quiet. The cheers and banging became ragged and then ceased. He felt a small sense of triumph and hoped Pastor

Winkelmann was marking how well he was handling things.

'Adults, return to your tasks. Children, you will finish your meal. Where is Casper? I was told he's been injured.'

'Here Sir,' rasped Casper, quietly from the shadows. 'It's not too bad, just a small cut I think. When she threw the plate at the wall it broke, and one of the shards caught my brow.' Saskia had made a pad from her cap, and was holding it against the crippled boy's face. Katjie the cook advanced with a cloth.

'It's nothing, Sir,' said Casper, propelling his chair forward so that the schoolmaster could see. 'Really, look, it's almost stopped bleeding.'

It was only when he and the pastor had retreated to the Regent's office once more that it crossed Roel Mulder's mind to wonder where Tomas was. The cut on Casper's face was indeed nothing serious, but he would have expected Tomas to be beside him, supporting his injured friend in his hour of need. Tomas had made himself scarce. Might the boy have had unfortunate experiences with drunkards? Have lost his parents to strong drink? He'd hardly got to know anything of these weeshuis children and their previous circumstances. It further crossed his mind that perhaps it was better not to know.

'Dries van Corte, he's the man we need,' said Pastor Winkelmann, subsiding once more into a chair, and producing and filling his cherry-wood pipe with slightly unsteady fingers. 'He runs the Infirmary. Proficient. *He'll* know what to do for the best. I really have little experience of this kind of thing. Van Corte may even know when we can expect Maarten to return. They're friends as well as colleagues.'

'Yes, I met him, briefly,' said Roel Mulder. 'Might it be appropriate to send this woman, Vrouw Schmit to his establishment? To be dried out?' He couldn't have said why he had taken a dislike to Directeur van Corte at their one brief meeting in the coffee shop. Only ten days since? It seemed like another life. Something about the director of the Infirmary had struck a false note, and an actor is sensitive to false notes. Too breezily cheerful, too smoothly persuasive. Too quick to recommend his friend Maarten de Hoop engage a chance met schoolmaster, whilst knowing nothing about him, and to urge him to rush away to Amsterdam. Was *he* somehow fraudulent? Not who he appeared to be?

Roel Mulder had no reason to think this, but, he reflected, perhaps it takes one to know one?

Chapter 28

Frans Rijnsberger Encounters a Setback, and Miss Mathilde Makes a Decision

'She's peaceful now, as you see,' Clara de Haan was telling Frans Rijnsberger, 'just sleeping quietly, but sometimes – why, even just an hour ago, she was so restless, turning her head this way and that. Quite often now her eyelids flicker, and I think she's going to wake.'

'That could happen soon. She's a much better colour than when I saw her last. See, there are faint roses in her cheeks?' said Frans, who had kept his promise to bring a soothing salve for his beloved's brow. He'd been somewhat disconcerted on approaching the de Haan house, to find another man was already plying the knocker, a stout older man in an old fashioned frieze coat and a muffler, whose pale bulging eyes seemed to regard Frans with immediate mistrust. Frans had been horribly afraid for a moment that this was yet another policeman. Then Cornelius appeared, and he wondered if he was going to be either arrested or barred admittance. Or possibly both.

However, while the Bridge Watcher barked a welcome to this stranger, Clara led Frans indoors murmuring that this was 'Rombouts, the lawyer, come to see Cornelius. We notified him, of course, of our niece's condition. He's been away on business in Breda, and only received the letter on his return. For some reason he felt he must hear all about it at first hand from my husband, although Cornelius didn't think it at all necessary. He'll probably want to see poor Mattie, but we'll just slip upstairs ahead of him, shall we? And you shall tell me how to apply the salve? I do want Heer Rombouts to see for himself that we are giving her the very *best* of care.'

She led Frans up the steep staircase, and into the sick room, saying, 'I've put a pot of coffee on the stove and set out some cold cuts. Anneke and Lotte have strict instructions to serve Heer Rombouts if he requires it, so we needn't worry ourselves about him! Now, show me how to apply the lotion, so I know exactly what I should do! See, here are the squares of linen the girls cut out for you this morning. They are *so* pleased to be of use to you, Heer Rijnsberg!'

Frans was beginning to find her manner a little too "confiding." She kept giving little girlish giggles, and patting his arm. He wondered if Mattie in her unconscious state was aware of what was said and done around her in the sick room. Clara was making him uncomfortable, so he hoped not.

He'd got no further than beginning to apply the salve to the girl's forehead when Cornelius stomped into the room with the lawyer at his heels. Rombouts was a short fat man with heavy jowls, which shone greasily as though he'd anointed himself with bacon fat.

'Here she is,' wheezed Cornelius, breathless from climbing the stairs, 'just the same! Doctor Saunders and this…apothecary fellow,' he waved a dismissive gesture in Frans' direction, 'keep telling us she's improving but she hasn't woken. Hasn't said a word, and it's been ten days.'

Rombouts was one of those corpulent men who teeter on tiny feet in buttoned boots. He pottered over to the bedside and peered down at the sleeping girl. Frans stood politely aside.

'Hump! I'm no medical man. She just looks as though she's asleep to me! What are ye dosing her with, young fellow? Try not to kill her, she's an heiress, ye know?'

'I'm just applying… a tincture of white willow… a pain reliever. Her aunt thought… to relieve the pain in her head…' Frans found himself stammering. Glancing around wildly, he saw that Clara de Haan was as startled as he was. Cornelius on the other hand, must have already been told this news, and was looking decidedly pleased with life.

'An heiress! *Mattie?* But Cornelius, you said your brother…?' exclaimed Clara, clasping her hands to her considerable bosom. 'You said Harald left so little!'

'So he did, Mevrouw, so he did, hardly a guilder to his name when he died,' said the little lawyer, rubbing his hands together as he stared down at the sleeping girl, 'He always believed his chemical experiments would come to something, sooner or later. Alas, that was not to be! *However*, he did invest in the railways… *and* in those people who have discovered how to extract the fat from cocoa beans, neither of which seemed at all profitable in the short term, but now! Now, those investments that seemed rather foolish gambles at the time are paying off. Miss Mathilde, *if* she recovers, will be a wealthy young woman. And so, Meester Apothecary,' he went on, turning to Frans, 'I trust whatever this concoction is that ye're dabbing on my client *will* speed her recovery?'

At this, Cornelius darted forward and flapped his hands at Frans. 'Leave her! Take you potions and go! I'll have nothing administered to my niece except under Doctor Saunders' direct supervision. How do we know that your interference won't make her worse?' He turned to the lawyer, 'My wife and daughters – all the females in this town – make much of this fellow, but to my mind he's quack! I won't have him meddling with Mathilde!'

'Cornelius! I'm sure Heer Rijnsberger means only the best for Mattie!' protested Clara.

Frans began to collect his things together. 'I don't stay where I'm not wanted,' he said stiffly, and walked from the room without meeting the eye of anyone present. As he pulled the door to behind him he heard Heer Rombouts say, 'Perhaps it's as well to dismiss him, m'dear, ye really mustn't take chances. Allow nothing that hasn't been approved absolutely by yer chief medical man. We must speed her recovery at all costs. All costs! She's reached her majority, and so can inherit outright... but of course she hasn't made a *Will*. If she should die intestate that uncle of hers, the mother's half-brother in s'Hertogenbosch... ye remember him? A very unsatisfactory individual...'

As soon as her uncle and aunt and the lawyer left the room, Mattie opened her eyes. She stared at the ceiling. She removed the damp pad of linen from her brow and dropped it on to the patchwork counterpane. Then she turned her head slightly so that she could see the candles that had been left flickering on top of the chest of drawers that held all her meagre possessions. Light glinted on the glaze of the delft bowl that held lavender and rose-petals.

'I'm an *heiress*,' she mouthed, not allowing a sound to escape her lips, although there was no one to hear. 'Papa made investments. *In the railways, of all things!* Poor Papa. And poor Mama too, always having to scrape and save, and then for them to be killed like that – not knowing that those investments would have made them rich one day.' She turned back on her pillow and stared up at the ceiling again, while tears trickled down her cheeks. Her chest hurt with each breath, although not so much as previously. Her head ached, but she found she could bear the light now, whereas before the wavering candle flames had made it worse.

'*Tomorrow*,' she thought, 'tomorrow, I'll plan how to get away from here.' She wondered if the house in the Herrensgracht had been sold. She had some dim recollection that her uncle had said it was rented. To provide money for her keep while she lived here with her cousins. 'I want it back. It's mine,' she whispered to the rafters.

Hearing feet on the stairs she scrabbled for the apothecary's pad and replaced it on her brow, but no one came into the room. She could hear Clara and Anneke's voices outside on the landing. Floor boards creaked, cupboards were opened and closed. They were getting clean bedding, going into the spare room to make up a bed. For the lawyer, she imagined. It must be Sara's night off, the evening the de Haan's maid went to visit her ancient father in Vlaardingen.

'I don't see *why*,' Anneke was saying, 'why she shouldn't? Why you and Papa couldn't at least *hint*. We've had to put up with the dreary girl living with us four whole years! It's not much to ask, dowries for me and Lottie? Is it?'

Clara's murmured response was inaudible.

'So she paid her way? Or this Heer Rombouts did. But *we've* had all the trouble of nursing her, haven't we? And wasn't it her own fault that man stabbed her? Going off on her own like that? She was always doing it. Too stuck up to walk home with us, her own cousins!' Again Clara's response was inaudible, but she sounded as though she was chiding her daughter, if not very effectively.

'Oh, very well, *you've* had to nurse her!' Their voices faded as, presumably, they went into the spare bed chamber to start making the lawyer's bed, and the door swung to behind them.

Mattie lay with her eyes wide open, staring above her as the candle flames created flickering spears of light across the ceiling. Thoughts spun through her head, tumbling and turning like dry leaves in a gale.

'Tomorrow,' she whispered, 'I'll start my life again.'

Chapter 29

Vos Rises Early and Learns More of Schiedam

Anders Vos rose whilst his two assistants slumbered on, snorting in their fevered sleep. It must, he decided, peering at his watch in the half light, be earlier than he'd thought, since neither his landlady nor the skivvy were visible when he went downstairs. He was restless, eager to be up and doing, although it was too early to call on any of those he wished to question. He thought he might break his fast in one of these comfortable coffee houses of which his assistants were so fond.

A bright morning, considering how early it was, and when he stepped outside he saw that winter had arrived overnight. Sharp frost under a pale blue sky had replaced yesterday's blustery showers, and a thin lace trim of ice now edged the canals. A depressed heron shuffled its feet on the seat of a row boat by the lock.

'Don't worry my friend,' said Anders Vos to the bird, since there was no one about to mock, 'I may be a fox, but I'm not after you today!' But the heron didn't believe him and flew off, the quills in its wing feathers creaking together like the hinges of an old door needing oil.

Turning onto the Lang Haven he became aware that others had risen even earlier than he had. Schiedam was already stirring. The chimneys of the distilleries were puffing forth clouds of steam which hung like fat grey-white pillows in the cold air. Warehouse doors were thrown open, and already men were hastening to and fro, trundling handcarts and rolling barrels. The sharp scent of juniper stung at the back of Vos's throat. There was no wind, and the sails of the windmills hung idle above the frosted roofs of the houses. Vos found them somehow menacing. He fancied they were giants waiting their chance to reach down and seize a handful of these ant-like workers scurrying below. Windmills, in his opinion, should stay in the countryside where they belonged. These great brick monstrosities, far taller than the surrounding buildings, made him uncomfortable. They seemed to be watching, standing guard, perhaps ready to attack.

There was a boat drifting on the far side of the Appelmarktbrug, brown sails drooping from the mast, waiting for a bridge watcher to raise the bridge and let it through to make the turn onto the Korte Haven. Vos, having risen with no immediate aim in view, had a sudden desire to make mischief. He stood and observed as that fussbudget Cornelius de Haan came bustling along the wharf. He watched as he hauled the key on its silver chain from his waistcoat pocket and unlocked the padlock which held the mechanism fast in the bed of the bridge. His assistant, an unhealthy looking stripling with cold-reddened nose, ears and fingers, stood idling on the far bank, until at a sharp command from Cornelius they both grabbed at the hanging chains on either side and pulled so that the two halves of the footbridge parted and rose up like prayerful hands the frosty air.

'Good morning, Heer de Haan,' said Vos, sidling up behind the Bridge Watcher, tickled by the notion of discomforting that strutting cockerel, 'a cold morning, eh? Winter has arrived, has it not?' He noticed that Cornelius wore stout leather gauntlets against the rough metal and biting cold but his assistant had none. 'Have you news of your poor niece?'

Cornelius was, as he'd hoped, startled to find Vos at his elbow, and stumbled back a pace. 'My niece? What about her...? Oh, you're the chief of those detectives, aren't you? My niece, I'm pleased to say, is *beginning* to show signs of recovery.' He paused, wrinkling his brow as though hardly believing what he'd just said. 'We never thought she'd pull through you know, it's been so long. But late last evening when my wife went into her room to settle her for the night, she opened her eyes, and mumbled *'Tante Clara,'* – very faint, you understand, but my wife said it was quite clear, and this morning she took a little oatmeal with milk from a spoon.'

'Splendid! Could I come and see her? Perhaps later today? If she's regained consciousness she'll be able to tell us who attacked her. Make a formal accusation.'

'A formal accusation? She needs to do that? Why, have you caught that devil?'

'Not yet,' said Vos, 'but we will.' Of this he was by no means certain, but he wasn't about to allow Cornelius de Hann to guess it.

'I don't want her bothered,' Cornelius fretted, 'If you come mithering her, it could set her back. We've already had the lawyer come peering at her, *and* that Apothecary fellow, Rijnsberger, trying to weasel his way into my household.'

'Oh, I wouldn't *bother* her,' lied Vos, who had every intention of asking Mattie some very searching questions, as soon as was humanly possible. She was, since Ambroos had proved so unsatisfactory, his only witness. He was still cherishing the theory that she'd been attacked by a disappointed lover, and the last thing he wanted was for her uncle and aunt and cousins to put alternative ideas into her head.

'I'd leave it a day or two if you would,' Cornelius prevaricated. 'I don't want her upset.' Not yet apprised of the fact that Mathilde was to inherit a fortune Vos was mildly surprised to find the Bridge Watcher so concerned for her welfare. Cornelius, at their previous meeting, had not struck him as a sensitive fellow.

'I'll call round later this morning,' he said firmly, 'and see what your wife thinks. I promise to be guided by her. The sooner we have Miss Mathilde's evidence the better. Young girls are easily influenced when they begin talking amongst their friends, and start thinking they remember things quite differently from how they truly were.'

'Mattie is not a girl to be influenced by *anyone*,' said Cornelius with some feeling. 'Look at that ridiculously shabby bonnet she wears all the time! My wife has often and often offered to buy her a new one, but will she let her? No! Goodness knows what people must think. We've never denied her anything, but what must she do but insist on traipsing around dressed like a pauper! It's been very upsetting and embarrassing for us.'

Now this sounded to Vos much more what he would have expected to hear from Cornelius de Haan!

'I promise to be guided by Vrouw de Haan,' he said, raising his eyebrows a little at this outburst. He strolled away while he waited for the barge to pass through and the bridge to be lowered once more. He was recalling what van Dyke had said about the de Haans, namely that Clara seemed fond of the girl in a rather shatter-brained fashion. But his assistant's impression had been that Cornelius and his daughters treated Mattie much as they might a maidservant.

Once the bridge was down Vos walked onto it without looking back, ignoring the fact that Cornelius was standing staring after him, chewing on his bottom lip.

As he crossed over the canal he noticed that the pace of work all around him was increasing by the minute. Although it was still early the Lang Haven hummed with activity. Men and boys darted to and fro. Barrels were being rolled out of Nolet's distillery onto the deck of a waiting boat. Metal wheels rumbled over cobblestones. Sacks of grain were being barrowed into storehouses, or carried on the bent backs of the zakkendragers, and heaved on or off barges. Some of the boat women were busy hanging out washing on lines strung between masts; others were handing up bowls of steaming food to their menfolk or their children from cook stoves below the deck. And over them all plumes of smoke were rising from the distillery chimneys, smudging the blue of the sky with dirty fingers.

'That Flemish fellow, Bruegel,' said Vos out loud as he paused for a moment with his hand on the rail at the end of the bridge, thinking no one would hear him above the clang of metal wheels and barrel hoops, and the warning shouts of the zakkendragers. '*He could have painted this.*' Vos had few interests outside of his police work – detection left him very little free time, but he liked to look at paintings, especially in the new museum in Rotterdam.

'Yes, I have often brought his paintings to mind myself, Sergeant,' said a voice at his back, and he found Pastor Winkelmann standing at his shoulder, making him start, exactly as he had startled Cornelius. 'Our own Hieronymus Bosch too, from time to time, unfortunately. Scenes of misery and degradation alas, and I'm due to visit such a one.'

Vos turned and blinked at the clergyman in some alarm. 'A scene of misery and degradation! So early in the day, Pastor?'

'Perhaps it won't be too bad,' said Jacob Winkelmann, doubtfully. 'My hope is that the worst will have passed, and we can dispatch her quietly to the infirmary without further unpleasant scenes. A woman who works at the orphanage. *Delirium tremens.* Very unfortunate. Horrid. The Regent is away and the schoolmaster, who has hardly been there five minutes, is having to deal with the situation. Dreadful that the children should see such things! Appalling! But Directeur van Corte at the Infirmary has come up trumps as I hoped he would, and has offered to take her in and see if they can, as it were, "dry her out."'

'You have to oversee her removal from the orphanage?'

'I promised I would. I'm a governor you see, and in the absence of the Regent.... This Heer Mulder seems a good enough fellow, and he's coped very well in the circumstances. The children have really taken to him, and he's managed to win considerable respect from the adults too, but *this* was more than he should have been asked to manage. Far more! This woman is the Matrone. Can you imagine it? She's supposed to care for the children's health and well-being, but instead she's been drinking herself senseless! I promised to go along this morning and see her taken away in a closed carriage before the children finish their breakfasts. It seemed the least I could do.'

'I keep being told there are some problems at the weeshuis,' said Vos, as they began to stroll up the slope together. Pastor Winkelmann seemed in no hurry to fulfil his errand. He fell short of actually taking his arm, but Vos thought he seemed relieved to have found someone to confide in. 'My colleagues and I, as you know, have been questioning the townsfolk about that unfortunate woman, Margriet van de Grote,' Vos continued, 'only to be told some rigmarole about another Margriet, Margriet de Hoop, the wife of the Regent at the orphanage? It almost seems as if they find her...*disappearance* more interesting than the murder of Vrouw van de Grote?'

'Human nature!' said Pastor Winkelmann, sadly. 'Vrouw van de Grote lost her reason. It's happened slowly, as these things do, over a long period of time. Those who have known her in better days are sorry, and sorry for Henke, her husband too, but she isn't – *news* anymore, someone they still take pleasure in gossiping about. Everyone supposes she must have attacked someone in one of her insane frenzies – you'll remember we discussed this with Henke himself? It's a sad thing, a wretched thing, but it doesn't give any satisfaction to the wagging tongues. Whereas, I regret to say,' here he lowered his voice almost to a whisper, 'in the case of Vrouw de Hoop, *she* has been a focus for salacious gossip in recent days. She inherited money a few years back, and this lead to a regrettable...change in her behaviour.'

'She takes lovers and skedaddles with them I understand?' said Vos.

'So it's said.'

'Is there any doubt?'

'I don't know it of my own knowledge,' said Jacob Winkelmann. 'Neither Maarten nor his wife has ever sought my advice, and the Dutch Reformed Church, as you will know, does not seek or require confessions of sin by individuals.'

Unlike the Maréchaussée, thought Vos, we certainly do seek them. Not that many do confess until they realise they've been found out.

They had reached the top of the slope now, in front of the fine wrought iron gates of Sint Jacob's Infirmary. A tall man in a well cut coat, and a top hat Prince Albert of England might have envied, and carrying a chased silver-topped cane, was descending the steps in front of the portico. Accompanying him was a large black and white spotted dog. Seeing the two men approaching the man raised his hat in greeting.

'Why here is van Corte himself!' exclaimed Pastor Winkelmann, surprised. 'I'd thought he'd have been at the weeshuis already, but no doubt some little emergency here at the infirmary held him up.'

Vos had not encountered the Directeur of the Infirmary before. A man of considerable private means he must be he thought, for I'm sure the good burgers of Schiedam would be surprised to know the price of that hat, that cane and those gloves!' And why, he wondered, is he bringing his dog?

Chapter 30

Unfortunate Events at the Orphanage

A carriage was drawn up outside the front entrance to the weeshuis. The doors on both sides swung open, and black curtains which were intended to obscure the windows from the eyes of the curious flapped in the cold breeze. A skinny horse had his nose deep in a nosebag; searching for the last wisp of hay. There was no sign of the driver.

'Oh, dear, that's the undertaker's carriage,' said Jacob Winkelmann, as the three men cleared the slope and began to walk the short distance along Lange Achterweg where the main entrance to the weeshuis was situated, 'I hope it may not upset Vrouw Schmit when she sees it.'

'It's the best I could do,' said Dries van Corte, sounding slightly miffed Vos thought. 'Carriages aren't easily obtained at short notice for *this* kind of affair, and Flanders likes to oblige me, since I give him steady business. You wouldn't want the woman dragged through the streets, now would you?'

Anders Vos considered van Corte's manner of speech somewhat affected. He was a handsome fellow with a wide mouth and lips that curled over at the corners when he smiled. His coat, his silk hat and his buttoned gloves were dove grey and perfectly matched. The dog, a thoroughbred Dalmatian was, in Vos's view (Vos liked dogs), even more handsome than his master.

He'd not intended to go any further than the Hoogstraat with these men. The affairs of the town's orphanage, he'd assumed, and was still assuming, had nothing to do with him. Vos, however, hadn't got where he was, holding rank as a successful detective in the Maréchaussée, if he'd not had a… a *nose?* A sense that here was something he should be taking note of? *Why* he had this feeling he couldn't have begun to give an account, but something tingled at the base of his skull and down his spine. So when the Pastor had introduced him to Heer Directeur van Corte and urged him to accompany them, he acquiesced. He told himself it was still too early to go and interrogate Mathilde de Haan, so he might as well fill the time.

The dog, which van Corte addressed as Boaz, ran ahead to fraternise with the horse. Those two plainly knew one another. As Vos supposed they inevitably would. A steady stream of elderly patients at the infirmary must die and the undertaker, his coffin-brake and his rather mean looking carriage for any mourners, would be frequent visitors at Sint Jacob's.

When they reached it, the orphanage's main doors stood open, but no one was visible. Van Corte and Jacob Winkelmann hurried inside.

Vos remained where he was, contemplating funeral carriages and death. And for some reason, the missing boy, Tomas. Was he alive or dead? Idly, he scratched the head of Boaz, who sniffed his newly mended boot with interest. The dead, as Vos knew well, dead from *any* cause, were not particularly easy to dispose of, anywhere in South Holland. There were well maintained cemeteries, of course. Most of the older churches had graveyards attached, but many of these were now reaching bursting point. Others were being created out in the countryside. Fine, for Oma who'd lived a long and virtuous life. A trip out to the new cemetery to lay flowers on her grave made a pleasant day's excursion for all the family. But what to do with an *inconvenient* body when you couldn't just send for this fellow Flanders, so willing to oblige? There were few forests, and farms were small, their fields flat, open and visible to anyone who might be passing. Faced with the problematically dead, Vos had observed only too often, people resorted to tipping them into lakes or canals. As indeed someone had done with poor Margriet van de Grote. The snag about this, which sometimes made Vos's life easier (and sometimes did not), was that unless securely weighted, the corpse quickly rose to the surface. Even if it didn't, if the water was still and not too deep, it would be spotted, sooner or later, by one of the boatmen.

Vos leaned against the side of the carriage and Boaz, either because he'd taken a fancy to Vos, or because he liked the smell of animal glue emanating from his boot, sat down and leaned heavily against Vos. The street remained empty.

'No one's reported finding a body,' said Vos to his new canine friend, 'so can we assume that the boy Tomas is still alive? Or has he left the district? I cannot imagine where he could hide in Schiedam for all this time. We know that there's been one sighting of his stepfather – or do we? Is that sighting to be relied on?'

Boaz, evidently eager to please his new friend, thumped his whip of a tail enthusiastically.

'You consider it is?' said Vos. 'Well, you may be right, but since according to those clowns van Dyke and Barends, the witness freely admits he was drunk at the time, you will understand that I have doubts.'

'Woof!' the dog Boaz sat up, ears alert, having heard something Vos had not. He straightened up and turned his eyes towards the front door of the weeshuis, expecting to see the Pastor, van Corte and the woman with *delirium tremens* emerge, but the only person on the doorstep was a small girl holding something in her hand.

Vos thought he recognised her. Wasn't she the child who hitched up her skirts to display her leg-iron, some days ago on the canal bank below the windmill? The one he suspected of telling him a whole string of lies about what she was doing there with the crippled boy in the wheeled-chair? Today, in her brown woollen dress and crisp white cap and apron (only minor grease spots on this so far) she was almost the double of the wooden figure perched on the roof above the weeshuis door.

'Nobody's here!' she called cheerfully over her shoulder to someone inside the building. 'I'm going to give this crust to the horse! Old Flanders half starves the poor beast. D'you want to come and help?'

Vos coughed, and stepped forward from his concealment behind the carriage. The effect of his sudden appearance was remarkable. The child's round blue eyes flew open, her lips parted in a shriek of horror, and she turned and bolted back into the building. Boaz, the dog, evidently thinking this reaction merited investigation, or perhaps interested in the crust, trotted after her.

Vos thought, what on earth was that about? Who were the children she had been calling to, inviting to join her? All he'd seen was a flurry of movement in the shadowy hallway as she fled. That crippled boy in his chair, he supposed, and another child spinning it around and pushing it rapidly out of sight.

Unlike Boaz, he hesitated to go after them. It was none of his business; let their teacher and the other adults in the place deal with disobedient scamps. He leaned back against the carriage, this time on the side nearest the front door, watching, waiting for the emergence of the drunken employee and her minders, but he couldn't help puzzling over the incident. Why had the girl fled? Did it matter? She'd certainly not done so on their previous encounter. She was a naughty little puss that much was evident, given to going where she should not be. He hadn't believed a word she'd said when he'd met her on the canal bank, but on that occasion she hadn't seemed worried to be found there, quite the opposite. Obviously, he mused, today was different. Those in charge of the orphanage had been intending that the drunken employee should be removed as quietly and discretely as possible, "while the orphans were eating breakfast" or so Pastor Winkelmann had maintained. Undoubtedly the children had had strict instructions to stay in the dining hall, and their ushers would have been given orders to keep them there. Despite this, he could guess that they'd fathomed that something unusual was happening, and some of them hadn't resisted sneaking out to see. Vos consulted his pocket watch. Van Corte and the Pastor had now been gone some time. The woman must be giving trouble, must be resisting removal. There was no question of his *arresting* the inebriate of course. She had committed no crime that he knew of. This was an internal matter for the weeshuis. However, the presence of a policeman in uniform might help to speed things along? He straightened his hat, pulled down the hem of his tunic, and stepped forward, intending to enter and find out what was happening.

The hurtling body hit him squarely in the chest, knocking him aside, whilst the knife she wielded jabbed into his left shoulder creating a sharp jolt of pain.

'Stop her! Stop her!' Half a dozen people in breathless pursuit jostled in the doorway. Vos registered that the one with the loudest voice, shouting at him to stop this frantic dervish, was the schoolmaster.

'You're under arrest!' said Vos, seizing her loose, flying hair with one hand, thus forcing her head back, and with the other, catching hold of the wrist that held the knife. 'Here, someone help me hold her!' Van Corte, the Pastor and several others remained open-mouthed and immoveable on the threshold in attitudes of frozen horror.

Only Heer Mulder stepped forward. 'Handcuffs?' he enquired, sounding gruff and official. Vos wasn't to know that Roel Mulder had once played a policeman in a murder drama. And therefore knew what the next line here should be.

'Lower left pocket,' gasped Vos, who was finding it difficult to keep a hold on his prisoner. Fortunately, his grasp on her wrist weakened her grip sufficiently and the knife clattered to the ground.

'This is the woman? The one you want to take to the infirmary?' he demanded of the men still crowded in the doorway.

'No...no,' Dries van Corte cried, shuddering. 'I won't have her there! She attacked me! She's turned lunatic!' He held up his hand. The back of one of his elegant grey gloves was soaked with blood. 'She must be sent to the prison at Brielle! Or Rotterdam! Somewhere with proper provision for the criminally insane!'

By now Mulder had extracted the handcuffs and Vos, with his assistance, managed to force them onto one of the woman's wrists. He then used the other to lock both them and her to the metal shank that held the step of the carriage.

'Hoy! Never mind afixin' 'er to my carriage! I doan'a want 'er if she ain't goin' to St Jacob's, and she'll likely frighten the hoss!' Flanders the undertaker now pushed his way forward from amongst the throng in the doorway. He was a round-shouldered fellow, his legs splayed by infant rickets, his voice soft but penetrating. Vos, who was becoming aware of the pain in his shoulder, didn't need to be told his name. He bent to retrieve the knife, which had skittered away under the wheels of the carriage. The horse stamped a foot, but appeared otherwise unperturbed. Vos thought that no doubt he'd seen a few hysterical mourners in his time.

'He doesn't seem bothered,' he said, ignoring the undertaker and picking up the blade to examine it. 'Where did she get this knife?' he demanded, holding it up.

'She ...*gasp*... must have picked it up in the kitchen,' said Pastor Winkelmann, gulping down lungs full of air. 'We went to collect her from her room as arranged... but first we couldn't rouse her, and then, when we got her on her feet, she broke away. Ran through the dining hall, and into kitchen. She was ahead of us, and must have grabbed hold of the knife there. When we were, err...*pursuing* her through the corridors, she lashed out at Heer Directeur and slashed the back of his hand.'

'She's severed a vein!' said van Corte, in tremulous tones, 'I'm losing a lot of blood here. I must get back to the infirmary and have

Dr Saunders attend me.' He began to tie up his hand, ineffectually, in his silk handkerchief.

Vos was exasperated. How had he got himself involved with these incompetents? But he could see that van Corte looked likely to faint, his face having turned a shade of grey that nicely matched his attire.

'Very well, perhaps we can take the lady somewhere else for the time being,' he decided. 'Have *you* any suggestions, Pastor? Closer at hand than Rotterdam or Brielle, that is?' Matrone Schmit, fastened to the step of the carriage, was sobbing quietly, and trying, with her free hand, to gather up the hem of her nightgown to wipe her eyes. Vos noted that despite obvious signs of dissipation, she was, or had been, a handsome woman. All her urge to fight off her captors had drained away, and she slumped miserably against the door of the coach.

'Oh, dear! The women's house of correction? I...err, believe they have a secure room there... for... for...women who are out of control.' said Jacob Winkelmann, his voice unsteady. The clergyman's hands were shaking. He was plainly out of his depth and much distressed by the whole unfortunate affair. 'It's over beyond the Nieuwe Haven. Flanders, you'll know it? Such a dreadful thing! Horrible! And that those innocent children should have been witnesses to it!' He shuddered at the memory.

'At least she didn't throw the crockery this time,' said Roel Mulder. 'Hoy, you lads! He addressed some of the older boys who were crowding in the back of the hallway, their tool bags slung on their shoulders, all ready for departure to their apprentice places, as they did every day at this time – but in no hurry to go whilst such excitement was taking place. 'Be off with you! Your masters'll be wondering where you are. Dirk, Ruud! Back to the dining hall you two, and round the children up. Have them sitting quietly at their desks in the schoolroom. I'll be coming to start morning lessons in a very short time!'

'Rather you than me, Sir!' said Vos, 'however, thank you for your prompt assistance. You haven't been in the police yourself at some time?'

'No, never, Sir,' said Roel Mulder, only just preventing himself from telling Vos how he had, when just starting out on the stage, played the junior detective in a production of "Maria Martin in de

Rode Schuur" – it had played for three weeks solid in Nijmegen – and one of his meagre portion of lines had been 'handcuffs?'

'By the way,' Vos continued, 'one of you pupils, a little girl with something wrong with her leg... was out here earlier, wanting to feed a crust to the horse.'

'Saskia,' said the schoolmaster immediately, with a grimace that suggested that nothing that young person did would entirely surprise him.

'Keep an eye on that one,' said Vos.

'I do, when I am not prevented by drunken females rampaging through the building. While we were trying to rouse the woman from her stupor and then get her under control, the ushers, never of much use at any time, abandoned supervising breakfast and let the children wander all over the place. I suppose I'd better go and see what Saskia and her particular pals are up to.'

The scene began to sort itself out. The unfortunate Vrouw Schmit was loaded into the carriage. Flanders accepted money from the purses of Pastor and van Corte to take her to the House of Correction. The kitchen boy was sent running ahead to warn of her arrival. The maid Roos was found cowering indoors and told to go with her. The apprentices left, regretfully, for their employment. Heer Mulder went indoors to start the morning's lessons. The Pastor set out to escort Dries van Corte back to his own hospital to receive treatment for his wound. Boaz went with them. Vos found himself standing quite alone in the street, holding the knife. He was noticing that it had a sharp point and a serrated blade, but couldn't think, just then, why this should be of any significance. He wondered, in a rather vague and confused manner, if he ought to go to the infirmary to have his own wound dressed. When he moved he could feel blood trickling down his arm and soaking his shirt.

Flanders had taken the coach up to the end of the street to turn, and now he drove back along the lane, making, Vos presumed from what he knew of the layout of Schiedam, for the bridge that would take him to the western edge of the town. As they passed him, the black curtain that covered the carriage window was dragged aside, and Matrone Schmit glared out at him. Her mouth was moving, and she seemed to be trying to speak, although the glass made her all but inaudible.

'Ruined me...' he thought she mouthed, and then, 'van Corte.'

Had she really said 'van Corte'? He couldn't be sure. He couldn't be sure of anything, except the knife, and the pain in his shoulder which was beginning to blot out everything else.

Chapter 31

The Peaceful Routine of the Orphanage is Further Interrupted

The dining hall had been in uproar. The younger children, badly frightened by the sight of their Matrone being chased through the building, were in tears. The older ones, excited rather than scared had wanted to join the chase, and only Dirk and Rudd lashing out with their canes had restored even a small amount of order. Roel Mulder, who had been present at a few outbreaks of hysteria in the theatre in his time, knew that the only way to go forward was to move onto the business of the day. No explanations (no matter how Felix pestered) no words of calm and consolation, just "next!"

'Mieke, Hanjie, pass out the readers. We'll begin at the top of page twelve! Saskia, you can start.'

Thus they read around the class, the older children prompting the little ones. Discipline and tranquillity were re-established. The struggle to spell out words quickly wiped the morning's events from their minds. A battery of problems in arithmetic to be copied onto their slates from the blackboard completed this. By mid-morning all was serene in the weeshuis schoolroom. Only Casper remained troubled and thoughtful. Roel Mulder laid a hand on his shoulder. 'I've sent someone to ask the doctor to call,' he said quietly, 'since it seems we shall be without a matron for some days at least.'

'Thank you, Sir. I find I am not feeling too well today. My chest is very tight. I hope it may ease.'

He moved on to Tomas, who had reached long division, two thirds of the way down the board, and was using his sleeve to do a lot of rubbing out. 'No, Tomas stop and think. Start with the tens. Let Casper show you again.'

Heer Mulder moved amongst his pupils, authoritative and apparently unmoved by the morning's events. His cane lay, visible but unused, on the desk. He was, however, doing a lot of thinking as he walked between the rows of desks, wondering what action the governors of the weeshuis would take and how quickly, and how this might affect his own irregular position. He wasn't particularly surprised when the schoolroom door opened and a man came in.

He was expecting it would be Pastor Winkelmann, on his way back from the infirmary, but it was a complete stranger, a tall heavy set man in a blue smock, his scarlet britches tucked into canvas spats, a navy blue neckerchief knotted at his throat. He pulled off his cap, and stood waiting to be acknowledged, his broad face pleasant and expectant. The orphans stared at him round-eyed, except for Tomas, who gave him a shy grin of recognition.

'Can I help you?' Roel Mulder now supposed he was one of the tradesmen come to collect payment, who'd refused to be discouraged by the kitchen staff. He wasn't going to get his money today.

'Henke van de Grote,' the man said, obviously thinking this would make all plain. 'I'd like a word, if I may? Can't get a clear picture from them in the kitchen. Running round aflapping, like a bunch of fowls when the fox gets into the pen, *they* are.'

'If you're owed some payment…' the teacher began.

'No, nothing like that, Sir. I wanted to ask… but perhaps not in front of the nippers?' he gestured that he and Roel Mulder might step outside the schoolroom. Then his eye registered the presence of Tomas, and he beamed, striding forward to pat the boy on the head.

'Ach, young Tomas! So the Pastor got a place here for you, eh? That was good of him. Does that fellow from the Maréchaussée know you're here? He was asking about you. Thought you'd gone missing. I'll be able to tell him if I see him that you're fine and dandy!'

'Yes, perhaps we could speak together outside?' Roel Mulder interposed; now more puzzled than ever by this visitor. 'The children are due to take their mid-morning break. Kinder, leave your chalk and your slates in your places. We'll finish this task later. Stand in your places. Now lead off from the window. Coats, mittens! It's a cold morning.'

'So who, exactly, are you? And what can I do for you?' he asked the Chief of the zakkendragers once they were outside in the biting cold of the playground. 'I usually give them their physical drill around this time, but we've had a very disturbed morning,' he added, 'so I think it best to leave them free to run about. Saskia! Go and fetch a blanket for Casper. Tomas, move his chair into the sun.'

'You've got 'em well in hand,' commented Henke, admiringly,

glancing round at the awestruck orphans. 'I'm glad young Tomas is here, I was proper worritted about him, after he never came back to the Guildhuis, and my wife was murdered. That policeman thought the brute might have murdered Tomas too.'

'Your wife was murdered?' Roel Mulder had been so concerned with maintaining his own precarious position in Schiedam that he'd taken little or no notice of local gossip. He'd known of course that *someone* had been murdered, and that the Maréchaussée were investigating. His cousin, Vrouw Hauberk, had them staying on the top floor of her lodging house, but he'd managed to avoid actually seeing them. Apart from leaving behind a few unpaid bills in Amsterdam, and talking his way into a position here for which he had no credentials, he'd nothing of importance on his conscience. Never the less, the police were a body of men he was inclined to avoid as a matter of principle.

'Yes, my wife, Margriet,' said this new acquaintance. 'Everyone says it was Ignaas van Damme, that's the steifvader to young Tomas, that killed her, but I'm not so sure. I wanted to ask Vrouw Schmit, that's the matron here, about it. She was a friend to my Margriet, *and* to Vrouw de Hoop, once upon a time. They were all friends for many years, since they were young women, new to the town in those days. But then there was a falling out, a bad falling out, between Vrouw de Hoop and Vrouw Schmit…probably over some man. I don't who he was, although I might be able to guess. Margriet, *my* Margriet, she tried to keep friends with each of them although she really didn't approve of Vrouw de Hoop's carryings on, but the other two, they were at daggers drawn, and once my Margriet began to lose her wits, neither came nigh her, said it was too upsetting.'

'I see,' said Roel Mulder, who didn't at all, 'but what can *I* do for you? You must have heard we had a dreadful upset here this morning and Vrouw Schmit had to be taken away?'

'I heard. And I don't suppose it was any affair of yours, but I thought, being a schoolmaster, an educated fellow, I'd get a straight story from you, with no extra folderols! The drink'd got to her, they're saying. Do you know where they took her?'

'To the Women's House of Correction is what they said, but I believe that's just a temporary measure, while they sober her up. We thought she'd be sober by this morning, but evidently she'd drink hidden away in her room, and she ran amok, stabbing the hand of the Director of the Infirmary. A policeman by the name of Vos was here at the time, and he put her under arrest.'

Henke nodded. 'That's more or less what the cook told me, although she didn't say it was temporary. Poor woman, to come to, and find herself in that place! She isn't a bad woman, Dorte Schmit, not one like *that*, those female riff-raff selling their bodies to all and sundry down on the harbour. I suppose his lordship at Sint Jacob's wouldn't have her?'

'Heer van Corte? No, but that's understandable. She slashed his hand with a knife.'

'Heer Directeur van Corte!' snorted the zakkendrager, 'Thinks he's God Almighty. Thinks he can do just as he pleases in this town! Anyway, I thank you, Sir, although I'm not much the wiser. But I'm pleased to see young Tomas here and benefitting. It sets my mind at rest. That Ignaas van Damme is a nasty fellow and Tomas shouldn't be left to his mercies, but I'm still not convinced it was he killed my Margriet.'

The shouts of the children made listening to Henke difficult, and Roel Mulder was by no means sure he'd understood everything he'd heard. 'You know that Vrouw de Hoop has gone to Amsterdam and the Regent has gone to fetch her back?' he asked him.

'I know that's what they're *saying*,' confirmed Henke, 'but I wonder if it's true? I've my doubts whether she'd as many lovers as folks credit her with. Mebbe she just liked folks to *think* she had.'

'You don't believe it? Even the older children seem to know...' Heer Mulder waved a hand to include Casper and Saskia, and Tomas who were examining an insect, made drowsy by the wintry cold, that was crawling across Casper's blanket. Casper seemed to be instructing Saskia and Tomas in entomology. Roel Mulder thought he'd have liked to hear what he was telling them, instead of this bewildering talk of murdered wives and phantom lovers. The bright day was clouding over, and the air was full of hovering smuts from the distillery chimneys.

'I've never met her, Vrouw de Hoop, that is,' he added. 'She was gone, supposedly to Amsterdam, before I arrived. I met Maarten de Hoop of course, when he set me on to teach the children in his absence.'

'They say she went with young Dekker, the jeweller's clerk, *this* time,' said Henke, 'but then someone else told me he's gone home to his parents in Maassluis, after a row with his employer. Which tale is true, I don't know.'

'I'm afraid I don't know any of these people,' said the schoolmaster, shrugging.

'No more you would,' said Henke, pacifically. 'I reckon maybe the drink turned Dorte Schmit's brain in a different way. Different to the way my wife lost her wits. She was always a jealous creature, Dorte, jealous over men and jealous even of Margriet's friendship with Margriet de Hoop, although those two had known each other since their childhoods' in Delft. Then Vrouw de Hoop inherited all that money – money makes all kinds of people act a bit strange.'

'So, what do you believe *has* happened?' Roel Mulder had never been particularly interested in finding out, but if Margriet de Hoop hadn't gone to Amsterdam after all, it would explain why it was taking her husband so long to find her. 'You surely can't think this Vrouw Schmit might be the one who murdered your wife?'

'I don't know,' said the zakkendrager. 'I don't think she'd do that, but I just don't know what *did* happen.'

He stood watching the children running about, shouting and tussling with one another, and clapped Roel Mulder on the shoulder, 'Childhood, eh? I lost my parents when I was a youngster, and was always taught to be grateful that my aunt took me in. I'd never a spell in the weeshuis. Folks shudder to think their children might end up here, but it's not so bad, is it? They're happy! You're a good man, teaching them all they need to know. I'm glad Tomas landed on his feet.'

After Henke was gone, Heer Mulder called the children together and put them in lines to do drill, bends and stretches and jumping on the spot. Saskia, he ordered to take Casper indoors. It had grown colder, the sky darker. The steam clouds from the distillery chimneys seemed to press down like grain sacks around their shoulders.

'Will it snow, Sir?' asked Felix. 'Will it snow for Sint' Klaas, next week?'

'Next week? Ah, yes, December,' said Heer Mulder, rather vaguely. He had been pondering on what Henke the zakkendrager had said. If Vrouw de Hoop wasn't in Amsterdam, where was she?

Was there anything in Henke's tale of female jealousies?

Was he, Roel Mulder, a good man, teaching these imps all they needed to know? That certainly wasn't a role he'd ever played before.

Chapter 32

Anders Vos, Faint but Pursuing

Vos began to make his way slowly back to the lodging house. It was still early. He was feeling dizzy, and sorting out the events of the morning in his own mind seemed a huge effort. Was this, he wondered, the result of the injury to his shoulder, or because he'd had no breakfast? The rent in his uniform coat wasn't large, but would still have to be accounted for once he returned to barracks. Passing the gates of the hospital he decided not to bother the dispensary for a dressing for his shoulder since he'd no wish to encounter Directeur van Corte, to whom he'd taken an unaccountable dislike. Midway across the Appelmarktbrug he paused, seeking to clear his head. His wound throbbed drearily.

Cold air rose up from the canal, but the noise and clangour made by the distillery workers seemed to make it even harder to think. The air was thick with the fumes from the brew-house chimneys.

He'd arrested that woman after all. Quite right, she was dangerous. Various things he must do about that. Paper work. Write a full report of the incident. Make out the charge, too. *Drunkenness. Grievous Bodily Harm. Resisting arrest. Attempted murder of a police officer. Brandishing a lethal weapon in a public place... and* she'd ruined his uniform tunic, no shortage of criminal behaviour there. He'd throw the book at her.

He should be arranging, once she had sobered up, to transfer her to Rotterdam. An arrest, but not the one his superiors were expecting. Getting himself involved in a local fracas! They wouldn't be pleased. He was still no nearer discovering who in this town had murdered Mad Margriet – *or* who'd stabbed Ambroos and Mathilde de Haan.

Mathilde de Haan. He wanted to see that young lady now that she was said to be conscious. Clear that one up. 'Now Missy, *was* it Ignaas van Damme who stabbed you, or Handsome Frans the apothecary, or some would-be lover boy your uncle and aunt don't know about?'

Spurred on by all he had to do, he began to hurry from the

bridge, but found himself swaying. His legs seemed suddenly powerless. He clutched at the guard rail, feeling unsafe. He must have lost more blood than he'd thought. Somehow he made it along the quay to the lodging house – must have done. He recalled, later, the look of alarm on the face of his landlady as he staggered through the front door. After that, until he awakened to find himself lying on his bed in the early afternoon, his arm bound across his chest in a makeshift sling, he remembered little more.

He woke to find Josef van Dyke seated at the foot of the bed, his glum features half buried in one of his outsized nosewipes.

'Have you recovered?' Vos demanded.

'Better than I was, Sir, just a nasty cold,' said van Dyke, 'how are *you* feeling? What happened to you?'

'I got involved in arresting a drunken woman. Orphanage. Probably nothing to do with the case,' he grunted. He gradually hauled himself up on one elbow. The other arm was incapacitated by the sling. It hurt like the devil. 'She stabbed me in the shoulder, the vixen. Where's my uniform tunic?'

'Vrouw Hauberk took it to wash the blood out and mend the rent, Sir. We padded the wound, and put your arm out of action to stem the bleeding. I hope we did right?' van Dyke had been a regular soldier. First aid on the battle field. Vos had to acknowledge he had his uses.

'Damnation!' he swore. 'Oh, that's not aimed at you, Corporal. I met that fool of a Bridge Watcher earlier, and he told me his niece is conscious at last. Once I'd cleaned myself up and had a bite to eat, I was intending to go round there. If she can say who stuck the knife between her ribs it'll be a step forward at least!'

'We found a knife in the pocket of your tunic, Sir,' said his lugubrious assistant. 'I laid it aside as it's got blood on it. I thought it might be a clue.'

'The blood's mine, unfortunately,' said Vos. 'They said the woman must have picked it up in the weeshuis kitchen whilst evading their efforts to catch her. I'd imagine there are similar knives in every kitchen in the town. It's unlikely to be anything we're interested in. However, I did think I might show it to Miss Mattie as a point of comparison. *If* she remembers what the knife looked like. Anyway,' he hauled himself upright, and swung his legs over the side of the bed, 'go and see if my tunic's wearable,

Corporal, and if it is we'll both go round to the de Haan's. You'd best keep well away from the young lady's sick bed, but you can sit in a corner and write down every word she says.'

'Yessir. What about Barends? He's trifle better, his fever's gone down. Do you want him?'

'No,' said Vos. 'You'll be carrying enough pestilence into the house. I ought to eat something before we set out. I believe I must have been light headed *before* that woman attacked me, or I'd never have allowed myself to get involved. What has our landlady on the go today?'

'Snert and rye bread. That's what we had at mid-day.'

Vos pulled face. Thick pea soup was not a favourite of his, but needs must. 'Fetch me some, Corporal,' he said.

They found Mathilde de Haan propped up on her pillows, gazing around the room dreamily, as though she was miles from this place.

'I can only allow you a few moments,' fretted Clara de Haan, her several chins quivering. 'My husband didn't want me to let you see her. Not yet. Doctor Saunders says she must be kept absolutely quiet, and not be worried about anything at all until she's stronger, but I quite see…'

'Never mind, Aunt,' said the girl on the bed, allowing her eyes to focus on Vos. 'I can tell them what happened. They ought to catch that man, before he succeeds in killing someone.'

Clara de Haan, puffing angrily, plumped herself down on a chair in the corner, evidently not trusting Vos and van Dyke alone with her niece. Presumably the Bridge Watcher was out watching bridges. As there was only the one chair in the sparsely furnished bedroom (one straight backed chair, one gloomy oak clothespress, one mean chest of drawers, those being considered sufficient Vos supposed, for the poor relation) At least there was a fire in the grate. Van Dyke had to fold himself into a corner of the window embrasure. He took out his pencil and notebook in a deliberate fashion.

'Well, Miss de Haan,' said Vos heartily, going to stand near the head of the bed, 'I'm very pleased to find you recovering from your ordeal. A most unpleasant experience for you and the last thing I want is over-tax you. So, perhaps you can recount to me, briefly, in your own words, exactly what happened? Corporal van Dyke will write it down as you speak.'

Mathilde de Haan allowed her dreamy gaze to rest on Vos's face. Vos was no connoisseur of female beauty, but even he was struck by her lovely eyes, their pupils still enlarged by laudanum. The scar he noted (that old accident on the railway he'd been told about) but it hardly registered.

'In my own words? Why, whose words would I use but my own?'

'That's...just an expression we use. We of the police. We want your own account, exactly what happened, not what others may have told you.'

'I was walking home. I'd been helping the apothecary... and Pastor Winkelmann, to take that man, the sack porter; to the infirmary...did he recover?' Her voice was faint, and Vos had to bend closer to hear. He beckoned to van Dyke to come nearer, and rest his note book on the foot board.

'I'm pleased to say, Miss, that Ambroos is well on the way to recovery but he doesn't have a clear recollection of what happened. We hope *you* may be able to tell us more.'

'I'm glad,' sighed Mattie, 'and the little boy? Tomas? He wanted me to tell him... the man who attacked me... *he* wanted to know where Tomas had gone. After he ran away from my uncle.' She closed her eyes for a moment, perhaps visualising the painful encounter.

'This was the man they call Ignaas van Damme, the binnenschipper?'

'Yes.'

'And he attacked you on the Hoogstraat?'

'Yes. He suddenly appeared... out of nowhere. He grabbed hold of me and... demanded to know what I'd done with Tomas. He said he'd seen me speaking to Tomas while we were on the bridge... or maybe he said he'd seen Tomas speak to me... I don't remember. I was so frightened.'

'Did he say why he wanted to know what you and the boy had said?'

'No... yes. I told him I hadn't spoken to Tomas, but he insisted. He seemed to think I'd sent him somewhere, or... told him to do something. But I hadn't!'

'But *he*, that boy, did speak to you, dear,' said her aunt from her position by the door. 'I was standing next to you, so I heard him. Tomas gave you a loaf of bread and...'

Vos scowled at her, ferociously. This was precisely what he didn't want, the witness prompted.

'Yes, that's right, he gave me a loaf of bread...' said Mattie, slowly, as if she was re-living the scene moment by moment, 'and he said... "Give this to the Reverend, Miss, please..." I don't think he knew Pastor Winkelmann's name. He said, "Ask him to give it Henke at the Guildhuis." And I did,' she recalled, 'I gave it to Pastor Winkelmann later. That's all, all I remember, anyway.'

'You told Ignaas that this was what the boy said?'

'*No*, at least I don't think I did. Not that last bit, about the loaf. I don't think he asked me what Tomas said to *me*. I know I told him I didn't know where Tomas went... then he got very angry when I mentioned my Uncle, Uncle Cornelius, and he stuck the knife in me. I honestly don't remember anything more. He was drunk. He smelt terribly of drink and was in a dreadful temper. I don't suppose he cared whether he killed me. He was just so drunk and mean. Beside himself. I wouldn't have told him where Tomas had gone, even if I knew.'

Vos recalled someone else saying that. Frans Rijnsberger had used the very same words. Or not quite. He'd actually said he wouldn't tell *Vos*, even if he knew.

'Why was that, Miss?'

'Because it was obvious he ill-treats him. Poor little boy! He'd great welts all over his back. You could see where the blood had soaked through his shirt.'

'Did he, van Damme, say *why* he wanted to find Tomas?'

'Oh...yes, he did. I remember now. He said he needed him, because he couldn't sail the boat without him. Something about his mother, Tomas's mother, who'd died...I think. And he said he would beat Tomas when he caught up with him. He said it was his right to do it, because he'd taken him and his mother on...that's how he put it, and therefore he'd a right to do as he pleased with the child.' She shuddered, 'Horrible, horrible man!'

So, they were back to Ignaas, thought Vos. He found rather to his dismay that he believed what Mattie was telling him. No Frans Rijnsberger, no secret lover. A clear enough account, quite enough to charge the elusive binnenschipper with attempted murder – not to mention child cruelty. She didn't remember the knife, but once she was well enough to leave the sick room Miss Mattie's evidence would stand up well in a court of law. But first they had to catch the villain. And they hadn't made progress at all with that.

Chapter 33

Trouble at the Mill

Joop Barends was feeling better. His fever had subsided, although his legs still felt as if they'd been stuffed with cotton wadding. His nose ran constantly. Vrouw Hauberk's proffered bowl of snert had turned his stomach. Never-the-less he felt restless, had the urge to be up and about. But doing what? Vos and van Dyke had gone off to interview Mathilde de Haan, making it clear that they didn't want his company In truth he didn't mind, wouldn't have felt alert enough to question a witness, even if Vos would have allowed him to get a word in edgeways. Which he knew he wouldn't. Perhaps a short stroll in the fresh air might clear his mucus clogged nasal passages? He hoped so. He thought he might go as far as the Hoogstraat and buy some handkerchiefs, his own stock being now exhausted. He'd already had to beg some from van Dyke.

Seeing him with his hat and coat on, the landlady, displaying hither-to undiscovered motherly impulses, informed him that he'd find it 'mighty cold out,' and that he'd "best wrap up warm, or you'll be back in your bed, young fellow," so he retreated and added a woollen waistcoat and a thick muffler, which were all he had in addition to what he stood up in.

Out on the Lange Haven, making for the bridge, he discovered how right she was about the cold. The sky, where it could be seen, was an icy blue. The steam from the distilleries hung like dense eiderdowns above the roof tops. Notwithstanding his being half-deaf with catarrh, Barends found the noise of rolling barrels and the clipping-clopping of clogs melded into a racket that hurt his ears. Thus he was at first unaware that a piping voice was calling him.

'That's 'im! Hey, Meester! Police feller!' The urchin Piet launched himself at Joop Barends, seizing the hem of his tunic with a filthy paw. 'Yer gotta come, there's trouble at t'mill!'

Startled, Barends looked first down at Piet, and then along the wharf in the direction from which Piet had sprung. Three or four mill workers in leather aprons were converging on him, breathlessly, in Piet's wake.

'You're the... police feller?' one of them gasped, promptly

bending himself at the waist to grasp his knees and catch his breath.

'E's in the mill!'

'Us seen 'im! 'E's gotta knife!'

'What? Who?' Joop Barends' brain didn't work quickly at the best of times, and this wasn't the best if times.

Piet gave his tunic hem a frustrated yank. 'Ignaas!' he yelled into his face. 'Ignaas van Damme! 'Im as yer wanted ter catch! 'Im as 'as bin amurderin' folk!'

'You've seen him? In the mill?'

'That's what we're tellin' yer! 'E's bin stealin' our stuff!' one of the mill workers said.

'Err, which mill?'

'The Walvisch!' other exasperated voices gasped, as though what other mill could there be? Although Barends, glancing around, could see the sails of three or four looming above the rooftops.

'Well, I'm...' he caught himself about to say, 'I'm on my own, my two senior officers have gone to question a witness,' then he pulled himself up sharp. Rise to the challenge, Joop Barends! This might be something... this could be your moment!

'Show me,' he commanded. Eager hands seized his elbows, hurrying him along the quay and through Walvisstrat onto Westvest.

In the wide doorway of the windmill they found an agitated crowd. Wenders the miller was attempting to soothe two men who were shouting angrily at one another. One of them had a torn smock; the other was sporting a rapidly swelling eye.

'Calm down! Hans didn't take your broodjes, Mattie! We know that, now!'

'He didn't need to punch me in the eye!'

'*You* didn't need to rip me good smock! Me wife'll kill me!'

Meester Wenders, seeing Barends approaching with an escort, left them to it.

'We've got a bit of a situation here, Officer,' he informed him, 'things have been going missing for a day or two. Sandwiches and such like, taken from lunch pails. The men started off thinking it must be one of their workmates, and it all got a bit nasty. Then today *these* fellows,' he nodded to Barends' escorts, 'came to tell me they'd found an intruder up in the maalzolder,' he tipped his head back, looking up as though he half expected to see the man clinging to the slowly rotating sails. 'And they believe he's still up there.'

'I went after 'im!' volunteered one of them. "E's bin hidin' out amongst the sacks of grain! We're behind this week, and they're all stacked up in piles in the maalzolder, an' 'e musta burrowed in there like a rat. I tried to go after 'im, but out comes 'is 'and wi' a knife! I wasn' goin' no further!'

Joop Barends took another deep breath and threw back his shoulders. In his head he heard the voice of his late father, chiding him. 'Don't be a coward boy! Being an idiot I suppose you can't help, but try not to be a coward as well!'

'Take me up to this maalzolder place, and show me!' Inwardly Barends might quake, but with his hand clutching the butt of his pistol he stepped forward, ready to uphold the honour of His Majesty King Wilhelm the third, the Netherlands, and the Maréchaussée.

The sounds of boots and clogs on the stairways must have warned Ignaas. Before they reached the maalzolder they heard sounds of scuffling and dull thuds as heavy bags of grain were thrust aside.

Barends entered in the van, Wenders and half a dozen mill hands right behind him. They were just in time to see a pair of boots disappear up the next ladder.

"E's goin' up! 'E's makin' fer the steenzolder! Stop 'im! We gotta stop 'im!'

As one, they charged after the binnenschipper. Barends found himself carried on up by the press of men behind him. Arriving in the steenzolder he saw Ignaas or to more accurately, *someone*, dodge behind the slowly rotating spoorwiel. The air up here was dim and hazy with grain dust. Only a little light penetrated this level of the mill from a tiny dirt-encrusted window set in the thick outer wall.

'Stop! In the name of the law!' panted Barends, astonished to hear his own voice proclaiming these words, words he'd hardly dared hope ever to utter. The only response was a snarl, and then a knife whistled through the air, glanced off the great cog wheel driving one of the grindstones, and imbedded itself in Barends' kepi, knocking it into the steenkoppel. It slid down between the grindstone and the trough where the meal was being slowly but relentlessly ground.

Without a conscious thought he snatched his pistol from its

212

holster and fired. There was a deafening report, followed by a yell, and his opponent toppled to the floor, dropping down behind one of the stone troughs.

"'Ere! You've shot 'im!' remarked one of the mill hands.

'Is 'e dead?'

'He's destroyed my cap!' said Barends, indignant. 'That's against the law, that is. Destroying a police officer's uniform.'

'Ach, very likely you'll have to pay for a new one,' agreed another mill hand. 'And the knife's gone into the meal too. Will we stop the spoorwiel and try and fish them out for you?'

'Hadn't we better see if you've killed him first?' enquired Wenders the miller, peering nervously around the stone basin at the victim. 'I don't want him bleeding to death up here. We'd never get the stains out of the floorboards.' Joop Barends, coming to his senses, followed after him.

Ignaas lay on the floor clutching his upper arm, and swearing under his breath in, alternately, Dutch, Flemish and Friesian. 'Vwijn!' he snarled weakly at Barends. 'Filthy swine!'

Joop Barends then spoke seven more words he'd barely hoped, even in his wildest dreams, to utter, 'Ignaas van Damme, you are under arrest!'

For a moment, complete silence fell. Barends suddenly discovered he'd no idea what came next. He felt dizzy, faint, disconnected from the world as though it were he and not Ignaas who'd been shot. Then the voices of those around him began clamouring suggestions.

'Shall us carry 'im downstairs?'

'Tie 'im up first!'

'Better fetch someone to 'is shoulder?'

'Nee! 'e ain't bleeding, or not much. Someone get 'im on 'is feet.'

'No!' Barends said, rousing himself. 'Can someone go... to the house of the Bridge Watcher... Heer de Haan? Inform my colleagues... Sergeant Vos and Corporal van Dyke...that I have the suspect here, under arrest. They'll want to see...where he was hiding. Question him on the spot.'

'I'll go, Meester!' The wharf rat, Piet, had somehow managed to wriggle through the crowd to get a happy eyeful of the man Barends had shot. 'I'll get 'em for you! Coo! I dint know there'd be shootin'! You winged 'im proper, Meester!'

Ignaas, rallying a little and naturally infuriated, rose up on one elbow and made a grab for Piet's foot, but the boy's broken down boot came away in his hand, and Piet skipped lightly out of reach and scuttled off down the nearest ladder.

Someone brought a length of rope, binding the man's ankles, and then tying his hands before him, despite his howls of pain and protest. Someone else had stopped the kruibok, and fished about with a hook down the side of the steenkoppel. He now handed Barends his kepi, battered beyond repair, and the knife.

The knife. Barends, unsure his trembling legs would support him, seated himself on the edge of the circular stone trough and held this in his hand. It was a short handled knife with a sharp point and a serrated blade. Ignaas, lying wounded and bound at his feet, glared up at him.

Something about the knife was puzzling Joop Barends. The tip of the blade was sharp indeed. Vicious. He calculated that it must be one Ignaas used to gut fish – into the fish's belly with the sharp end, then a sawing motion to open it up and extract the entrails. Easy to see how he might have used it to score Ambroos' belly, bearing down from above – and to push that cruel point between Miss Mattie's ribs. He held it up against his own neck, trying to envisage how it might be used in a sideways sawing movement, to cut the throat of Margriet van de Grote. The serrated edge didn't seem sharp enough.

'Is this your *only* knife?' he asked Ignaas, but the fallen binnenschipper clamped his mouth firmly shut and closed his eyes.

Some time elapsed before Vos and van Dyke came stumbling up the mill's staircase. Piet had encountered some difficulties, first in gaining admittance to the de Haan house, and then in persuading the detectives that Barends really had sent for them. Vos fully expected to find the whole thing was a hoax. Some ill-wisher might have bribed the artful Piet to waste his time. So he was duly flabbergasted and more than a little exasperated to find van Damme trussed up like a boiling fowl, and Joop Barends sitting dazed and confused, examining the knife as though he'd never seen one before.

'Well!' he barked, 'don't just sit there dreaming lad, we need to take him in! They promised me a cellar at the Gemeentehuis. Get him upright! Remove the rope! He can walk down on his own two feet.'

''E shot me,' growled Ignaas.

'In your shoulder not in your foot, he didn't,' Miller Wenders pointed out. 'You haven't lost much blood. If we untie your feet you can walk. I was wondering how we'd get him out of here,' he told Vos. Take him and the sooner the better. He's holding up production.'

'I'll hold you up no longer!' growled the binnenschipper as the rope was unbound from around his ankles, and, though his hands were still tied – but not, in the event, tightly enough – he barged his way through the gawping crowd, grabbed at the hoist that lowered the meal sacks, and, clinging desperately, swung himself through the trap door and disappeared through the floor.

'After him!' roared Vos, running for the doorway. Police and mill workers collided, scrambled, toppled over one another and swore horribly. Limbs became entangled. Bodies flailed and fought to free themselves. By the time the jumbled mass of men had fallen down three flights of stairs and disentangled themselves at the bottom, Ignaas van Damme was gone.

Chapter 34

A Wanderer Returns

The Reverend Jacob Winkelmann was sitting in the Regent's office at the weeshuis, counting money. It was evening, darkness was approaching, and he was working by the light of a pair of hanging lamps. Their wicks were poorly adjusted and flickered a good deal, but he'd no idea how to rectify this. In his own house he relied on his housekeeper to deal with such matters. Like Barends and van Dyke, he was suffering from a cold, and had to pause frequently to sneeze into a large handkerchief. Each pile of coins represented a sum owed to a tradesman or the wages of one of the weeshuis servants. Accounting was not an occupation he took any pleasure in, or indeed was very good at. At Sint Jan's, he had a kerkdienaar, a churchwarden, to do this on receipt of the Sunday collections, but the schoolmaster – what was his name again? – *Mulder*, yes, Heer Mulder had asked him for help, and Jacob Winkelmann was doing his best. Roel Mulder had been loath to call in the Governing body for his own reasons, and little though he was aware of it, Jacob Winkelmann was equally loath.

Indeed, the Pastor was suffering not only from coughs and sneezes but a severe attack of guilt. He knew he should have been aware of the situation at the orphanage long before Mulder brought it to his attention, but he'd been immersed this last week, both in his developing cold and an epic poem he was composing based on the tragic tale of Hagar and Ishmael in the book of Genesis. Somehow he'd completely lost track of the days. What could be keeping his friend Marten de Hoop in Amsterdam all this time? He supposed Vrouw de Hoop must be proving more intransigent than usual.

Wives really were more trouble than they were worth he decided, as a pile of stuivers, owed to the boiler man, slid sideways and collapsed into the pile owed to the greengrocer. He sighed and counted and straightened these piles once more, not allowing his eyes to travel to the lady with the naked bosom above the fireplace. From time to time the image of Mathilde de Haan floated before him, although he was careful to steer his thoughts away from any considerations of her anatomy. Perhaps, he reflected, it had been Mattie's air of being oppressed and unhappy that had drawn him to the sad tale of Hagar, so shabbily treated by those who ought to have cared for her. At least, he thought, brightening, Our Lord has seen fit to preserve Miss Mattie. He had not yet called to see her (being too absorbed in composing rhyming couplets for Hagar and her son) but everyone was now saying that the young lady had made a miraculous recovery. There was talk of her being well enough to drive out, wrapped in shawls, in a pony cart to Negenhuizen to visit a distant cousin of the de Haans if the weather didn't turn too bitter. His aged housekeeper, who saw it as a duty to keep abreast of local news on his behalf, had told him that the family, having taken their niece for granted for so long, now appeared almost over protective in their care of her.

Jacob Winkelmann dragged his attention back to the many piles of coins he'd set out before him, and grunted in dismay. Surely this pile should be taller than the one next to it? More must be owed to the man who stoked the stoves than to the potato merchant, must it not? He glanced around him for the list Heer Mulder had provided. Light glinted on the sumptuous gilt leather covering the cupboard doors and walls whenever one of the lamps flared up. Perhaps he'd put it down on a shelf when he took out the money chest? He was just rising from his chair, when the door was pushed open.

'Maarten!'

'Jacob! What are you doing here?'

'Err, helping. Helping your new schoolmaster fellow. Bills, you know? Tradesmen and so forth. They were piling up. How are you Maarten? Did you find Margriet?'

Even as he asked the question he could see the answer for himself. Maarten de Hoop was alone, and there was no sound of voices from the corridor, no suggestion of a wife arriving home from a trip, and commanding attention as she disposed of cape, bonnet, bags and parcels.

'Jacob, she's not there! I went…to all the hotels. No one has seen her, or…or the young man either.' Jacob Winkelmann was now registering how pale and dishevelled Maarten de Hoop appeared, almost as though in his tireless search for his wife he'd neglected to eat, sleep or change his clothes over the last ten days.

'You're exhausted, Maarten! Here, give me your coat, take this chair. I'll ring for someone to bring you some broth!'

But Maarten de Hoop seemed incapable of even the simple act of removing his top coat. His hat dropped from his fingers and bowled across the floor on its brim. His gloves and cane he seemed to have mislaid.

'Sit down, man, sit down!' the Pastor took his friend's arm and guided him bodily to a seat. He took up the hand bell from the table and rang it vigorously, but then realised that this was unlikely to be heard, let alone answered at this hour. The staff would be upstairs supervising the dormitories. He went to the door and rang again. Nobody appeared, so he stepped over threshold into the corridor. There he caught sight of a small boy scuttling along in the shadows.

'You! Boy! Fetch...' then he realised he didn't know who to ask for. Matron Schmit must now be in Rotterdam being held by the police on all kinds of charges. Should Dirk or Ruud see the Regent like this? Or any of the maids?

'Is Heer Mulder still here? Fetch him for me, please, child!'

'Yes Sir,' mumbled the boy, shrinking back into the shadowy passageway before turning tail and hurrying way. It crossed his mind, fleetingly, to wonder why a boy should be wandering alone in this gloomy lower corridor so late in the evening, but he turned his attention back to Maarten de Hoop.

He found him slumped in the chair too fatigued it seemed, even to warm his hands at the fire's blaze.

'I've sent one of the boys to fetch Mulder,' he assured the Regent. 'You're exhausted, man! He'll organise some broth. I'm not sure which of the kitchen staff are still on the premises, but he'll know. Seems a capable fellow, very capable indeed. No sign of Vrouw de Hoop at all, eh?'

'She's not in Amsterdam, I'm sure of it. Yet people here seemed certain she and Dekker had gone there. Why, Dries told me everyone was saying so! The jeweller, Kooperman the Jew, told him young Dekker had walked off the job.'

'Yeees...although I've heard, or rather my housekeeper heard it at the Friday Market, that Heer Kooperman has since learned that Dekker may've gone home to his parents in Maassluis,' said Jacob Winkelmann doubtfully. 'Some tiff about how figures were entered in the accounts book. But now Kooperman is acknowledging it was an honest mistake and is offering to take the young fellow back.'

The pastor glanced ruefully at the piles of money he'd been counting. He had considerable sympathy with young Meester Dekker. He'd never remember now, which piles he'd assigned to which tradespeople. All that to do again.

'So perhaps Margriet went to Amsterdam alone?'

'I didn't ask after a woman alone... She's never gone alone on one of these sprees of hers... always with some man. Always.'

'But she might have. Perhaps not to Amsterdam. Den Hague? Utrecht? I'd assume you'd have heard if she were just up in Rotterdam. Someone would have seen her there...' Pastor Winkelmann allowed his voice to trail away. Maarten de Hoop's head had drooped on to his chest. He was apparently too weary to speculate.

Just then, Roel Mulder appeared in the doorway. He may have been tempted to say, in the manner of a butler in some play he'd performed, 'You rang, Sir?' Certainly his lips moved, but he said nothing.

'Ah, Heer Mulder! The boy found you. Good, good! You've met Heer Regent de Hoop of course? I wasn't sure who might be still on the premises at this hour... The Regent's had a very tiring journey; he's quite exhausted. I thought some hot broth? Is there anyone in the kitchens at this hour?'

'Katjie, the cook, I'd imagine. Preparing tomorrow's meals. The children had snert with a little bacon crumbled in it at supper. If there's any left I'm sure it could be quickly heated up. I'll go and see,' said Roel Mulder. His rather rigid expression suggested that the commission was inconvenient. However, he gave no hint of refusal, but turned and left, closing the door behind him.

'That's exactly the kind of fellow,' said Maarten de Hoop, mumbling into the muffler he had not yet removed, 'a smooth talker like that, I'd expect Margriet to go off with.'

'Surely not!' exclaimed the Pastor. 'He's been here all along. Teaching the children, just as you asked him to. A very able fellow, I think. The children have responded well to his teaching. Has some unusual methods, I'll grant you. Why, he's taken them to the town hall to learn about civic government, and even up into one of the windmills to learn how the mechanism works. He showed me some of the reports they've written, and they've obviously learned a great deal. Things I didn't know myself! You *can't* be imagining…?

'That Margriet's *here*, all along, somewhere in Shiedam? Hiding out? Seeing this fellow behind my back? While I traipse off to Amsterdam like a fool, trying to find her? It wouldn't surprise me. I can think of no other explanation. Can you?'

'No, surely, Marten, that *cannot* be. You're over-wrought, worn out. It's not conceivable!' But was it? What did de Hoop, what did *anyone* know of this Roel Mulder?

'If they were having a liaison someone would have seen them,' the pastor continued. 'It's not *possible* to keep that kind of thing secret in a town like Schiedam. Where could they meet? From whom could they hire a room, man? Mevrouw de Hoop is well known in the town – anything unusual, anything…*scandalous*, everyone here knows of it in a trice!'

But even as he said this Jacob Winkelmann realised that although many people knew or suspected Margriet de Hoop of immoral behaviour, everyone pretended they didn't for her husband's sake. Also, many things had happened since Maarten de Hoop's departure – so many unexpected and indeed alarming events – the murder of Henke's wife, Margriet van de Grote, the attack on the zakkendrager, Ambroos, the near fatal stabbing of Mathilde de Haan, the disappearance of the boy Tomas, the truly shocking public breakdown of Vrouw Schmit… so *many* unusual things that a spot of adultery might, just for once, have escaped the townsfolks' attention.

The door opened and Roel Mulder entered, carrying a tray which he set down on the table, being careful, the pastor was relieved to see, not to dislodge the piles of coins.

'There you are, Regent,' he said, deferentially, still playing the butler, 'A bowl of soup with rye bread and a piece of Gouda – and a hot gin and lemon. I trust that will revive you, Sir. I was intending to sleep here tonight, in the room off the senior boy's dormitory. Quite a few of the youngsters have caught this cold that's going around, so I feel I should be available. Send for me if either of you need anything further.'

Something in the cool tightness of his tone, though polite, suggested that he would much prefer that they didn't. Roel Mulder evidently had other things on his mind.

Chapter 35

Tomas and Roel Mulder Exchange Confidences

'Sir? Heer Mulder?'

Tomas had discovered the teacher sitting at his desk in the deserted schoolroom, puzzling over a letter to which he was in the process of composing a reply. A candle at his elbow guttered in the draught from the open door.

'Yes, Tomas, what do you want? Why aren't you in bed?'

Tomas wasn't sure which of these two questions he should answer. He stood for a moment, stepping from foot to foot in his ungainly boots. They fitted him better than they once had, but he still felt awkward in them. He twined his fingers around one another.

'Sir, the Pastor sent me,' he said, hoping that answered question number two. 'He called to me in the corridor and asked me to get you to come, Sir.'

'Come where?'

'To the Regent's office. Someone is there, and he wants you.'

'Do you know who?'

'No, Sir, he didn't say. There was someone, a man I think, sitting there. I could see him when the door was open.'

'And how did you happen to be in the corridor near the Regent's office? When you ought to be in bed?'

'I was walking back from the privy, Sir. I share a room downstairs with Casper.'

'Yes, so I gather. Several people have told me you ought to be in the dormitory now your skin complaint has healed, but I suppose we haven't time to discuss that now.' He rose to his feet, 'I'd better go and see what Pastor Winkelmann wants. We'll talk about your sleeping arrangements some other time, eh?'

'No, Sir.'

'No?'

Tomas took a deep breath. 'Please Sir; I'd like to talk *now*. About Casper, I'm worried about him. He's ill... but I'll wait. I'll wait until you come back, Sir.'

Roel Mulder looked at Tomas for a long minute, and then he

placed his pen in the inkwell and walked towards the door. 'Very well, I'll attend to what the Pastor wants. I'll come back as soon as I can.'

Tomas went to the stool he habitually used, at Casper's special table, and seated himself. He folded his arms on the desk top and settled down to wait. And wait. And worry. He ought to have told Casper about this errand. Casper might be fretting, unable to settle down and sleep, wondering where his friend had gone and what he was doing. Casper's chest was bothering him. He was struggling to breathe, particularly at night, and although Heer Mulder had mentioned sending for the doctor, no doctor had come.

Tomas had said to Casper, 'I'm going to ask Heer Mulder about the doctor. Maybe he forgot.'

'Maybe he's too busy... the doctor that is,' Casper wheezed. 'I heard Dirk say there's lot of people sick in the town. Even Pastor Winkelmann's got a fearsome cold. He was sneezing so much when he said grace... before lunch today... that he never had his head out of his nose-rag long enough to spot you! I expect Doctor Saunders'll come when he has time.'

Tomas decided this wasn't good enough. *A cold*, he thought scornfully, a cold is a *nothing*. (Not that he ever caught colds himself). Most people could get over a cold without any doctoring, but not Casper. If the infection goes to his chest, with his twisted spine and crushed lungs, he wouldn't be able to breathe. If he couldn't breathe he'd *die*. He'd talked to Saskia about this, but Saskia was coming down with the cold too, and feeling sorry for herself.

All she could say, or rather croak, was, 'I'd better stay away from him. He was like this last winter, and all the doctor did was send out for some medicine from Heer Rijnsberger. It worked then, so perhaps – *atishoo!* – it will again.'

Casper insisted it didn't matter, don't worry, but Tomas did. He decided to speak to Heer Mulder if he could catch him alone, and Pastor Winkelmann's summons had given him his first opportunity.

So he sat in the cold schoolroom, lit by a single candle, and waited. He tried to concentrate on the map of South Holland that Heer Mulder had left hanging on the blackboard easel, reciting the names of the rivers, and then the towns along those rivers, to keep himself awake. But he couldn't see it very well by the light of one wavering candle, and gradually his eyelids began to droop and his head fell forward onto his folded arms. Tomas, keeping his lonely vigil, slept.

Time elapsed. Heer Mulder, not at all delighted at the return of the Regent, never the less carried out the errand. Katjie in the kitchen (to his surprise she was not delighted either) 'Oh, trust him! Just when we've about got ourselves straight!' made up a tray of food and heated a tankard of gin and lemon. He delivered it. Then, having forgotten all about Tomas, he returned to the schoolroom and his correspondence, deep in thought.

The candle had by now melted down within the base of the candlestick, its wick floating in melted grease, and little light now penetrated beyond the edge of his desk. Roel Mulder sat and turned his attention to the letter that was perplexing him. It had arrived two days ago at the lodging house, but his cousin, Vrouw Hauberk, had only today sent her maidservant round to the orphanage with it. It was from a fellow thespian and it brought him news of a possible engagement. An opportunity to tour Holland and other parts of the Low Countries in a production of Macbeth! Tempting, very tempting.

Hamlet was very familiar to the people of the Netherlands, but he knew Macbeth, perhaps because of a poor translation, or because the first actor ever to essay the lead had dropped dead of a heart attack in mid-performance, had never been so popular. However, someone was mounting a new production, and it seemed his acquaintance had already secured a part (his handwriting was atrocious). Unfortunately, whilst celebrating this triumph a little too lavishly he'd slipped and broken a leg, so would his old comrade Roel be willing to substitute for him for a few weeks while the leg healed?

Roel Mulder was surprised to discover himself to be in a dilemma. Never before had he considered refusing *any* part. Should he accept, abandoning the weeshuis and the orphans for his former, true, profession? On re-reading the crossed lines with care, he saw that it wasn't a particularly splendid part. And if he left before the month was out he thought it unlikely that the weeshuis governors would pay him. The main role was as one of Macbeth's henchmen, who later becomes First Murderer. First Murderer! Heer Mulder smiled wryly, recalling a previous occasion when he'd been cast in this play. Wasn't First Murderer required to cut the throat of MacDuff's young son? Was he to go straight from playing stern but kindly schoolmaster to snuffer out of infant lives? Well, some would say... A rueful chuckle escaped him.

At this sudden sound in the empty room Tomas stirred in his sleep, and then raised his head to gaze heavy-eyed at the teacher.

'Ah, Tomas. You're still here. Come and tell me quickly what it was you wanted to say. You ought to be in bed.'

Tomas rose to his feet and came and stood before the master's desk, hands clasped behind his back. Roel Mulder regarded him. Tousled hair, grimy face, two buttons missing from his jacket. Poor child, poor children! The care of these orphaned mites had been sadly neglected these last few weeks.

'Casper is your particular friend and you feel responsible for him, don't you?'

'Sir, I don't want him to die.'

'You think he may?'

'Yes, Sir, if he doesn't get medicine soon. You said you'd send for Doctor Saunders, Sir, but he hasn't been yet.'

'I did send for him, Tomas, after Matron Schmit... left us, but I'd a message back that he, too, is suffering from this heavy cold and fever that so many people in the town seem to have caught. He didn't want to bring the infection here. Do you know if there are other doctors in Schiedam? You see, Tomas, I'm not a native of this place, I don't know Schiedam well.'

'*I* don't know any doctors, Sir,' replied Tomas, sleepy and puzzled. He'd always thought that those who didn't live on boats stayed in the towns where they were born unless they went to live in one of the big cities like Amsterdam or Rotterdam, but it seemed Heer Mulder knew even less of Schiedam than he did. 'But we could ask Heer Rijnsberger to come?'

'Heer Rijnsberger?'

'He's the apoth ... apothecary, Sir. He comes sometimes, to bring medicines. Saskia told me so. She reckons he'd know what Casper ought to have. He would, wouldn't he?'

'I suppose he would, since he supplies the medicines,' said Roel Mulder slowly, 'but perhaps it isn't up to us to send for him now that the Regent has returned? Can it wait until the morning?'

Tomas's face crumpled and he dropped his chin, but he wouldn't allow himself to cry. Then his head came up and he met the teacher's gaze.

'No, Sir. His breathing is worse than I've ever heard it, and his cheeks are burning. I'm sure he has a fever. He didn't eat any supper, Sir, although I took him some soup and tried to get him to swallow...but he just turned his head away.'

'You've always looked after him, slept in his room? The Regent allows you to do this?'

'Oh, no, Sir, only since...since I came.' Tomas took a deep breath. 'The Regent doesn't know about me, Sir. I'm not supposed to be here.'

Man and boy stared at one another. The only sound was the schoolroom clock loudly ticking off the seconds in the cold empty room.

'I ran away, Sir, from my steifvader, because he beat me... and did other things. I needed somewhere to hide. I knew he wouldn't look for me here. When the Regent finds out I expect he'll send me away.' Tomas stopped, surprised to see that Heer Mulder was smiling.

'So, you're an interloper! Well, Tomas, that makes us two of a kind! I'm an interloper too. Heer de Hoop wanted to rush away and find his wife, and when I led him to believe I was a schoolmaster he hired me. But I'm afraid I told him a lie. The truth is, Tomas, I'm not a teacher at all, I'm an actor. You know what an actor is?' Tomas nodded, although he wasn't entirely certain.

'I've only ever acted the part of a school teacher in a play. I needed to earn some money you see, and I thought it might be amusing to pretend to be a teacher.'

Tomas considered this for long moment. 'Did it make you laugh, Sir?'

Roel Mulder chuckled. 'Yes, it did Tomas. Saskia, who has an answer for everything! Felix, who doesn't seem to know what the question is, never mind the answer! Mieke who practically swoons with relief when she answers correctly! *You*, fussing so importantly over Casper as though *your* life depended on it! You're a wonderful bunch! But Tomas, when that fellow came, earlier in the week, the sack porter, *he* seemed to believe you were here on Pastor Winkelmann's recommendation?'

'I know, Sir, but Henke got that wrong. Pastor Winkelmann doesn't know I'm here. He hasn't noticed me yet, but I expect he will.'

'Surely he saw you, just now, when he asked you to come and fetch me?'

'No, Sir. It was dark in the corridor. He came to the door of the Regent's office, and saw *someone* was there, and called out. He just said, "Boy!" He didn't know who I was. *Anyway*, Sir…'

Tomas took a huge inbreath and clenched his fists at the seams of his purloined orphanage britches. For Casper's sake he must keep trying, 'Sir, I think you should send for Heer Rijnsberger, *now, tonight*. I could go! I'm sure I could find his shop. It's beyond the windmill. The one you took us to see.'

'But Tomas it's dark already and I think it's beginning to snow.'

Roel Mulder knew this responsibility belonged to the Regent, but he'd seen the state the man was in, too exhausted, too wrapped up in his own trouble, surely, to deal with this right now? Damn that wretched Matrone Schmit, *she* should have been looking after these brats when they fell ill.

'I don't mind the dark, Sir. I often ran errands in the dark when…I lived on the boat.' Despite his determination, Tomas could feel tears begin to collect in his throat and behind his eyes, and sniffed loudly trying to swallow them back. Meanwhile he watched Heer Mulder, who was staring into the dying candle flame, his chin propped in his hand. Tomas stood quite still, wondering what the man would decide.

'Very well,' he said, opening the drawer in the desk and removing a fresh candle, which he lit from the last stuttering sparks of the old one. 'First let's see how Casper is. The Regent is…exhausted after his journey. If Pastor Winkelmann's still here, I'll speak to him and explain the need… if there is a need. *Then*, you and I will go together, Tomas.

Chapter 36

Roel Mulder is Unjustly Accused

Roel Mulder had never had much to do with sickness. His own health had always been robust, and living a largely rootless life, travelling from town to town (and even when settled in one place, frequently flitting from one lodging to another whenever the rent was due) he'd had little experience of illness. However, entering the dark, poky cubicle that Casper and Tomas shared so companionably, he was immediately in no doubt that the boy was seriously unwell. The whole room seemed full of the harsh sound of his laboured breathing, and when he placed a hesitant hand on his forehead it burned with fever. Casper seemed to be sleeping, and when his eyelids flickered open at his touch, he gave no indication that he knew his friend and his teacher were at his bedside.

'I found these in the storeroom and I've propped him up as much as I can, Sir,' said Tomas anxiously, and Roel Mulder saw that this was true. Tomas had somehow acquired additional shabby pillows which he'd placed around the sick boy to raise him up and ease his breathing as well as cushioning his distorted spine. 'But it doesn't seem to be helping.'

'No, Tomas, you've done your best but we need a doctor, or at the very least someone who can dispense the right medicine. It ought to be a doctor, but unless we can find where he lives, we may have to settle for the apothecary. You're sure you can find this Heer Rijnsberger, and he'll know what to proscribe? What time is it now?'

From his waistcoat pocket Roel Mulder produced his watch, and registered a moment of surprise at finding it there. Two weeks had now passed since he'd last retrieved it from the pawn shop in Amsterdam. This must be the longest spell it had spent in his possession in many months. 'If I'm not careful I'll be turning respectable in my middle years!' he thought with a rueful grimace. 'It's late already, Tomas. If we don't act soon we'll find either or both have retired to bed.'

Tomas walked over to the narrow wall shelf, and returned

holding a small brown glass bottle. 'This is what Casper had,' he said, 'but he says it doesn't do much good. We could show it to Heer Rijnsberger and then he might find something…better. Stronger?'

'It's empty. Casper's been taking this recently?'

Tomas dropped his eyes to the floor and shuffled his feet. 'No, Sir. He said it didn't help, and then… Well, you see, Sir, Saskia told everyone I had a skin disease, so that no one would ask why I was sleeping downstairs…'

'*Scabies,* or so she led me to believe?'

'Well I didn't, not really, but you see Sir, when we have our baths, I had to have something to…dab on my skin. Otherwise Dirk would have known it wasn't true. Casper didn't mind, Sir! Truly! He said it didn't work for his chest, so I might as well.'

'So you used it all up on your imaginary skin disease.'

'Yes Sir. Casper thought it was a clever joke to play on Dirk. Dirk isn't very kind to him, he calls him 'the cripple' and he always pretends he's going to drop him when he's getting him in and out of the bathtub. But I'm really sorry now, Sir, because if there was any left we could've tried to get Casper to swallow it, and it *might* have helped….'

'But it might not. At least we could show this apothecary fellow what *doesn't* work.' He looked down on the sleeping boy, whose breathing sounded ever harsher to his ears. Was he sleeping? Or had he already slipped into an unconscious state from which he might never wake? Roel Mulder didn't have sufficient knowledge to judge, and feared the worst. 'Tomas, you stay here with him for the moment. I'll go and find either the Regent if he is still about – or Pastor Winkelmann if he hasn't already gone. Either of them should know where this Doctor Saunders resides.'

At first he thought the Regent's office was empty. The fire had burned down and one of the oil lamps was flaring sluggishly, its wick now in dire need of trimming, sending dancing shadows around the room. The coins the Pastor had been so industriously counting were still set out on the table although some of the piles had toppled into one another. He turned to leave, but then a soft snoring sound alerted him and he realised that someone was seated in the armchair; his head sunk low on his chest. The creak of the opening door must have penetrated the sleeper's consciousness.

Maarten de Hoop sat up suddenly.

'What? Who's there?'

'I'm sorry to disturb you, Regent. Roel Mulder here. I daresay Pastor Winkelmann will have told you we're without Matron Schmit? And Casper, one of the boys – you'll know who I mean of course – has fallen sick, and I wonder if you could give me the address of Doctor Saunders? I want to fetch him.'

To his astonishment, Maarten de Hoop leapt from his chair shouting, 'You! Scoundrel! *Where is my wife?* Winkelmann keeps insisting… but you're *just* the kind of villain she'd fall for! A smooth and slimy toad! All that fol-de-rol about being a schoolmaster fallen upon hard times! How many weeks had you been here in Schiedam laying siege to Margriet before you came sidling up to me wanting a job? You overheard van Corte, that morning in the café, encouraging me to leave for Amsterdam. You *knew* it was safe to come here. Carrying on, I wouldn't wonder, under this very roof! No doubt Margriet suggested it, damn her eyes!'

Roel Mulder was rarely dumbfounded, but the words that came spewing forth from the Regent's mouth rendered him speechless. That de Hoop should have discovered that he was not a schoolmaster and be extremely angry at the deception, he could have understood. But where on earth did Vrouw de Hoop whom he'd never met, come into it? Roel Mulder was an actor. His tongue was ever smooth, he never stammered, but now he found himself doing so, 'W-what, who? Sir, I've no idea…'

'*You* know where my wife is. Waiting for you in some sordid room in the back streets, I suppose?' Vaguely, Roel Mulder observed that the Regent's food tray remained on a side table, untouched, and wondered how ill the man was?

He pulled himself up to his full height and marshalled the spirit in which he'd comported himself when cast on one occasion, as Napoleon. (He'd been roundly booed; memories are long in the Low Countries)

'Sir! You insult me! I have a…a… sick child in my care, whose life is in danger!' (In the play he'd said he had no time to waste as he had a battle to fight, but it amounted to the same thing) 'I can only think that you have been imbibing strong drink. Go to your bed, Sir, and in the morning, when you're sober, I trust you'll render me an apology!'

'You lie, Sir! I feel sure you know where Margriet is...'

Roel Mulder spun on his heel and made to stride from the room. His exit was spoiled by finding himself immediately chest to chest in the dim corridor with a man he couldn't at first place. Then he realised he'd seen him before, on two occasions, once during that fateful coffee shop encounter, and once during the equally fateful attempt to remove the inebriated Matrone from the premises. He was Heer Directeur Dries van Corte, stylishly clad as always despite a heavily bandaged hand. With him was Jacob Winkelmann.

'Ah, Heer Mulder, Heer van Corte is here from the Infirmary. I was so worried about our Regent,' babbled the Pastor, 'he seems not himself at all.'

'So I observe,' said the schoolmaster in fierce tones for he was still in Napoleonic vein, 'he's just accused me, *me*, of seducing his wife! Gentlemen, I've never met his wife!'

'How fortunate for you, Sir,' stated van Corte wearily, 'Margriet's whereabouts have become something of an obsession with our unhappy friend.'

'*My* concern is young Casper. He's not at all well. I want to fetch the doctor. Do you know where he lives?'

Jacob Winkelmann looked perplexed. On those occasions when he needed a doctor, he sent his housekeeper out with a message.

'Doctor Saunders *was* at St Jacob's a while ago,' offered the Directeur, languidly waving his wounded hand, as he moved into the room, and stood behind the Regent, laying a soothing hand on the afflicted man's shoulder, 're-dressing this wound of mine, and I know he was visiting that zakkendrager fellow, who ought to be discharged but is feigning. His wife's a virago apparently. You *might* catch him there.'

'I'll do that,' decided Roel Mulder, turning, once more, to go.

'Really, I wouldn't waste time on it,' drawled Dries van Corte 'he lives at quite a distance, out on the Rotterdam road. The apothecary would do just as well. That boy isn't long for this world anyway. You must realise with such a degree of deformity it's only a matter of time. *Don't*, I beg of you, grow too attached to him. If we behaved rationally we would see that such children don't survive infancy, drown them at birth as we would the deformed runt of a litter of pups.'

So stunned was Roel Mulder by this heartless speech that he paused opened-mouthed in the doorway, unable to find words to respond.

'You should drink your gin and lemon,' van Corte was bending over the Regent, apparently dismissing Mulder from his mind. 'You haven't touched it. It would do you good.'

Maarten de Hoop stirred restlessly in his chair. 'Can't stomach it. For all I know this...this *interloper*, has poisoned it, the better to have his way with my wife!'

This brought Roel Mulder to a sudden halt. Furious, he turned again, snatched the tankard and downed the contents. It was a dramatic gesture from a man who frequently made dramatic gestures for a living, and he thought nothing of it.

Determinedly, he strode forth into the corridor to return to the sick room. Half way there he observed that such lamps were lit seemed to be dimming. He had time to wonder why this should be. Then he began to sense that his legs were no longer able to support him, and darkness closed in.

Chapter 37

Joop Barends Acts Over and Above the Call of Duty

Although Vos was clearly embarrassed to have been outwitted by Ignaas, and must have known full well that he owed his junior officer an apology, he wasn't a man who ever admitted he was wrong.

'Those fools!' he blustered, as the three policemen sat over the remains of a herring supper in the lodging house that evening, 'if they'd only warned me about that hoist mechanism! If they hadn't then all started rushing about, blocking the stairway, we'd have recaptured van Damme easily! Anyway, he can't have gone far. We'd better alert all the mills. Have them searched. It's an obvious place for the man to go to earth, amongst all those sacks of grain. Under cover, dry; warm even, now the weather has turned bitter. Why they took so long to notice he was there is a mystery to me, especially when their mid-day snacks began to go missing. Addlepated fools, the lot of them!

'Search the windmills, Sergeant? Every one of 'em?' gloomed Josef van Dyke, lighting one of his evil-smelling cheroots. 'Have you any idea how many there are in this town? Around twenty or so I've been told. Can three of us search twenty mills?'

'Of course not. No, I'll ask, I'll *demand*,' huffed Vos, 'that the managers have some of their men do it. Barends!' he barked suddenly, 'Find me the names of the four or five nearest to the Walvisch. You know some of the mill hands by sight now. Go immediately, *now*, find which taverns they frequent, and get a list. I can't see Ignaas going much further afield. He's stealing to eat. He doesn't have money. He doesn't have his boat. He'll need to rest up now you've been daft enough to put that bullet in his shoulder.'

Barends swallowed his last mouthful, got to his feet, wound a scarf around his neck, commandeered van Dyke's kepi (his own uniform cap was beyond saving) and trudged out. His head was clearer. His cold was on the mend, but his spirits were fast in the mud at the bottom of the Korte Haven. To think that he'd actually *caught* that man! And then Vos had come bumbling up, bellowing orders (stupid orders as it turned out) and ruined everything. The credit for capturing Ignaas should have been his, Barends, but now he knew that instead, once they got back to Rotterdam, all he'd hear would be unpleasant questions about why he'd fired that shot. Life was so unfair!

It was twilight and colder than ever. He plodded along the Lang Haven, intending to cut through Walvisstrat and knock up Wenders the miller (why trail around the taverns when Heer Wenders was sure to know the names of rival mills?) But so wrapped up was he in his muffler and his sense of ill-usage, that he completely missed the turning, and found himself, to his surprise, climbing the slope to the Koemarkt Bridge.

The bridge was open; Cornelius de Haan was on the other side of the canal, fussily supervising the last few boats of the day as they made their way through. Barends stood and watched as he exchanged angry words with an unknown binnenschipper who wanted a berth inside the Haven, although Cornelius was insisting none were free.

No one seems to like de Haan, he thought, so cocksure, so certain he knows it all, and this brought him back to his gloomy reflections on his superior officer, Anders Vos, another one who thinks he knows it all! But even as his musings strayed in that direction his eye was caught by a furtive movement behind the Bridge Watcher's back. A young lady in an old fashioned poke bonnet had stepped out cautiously from a side door into the street behind Cornelius and paused (alarmed?) as though she hadn't realised that there might be people around at this hour to observe her. However, instead of retreating, she sidled around the corner into the mouth of a passageway, drawing her dark cloak close about her. Concealed there, should Cornelius happen to turn his head, he'd never see her. Strange, thought Joop Barends, this must surely be Miss Mathilde de Haan? According to Vos, earlier today she'd been too weak to rise from her bed. Yet here she is wandering abroad. Whatever can she be up to?

He hoped against hope that Cornelius would go away, (so that he could ask her) and sure enough, the Bridge Watcher and his scrawny assistant brought the two halves of the bridge down with a satisfying thump, leaving the belligerent binnenschipper on the wrong side of both bridge and argument. Then Cornelius, lantern in hand, beak of a nose in the air, and without even wishing his assistant 'goede nacht' stalked away down the opposite slope towards the Appelmarkt. He never even glanced towards the passageway where his niece was hiding.

'Miss Mathilde de Haan?' Joop Barends marched across the bridge and straight up to the girl who gasped aloud, and pulled her fur muff across her face. He doffed his borrowed kepi. 'May I ask what you're doing out here, Miss?' Mattie said nothing, gazing at him in horror. 'I'd been given to understand, Miss de Haan, that you've been seriously ill. It's a very cold night,' he went on; 'Surely you shouldn't be out of doors?' He waited, partly because he couldn't think of anything else to say. (She had the most remarkable eyes!)

Miss Mattie tossed her head and returned his stare, defiantly. 'It's true I've been ...unwell, *officer*, but I'm much better, thank you. I wanted a little fresh air to help me sleep. There's no law against that is there?'

'No, Miss, but it's very cold, and too late don't you think for your first outing?' He grinned at her. He reminded himself that she was the victim of a crime and not a criminal. He mustn't frighten her. 'I'd understood from my colleagues, Sergeant Vos and Corporal van Dyke, that you were still very weak.'

'Oh, them!' said Mattie, scornfully. 'They, *you*, the Police, caught that man, van Damme, this afternoon did you not? My Aunt told me. So I know it's quite safe for me to go out. And I do so want... to get out of the house and get some air!'

'Err... well, Miss, actually *no*. Ignaas van Damme *was* captured, but unfortunately he escaped. So we of the Police would really prefer you to stay safe indoors. For the present, that is.' Joop Barends tried to make this statement sound as official as possible, although he wondered why he was being so loyal. Damn Vos! (Until today Barends had never been swearing man, not even under his breath).

Mattie's eyes widened. 'Oh dear, I didn't know that...but it's my relatives you see, my uncle and aunt and my cousins... *Oh, can you understand?* I feel smothered by them, and yet bullied too. If I don't get away from them for a while I'll go mad!'

She had found an understanding listener in Joop Barends. As an only child, he'd been alternately mollycoddled by his mother and bullied and despised by his father. His father's words were ever present. 'You can't help being an idiot lad; but try not to be a milksop.'

'You certainly shouldn't be out alone, Miss,' he said, 'but perhaps you'd let me accompany you to a coffee house?'

Mathilde gasped, 'Oh, I couldn't! That wouldn't be...! My mother always said it wasn't...'

'A respectable thing for a young lady to do? No, but it's too cold to walk about out of doors, and if I'm with you, and perhaps if you removed your bonnet? Pulled the hood of your cloak up around your head against the cold? People here all talk about your bonnet you know? I'm sure most of them have never seen you without it. When there are so many strangers here, boat people and so forth, you probably won't even be recognised.' If Barends was surprised to hear himself offering this invitation, he didn't stop to think about it.

Mattie lowered her muff. 'You must know why I wear this bonnet?'

Joop Barends studied her face by the light of a lantern swaying gently on the bowsprit of a nearby boat. 'You don't need to,' he said. 'The scar's nothing! Really! It just looks as though a moth has settled on your face. You shouldn't hide it, it's rather...attractive.' He'd never said such a thing to a young lady before. He said it earnestly. And because it was true.

'Very well,' said Miss Mattie, untying her bonnet strings, pulling on her hood and taking his arm, as though this was the most natural thing in the world. 'Can we walk a little way up Broersvest? I'd prefer one not too close in case my uncle should come by.'

It was already late; the coffee shop they chose was more or less deserted. An ancient fellow, a retired zakkendrager by his smock, sat in a corner smoking his long-stemmed clay pipe and paying no attention to newcomers. Only two lamps burned at opposite ends of the dark wood-lined room. The waitress, a plump bundle in oil-stained apron, her grey hair straggling down from an untidy knot, was engaged in poring paraffin into the base of a third lamp which stood on a table at the rear of the shop.

'Yes?' she demanded without looking up, none too pleased to have late customers.

'Two coffees Ma'am, and *err*, if you still have it, two slices of your apple cake?'

'Where were you planning to go, Miss, sneaking out in the dark like that?' Joop Barends asked, as soon as they were alone at a table with their coffee. Two slices of apple cake were set on a chipped dish before them.

'Out,' she replied, shrugging and nibbling cake, 'just...out, *anywhere*. I've been lying in bed for nearly two weeks. I wanted to see if my feet might carry me as far as the mail-coach office tomorrow. They gave me far too much laudanum, you know? I wanted to tell that fool of an apothecary so when he came sneaking round while my uncle was out.' She sighed. 'It wasn't entirely his fault; I pretended I was much sicker than I was.'

'Why?' asked Barends, who never attempted subtlety.

'I don't know,' said Mattie. A tear leaked from the corner of her eye, and she dabbed it fiercely with a crumpled handkerchief. 'My spirits have been so dreadfully low, even before that dreadful man attacked me. I thought he was going to kill me... and then I wished he had. I just wanted... not to be *here*, in this boring town, living with my aunt and uncle and my stupid cousins!'

'Whe' d'you wanna be?' he enquired, masticating cake (which was better than the appearance of the proprietor and her shop had suggested).

'Amsterdam!' said Mattie, her face brightening. 'And now I can! When he heard I'd been stabbed, old Rombouts who was my father's lawyer, came to find out whether I was likely to recover or not. He said they must on no account let me die, because I'm an heiress! Imagine! You know that my parents were killed in a railway accident just outside the station here in Schiedam? Well, it seems Papa made some good investments, and now they're worth a lot of money.'

'Uhn,' grunted Barends, because the cake was sticking to the roof of his mouth.

'That's why I want to find the mail-coach office. I want to go back to Amsterdam, but I'm frightened... after the train crash. I know the train would get me there in less than a day, but I can't face it.' Her large eyes met his, seeking reassurance.

'Can unner...stand that you'd be scared, after wha' happened,' agreed Barends. 'We came down... on the train, from Rot...dam.' He grinned, and swallowed cake. 'I liked it, but I can understand how you'd feel. What are you planning to do when you get there?'

'Go home,' said Mattie. 'The house has been let out... since the accident, but Heer Rombouts says the most recent tenants are gone.' She took a deep breath and winced slightly as the lingering pain caught in her chest. 'So the house is mine again. I'll engage a maid...and someone to do the cooking...'

'And then?'

'I'll start a school, a school for girls, young women.'

Joop Barends blinked. '*A school?* Whatever for? If you're an heiress, like you said?'

'Why not? I want to! I shall have them all learn the sciences! Biology, chemistry, anatomy! People think young women can't learn such things, but they're wrong! I shall teach them as my father taught me. Then they shall all have careers – as scientists, apothecaries, and teachers. Perhaps even Doctors!'

Joop Barends' mouth sagged open. To him such ambitions were unimaginable – for members of either sex, 'These young women,' he asked, doubtfully, 'are they what they call "bluestockings?"'

'I suppose so. I do believe that in twenty years from now, we shall have the first woman doctor here in the Netherlands, and I'm going to help that to happen!'

Tonight, in her shabby cloak, with her face partly hidden within her hood, Barends thought she could be easily mistaken for some drab young creature from one of the tumbledown hovels that crowded around the skirts of the distilleries. He blew out his cheeks, baffled as always by the remarkable things that seemed to go on in the minds of other people.

'Wouldn't *you* like to do something amazing like that? Or your sister?' she demanded.

'Not me! And I don't have a sister. I know I wouldn't like to have to do some of the things a doctor has to do.' He shuddered, recalling sights he'd seen as a policeman, the mangled limbs of children run over by carts, men crushed in machinery at their work. 'I've always wanted to join the Maréchaussée.'

'You enjoy your work? Catching villains?'

His shoulders sagged, and he sighed long and deep. 'I was over the moon at catching Ignaas – and then my boss, Anders Vos, ruined it all!'

'No! Why? How?'

Joop Barends sat for a time, head bowed, staring at his boots, fiddling with his coffee spoon. 'I suppose it was partly my fault. I was just so surprised – after I shot him, and really you know, that was a fluke, I never meant to hit him – I didn't think to tell the mill workers to fasten his hands *behind* him. So when Sergeant Vos told them to untie his feet and walk him down the stairs... although his hands were bound, he could still grasp the rope on one of those hoist affairs they have for raising and lowering the grain sacks, and swing himself down through the opening in the floor. Then everyone collided with one another in the doorway and on the stairs. He was long gone by the time they got to the bottom.'

'But if you wounded him...? Surely he won't get far?'

'I don't think I did him *much* damage. I hope not because I'll probably be up on a charge when we get back to barracks.' Vos hadn't actually said so, but both he and van Dyke had treated him to pursed-lipped disapproval. 'We're not supposed to shoot people,' he explained, 'all I was trying to do was warn him. He threw his knife at me... and I just fired without thinking.'

'You can't have hurt him very badly, not if he could still cling to the rope and swing himself down. Otherwise he'd have fallen and been killed, wouldn't he?'

'People do attempt some really desperate things when they're trapped,' Barends said, gloomily.

'Yes,' acknowledged Mattie in a small voice. 'They do. Or at least they *think* of attempting something desperate, I know I have. Did the Police ever find the little boy who ran off? Tomas? He'd been badly beaten, poor little fellow, and then my uncle frightened him half to death... he must have been terrified to run off like that.'

'No, he disappeared. Sergeant Vos has had us ask around of course, but we've received no reports of sightings. Vos thinks Ignaas must have killed him, and got rid of the body.'

'Oh, how dreadful...' Mattie began, when they were interrupted.

'Hoy, youse two! I wanna shut shop!' said the slatternly woman, swiping at their table with a grubby cloth. 'Out you go, back to your stinking barge or wherever you came from, the pair o' you!'

Joop Barends took up his (no, van Dyke's) uniform cap and settled it on his head in a pointed rebuke. 'Certainly, *Ma'am*. This *lady* has been most helpful to the police with their inquiries.'

'I don't think she was impressed!' giggled Mattie, as they left the shop.

'You're even prettier when you laugh,' said Barends.

They walked companionably arm in arm up Broersvest. Mattie prattled of her plans for the future (those who'd seldom heard her speak would have been astonished at this fountain of words). Joop Barends listened without comment, happy only to be escorting such a charming young lady. Brief flurries of snow were beginning to settle in the roadway and they quickened their steps until reaching the Koemarkt where they came to a sudden halt.

A fight was in progress. A fight that at first appeared most unequal, being between a large lumbering fellow armed with a short bladed knife and a slight youth shod in a single boot. But as they approached, the lad fended off the older man, dashed into a wooden lean-to next to the baker's shop, and emerged with an armful of logs which he began to pitch at his opponent's head. Most missed their target, but as the man roared and lunged at his young adversary, a log rolled beneath his feet and brought him down on his back amidst howls of agony. His knife flew from his hand and skittered away across the cobbles. The youth dropped his ammunition, and hurled himself astride the stomach of his fallen foe.

'Got 'im for yer!' panted Piet, as Barends rushed forward, his hand once more on the butt of his pistol. "E wus tryin' to pinch my spot, Meester. *I* kips in ol' Maurits's wood store, an' 'e came an' tried to kick me out!'

Barends' words rolled off his tongue more easily this time, 'Ignaas van Damme you're under arrest!' A small crowd began to form. Mattie was at his elbow, the baker and his assistant in their nightshirts came hurrying up, roused by the noise. All round the square shutters were thrust back, doors were flung open and heads poked out.

'I niver killed nobody,' gasped the fallen man. 'An' yer can't prove I did!'

Chapter 38

What Ignaas (and Everyone Else) Had to Say

'He'll go before the firing squad,' pronounced Cornelius (he would turn up to remind them of his status as a member of the Watch Committee, thought Barends. He and Vos were two of a kind.). 'But what should we do with him in the meanwhile?'

'The Steen?' Barends had no idea where Vos would put the prisoner. Clearly he couldn't be stashed in the home for fallen women, like the luckless Vrouw Schmit.

'Doubt if it's secure,' said Aarte the glassblower who'd joined those assembled around the fallen binnenschipper. Several of them were in their nightclothes under hastily donned cloaks and greatcoats. The hard-working burgers of Schiedam retired early and rose with the dawn.

'The castle's been falling down for years,' Maurits explained to Barends, fastening his topcoat and pulling his nightcap down over his chapped ears. 'Ever since the Countess Aleida built it in days long forgotten or so I understand.'

'Us could shut 'im one of the bread ovens?' offered Augustijn. 'Us don' fire 'em up 'til four of the clock.'

An argument broke out between those for and against this suggestion.

'Silence!' roared Barends. He waved the pistol at them to underline his point. 'This man's under arrest. It's for the Maréchaussée to deal with him.'

'Well I ain't goin' to fetch yer big chief *this* time!' said Piet, shifting his position onto the captive's chest. 'I went last time, and ye dafties let 'im go!'

Mattie, who'd retreated behind Barends on the arrival of her uncle, stretched out a slippered foot to prod at Ignaas. 'What have you done with that boy of yours, you wicked, *wicked* creature?' she demanded. Barends was startled to realise what the lace-edged garment now visible beneath her cloak must be. He blushed. He'd not only daringly escorted a young female to a coffee house, but one who'd absconded from her home with only a cloak thrown over her nightdress! He could only be grateful it was too dark for his embarrassment to be observed.

'Ain't done nothin' to 'im!' Ignaas grunted in reply. 'Saw 'im a while back at t'mill. All dressed up 'e was…in…some kind o' *uni…form*…an' he dint come to no harm from 'is fall neither. …I sees him jump down from that tree an' go off with 'is pals.' His speech was becoming faint and slurred, and those standing around crowded forward, struggling to make any sense of this. His eyes rolled back in his head and his breathing was becoming laboured.

'Perhaps,' said Barends, rather alarmed, 'you should leave off sitting on his chest, Piet.'

'Olright,' said Piet, 'what's it worth then? If I goes fer yer big boss man?'

'No, no, it should be someone *responsible*!' Cornelius interrupted. Not wishing to go himself Barends guessed. He looked around the assembled company but found no volunteers. His niece's presence de Haan hadn't, thank goodness, yet registed. Joop Barends rooted in his pockets. 'Piet did it before,' he told Cornelius, 'so he knows who he's looking for.' Unfortunately his pockets came up empty. He'd spent every stuiver he had buying coffee and cake for Miss Mattie.

'Sorry, Piet, I'm cleaned out.' He looked meaningfully at her uncle, but the Bridge Watcher avoided his eye. As did everyone.

At this impasse, a tall figure in an unstable top hat wobbled into view astride his velocipede 'What's going on here?' demanded Frans Rijnsberger. He was returning from delivering medicines to a sick patient.

'We've caught 'im! Ignaas!' answered a dozen voices. 'Him that's murdered more than a few!'

'I never!' said Ignaas protested weakly.

'He's been injured?' Frans dismounted and handed the velo to Piet to hold. Piet seized on it enthusiastically, bestrode it, and pushed off. 'I'll get yer boss for yer!' he yelled over his shoulder to Barends, and careered away before its owner could protest.

Frans, however, had just spotted Mattie, and was gawking at her in astonishment.

'I'm better!' she snapped. 'I'd have been up and about sooner if you hadn't overdosed me on laudanum. And don't waste those sheep's eyes on me, either.' Frans' face fell, and Barends felt sorry for him.

'Shall us move *'im* indoors?' queried Augustijn, whose bulging knees below the hem of his nightshirt were turning blue. He prodded at Ignaas's ribs with the toe of his clog.

'Yes. Get up you, and walk!' commanded Maurits the baker.

'Doubt I can,' said the fallen binnenschipper, subsiding onto the cobbles once more. 'Think I've broke summat.' Even in the weak light of the various lanterns the neighbours had brought to the scene, Barends could see he looked grey with pain and fatigue.

'In that case, better not. We don't want him dying on us before we can put him on trial,' he told the crowd. 'If he has broken his back, we need to get him to the hospital.'

'Chain him fast to the bed when you get him there!' opined Maurits. 'He's wily bastard!'

Murmurs of agreement rose from the assembled company.

'He's faking it, to be sure!'

'Who cares about his back, let him die of it!'

'He never thinks of others when he's slashing at 'em with that knife of his!'

'A stretcher,' said Frans, dragging his thoughts back from Miss Mattie's cruel dismissal, 'to carry him indoors somewhere. Otherwise we'll all be down with inflammation of the lungs.' Snowflakes, though they melted as they met the slick wet cobbles, were falling more thickly now.

'The wood store,' decided Maurits. 'The wife won't want his sort in the house. I'll let Piet come in the kitchen for tonight. She don't care for him either, says nothing smells worse than that young urn's feet, but better Piet than *this* fellow.'

'Doesn't Piet have a home?' asked Barends, who had been wondering about this since his first encounter with Piet on Westvest.

'No,' said a number of voices, flatly. 'Leastways, he does by rights,' explained Maurits, 'being as his mother has a room down by the harbour, but mostly she's *entertaining*, plying her trade, if you take my meaning, and she don't want Piet underfoot. I let him sleep in the wood store many a night. It's warm and dry.'

Finding something suitable to convey the fallen rogue to the shelter of the wood store took time. Several trips to nearby houses produced hempen flour bags (too small) tablecloths (fabric not strong enough) and a cracked door (liable to break in half) until finally Aarte went unwillingly, unlocked his workshop and brought forth the little cart on which Ignaas's first victim, (if he would ever admit it), Ambroos, had been transported to the infirmary, nearly two weeks before.

Heaving the stricken binnenschipper onto it proved more than difficult. At every attempt the man struggled and howled that his back was broken. Barends, having witnessed the fall, doubted this, but the apothecary insisted it was possible. They should proceed with the greatest caution. 'If the spinal cord is severed, he'll die, that's certain.' Several of the onlookers, growing cold and wet in their nightgowns, retreated to their homes and left the two men to it. Mattie had retreated to a sheltering doorway, wrapping her cloak tightly around her. Ignaas continued to resist.

'Co-operate, you fool!' snarled Frans at last. 'We can't leave you here. Cold is injurious, even to those in good health. At Sint Jacob's they often lose elderly patients to its effects. However, I don't believe there's a single bed available there, not somewhere where he could be kept securely. There's so much sickness about, chest complaints, and the staff are run off their feet.' Ignaas, however, showed no signs of co-operating, and the apothecary and the policeman paused in their efforts to catch their breaths.

'No!' shrieked Miss Mattie from her doorway refuge, as the fallen man suddenly leapt to his feet and staggered away. His back, though it clearly pained him, wasn't broken at all.

'He's getting away! After him!' cried the assembled spectators as Joop Barends and Frans leapt to intercept him.

Ignaas had a start on them, but the pain in his back must have been agonising and it caused him to lurch wildly. He was making for the Koemarkt Bridge, but hearing feet pounding close behind him, and at the same time seeing through the swirling snow figures approaching, he swerved aside to go down the slope to the canal – only to collide with Piet, returning astride the velo. Crashing sounds, and yells from both Piet and the escaping prisoner filled the air. Then Piet managed to scramble aside as both Ignaas and the velocipede slithered down into the canal, tumbling through the thin layer of ice with a tinkle and a splash.

Joop Barends stood regarding the dark hole. He took off van Dyke's cap, and tore at his hair.

'Done it again, has he?' said the owner of the cap. It was he, together with Vos who had been approaching over the bridge. Summonsed by Piet, they'd hurried along the opposite side of the Lang Haven.

Bubbles appeared on the surface of the dark water. The rim of one of the velocipede's wheels could just be discerned, but of Ignaas van Damme there was no sign.

'Hit his head, I'd imagine,' said Frans.

'What's my *niece* doing here?' cried Cornelius, who'd only just perceived Mattie's presence.

'Ain't anybody gonna jump in and save 'im?' enquired Piet. 'I ain't. I can't swim.'

Chapter 39

Tomas Makes a Big Decision

An hour or so before the events in the cattle market square Tomas was crouching at his friend's bedside. He'd waited a long time, listening to Casper's laboured breathing. His fingernails were chewed to the quick and his own chest felt tight with worry. Surely Heer Mulder *must* come soon? Then he was startled to hear the sound of something falling outside, and tiptoed to the door, opening it a crack to peer into the dimly-lit corridor. A man lay sprawled on the floor there, and as he watched, two other men advanced and bent over him.

'I didn't have *Mulder* down for a drunkard!' said the first. Tomas recognised his voice as that of Pastor Winkelmann.

'Maarten was right, then,' said the other, sounding satisfied. 'He *had* poisoned his drink.'

'You think so? Then why did he drink it off himself?' Tomas thought the Pastor sounded both puzzled and upset.

Peeking through the crack, he studied this other man, a tall person with a bandaged hand. Presently the man straightened up so that the light from the wall bracket lit his face. Tomas knew he'd seen this well-dressed stranger before, though he had no name for him. Wasn't he one of the men who had been present the day they took Matron Schmit away in a carriage? Hairs rose on Tomas's arms. He knew nothing of this person, but instinctively mistrusted him. He could see now that the figure sprawled on the floor was Heer Mulder. What was the man with the bandaged hand talking about? This was *wrong*. Heer Mulder didn't drink, didn't smell of it, as Ignaas and other habitual drunkards did. Tomas had learned from bitter experience to recognise the signs. And why was he saying that the teacher had tried to poison someone? *Poison?* If Heer Mulder was poisoned, did that mean he was dead?

Afraid, suddenly, that this stranger might sense his presence; Tomas retreated into the room, pulling the door to as quietly as he could. Now the voices of the men in the corridor were muffled. He could barely hear them above the rasping sound of Casper's breathing, but he guessed they must be deciding what to do. There were scuffling sounds. He could hear no words. They must be lifting Heer Mulder. He heard a door creak open on the other side of the corridor. Now that they'd moved closer, he could just make out the drawling voice of the stranger saying, 'Don't worry, man, he won't die! It's probably just some form of opiate, we'll put him in here to sleep it off.'

They were carrying Heer Mulder into the storeroom; the one in which Tomas himself had once hidden. He heard the soft thud of the door being pushed open against a pile of discarded matrasses, and their muffled footsteps as they manoeuvred with their burden. With his ear pressed hard against the door panel he could just make out Pastor Winkelmann's voice, sounding more bewildered than ever, 'Don't understand,' he was saying, '...sure Mulder isn't involved with Vrouw de Hoop! ...done a very good job with the children ... always struck me as a sensible fellow. Why would he do this? Drug poor Maarten's drink? ...and then swallow it himself?'

Tomas couldn't hear what the other man replied, but his heart filled with misery and anger. *Now* what should he do? Heer Mulder had promised to go with him to find the Doctor, or failing him, Heer Rijnsberger.

He went back to Casper's bedside. His friend's breathing seemed a little quieter, but no less ragged. Tomas would have liked to wipe the perspiration from his brow, but he'd no cloth, no cooling water to wet his friend's lips, and he was afraid to make an expedition to the stand pipe. Discovery would, he was now certain, mean disaster. They would realise that he'd no right to be there and turn him out into the night. He imagined himself barred from the weeshuis and unable to get back in. If only he could call on Saskia! But an attempt to enter the girls' dormitory was unthinkable. He didn't even know where it was, never having had cause to go to the upper floor. He'd no idea where in the building the Ushers might to be found, and he shared Casper's poor opinion of them. He might have risked trying to enlist the Pastor's help, but not while the sinister stranger with the bandaged hand was with him. His presence, which he could only think was linked to the strange collapse of Heer Mulder, filled him with dismay.

'I'm sorry, Casper,' Tomas whispered, tears of frustration trickling down his cheeks, 'I'll try to get help. I will! I'll have to leave you and go for Heer Rijnsberger. I just hope I can find him!'

He heard the sound of the door to the storeroom closing and the two men's voices grew louder as they crossed the corridor.

Pastor Winkelmann was saying, 'I feel I should look in. He sleeps down here, the crippled boy. I believe the idea was that Matron Schmit would be close at hand, but of course she's here no longer. It's probably not as serious as Heer Mulder thinks, but really, poor Maarten is in a state of mental collapse. One wouldn't want him to be worried by anything more tonight.'

They were immediately outside the room. The door handle turned. They were coming in!

Before it could be thrust open, Tomas had dived under the bed onto his own tattered matrass which he stored there each day until it was time to sleep. He crouched as near to the wall as he could, and tucked his legs in close to his body, remembering the time Casper had told him that Matron Schmit would have spotted his boots if she hadn't been sozzled. He prayed that the two men wouldn't look down, and hoping that Casper's noisy breathing would cover any movements he made. For a moment he kept his eyes shut, in the superstitious hope that if he couldn't see he couldn't be seen. There was a great deal of dust beneath the bed. He pinched the bridge of his nose tightly, frightened of sneezing.

'Ah, yes, I know how concerned Maarten has always been for this boy,' Heer van Corte was saying, 'a hopeless case. I'm surprised the child has lasted as long as he has. Maarten insisted on sending for specialists to see if anything could be done – in vain of course. As I recall, he even sent for one doctor from Amsterdam. Set a lot of store by what he'd heard of him. Alas, the poor fellow and his wife were killed in the railway crash. Not that I believe for a moment that he could have done anything. Maarten can be terribly sentimental about some of these sickly children. I've wondered sometimes if it's because he and Margriet have had no children of their own.'

'I feel... perhaps a prayer?' murmured Jacob Winkelmann. 'There doesn't seem to be anything else one can do. It's so unfortunate that this should happen when the weeshuis is without a Matrone to look after the children when they fall sick. I suppose we should ask one of the servants to come and sit with him. I imagine Mulder intended to do that.'

Tomas could tell from the tone of his voice that the Pastor was unhappy, but whether this was because he was upset to see Casper so desperately ill, or by his companion's heartless words, he didn't know. He waited to hear the prayer, wondering if would be one recognised from one of his excursions to church with Mama, but it seemed Heer Winkelmann didn't intend to utter it aloud. Now he'd opened his eyes as well as his ears, Tomas could see two sets of trousered legs, and two pairs of well-polished boots. There followed a silence during which Heer Winkelmann presumably prayed, and the other man tapped his foot, impatient to be gone.

'Yes, *that's* what I shall do,' said Jacob Winkelmann, breaking the silence, having Tomas imagined, sought God's advice. 'I'll find one of the servants – not that Dirk fellow, he'd probably fall straight to sleep – one of the maids perhaps, and ask her, no I'll *tell* her she must sit with this poor lad. Perhaps two of them to keep one another company? I think that would be best. Even if nothing can be done it seems wrong to leave the poor child quite unattended. Perhaps by morning Maarten will feel able to deal with the situation? Or *you* might send the doctor round?'

'I could do that,' agreed the unknown one, 'although I think it would be a waste of his time and the town's money. However, no doubt Maarten would wish everything to be done for the boy that can be done.'

'We must go back, and get him to his bed. Perhaps you would do that, van Corte? Whilst I rustle up a couple of servants to sit with this poor little soul or at least look in on him from time to time?'

'*Yeees*, I'll do that. Persuade Maarten to take a sedative – but a lower dose than the one Heer Mulder was so intemperate as to swallow!' The man, Tomas now knew his name to be van Corte, laughed. He actually laughed aloud, and Tomas knew then that it was he and not Roel Mulder who'd drugged the Regent's drink. Although he could see nothing but their legs below the knees, Tomas sensed that the Pastor had realised it too, and was not at all amused. One pair of trousered legs tensed sharply

'You mean it was *you* who administered...?' he heard him say, but van Corte was already opening the door to leave. 'I'm afraid I must hurry,' he drawled, 'I have another appointment that I simply must keep...'

As soon as the door closed behind the two men, Tomas scuttled out from his hiding place. It must be now! Soon Pastor Winkelmann would send some of the maids to "look in on" Casper. Tomas didn't believe for a moment that they'd stay with him. There was no chair in the little room, and no space for one. He placed his fingers lightly on Casper's burning brow.

'I'm going for Heer Rijnsberger,' he said, bending close to whisper in his friend's ear in case anyone should be listening outside the door, 'before anyone stops me!'

Casper's lips moved, and he made a small sound. Tomas didn't know if he was trying to say something. It was little more than a grunt, but it cheered him to suppose that his friend knew he was there, knew he was trying to help.

'I'll be back just as quickly as I can,' he repeated. What else could he say? He wanted to ask Casper to hold on, keep breathing, *please*, *please* don't die!

He tiptoed to the door and peered out. The corridor was deserted. He waited a few more minutes to be sure no one was about, then, sparing a thought for Heer Mulder, although he dared not stop to see how he was, he sidled into the corridor, quietly pulling the door to behind him. This was his chance to go for help, and he mustn't waste it.

Chapter 40

Tomas, Running Through the Town Once Again

Carefully, quietly, he took his orphanage coat and cap from the peg in the corridor, and crept along the passageway. It was empty, all the doors closed. He slid along the wall to the entrance hall, trying hard not to make the smallest sound for fear someone should hear him, and ask what he was doing, or why he was wearing outdoor clothes at this time of night? The front door, to his surprise, stood slightly ajar, as though someone had either come in or left in a hurry and failed to close it properly. It should surely have been locked if not barred at this hour? It was a relief however, to find how easy it would be to slip out, no keys, bars or bolts to wrestle with.

Night had come on, it was dark, a dim lamp hung from the hall ceiling and the white squares in the chequerboard floor gleamed in its faint light. Despite his caution his boots thudded on the tiles. *That* day, how many days ago was it? He'd lost count. On that day he had been barefoot he remembered, and the cold had made his toes curl. He recalled too, how scared he'd been of being found within these walls. Strange how this place had come to feel safe, to feel like home.

Tonight was colder, much colder than it had been then. He felt the sting of frost on his wet cheeks as he stepped over the threshold. The sky above was patched with clouds, a fine veil of snowflakes swirled across the empty street ahead of him. A lone lantern swung at the corner of the orphanage building. The shadows of tree branches swayed and danced across the roadway, tossed and tousled in its unsteady amber beam. Above him, between the clouds he could see the high dome of Heaven; the stars diamond pin-ricks in the never-ending darkness. The moon was a slender scimitar, a sword for Sinterklaas's fearsome assistant, Black Piet.

Thousands of miles away the stars were, Mama used to say – *Mama*. If only she was here to guide him! Mama would have known what to do, how to help Casper. How to make him better with one of her hot flannel, onion and ginger poultices, but perhaps even

Mama couldn't save him? Fear was a stone, heavy in the pit of his stomach. Then he pictured Mama high above him, sailing amongst the stars in a cloud boat, with Papa and Opa and Prins, and the thought comforted him.

A little snow was settling now on the cobbles and he slipped and slithered in his still unfamiliar boots, and righted himself and struggled up the slope onto the Hoogstraat. It was a shadowy place at night. Lights still spilled from occasional shop windows, although their doors were closed and barred. Merchandise displayed out of doors during the daytime, the flowers and vegetables, mops and brooms, had been taken in, and now and then the storekeepers could be glimpsed, sitting in lighted rooms at the back of their shops, supping soup or counting the day's takings. Tomas saw one or two windows which displayed pairs of clogs neatly lined up and filled with iced gingerbreads, packets of glass marbles and little wooden toys. Behind them stood hoops and even a hobby-horse, reminding parents – as though, thought Tomas, their children might not! – that Sinterklaas would soon be calling. He would have liked to stop and look, and tell Saskia all about them later, but he mustn't.

The Hoogstraat was quiet. At first he saw nobody, although raucous singing could be heard from a tavern at the end of the furthest alleyway leading down to the Lang Haven. A woman, her head wrapped in a black cloak and carrying a portmanteau, passed him, walking quickly. She glanced in his direction but didn't stop.

Tomas paused in a darkened doorway and removed his cap. Belatedly, he'd realised that the cap more than the coat marked him out as an orphanage brat. Someone might stop him and take him back, thinking he'd run away. He stuffed it down the front of his jacket as Casper had once recommended, and thought once more of Saskia, outraged when they first met, by the idea of his running away *to* the weeshuis, when other children only tried to run away *from* it.

He was uncertain whether to continue along the street or duck down onto the canal side. Either would eventually bring him to the Koemarkt Bridge where he must begin his search. It had been on the bridge, the day he discovered Ambroos with his belly cut open, that he'd first met Frans Rijnsberger. Heer Rijnsberger had been coming *across* the bridge towards Koemarkt, dressed Tomas had supposed, for church. Therefore he'd assumed, he must live somewhere over on the Nieuwe Haven. Indeed he'd confidently told Heer Mulder so, but now he worried that he might have been mistaken. He'd nothing else to go on. He must start by crossing the bridge.

Mama. He remembered what she would have said... 'In a strange place, where you don't know your way, *ask*. Choose someone who looks trustworthy. Ask politely, Tomas, someone will put you right.'

There was a roar of drunken laughter from the tavern ahead, and two men tumbled out into the street, lashing out at one another with their fists, rolling over and over in the slush. It didn't look to be a very serious fight, one of them quickly scrambled to his feet and ran off, but it decided him. It would be of no use to ask any of *those* people.

He slipped down one of the alleyways and found himself once more running through the dark along the side of the Lang Haven. *This* time he was running *towards* the bridge and the Buitenhaven wharf. The Nieuwe Kerk and the Appelmarktbrug were behind him. Snowflakes settled on his lashes and he blinked them away. He'd never acquired a pair of regulation orphanage mittens and the cold nipped at his fingers. He thought of Henke in the warmth and light of Guildhuis to which he had run that evening. It must be nearly two weeks ago. He wished he was going there now. But no, he must keep going, must find the apothecary.

Boats were tied up as was usual, all along the quay. He could smell suppers cooking, and saw one or two of the binnenschippers lighting lamps to dangle from their yardarms or bowsprits. A few glanced his way, but no one asked where he was going. Just a boy running home to his supper through the cold and dark, that's all they'd see. These men were travellers, bargees, they might visit Schiedam regularly, but it would be useless to ask any of them where Heer Rijnsberger lived. The binnenschippers and their wives were a hardy breed. They always had their own remedies on hand for illnesses and accidents. He didn't remember Mama or Papa ever consulting a doctor or an apothecary. Tomas kept running.

But ahead, now, as he got closer to his goal, he could see a small crowd eddying around the foot of the bridge. Not drunks, like the men who had spilled out of the Hoogstraat tavern, but people involved in a noisy skirmish, none the less. Tomas shrank under the prow of the closest boat, his heart racing. Who were these folk? What were they doing? How was he to slip past them in order to cross the bridge?

Although it was dark, they'd brought a number of lanterns to the scene. One, a young fellow, was up on the bridge, busy fastening a lamp to one of the struts so that its bright beams fell onto the canal below. Tomas had never met Joop Barends, but he knew he must be a policeman by his uniform coat and epaulettes. There were plenty of policemen to be seen in Rotterdam. Two other men he also recognised as policemen by their coats and kepis, and one of them was the man whom Casper and Saskia had encountered on Westvest. The sergeant, the man in charge. These fellows had ropes and a grappling hook which they seemed to be preparing to drop into the canal. Something overboard? There was a large hole in the thin crust of ice. As a boat child he was familiar with this kind of happening. He thought it must be something very valuable that the police were attempting to raise it in the dark.

And who were all these other people, the ones who were not police? A goodly proportion of the town seemed to have gathered. His heart which had steadied beat faster when he realised that one of them was Cornelius the cockerel. *He* alone seemed uninterested in what the policemen were doing, but was berating a young woman tightly wrapped in a long cloak who, by his gestures, he was ordering to leave immediately. She however was defying him, head in the air, intent on watching the young policeman who was now scrambling down from the bridge in triumph, his task complete.

'Oh, well done!' The young woman he now recognised as Miss Mathilde de Haan, (she wasn't wearing her bonnet) clapped her hands together, and the young policeman grinned at her. Perhaps he was blushing too, but Tomas couldn't tell at a distance. Meanwhile, the other two policemen were engaged in dropping the grappling hook into the water watched by an expectant crowd. Curiosity overcoming doubt, Tomas took a few steps forward, straining to see better what was happening. Whereupon one of the shorter figures spotted him, and came trotting over to join him, (dot one and carry one as he only had one boot).

'Oy, whatcha doin' 'ere kid?' demanded Piet. 'Youse s'posed to be dead, ain't yer?'

Tomas was baffled and indignant. 'No! I'm not dead! Who told you that?'

'Them p'lice fellers reckon yer dead.' He jerked his head in the direction of the men with the grappling hook. 'Youse sure yer ain't a ghost? They reckon yer steifvader done yer in.'

'He ain't! *Hasn't!*' Mama had always urged him to speak properly. He opened his mouth to explain that he was living in the weeshuis nowadays, and then thought better of it. Ignaas hadn't "done him in" but it had been a near thing. He didn't want Piet telling the whole town where he was. Already he was eying Tomas's feet.

'Where d'yer get them boots?'

'Never you mind!'

'Pinched 'em, eh?'

'No, I didn't!' but Tomas had an uncomfortable feeling Mama might not have agreed. He changed the subject hastily. 'What are they looking for, those policemen?'

'Yer steifvader o'course. Reckon 'e's drowned. 'E didn't 'alf go in wiv a splash! An' Heer Rijnsberger's contraption's on top of 'im! *An'* 'e's bin shot an' all! Reckon 'e's dead as a lobworm down there,' said Piet.

'Oh,' said Tomas. He felt very strange suddenly, as though black snowflakes were dancing in front of his eyes, and he would have liked to sit down. He wasn't sorry exactly, although Mama had said he should be sorry when *anyone* died, perhaps all the more so when that person 'hadn't made things right with God,' and was sure to go to hell. It was a peculiar sensation he discovered, a mixture of relief and sorrow. Now he needn't be afraid of Ignaas anymore. But now... he had no one. Now he really was an orphan.

'Come an' 'ave a look!' said Piet. 'See, they've got the velo!' Sure enough, van Dyke and Barends were hauling up the velocipede by one of its wheels, and now he saw that Frans Rijnsberger was there amongst the crowd, watching, hands in his trouser pockets, shoulders slumped and a strange sorrowful expression on his face. He wouldn't need to find his shop now, after all.

'Reckon that's done for!' said Piet, as the velocipede was pulled clear. 'Niver the same again, it won't be. That front wheel's smashed.'

'It'll dry out though,' said Tomas. 'Wood dries all right if you do it slow and careful. My Papa had a few things fall off the boat. We just had to dry them out careful. Then he can get someone to mend it.'

'Yer'd better tell 'im. Cheer 'im up, since Miss Mattie's making eyes at that young rakker.'

'I thought she was poorly?'

'Nah, she's better. Yer steifvader niver killed 'er after all.' Tomas could tell Piet thought that disappointing.

No hesitating. It was now or never. He left Piet's side and ran across to where Frans Rijnsberger bent despondently over his broken velocipede, which lay streaming canal water onto the quayside.

'Sir! Heer Rijnsberger, Sir!'

Frans looked up. 'Sir, you remember me?' Frans regarded him blankly. Evidently that fateful encounter on the bridge had faded from his mind.

'Sir, you know Casper, the boy at the orphanage, the one with the hunched back?'

Frans' eyes sought Tomas's, his expression one of puzzlement. 'What about him?'

'Sir, you must come!' he seized the man's coat cuff and tugged on it. 'To the weeshuis, he's ever so ill! Really, really ill. Please come!'

Frans straightened up. 'Casper? Yes, of course I know Casper, but surely Heer Doctor Saunders...?'

'I don't know where he lives!' Tomas wailed. 'I've come to find *you* because you're only person who can help!'

'But who sent you? Did Matron Schmit send you? Or the Regent?'

'No, Sir! We...we don't have Matron Schmit anymore... they sent her away. It was... it was Heer Mulder, our teacher. He was going to come with me, but then... something happened, and he couldn't...'

Something was happening here on the quay. There were shouts and exclamations from the watchers as the grappling hook broke through the surface once more and the policeman with the drooping moustache made a grab for a bundle of clothes.

'Stand back, everyone! Stand back! This is police business, not something to gawp at! Move!' roared the policeman with the strange

North Country accent. Tomas recognised his voice from the time he'd heard him interrogating Saskia near the windmill. The crowd shuffled back a few metres but continued to stare. Something heavy was landed with a wallop on the stones, streaming water like a huge fish.

Frans Rijnsberger's eyes darted to this sight, and then he seemed to make up his mind. 'I'll come,' he told Tomas. He took one more glance, shuddered and then taking Tomas by the shoulder turned him about and led him away. 'You shouldn't see this, the man's dead. It's no sight for a child.'

As they began to walk along the gracht together they passed Miss Mathilde de Haan who'd obeyed the command to step back, but was still watching the scene avidly from a distance.

Frans Rijnsberger paused, tipped his hat to her, and spoke, 'Miss Mathilde, I beg of you! I cannot but agree with your uncle. You shouldn't be out here in the cold. You've been seriously ill!' Mattie ignored him, staring past him, and intent on observing the three policemen as they examined their "catch."

'Oh, go away do!' she snapped when he didn't move. 'I shall do as I please from now on. Don't come sidling around with your doses to put me out of my senses! Aunt Clara and my cousins may think the sun shines out of your eyes, but I do not!'

Chapter 41

A Vigil at a Sick Bed

Frans Rijnsberger and Tomas walked in silence for a while along the quay. Frans seemed dejected, lost in painful thoughts. Spiteful gusts of wind blew sharp spicules of snow in their faces.

'Heer Rijnsberger,' Tomas said, having observed that Frans wasn't carrying his medical bag. 'What about medicines? Have you any medicines to make Casper better? Don't we need to go first to your shop?'

'What? Oh, no. We'll try a camphor and turpentine plaster. And, if we can, steam. There'll be camphor in Matron Schmit's cupboard. Have they really sent her away?'

'Yes, because she was drunk and she threw the plates and smashed them,' said Tomas, looking sideways at the apothecary to see how he took this information. Frans merely grunted. They walked on.

'Sir, now my stepfather is dead, what'll happen to our boat? The Appelbloesem?' Despite his fears for Casper, Tomas couldn't stop himself from asking this. The cold weather had arrived early this year. If this kept up it would soon be time to lift her out of the water for winter storage and repairs. Would someone do this? He knew it was beyond his own powers.

Startled out of his preoccupations, Frans Rijnsberger stopped in his tracks.

'*You're Tomas!*' he exclaimed, 'the missing boy! That was...that man... the man they just fished out of the canal was your father?'

'Steifvader,' said Tomas, firmly. 'I don't mind that he's dead, he used to beat me a lot. I just want to know about the boat. I've been living at the weeshuis, but I'm not supposed to. Do you think they'll let me have my boat back? It *is* mine, truly it is! It belonged to my grandfather.'

But Frans seemed bewildered by these considerations and did not reply. 'How does it come that you're the one who's been sent to get help for Casper?' he asked.

'Nobody sent me! Casper's my friend. Heer Mulder said we'd come together when I told him how poorly Casper is, but then he couldn't.'

'Why not?'

How exasperating grown-ups are, Tomas thought. It would take too long to explain, (not that he really knew what *had* befallen the schoolmaster) and he wanted the apothecary to hurry. 'Something happened. I think he swallowed a sleeping draught by mistake. Do please, hurry, Sir! I don't want Casper to die!'

They crossed the spine of the Hoogstraat and skidded down the slope to the weeshuis. Tomas slipped and fell. Frans hauled him onto his feet again.

'Sorry, Sir, thank you Sir! I'm still not used to wearing boots,' he panted, brushing the snow from the seat of his britches with reddened fingers.

The great front door to the orphanage was still unlatched. Tomas pushed it open and they stepped inside, stamping the wet slush from their feet in the dim hallway. Immediately a small figure in a nightgown came running to meet them, half enveloped in a trailing blanket.

'Saskia! Oh, Saskia, Casper isn't...?'

Saskia's face was blotched with tears and she had to sniff hard and gulp them down before she could speak. 'No, but Katjie thinks he's going to. He said my name, so she came and woke me. And he asked for *you*, Tomas! *Where have you been?* On this last her voice rose to a wail.

'To fetch Heer Rijnsberger of course! It took me a while to find him. I told Casper I would, and here he is!'

'Take me to the patient,' said Frans, becoming, thankfully, before the children's eyes a grown-up, someone who knew what to do. Since he must have known where Casper slept there was no need for them to do this, but they pattered alongside him to the door of the room.

It was of course a very small room and it was full of people. Tomas was surprised and relieved to see Roel Mulder perched on a stool under the window. He looked white and ill, and as though recovering from what, (wise child of the waterways that he was) Tomas would in other circumstances have supposed a hangover. He was relieved to find him neither unconscious nor dead. Heer Mulder attempted to nod to him, but it seemed his head hurt and he didn't try to speak. Pastor Winkelmann was standing, his back against the shutters. His lips were moving in prayer, his eyes were closed, but on hearing the arrival of the newcomers, they snapped open.

'Ah, yes,' he said, to no one in particular, 'that is indeed Tomas, the very boy.' He closed his eyes again and continued to pray inaudibly.

At the bedside, slatternly snaggle-toothed Katjie the cook, her head still bound its perpetual gravy-stained cloth was wrapping hot stone bottles in torn sheeting and placing them down each side of Casper's body. To Tomas's astonishment the fellow filling and passing the bottles to be wrapped was Dirk!

Katjie turned and saw Frans Rijnsberger hovering behind the children in the doorway.

'Doin' me best, Sir!' she told him. 'It's what me old mother done when any of us kids took bad. Hot bricks, she used to use. Heat 'em on the fire but then wrap 'em so youse don't burn the poor kiddie. But we got these stone bottles that last cold winter when the maids in the attics said they couldn't sleep for it, and I thought they're better'un bricks. Just fill 'em with piping hot water is what I done. I boiled some, and Dirk 'ere ran across to the distillery wiv jugs. I hope I done right?'

'An' 'e ain't no worse,' mumbled Dirk in his thick speech. 'No better 'e ain't, but still breathin'.'

The two children crept forward then and knelt down at the bedside.

'Here's Tomas, Casper!' whispered Saskia. 'I said he'd come back. He didn't run away. He fetched Heer Rijnsberger to make you better!'

Casper's eyes flickered open for a moment and he stretched out a hand and placed it on Tomas's wind-tousled head. 'Thanks... for trying,' he murmured so low that only the children heard him, 'Probably... a waste... of time, but thanks.'

Meanwhile, above their heads, Frans Rijnsberger was speaking softly to Katjie. 'Heat is good, so far as it goes,' he was murmuring, 'and I commend your efforts, but we need to do more. I propose using camphor mixed with turpentine oil applied to the boy's chest. And bowls of steaming camphor vapour set about the room might help. Do you happen to have a key to Matrone Schmit's cupboard?' Katjie was shaking her head. 'I s'pose the Regent 'as it.' She looked across at Jacob Winkelmann, who had opened his eyes again on hearing these words. He looked bewildered.

'The Regent, yes. But I don't know if ...'

'F'get 'im, I'll smash 'un!' mouthed Dirk, striding for the door, and shortly they heard the sound of wood cracking and splintering.

'Mercy!' breathed Frans and went out hastily to rescue the contents of the medicine cupboard. Katjie went on rearranging the hot stone bottles which varied in size. She kept placing them on each side of Casper's ribs until she had them to her liking. 'Camphor an' turpentine! Wha's turpentine? Summat painters use, isn' it? New-fangled notions!' she muttered under her breath as she worked.

Tomas and Saskia continued to kneel at the bedside, side by side. Saskia grasped Casper's hand; Tomas laid his cheek on his forearm. The boy's breathing rose and fell, occasionally faltering and falling away, then rising again, deep, painful and slow.

'Children, you mustn't stay, you'll be in Heer Rijnsberger's way,' the Pastor came and stood over them. 'He wants to try a special treatment, and you wouldn't want to hinder that, would you? Why don't we say a prayer together and then you can go to your beds?'

'No!' said Saskia. '*I* won't get in the way. You shan't turn me out!' She began to sob.

'We can go *under* this bed if we have to,' said Tomas, equally stubborn. 'I keep my sleeping mattress under here anyway. We're Casper's *friends*, we have to be here!'

'We're his *friends*,' Saskia repeated, 'nobody else loves him like we do. If he has to go to Heaven we want to see him over...over the bridge!'

'Over the bridge,' Roel Mulder murmured, the first words he had spoken since Tomas arrived. He stood with effort and came across to the bed. He was squeezing his forehead which obviously pained him, between his palms. 'That's a nice image, Saskia. We all have to cross the bridge from life to death one day, Pastor. Do we not? Over the bridge across the canal and down through the green meadows beyond. That's what we all hope for. Let the children stay.'

Chapter 42

The Longest Night

The clock in the weeshuis schoolroom ticked through the hours but no one heard it. In the dormitories, children coughed and sighed and turned in their sleep. The apprentices dreamed of days free of exacting masters to go fishing or skating above the lock. Maids dreamt of sweethearts and new ribbons for their Kirstmis bonnets. Above stairs the building was deeply silent except for the occasional skittering of mice in the wainscoting.

Downstairs all was frenzied activity. In the kitchen Dirk stoked the fire and plodded back and forth with cans of boiling water. Katjie filled and refilled her stone bottles. In the sickroom Frans Rijnsberger was in his shirt sleeves, collar and waistcoat discarded, hair flopping across his brow, applying his camphor and turpentine plasters to Casper's chest, filling and deploying bowls of steaming camphor around the bed. Roel Mulder helped him create an overarching canopy of sheets to contain the fumes.

Moved out of the way while this was constructed, Tomas and Saskia were curled like two puppies on the floor at Pastor Winkelmann's feet.

'I'll wake you,' he promised them, 'if seems that...' He didn't know whether he would or not. He'd already said the same to Heer Mulder. Still half stupefied by his overdose of opiate, Roel Mulder had been persuaded to go and lie down. 'I'll send someone to fetch you if the boy's condition worsens,' the Pastor had assured him, although he had sat at other bedsides, and in the end the change had come too quickly for the relatives to be called. Now and then he consulted his pocket watch. Eleven of the night, midnight, the hour hand moved slowly. He'd commandeered the schoolmaster's stool once he left, but his back ached without the comfort of his armchair. He wondered if it would be so wrong, after all, to go and wake the Regent and ask him to take a turn. And how much of the opiate Dries van Corte might have given him to 'help him sleep.'

Van Corte's behaviour earlier that evening had bewildered Jacob Winkelmann. They had known each other for years, although they'd never been close friends in the way that Maarten de Hoop and the

Directeur of the Infirmary had been, and presumably were. Naturally, he understood van Corte had been concerned for his friend, arriving back heart-broken, frustrated and exhausted after so many days searching for his wife. A little sedative to help the poor fellow relax and sleep away his cares, yes, that he could comprehend. But why had van Corte administered it surreptitiously, not appearing to want Maarten to know he was doing it? And how was it that the original dose had been so wildly over generous that when Roel Mulder accidently swallowed it, it had rendered him unconscious within minutes?

Van Corte wasn't a doctor despite the fact that he ran the hospital. However, he must have easy access to drugs of all kinds. Perhaps he regularly administered them to avoid having to call out Xander Saunders? Every call on the little Scottish doctor cost time and money, and van Corte was always complaining that the hospital was underfunded. But if this was so, one would have thought he'd have learned what the correct dosage for a grown man was?

The camphor fumes were making his head feel light, but were they alone the cause of the uncomfortable thoughts that now invaded his mind? There were many, many deaths on the hospital's wards and amongst the elderly "alms house" inmates housed there. That was inevitable. That was the nature of things. But had some of them come sooner than they should have? When he'd taken weekly services there amongst the ambulant oldsters, had he not sometimes been surprised to miss a face that only the previous week had seemed hale and hearty? Only to be told that Klaas or Hanjie had 'passed'?

Now he was really uneasy. Should he go and see if Maarten was all right? In the Regent's debilitated state, Jacob Winkelmann wondered, could even a measured dose prove fatal? He glanced again to the bed where he now noticed Casper's breathing seemed to have eased a little under the young apothecary's ministrations. The Pastor had been profoundly shocked by the callous attitude Dries van Corte had expressed towards the crippled boy. He could make excuses for him – the man had to deal with the sick and dying daily. He'd become inured to death, probably seeing it as the kindest option for the old, the feeble, and the incurable. Perhaps it was only possible for the Directeur of St Jacob's to do his job day after day by hardening his heart to suffering?

Jacob Winkelmann was aware that he himself was no saint. Dealing with the sick and dying had always been a part of his work that he dreaded. However, although his heart sank every time he was called out to a parishioner at death's door, he'd never shirked it, never, he hoped, grown hard and uncaring. He'd always found sufficient reserves of compassion to carry him through. Never had he thought that even the most hopeless case, as he supposed Casper must appear, should be hurried out of the world before the Good Lord decided so.

He shifted unhappily on his stool. The camphor fumes were making his head ache. Saskia's fair curls, loosed from her pigtails, spread over his feet. She was sound asleep with her thumb in her mouth. Tomas stirred now and then. His head lay on his folded hands, as though, the Pastor thought, sentimentally, he was praying for his friend even as he slept. Such innocence! To think the boy had, while everyone in the town was looking for him, been safe here in the weeshuis!

'He told me he thought his stepfather wouldn't look for him here,' Roel Mulder had explained to the Pastor in a low voice, before he was persuaded to go and lie down. 'And because the Regent left for Amsterdam, and I was new and didn't know any different – no one questioned it.' He glanced down at Saskia, asleep on the floor. 'Of course Casper and Saskia knew! I believe those two cooked it up between them! You should have heard the way Saskia convinced everyone that the new boy had some dreadful skin disease and had to sleep down here so as not to spread the infection. I was completely deceived, and so was everyone else!'

At this point Dirk had appeared in the room toting one of his cans of water. 'Th's p'lice 'ere,' he mouthed. 'They called in t'kitchen, seein' the lights. They want t'know if the boy's 'ere. Tomas? 'E's drownded, is tha' man, 'is Dad. One of t'kids, Piet, telled 'em Tomas might be 'ere.'

Roel Mulder roused himself. 'Tell them yes, Tomas is here. He's quite safe. He's sound asleep. They can speak to him in the morning.'

'Poor little mite,' said Katjie, stoppering a hot water bottle. 'He's a nice little fellow and so good to poor Casper. I wonder how the steifvader came to drown?'

'Collided with my velocipede,' said Frans, who was adjusting the canopy. 'I saw it. That scamp Piet had borrowed it from me. Ignaas was running off from one of the policemen, but he ran into Piet. Piet was nimble and jumped out of the way. Ignaas and the velo went tumbling into the canal by the Koemarkt Bridge. Perhaps Ignaas couldn't swim? I believe a surprising number of the watermen can't. Also, he'd a bullet in his shoulder from a run in with the police earlier, and he'd hurt his back in a fall.'

The room fell silent, apart from the rasp of Casper's tortured in-breaths, as they contemplated Ignaas's unlucky end.

'What'll happen to Tomas now?' Roel Mulder had asked then, looking down at the boy asleep at his feet. 'He confessed his story to me earlier this evening. He told me his parents are dead. This Ignaas, the step-father ill-treated him, beat him savagely.'

'I saw the evidence myself,' said Frans, stirring camphor. 'I regret now that I didn't try to help the boy. I was more concerned about Ambroos at the time… and other things.' A sharp spasm passed across the apothecary's face as he said this, as though at some memory of blunders he'd made.

Jacob Winkelmann agreed, 'I regret that *I* did so little. Henke van de Grote asked me to help the boy, but then he disappeared and I'm afraid I largely forgot about him. Little did I imagine that he was here all the time.'

For a long time after Roel Mulder left he sat listening to Casper's desperate gasps for air, watching the sleeping children, regretting the cramping pains in his legs. He dared not rise and walk about to ease them. Eventually, despite his discomfort his head drooped onto his chest and he too slept.

Frans and Katjie worked on. Dirk, though willing began to flag, and by the time the clock of Grote Sint Jan chimed three Katjie found him snoring by the kitchen fire, an empty can dangling from his hand. She carefully removed it, filled it, and went back.

'Katjie, I think…' Frans' voice was low but excited, as she re-entered the room. 'I think he's responding. Listen! His breath is coming more easily. I believe the fever has broken.'

Katjie placed a hand on Casper's brow. 'Yessir. E's cooler. If 'e can make it through to the daylight, as me Mam used t'say.'

'That's a way off yet, but I'm beginning to believe we've done it, Katjie!'

'*This* time,' said Katjie, whom life had made a realist. 'We done it this time.'

Laughing, Frans bowed low to her, and she sketched a curtsy and executed a few steps from a country clog dance. Casper sighed and suddenly opened his eyes.

'Still here,' he remarked in a wondering voice. 'Seems as though God doesn't…want me yet.'

'Shall us wake 'em?' asked Katjie, indicating the sleeping children, the nodding priest.

'Not yet. Let's leave it another half hour. We want to be sure. We mustn't raise their hopes too soon. Why don't you go and put your feet up by the kitchen fire for an hour Katjie? I'll stay with the boy. Then you can come with fresh hot water and relieve me.' Frans looked around the tiny cramped room. His shoulders sagged; he was tired to the bone. 'I can sit on the floor for a spell.'

'Whatever for?' said a voice. A most unexpected voice, quite the last voice they might have expected, though certainly one they both recognised.

'Goodness me, this looks like the Friday Market in here!' Mevrouw Margriet de Hoop stepped into the room, casting her heavy, concealing cloak to the floor. 'Whatever's going on? Is the hunchback sick? Where is Dorte Schmit, why isn't she attending to him? What are you doing in here, Katjie? And Pastor Winkelmann!'

Jacob Winkelmann woke up with a start, and staggered to his feet, amazed.

'Margriet!' he cried, while Frans and the cook stood open-mouthed at this astonishing apparition. Mevrouw de Hoop was fashionably dressed as always. Instead of a bonnet she wore a hat in the very latest mode, furnished about with ostrich feathers. Her jacket of finest wool was a deep dark forest green. Her shoes, her gloves and even her travelling bag, matched it perfectly. In her right hand, quite casually, she held a knife.

'I heard voices,' she said, 'and wondered who could be here. I looked in on Maarten and he was fathoms under. He didn't even stir.'

'He's been looking for you, Margriet,' croaked Jacob Winkelmann. 'He's exhausted himself.' Observing the knife his face suddenly drained of colour.

'Yes, I heard. Looking for me in all the *wrong* places!' said

Margriet de Hoop with a tinkling laugh. 'I haven't been far, not at all. A little apartment over by the Plantage, very elegant, very discreet! What are these brats doing here?' She waved beringed fingers at Saskia and Tomas who were sitting up and rubbing their eyes. 'The boy I don't recognise. Has poor Maarten been cozened into taking another "hard luck" case?'

'Casper?' Tomas questioned, ignoring the newcomer, not even noticing the knife. He staggered to his feet and ran over to the bed.

'Still here,' grated Casper. 'Still alive, but I need to sleep now.'

'Oh you shall, you shall! Oh how glad we are to have you back with us!' cried Saskia stumbling after Tomas. 'Thank you, Heer Rijnsberger... and Katjie. Thank you both for making Casper well again!'

Vrouw de Hoop drew herself up, her face a picture of disdain. 'These children should be in their dormitories. Jacob, I'm astonished that you allowed them into the sick room. Things have come to a pretty pass if I can't go away for a few days without every rule of behaviour, every trace of discipline being abandoned here!'

Chapter 43

An Encounter with a Murderer

Frans Rijnsberger had straightened, all his weariness banished. He might be merely an apothecary, a dispenser of potions, but he could recognise lunacy when he was confronted with it.

'I imagine, Mevrouw that you are looking for someone who's not here? Can I relieve you of that knife? Then the children can go to their beds.'

He kept his voice low and controlled, having noted that the knife had fresh rust coloured stains. Katjie and Pastor Winkelmann stood frozen, alarm flooding into their eyes. Even the children realised that something was amiss, and were staring at Margriet de Hoop in bewilderment.

'Yes, I came to find someone,' she snapped. 'Someone who *should* have been here – here outside this building to meet me and take me to London as he promised!' She lifted her hand and consulted a slim jewelled timepiece. 'The boat sails from the harbour in precisely one hour! He promised he'd have a carriage waiting. I came only to collect some of my clothes. When I got here I found no carriage had been ordered. The coward reneged on his promises!'

'This someone would be Heer van Corte?' Frans asked quietly. 'He was here earlier I believe, was he not, Pastor?'

Appealed to, Jacob Winkelmann spluttered, helpless and horrified, 'Yes, that is… he *was*, but I believe…'

Ignoring him, Margriet turned on Frans. '*You knew!* You knew all along you filthy sneaking…*upstart*! Dries said he was afraid you did. He thought you were trying to blackmail him. Dropping little hints. He was frightened you'd go to the Watch Committee, and he'd lose his job, his position in the town, his *standing* that he was so proud of! I'll teach you to spoil all my plans…'

She lunged forward arm raised, ready to drive the knife into Frans' larynx. Katjie screamed. Jacob Winkelmann croaked in alarm. Saskia and Tomas clung to one another in terror. Then someone came quickly in at the door and seized her from behind, pulling her back and away, one arm encircling and crushing her throat, the other reaching out to imprison the wrist that held the knife.

'It's much easier from behind,' said Roel Mulder, conversationally, 'and more convincing for an audience. I was an actor you know? – I played Macbeth's henchman, killing the young MacDuff.' He applied more pressure to Margriet's windpipe and twisted her wrist. The knife dropped. 'What shall we do with her? There's an empty storeroom across the way, as I discovered when I was dumped there earlier. Does anyone have a key to the door? Or we could tie a rope from the handle to the one next door as a temporary measure, while we send for the police?'

'I knows where the key's kept,' breathed Katjie. 'Regent's office. I'll get 'un. Come wiv us, kinder, to the kitchen. I'll wake Dirk an' he'll mak ye a hot drink.'

'Could I have one, please?' quavered a voice from the bed. Unbelievably it seemed to all of them; in their alarm Casper had been almost forgotten.

'I'll fetch it!' cried Tomas.

'No, *I'll* fetch it!' insisted Saskia.

'Dirk'll fetch it,' said Katjie. 'He's bin a good lad over this, 'elped me no end. I'd guess 'e's found out 'e's fonder of Casper than ever 'e knew.'

'Splendid! You're better, my best and brightest pupil,' said Heer Mulder, smiling at the boy in the bed.

There was no need to send for the police. They had already reappeared in the kitchen. Anders Vos was demanding to speak to someone in authority, and refusing to take 'no' for an answer. He was in the process of frightening Dirk out of his slow and sleepy wits. Katjie took in the situation at a glance, and chased the children back to Casper's room with glasses and a jug of milk, gin and hot water.

'Who is this woman?' Vos demanded when led to the storeroom. Margriet de Hoop was a sorry sight. All her ferocity seemed to have drained out of her. She sat miserably on the floor, her arms around her knees, rocking to and fro and mewing softly. Her fashionable hat lay discarded, its feathers trampled and broken.

'She is… Vrouw Margriet de Hoop,' quavered Pastor Winkelmann, 'the Regent's wife. She seems to have run mad. I fear she may have killed her husband.'

'Someone has certainly been killed,' said Vos. 'We found his body in the lane outside. 'Nattily dressed fellow, it was too dark to be sure, but I think it was the one who was here the other day. The one whose hand that Schmit woman slashed with a knife?'

'Dries van Corte,' said the Pastor sadly, 'he is… *was*, very much a lady's man. He could be very charming, but it was all a game with him. I daresay he was playing these poor deluded women off against one another. I blame myself. I knew he'd an eye for the women and was apt to lead them on. I should have spoken to him, warned him he was playing with fire. I suppose he met her tonight and told her he couldn't or wouldn't take her to London after all.'

'I believe he'd set up some sort of a love nest over towards the Plantage,' offered Frans. 'Living as I do down on the Nieuwe Haven, I used often to see him strolling in that direction. I wondered if he'd a mistress. I'll admit I dropped a hint or two that I suspected it. That may be why he decided not to take Vrouw de Hoop to London, and why *she* wanted to kill me just now.'

'I'd wager she killed the other one too, the other Margriet' said van Dyke. Together with Barends, he was standing gloomily by; van Dyke because gloom was his natural element and Joop Barends because it was long past his bed time. The dog Boaz, who had followed them in whined softy. There were flecks of blood on his muzzle.

'I said all along that the other Margriet must come into it somewhere,' Barends agreed, although even he probably had no idea what he was talking about. He was too tired after the earlier events of the day to make much sense.

'Margriet van de Grote!' the woman on the floor suddenly spat, 'Such a prude! She was going to tell my husband. Even with her wits gone, she was a prude. She knew me, even in my cloak, no one else did. She saw me meeting Dries by the dam and came storming at us, shrieking that she'd tell. Dries made off in a hurry like the coward he was, and left me to deal with her.'

'Margriet de Hoop, I'm arresting you on a charge of murder,' intoned Vos before she could confess to anything else. He added, 'We'll lock her in that cellar at the Gemeentehuis I'd arranged for Ignaas – now it turns out he doesn't need it. I don't know exactly *which* murder we'll charge you with, Mevrouw, but we'll work that out in the morning.'

'So Ignaas van Damme didn't murder anyone after all?' asked Jacob Winkelmann, bewildered.

'Apparently not,' said Vos.

'He always said he didn't,' said Barends. 'He attacked Ambroos, he attacked Mathilde de Haan, but he didn't kill either of them.'

'Came damned close!' grunted van Dyke.

'He's dead, and from all I hear, no loss,' agreed Frans. 'Shouldn't someone go and see if this one killed her husband?'

'That I didn't do,' growled the woman crouched before them. 'I thought of it, I'll admit, but in the end…he was a good man. He was fast asleep, didn't even stir when I touched his shoulder! I couldn't kill him in his sleep. If only he wasn't such a bore, always maundering on about the "poor dear children!" Years of it I suffered, even after I inherited my grandmother's fortune and we could've had a comfortable life, left this dreary orphans' home and this dirty town behind and gone traveling. Seen something of London, Paris and New York! But he wouldn't leave the children.'

Chapter 44

Loose Ends are Tied

Vos stood to attention in the presence of his superior officer, the Big Cheese. Outside sleet slanted across the fronts of the tall houses. The cobbles that lined the streets of Rotterdam were as black and shiny as sucked liquorice.

'This was not the Maréchaussée's finest hour, Vos,' said that worthy, holding his report at arm's length once more in order to read it. Vos longed to tell him where one could purchase spectacles to correct long sight. 'Did you really manage to arrest this Ignaas van Damme *twice*, only to have him escape?'

'Yes, Sir,' Vos admitted, 'that is, Barends arrested him twice, only for him to evade capture just as I came upon the scene.' He realised, hearing himself say this, that this was unfair. 'I should say Sir, in mitigation, Barends did his best. He is inexperienced.'

'He is an idiot, and so is Josef van Dyke.'

'Not entirely, Sir. They did their best.'

'If you say so. So, what do we have? Ignaas van Damme was *probably* guilty of grievous bodily harm to the zakkendrager and *definitely* guilty of the attempted murder of Miss de Haan, and also of child cruelty in respect of his stepson?'

'Yes Sir.'

'He didn't murder anybody?'

'No Sir.'

'And has himself perished as a result of a collision with a …?'

'A velocipede, Sir. A two wheeled vehicle upon which the rider sits astride, propelling it forward with his feet.'

'Frightful things! You don't suppose they'll catch on?'

'Extremely unlikely I'd think, Sir.'

'So you've brought me a *murderess*?'

'That is so, Sir.'

'Vrouw Margriet de Hoop wife of…? Vos, your handwriting is little better than Barends'… wife of Maarten de Hoop, Regent of the Schiedam weeshuis. And she, it appears, did murder the wife of the Chief of the zakkendragers, and also her lover, Dries van Corte.'

'Yes Sir.'

'She's mad, of course.'

'I understand she has always been... *wayward*. She inherited money and this seems to have encouraged her to behave exactly as she chose. She would flounce off with some man whenever she felt bored with her life at the weeshuis. I understand that this Dries van Corte was an equally unsteady individual. He'd been paying marked attentions to the Matrone, Dorte Schmit, a widow, and clearly she expected him to offer matrimony. When this Margriet de Hoop cut her out she took to drink...'

'Yes, yes!' said the Big Cheese impatiently, 'the eternal triangle. I suppose there's little else to do in these small provincial places. I imagine it's the same in...is it Groningen you hale from? *He* set up a love nest at the other end of town to entertain his lady friends, but *she* became bored of "playing house" with him under her husband's nose, and decided they should take a trip to London?'

'Yes Sir, but of course if they both disappeared at the same time, that would have let the cat out of the sack. Part of the thrill for both of them was carrying on their affair under the nose of her poor overworked husband and the rest of the town worthies. Sending him off to Amsterdam was probably van Corte's idea of a joke. Then he became alarmed by her erratic behaviour, and wanted to postpone the London trip. Maybe he never really intended to go. He drugged the husband to give him time to meet her and disabuse her. She was furious and stabbed him to death.'

'Yes, now tell me why she killed the other woman, the other Margriet?'

'They'd been friends. – Vrouw de Hoop, Vrouw Schmit, and Margriet van de Grote. Margriet van de Grote was happy in her marriage, and until she lost her reason, content. She didn't approve of Vrouw de Hoop's carryings on, and when she happened to see her meeting van Corte at the lock, she ran out to remonstrate. Vrouw de Hoop was heavily cloaked of course, but the other Margriet would recognise her, even so. She might not recall what she'd had for breakfast, but she would recognise her old friend's gait, her body shape.'

'So, van Corte hurried off and left her to deal with this harridan, but then heard about the woman's body being found later in the day? No wonder he began to have doubts! Now, the knife, Vos, you spent a lot of time looking for the knife. Where did she get it?'

'From the weeshuis kitchen, the cook identified it. She said they had several but they were always going missing because the maids are careless and throw them out with the peelings.'

'Ah, yes. My wife makes similar complaints. So, the case is over. The woman will undoubtedly be sent to an asylum. *Now*, next I would like you to go to...where was it?' He shuffled through the papers on his desk.

Vos straightened his shoulders, ready to hear where the axe would fall this time. At his feet, the dog Boaz thumped an encouraging tail.

To Hendrick Hendricks,
c/o the stage doorkeeper,
Stadsshouwburg Theatre,
Amsterdam

Schiedam, 11th December

Dear old friend,

I am sorry not to have answered your missive of 28th November before this, events my dear fellow, events! I trust you discovered someone to play first murderer in the Scottish play whilst your leg heals? You will no doubt be astonished to hear that I am currently acting (no, not on the stage) as Regent and schoolmaster in an orphanage. Not a career I'd ever envisioned for myself. As you may recall I originally came here in hopes of a part in a production at the playhouse in Rotterdam, but that was not to be. One of the proposed backers defaulted, and there were insufficient funds to continue. With hardly a stuiver left to my name I therefore embarked on what I thought would amount to only a week or two of teaching school. Well, here we are fast approaching Kirstmis and due to the collapse of the Regent (his wife had murdered two of the townsfolk, and he's been sent on a sea voyage to recover from the shock) I am not only teaching the weeshuis brats but have been entrusted with the day to day running of the place. This is a grave responsibility and quite a departure for me, although it has its rewards. Almost I feel like the gent in that novel (I think it was *another by that Dickens fellow) who said "It is a far, far better thing I do now than ever I did before" or some such tosh. Anyway, I'm sticking at it until a better opportunity arises. Money is so useful I find.*

Reading, writing and arithmetic soon lose their charms however, for me as well as my pupils, so we are currently rehearsing a small dramatic performance, "A Short History of the Netherlands" in rhyming couplets (the orphanage Chaplain who is apparently quite well known as a poet is assisting me with this). The children are most enthusiastic, especially when we stage the assassination of Wilhelm the Silent at Delft. We're due to present this little offering to the Governors and their wives in a week's time. Wish me a loan of your broken leg!

Your old friend and companion on the boards,

Roel Mulder

*Herrensgracht,
Amsterdam,
21st December*

Dear Corporal Barends,
I was charmed to receive your letter, and not all offended although I have to say your 'fist' is not easy to decipher. You could benefit, I feel, from a course on spelling and handwriting in my school! You sent me your direction in Arnhem, and I hope I have it correctly.

You say you have been 'banished' there because Sergeant Vos and his superiors do not like you. That may be, but you have surely already proved your worth? You tell me that on your very first day on patrol there you caught a burglar descending from an upstairs window. I'm sorry to hear that your uniform cap was destroyed when he fell on top of you, what a shock that must have been for you both! However, the point is that you caught him, a fine start to your new posting.

Yes, I do hear about happenings in Schiedam. My cousin Lottie sends me a budget of news on an almost weekly basis. She hopes, of course, that I will invite her and her mother and sister to stay so that they can enjoy the heady delights of

Amsterdam. I may relent once I have my school up and running. I think I would be spared Uncle Cornelius as he is still furious with me.

I advertised my proposed school in the Courante and have already received numerous enquiries. Happily for me the previous tenants here left my father's laboratory untouched and once the decorators complete their work I'll be ready to throw open the doors to my first pupils! I've already engaged a promising woman to teach mathematics.

What can I tell you of Schiedam? Lottie mentioned in her first letter that Heer Rijnsberger the apothecary was heartbroken that I did not return his regard. However, by her fourth missive she was reporting that he was showing a decided partiality for the printer's niece, said to be a very pretty girl of nineteen, newly arrived from Enkhuizen. I wish her well! He and I would not have suited. I didn't want to spend the rest of my life pasting labels on medicine bottles in his poky little shop, which I feel certain would have been my fate. This Sofie will surely feel entirely at home amongst the labels?

What else? You asked about Piet, the rascally lad who used to hang about on the wharf. He has been taken on by, of all people, Aarte the glassblower! Aarte is a grouch, not known for his generosity, but he says Piet has a good pair of lungs and plenty of energy, so he has given him a home and is teaching him his trade. I was glad they found Tomas safe and well, although I hear they sold the family's boat to pay for Ignaas's funeral and Tomas's continuing schooling. A pity of course, but I hope Tomas may benefit from an education.

You probably heard already that Vrouw de Hoop is sent to a secure asylum near Assen? Her husband suffered a complete nervous collapse on discovering her crimes and a subscription was taken up to send him on a sea voyage to Madeira. Everyone hopes it will do him good.

In his absence Lottie tells me that the schoolmaster and Katjie the cook are running the weeshuis with some assistance from the Reverend Winkelmann. He, Heer Winkelmann, has a new poem published in some magazine of which people speak highly, but I haven't had sight of it yet.

I hope your time in Arnhem continues to go well, and if you are ever in Amsterdam, do call.

With kindest regards, from your "bluestocking" friend,

Mathilde de Haan.

It was a sunny afternoon, though a chilly breeze was stirring. The sails of the Three Cornflowers' windmill were turning lazily. After the early cold snap at the beginning of December the weather had turned deceptively mild, but now a hard frost was once again predicted. Three children in weeshuis uniforms were crossing the Korenbeurs Bridge. They were warmly dressed and cheerful, secure in the knowledge that if anyone queried their right to be out and about on their own they had "permission." They were off to visit Henke van de Grote at the Guildhuis.

The lock at the dam was closed, and there were few boats about. Some had already been hoisted from the water for inspection and refurbishment. Other binnenschippers were making last runs up to Rotterdam and Dordrecht to make a little money before winter set in and the canals froze.

Casper, tightly swaddled in rugs, sat in his chair peering over the edge of a blanket and commenting on this, 'So few boats. D'you know who bought the Appelbloesem, Tomas?' Since his illness his voice was barely a thread, and Tomas had to bend close to hear.

Tomas sighed and paused in the middle of the bridge. 'No idea. I hope it's someone who'll take care of her.'

'Are you really goin' t'be Henke's apprentice, Tomas? When you're twelve I mean?' enquired Saskia who was busy eating an orange, and thus mumbled indistinctly. The oranges had been part of a 'Sinterklaas' treat for the weeshuis children. One of the Governors, perhaps feeling that he should have taken more interest these last few months, had ordered numerous ponds of oranges and nuts, and bowls of these had been appearing on the dining tables in addition to the usual fare. Katjie had been urging the children to eat up the oranges before they went mouldy. 'I mean,' Saskia went on, 'ye arn' ver big, to carry sacks.' She found a pip in her orange segment and spat it out into the lock.

'I'm not going to carry sacks. Heer Mulder says Henke wants me to learn from Geert, his assistant, how to keep the account books and dole out the zakkendragers' pay. And I'll be checking bills of lading and running errands.'

'Better work on your long division then,' wheezed Casper indistinctly. He didn't laugh anymore, it exhausted him too much.

'I *think* I understand it now,' said Tomas, 'but I'll mostly be adding and subtracting. Money in, in one column money out in the other. Geert will help me a lot to begin with.'

'I'm goin' to be a *maid-and-companion* next March. Tomas is goin' t'be an apprentice i' June,' said Saskia, spitting out another pip, 'What'll you do without us, Casper?'

Casper was silent for a moment, then he said, so quietly that they both had to lean close to hear, 'I might be God's apprentice, writing people's good deeds in one column, and their bad ones in another. God must want that information kept up to date.' He risked a tiny soundless chuckle.

Tomas grinned at the joke, but in his heart he knew it wasn't really a joke. Casper was slowly fading away, just as Mama had. Dirk came faithfully every day now to undress and dress him. Since the night when Casper had so nearly died, he was kindness itself. No more calling him 'the cripple', no more lifting him roughly and threatening to drop him. Undressed, Tomas saw how much weight Casper had lost. His body was slowly shrinking so that only his humped back, his oversized nose and his wide smile remained. The wheeled chair felt ever lighter when Tomas pushed it.

'I'll keep busy enough,' Casper continued, 'reading all those encyclopaedias Pastor Winkelmann has lent me, ten volumes!'

They marched on, past the Korenbeurs, where they could hear the buzz of the traders' voices through the open doorways as they haggled over the sacks of grain, and on down the slope to the Guildhuis. Henke was out on the quay, marshalling his ducks onto the shore.

'Hallo!' the children called, 'Hallo, Henke!'

'Hallo!' he called back, 'Just been giving my feathered friends an extra swim. The big freeze is coming. Soon all this'll be ice and they mebbe won't get another 'til spring. So, young Tomas, they say you can't come and work for me until June, is that right?'

'That's when I'll be twelve, and we're allowed to start our apprenticeships,' Tomas replied. Then, something caught his eye and he started in astonishment. There was a trim boat tied further along the quay.

'Henke, that's the Appelbloesem!'

'Certainly is. Nice little craft. When the Watch Committee put her up for sale, I bought her. Useful. Geert and I took her up to Delft to get some crockery the other day. My poor Margriet broke so many pots when she was in one of her wild moods!' He licked his forefinger and held it up to test the breeze. 'Reckon there's *just* enough wind. Shall we go for a sail? Not too far, because the wind's tricky and we don't want to have to tow her.'

'Casper and me too?' gasped Saskia, wide-eyed.

'Why not? I'll just shoo the ducks into their pen. Geert? We're coming aboard, going for a sail,' he called, and Geert's head popped up from below the deck. He had a paint brush in his hand.

'We're smartening her up,' Henke said. 'In a day or two we'll have her out and see what's what below the water line, although Geert reckons she's sound.'

It was cold out on the Schie away from the town and its sheltering buildings. Mist dimmed the woods to the west, and the water-filled ditches which criss-crossed the meadows blazed, set afire by the sinking sun. A teasing breeze filled the brown sails so that they bellied and swung about, causing Saskia, seated on the deck, to squeal and duck. Casper's chair was wedged in the prow, where he sat wrapped in more layers than the Egyptian mummy Heer Mulder had told them about. He was smiling. Tomas moved between his friend and Henke at the tiller, important and serious. Geert trimmed the sails. Then, at a signal they turned for home, tacking back and forth to use the capricious breeze.

'Look!' cried Saskia, gazing ahead, 'Schiedam! It's…like a soap bubble! It's beautiful!'

'Trick o' the light,' said Henke.

The town, its sooty buildings, its tall chimneys and taller windmills seemed to float above the earth inside a dome of light, iridescent as pearl, and tinged with gold.

'It's an optical illusion. I've read about them,' said Casper.

Tomas laughed. 'Not Black Nazareth today!'

'No,' whispered Casper so softly that Tomas barely heard, 'It could almost be Paradise.'

Schiedam – Historical Note

Schiedam today is a pleasant dormitory town only five minutes from Rotterdam by train. The old centre with its traditional gabled town houses, converted grain stores, tree lined canals, and restored sailing barges, is very attractive. Traces of course remain of the town's darker history as the 'gin capital' of Europe in the eighteenth and nineteenth centuries; notably the huge brick-built windmills that tower over the roof tops, the grain stores now converted into houses and apartments, the elegant Corn Exchange, and the monumental hospital building now the Municipal Museum of Modern Art. Then there are the elaborate houses built for the rich distillers, ship builders and sea captains on the Lange Haven and around the Plantage (said to have been the first public park to be created in the Netherlands). And not forgetting the tall Zakkendragershuis, the guild house of the men who literally dragged the sacks of grain on and off the sailing barges which brought the grain from inland farms to the mills of Schiedam.

All this was built on gin. Many people in the UK will know of the famous, horrific, engraving, 'Gin Alley' from 1751 by William Hogarth, which depicts the poor of London, drinking themselves to death on cheap gin. Labourers sell their tools, mothers drop their babies on their heads, drunks fall down in the street, and all manner of crimes are committed to get money to feed their addiction. In the novels of Charles Dickens and Elizabeth Gaskell gin is shown affecting people's lives adversely. The poor drank it to dull the misery of their lives and fed it to their children to keep them quiet. It was referred to as 'Hollands' or sometimes just 'Schiedam' and was the equivalent of heroin today, although perfectly legal and much cheaper. Towards the end of his life, Branwell Brontë, brother of the novelists Charlotte, Emily and Anne, became an alcoholic. He wrote a letter to a friend asking, pathetically, "for five pence for gin."

Nearly all of it was shipped across the North Sea directly from Schiedam. A Dutch acquaintance told me that during the eighteenth and nineteenth centuries the Netherlands suffered economic decline. They were hard times, except in Schiedam. In Schiedam at the height of the industry gin could even be obtained free. Surplus hot water is created as part of the distilling process. Wives and servants had permission to go with jugs and buckets to collect hot water from the distilleries for washing and cooking, but somehow, or so I was told, "the wrong tap was turned and they took home gin instead!"

Despite the "evils of gin", the inhabitants weren't wicked people. Many of the gin distillers were pious and caring. Catholic and Protestant alike, they built churches, orphanages, hospitals and alms houses for the poor, handsome buildings which can still be seen today.

Black Nazareth

There seem to be several explanations of how Schiedam got its nickname. At one time there were said to be as many as 200 gin distilleries, and the smoke from their chimneys would have stained all the buildings black. The C19th pastor and poet Piet Paaltjans is said to have referred to 'black Schiedam' in one of his poems. It is also said that a delegation of distillers from the Belgian village of Nazareth visited and thought the town resembled theirs except that it was 'black'. (Presumably they had fewer distilleries or hadn't been making gin for as long). Then there is the uneasy association between apparently hard working, pious townsfolk living on the proceeds of an evil trade, in contrast to Jesus' home in Palestine, which some claimed the town resembled, in that it had small twisting streets, although this seems somewhat fanciful.

Piet Paaltjans, Priest and Poet

Schiedam really did have a Minister of the (protestant) Dutch Reformed Church in the C19th who was also a poet. His name was Francois Haverschmit (1835 – 1894) He wrote under the pen name Piet Paaltjans, and was well known in Dutch literary circles. The only poem of his I have managed to find in translation is rather melancholy in tone, but I understand that he also wrote comic verse. I feel certain that the Reverend Jacob Winkelmann in this story would only have written poems on serious biblical themes.

Made in the USA
Columbia, SC
10 August 2017